MW01119235

Jodi

Guardian Angel in Training

Book I of The Jodi Trilogy

By
Karin E. Olson, MD

RoseDog Books
PITTSBURGH, PENNSYLVANIA 15222

The contents of this work, including, but not limited to, the accuracy of events, people, and places depicted; opinions expressed; permission to use previously published materials included; and any advice given or actions advocated are solely the responsibility of the author, who assumes all liability for said work and indemnifies the publisher against any claims stemming from publication of the work.

All Rights Reserved
Copyright © 2014 by Karin Olson, MD

No part of this book may be reproduced or transmitted, downloaded, distributed, reverse engineered, or stored in or introduced into any information storage and retrieval system, in any form or by any means, including photocopying and recording, whether electronic or mechanical, now known or hereinafter invented without permission in writing from the publisher.

RoseDog Books
701 Smithfield Street
Pittsburgh, PA 15222
Visit our website at www.rosedogbookstore.com

ISBN: 978-1-4809-0610-5
eISBN: 978-1-4809-0633-4

Dedication

Jodi: Guardian Angel in Training is dedicated to my sister, Kristin Lauer, PhD, who always believed in her and to my editor, Vanessa Page, who thought of Jodi as her godchild.

Acknowledgments

Vanessa Page, my editor, turned Jodi: Guardian Angel in Training into a professionally written novel.

My sister, Kristin Lauer, has guided many of her students at Fordham University at Lincoln Center in New York City into successful careers as novelists. I was truly blessed that she believed in Jodi: a belief that was supplemented by numerous helpful suggestions regarding plot and content as well as gentle prods to complete the telling of Jodi's story.

PART I

Chapter 1

Jodi's memories wandered back eighty-some years to one late summer afternoon. Tranquil, yet alert, Jodi was attentively guarding Gerald, who could contrive serious mischief within minutes. On that day her fearless charge sat on his diapered round bottom on the kitchen floor, playing with his ball — a gigantic red one. He grabbed for it, knocked it away, scrambled after it; reaching it, he rolled onto his side with a giggle. She delighted in these quiet moments, watching him develop. In this warm weather, a diaper was enough, so his mother didn't insist on more clothing. He did detest the handicap of constricting garments and yanked them off as soon as he found himself unobserved.

In the parlor off the kitchen, rocking in the same wicker chair her own mother had used, Sue nursed Gerald's baby sister, Sally. The woman's loose-fitting blue-green gingham blended with her apron and bib. Since she felt most relaxed when her house, children, and clothing harmonized, she coordinated color combinations even on the days she spent alone at home.

The nurturing mother of two lifted her infant to her shoulder while she gently rubbed the little girl's back. Bending to kiss the cherubic head with its few strands of blond hair, she unconsciously held the pose artists strive to capture. The afternoon sun accentuated the auburn cast of the braids that lay twisted high on her head out of reach of grasping baby fingers. The young woman nuzzled the infant who was swaddled snugly in the yellow bunting worn by Gerald a couple years earlier. How fast he was growing! And active: he could barely spare time for a brief hug.

When she rocked Sally, Sue often reminisced back to her courting days: an attractive woman of 28, she taught school while waiting patiently for the right man. At a church social she met and rapidly fell in love with Dan, a sun-tanned, muscular, infantryman-turned-farmer. She adored his exotic-sounding clipped accent so unusual for the community. He had migrated to the area after he inherited his uncle's farm. Soon the two became a pair and, before many months, wedding bans were posted. His blue eyes and sandy hair so contrasted with her darker features that they questioned whom the children would resemble. Gerald did take after her though his hair curled like his father's. *It's a little early to be certain about you, my baby girl,* Sue mused as she studied her daughter's features.

Sue savored her life as a farm wife and mother; she planned to have six children whom she would teach to know God, cherish their home and family, respect their planet. Her many duties around their farm kept her figure trim despite two pregnancies. In addition to full responsibility for child care, she maintained a tidy house, dressed the little ones in home-sewn outfits, prepared nourishing meals and grew vegetables for the family table in the kitchen garden. Sue didn't dwell on her accomplishments: these she deemed normal chores. She wouldn't change a thing, except, perhaps, to slow Gerald down a bit.

When not tending a child or household duty, her never-idle hands busily mended and knitted or crocheted rugs and afghans. She attended church quilting bees with Emma, her best friend since first grade. Emma, who married soon after high school graduation, had three older children, followed by Teddy, born a month before Gerald.

Sue snapped out of her reverie to listen for Gerald but relaxed when she heard his belly laughs and the swish of his amazing ball, a whole foot in diameter. *Dan was so excited last night when he rolled the new ball to Gerald.* A smile lit her eyes as she thought of her adored husband. *He's such a great father. To notice that ball when he had so many items on his list. How am I so blessed to have married him?*

While Sue stayed constantly attuned to the children, she eagerly anticipated the day when the pair could safely play together. But Gerald considered Sally, "me baby," and their mother had to intervene during his frequent attempts to lift his tiny sister from the cradle.

Meanwhile in the kitchen, Gerald spied Mister Jack, the family cat, sprawled on top of the highest cupboard. He pulled the stool next to the counter and began his ascent. *I must stop him!* Jodi shifted into crisis-solving mode. *If only he makes a noise to alert Sue. Maybe he'll knock over that tall glass near the edge*; no, he barely missed it.

Get down! Jodi screamed into the boy's thought patterns, but he didn't heed her. *Oooh, if only I could materialize,* she lamented and not for the first time. As a Guardian Angel she was required to communicate through intuition, dreams, or occasionally telepathy. She sent thought-wave warnings to Sue but Sally distracted the normally vigilant mother.

With Gerald's sturdy knees planted on the countertop, his hands gripped the edge of the first shelf; he drew his feet under him to stand. His determined countenance hardened as his arms maneuvered between bowls and plates to feel for the farther rim of the ledge. Once he got hold of it, he pulled his legs one at a time up to the new level and, kneeling there, beamed from his perch. "Miher Yak. Miher Yak," he muttered, gazing up at his objective, still far overhead.

Mister Jack watched his nemesis approach. Jodi intuited the large cat's impulses as he remembered having his tail pulled and his tawny body smothered in hugs; he waited, tail swishing to and fro. Maybe the angel could induce Mister Jack to leap down. She beamed strong impressions toward the animal but the wily creature skillfully avoided her psychic energy. *Cats are such independent creatures*, she fumed.

Gerald climbed to the second shelf that stored the blue and white serving platters. Jodi imagined Mister Jack thinking, *When he's near enough, I'll swipe his cheek...he'll fall back...down to the floor...end the pestering.*

What to do? She projected her thought-waves with the intensity of a vocal yell, *Ger! Stop!* She could rouse no fear in him. Never had been able to. He didn't understand the notion of caution. Gerald stood, readying himself for the next plateau. As he drew his leg after him, his foot grazed the bear-shaped cookie jar; the rub of pottery against wood proved too low-pitched for his mother's perception. Then, inches below Mister Jack, he reached for the edge of the cat's sanctuary.

Jodi desperately surveyed the surroundings for anything that might prevent the impending catastrophe. She caught sight of George, the mailman, striding toward the door. A former football star, George maintained his athletic skills by participating in Friday night ball games with his buddies. And it showed: his postal uniform fit perfectly – no creeping folds of fat. Jodi broadcasted images of Gerald at him which influenced George to peek into the kitchen intending to tease his favorite youngster. The moment he glanced in, Mister Jack swiped; Gerald screamed, lost his balance, and fell backwards.

Jodi flashed a picture to George of catching Gerald. The vision triggered his reflexes: he jumped and intercepted the boy midair as adroitly as he caught the softball on the sandlot. Sue, alerted by Gerald's anguished cry, came running, snatched her sobbing boy, then noticed his bloodied cheek. Before the aroused mother could turn on their mailman, Jodi sent her an image of their pet's offensive swipe. Sue glimpsed the would-be murderer sneakily squeezing around the uppermost cupboards and scolded, "Mister Jack! How could you?" Gerald's harried mother turned a warm smile on his rescuer, "Thank you, George."

"Uh, was nothing. Glad I was here." The dazed man reddened, dropped a letter on the table, and escaped out the door.

Sue, cognizant of Jodi's role in Gerald's life, transmitted a quick, *Thank you!* prior to whisking the boy off to scrub the scratches on his cheek. Jodi glowed. As with similar near-misses involving Gerald, Sue and Dan fretted together that evening. After such events they opined, half-jokingly, half-seriously, that, if they could keep their son alive until age seven, he might reach adulthood.

Sue and Jodi had become acquainted a few months before Mister Jack's attempt to rid himself of Gerald. The toddler had proved himself exceptionally mobile. He possessed two speeds—asleep or go; and when not slumbering, he ran. His parents reckoned that he never paused from the time he woke in the morning until night when he collapsed into dreams.

On the warm spring day his mother and Guardian Angel would meet, Sue had opened the back door so the refreshing breeze could circulate through the house. Gerald played quietly on the kitchen floor while Jodi hovered nearby relishing the peaceful respite. As she watched him industriously load wood chips into the wagon his father built last winter from scraps, the angel mused, *Who'd dream a child, not-yet-two, could be this active?*

Lunch over and dishes done, Sue settled comfortably in her rocking chair; Mister Jack purred on her lap. Since she hadn't slept much the previous two nights with baby Sally restless and colicky, she had tried rocking Gerald to sleep. Naturally Gerald resisted napping; he wriggled and vocalized a steady crescendo of "No, No, No...." that would certainly awaken his sister. So his mother relented. She needed rest but couldn't allow herself to doze off with Gerald up and about. I'll just rock quietly while he plays was her last conscious thought.

Jodi, hovering beside Gerald's shoulder, gazed out at the kitchen garden with its nearly full-grown lettuce and spinach. The peas and beans climbed their poles. Next to them the baby squash and cucumber plants leafed, preparing to cover the rich black loam with their summer carpet.

Suddenly the strawberry leaves rustled exposing the bright berries underneath. Gerald and Jodi both spied the creature that caused the disturbance as it darted through the garden and across the open yard. Abruptly, the toddler leapt up to give chase. The chipmunk, fearful of the stumbling child, scampered into the weeds and startled a crow. Off flew the cawing bird from the tall grass into the woods beyond with Gerald in pursuit. Jodi assumed her charge was protected from bad scratches with his coveralls and shirt; his sturdy shoes should prevent cuts from rocks.

The crow almost instantly disappeared. Surprised, the child looked around. Then a yellow pansy sparkling in the sun begged his inspection. A squirrel jumped between the trees and, as the little boy reached the place where he last saw it, a black-and-gold butterfly fluttered above columbine in the opposite direction.

Jodi stayed at his shoulder as each new intriguing animal or beauteous flower attracted him farther from the house. The sights and sounds enticed him more than the likeness of Sue that Jodi implanted into his mind. If only he would miss his mother so his angel could lure him home.

Several yards into the woods he waddled into a clearing where he beheld an old stump on a grassy knoll; a caterpillar crawled along its bark. Breathless from his romp, he plopped down to examine the funny bug then glanced around to show off his discovery. He didn't see his mother and yelled, "Mamma!" She didn't race to his side or cry out, "Here I am!" Previously, she'd always come when he called.

Realizing that she wasn't nearby, he finally grew frightened — maybe for the first time in his life. He screamed, then whimpered. Very tired after such an extended hike for a little fellow, he soon dozed off lulled by the familiar melody Jodi hummed into his head. Once Gerald slept, Jodi flew off to fetch

Sue. The Guardian Angel had to leave her ward alone, lying beside the old stump, but he was safely shaded by a nearby pine and she would keep in touch mentally. She could fly to his side in an instant if trouble developed.

Jodi vibrated near Sue's shoulder while she whispered a dream into the mother's sleep. The angel transmitted the image of a young woman with golden hair, wearing a powder-blue gown trimmed with twinkling stars; she added silvery wings and a sparkling halo in order to fit Sue's concept of an angel.

Next, in Sue's dream, Jodi painted the knoll in the woods, with Gerald napping in the corduroy coveralls and yellow-and-red plaid shirt he had on that day. She nestled him beside her with his curls resting in her lap. The celestial being smiled out of the scene at Sue who, while still in her dream, glimpsed the angel through the bedroom window.

"Hello, Sue," Jodi spoke into the mother's dream. "I'm Jodi, Gerald's Guardian Angel. He's lost in the woods." Into Sue's mind Jodi carefully sketched the route from the garden through the thicket of trees to the grassy clearing; she detailed landmarks along the way. Then she awakened Sue by imitating Gerald calling "Mamma, Mamma."

Sue sat upright, ashamed that she'd dozed: she checked on Sally and hunted for Gerald. He was missing; she panicked. Then, she recalled the angel in her dream. The mother's forehead wrinkled as her eyes widened: angel communication, after all, was not an everyday occurrence.

Frantically, she rushed out the back door and sighted the dream's first landmark. She forced herself to breathe slowly and deeply as she painstakingly retraced the directions imprinted in her brain. Although only a few hundred yards, it seemed miles to Sue. She noted the scattered pansies that extended to the daintily swaying columbine and dashed toward the patch, oblivious to their fragrant scents wafting on the breeze. She turned to her left, darted into the trees, and followed the path made by deer and dogs through the dense underbrush. Soon she arrived at the knoll in the shade of the large Scotch pine.

Although Jodi had primed Sue well, the angel lingered beside the frightened mother. The woman sensed the Guardian's presence; that awareness prevented true hysteria. On reaching the edge of the clearing, Sue spotted the curled-up child – how angelic the sleeping toddler appeared! She sprinted to him, lifted him into her arms, and hugged him to her heart. As the tension drained from her muscles, she marveled at her incredible experience that day, complete with the glorious vision of her son's angel. But the indisputable knowledge an angel assisted her with Gerald made the boy no less grueling to parent.

Dan learned Jodi was more than Sue's fantasy while babysitting one summer day shortly after Gerald's third birthday. The father enjoyed his young son more and more as he transformed from a baby into a young boy with a unique personality and developing skills. Plus, Gerald could catch a ball if his father lofted it straight to him. When Dan did chores, his apprentice shadowed him with his miniature hammer at the ready to pound any nail.

Like his neighbors, Dan spent those days toiling in the fields. Situated on the banks of a tumultuous river, the family's few hundred acres were mainly devoted to oats and wheat although Dan set aside plots for experiments with various vegetables. He owned a team of plow horses and a few cows to provide milk for the household; Sue raised pigs and chickens.

Dan, a capable and competent man in his middle thirties, could fix anything; the conscientious, God-fearing husband and father had easily earned the respect of his adopted community during the past five years. Mostly, he entrusted the children to Sue since he felt inadequate to do more than love and provide for them. Yet, on that particular morning, Sue couldn't budge. After vomiting all night, she continued to feel nauseous if she tried to lift her head from the pillow. So Dan, already tired from his night at his wife's side, was in charge of Gerald and Sally.

Although she'd shared her apprehensions about Gerald's activity level, Dan believed they were exaggerated. He never imagined what an entire day with his children entailed.

Gerald characteristically rose at dawn with his father. Thus, before he needed to care for Sally, Dan figured he could dress and feed his son. To avoid bothering Sue, the considerate husband carried his own coveralls and shirt, socks and boots into Gerald's room. While he readied himself, he told his boy, not one but three times, "Get your things on, son." The task of clothing Gerald, a child interested in everything except dressing, proved the first major project of his day.

Dan determined direct supervision was required and handed Gerald his underpants, "Put these on." Gerald complied. But immediately after, he scurried to his toy box to fetch the crystal rock which he tilted so it sparkled in the sunbeams and brought to his father for admiration. He didn't notice the shirt Dan held out, let alone pause to consider slipping his arms into the sleeves.

Dan lifted up his son, plopped on the corner of the bed, and positioned his own legs to corral the boy. This was becoming an ordeal! He shook out the shirt, "Put this on now!" Dan repeated his words with the coveralls for which he spread his legs so Gerald could sit to pull them on. In order to secure the straps, Dan had to restrain the wiggling child with both arms and a leg around the boy's chest; only then could he fasten the buttons with two hands.

There was more. Dan wiped his brow as he contemplated the socks and shoes and opted for a shortcut: he'd put them on for Gerald. But, he soon was impressed with how tough it is to shoe a three year old who won't cease moving for 10 seconds. After much effort and a few harsh commands of "Hold still, boy!" he gave Gerald the socks and shoes one at a time. That way he only needed to tie the laces. It worked.

With his son clothed, Dan reckoned he'd accomplished the trickiest task for that day. The rest should be easy street. Moreover, the next chore proved simple and quite fun. He prepared oatmeal and set out milk, his and Gerald's routine breakfast, no difficulties worse than minor spills. Gerald chattered happily about the birds he spied out the window, the roof he'd watched his

father repair yesterday, and his baby bunny out in the shed. After the two finished their porridge, Dan pulled Gerald's blocks out of the cupboard and put
them on the throw rug in the sitting room, "Here you are. Now build a house
for Papa. I must take care of Sally."

Unexpectedly, his daughter dressed far more easily. He did prick himself
while changing her diapers; but, at least he foresaw such a possibility and had
positioned his fingers to avoid poking her. Her frock, laid out by Sue the previous evening, slipped over her head without a hitch; her tiny toes inserted
themselves into the stiff miniature footwear with no difficulty. He brushed her
sandy curls as she gazed up at him with her widened bright blue eyes full of
the anxiety of a child wondering, *Where's Mamma?*

"How come it's much easier to dress you?" her father spoke aloud. "You're
younger, more fragile, a girl. Are girl's outfits simpler?" Dan didn't connect her
sitting quietly, without squirms and wiggles, to the difference between his offspring.

To feed her was a challenge. Sally busily looked all around, searching for
Mamma; she pursed her lips refusing the porridge. Dan decided to coax his
daughter by touching spoonfuls to her lips while he commented, "I sure hope
your Aunt Jean shows up soon. Changing diapers once is enough. Aunt Jean
drops by to chat with your mother every morning." At the sound of "mother"
and her aunt's name, Sally swiveled in her seat and peered right and left; her
hair brushed the spoon. Dan grabbed a cloth and wiped away cereal. "Please,
God, don't let Jean decide to do something else today." He turned to the baby
and sighed, "She could get you to eat."

But Jean didn't arrive. She'd caught an early train for a shopping trip in
town and wouldn't be back until evening. Although she and Sue had discussed
the excursion over tea and biscuits the previous morning, Sue had no reason
at the time to tell Dan. No one would miraculously knock on the door to relieve
him of childcare responsibilities.

"Mamma?" Sally whined; increasingly restless, she scanned her surroundings.

When she tried to snatch the spoon from him, Dan offered, "Here, you take
it." Exactly what she wished: across the room she flung the porridge-filled
utensil with a shriek of glee and broke into her first grin of the day. "We make
quite the pair," he grumbled. "Where's your Aunt Jean? I'm no expert at feeding
babies and you're the world's least hungry." He assumed there was no harm
if his daughter skipped breakfast; that's what she obviously desired. Nevertheless, he was concerned: Shouldn't a responsible father feed his child? Aren't
children supposed to eat? *Tomorrow gotta watch how Sue feeds her.*

As Dan concentrated on Sally, he kept an ear out for Gerald, who played
so quietly his father felt proud. *He's sure acting grown up. Look how he's keeping himself busy so I can take care of Sally. Must take time to admire the house
he's building.* In a similar situation, Sue would sense the sitting room suspi-
ciously quiet for a three year old. Jodi, on high alert, monitored Gerald closely;
she was well aware that Dan did not appreciate his son's expertise at mischief-
making and danger-finding.

Dan outlined his day as he made one more attempt with Sally. *Might finish shingle repairs. Got about a fourth done last night.* "C'mon, Sally, just a little for Papa," but the pretty head automatically turned away from the spoon. Sighing, Dan waited for Sally to refocus on him while he continued his mental to-do list: *Ladder and tools still out. That'll keep me close to home. For certain, can't be out in the fields.*

While Dan was wheedling Sally to eat, Gerald strayed into the yard. The ladder, propped against the side of the house, reminded him that his father had been fixing those shingles. "Papa pulled on 'em. And ones that wiggled, he pounded nails in. Me do that," Gerald announced to the barnyard. "That'll help Papa." Gleefully he trotted to his father's toolbox and continued his monologue for the edification of the farmyard hens and pigs. "Papa feeding Sally. And me help Mamma when I dust. And Mamma hugs me and says, 'Ger, you're my special helper.'"

Gerald selected the hammer his father had crafted just for him and stuffed a handful of nails into his pockets like he'd observed Dan do. He fearlessly scooted up the ladder, gripped the eaves and hoisted himself onto the roof. Since Gerald had concluded that his father needed his help, he tuned out the soft voice inside his head that kept warning, *No! Gerald! Stay on the ground!*

Jodi was frantic. When a notion entered Gerald's head, she was powerless to influence him. At those times his thoughts sped down a single track along a route she couldn't enter. She desperately sent warnings to Dan but he was too preoccupied with Sally to discern her psychic voice. The frustration — how to force her angelic message through the ambient distractions — comprised one of the chief dilemmas she lived with on a day-to-day basis.

Jodi spotted a butterfly in the garden and recalled how the insects attracted Gerald's attention. That one, patterned with gold, red and brown, vividly contrasted against the azure sky. Maybe she could influence it to fly up near the kitchen window to entice Sally. When the fluttering creature rose into view, Sally shrieked with delight, precisely as Jodi schemed.

Dan, following the child's excited gestures with his eyes, recognized the possibility of a respite. He lifted her from the highchair and carried her to the window: the captivating dance of the swarm of delicate beings flitting around the pansy bed delighted both father and daughter. Sally squealed, kicked her legs and squirmed as she stretched toward the tiny beauties on the other side of the glass. Dan realized he could give her a snack later and strode outside for a closer peek. But, as soon as he put one foot out the door, he caught sight of Gerald's red shirt above — on the roof.

Perspiration broke out on Dan's forehead. His throat clenched. Later he would be thankful he had been speechless since any sound might have startled his small boy into losing his footing. For a few seconds Dan stood immobilized until his infantry training took over. He sized up the situation and decided the butterfly patch would provide several minutes of enchantment for his youngest.

Once Sally, cooing and crowing, stumbled after the colorful critters, Dan sprinted to the ladder and stealthily, but rapidly, ascended. He forced himself to breathe deeply as trained when under attack. From the eaves, he saw Gerald about twenty feet ahead of him. The child yanked on a shingle, hammered it, stood, teetered a bit and scooted farther up the steep incline.

Carefully Dan inched along the slope to reach his son. When within arm's length, he snagged Gerald by the belt and pulled him to his chest. There atop the house, dread turned into intense anger. He gave the miscreant the scolding of his short life.

"B-But, Papa, s-see, Me helping. You're busy with Sally. Me fix the roof." Gerald beamed and his father's heart started to melt.

But, as Dan held his boy, he spoke sternly, "Gerald, You wanted to help me. But you are never to go on the roof again. Understand?"

"Y-Yes…," his son whimpered. "—B-But…"

"Gerald. Do you understand?"

"Yes, P-Papa."

One lesson had been learned that morning: Dan would never leave a ladder against the house again.

He boosted Gerald up on his shoulders and climbed down. Then Dan flung the ladder into the grass. Scooping up Sally, he situated both children in the kitchen with him while he washed the dishes. No roofs today. He must choose work that permitted visual monitoring of the pair.

He managed occasionally to check on Sue. She slept until about one, when, even though a bit stronger, she experienced the room spinning if she sat up. Maybe food would alleviate her weakness; he brought her a piece of dry toast and tea.

"How are Ger and Sal, honey?" she inquired as she stroked the warm fur of the purring Mister Jack nestled contentedly beside her.

"Doing great. Sally's taking a nap and Gerald's building a tower." Dan frowned, then swallowed. "My younger brothers and cousins used to nap until they were five or so, I reckon. I had to play quietly while they slept, but…"

"Not our Ger," interrupted Sue with a faint laugh. He stayed with her a few more minutes until she nodded off.

Dan returned the teapot, cup and plate to the kitchen and cleaned them, plus the children's and his lunch dishes. Barney, their shaggy sheepdog, influenced by Jodi, tugged at his sleeve. "What's with you, Barney? I got enough besetting me with these young'uns? No time to play," Dan fumed. Yet Barney persisted and his master eventually heeded because the behavior was unusual for their dog.

Barney led the farmer to the barn where Gerald was in the stallion's stall. To Dan it seemed that Blackie had decided to stomp on that pesky intruder. At least, he'd raised his right hoof ominously over the boy's head. His owner's quick, "Atta boy", along with the rub on his neck, calmed the agitated animal. Dan snatched his son away; once outside he prohibited Gerald in no uncertain terms from trespassing into the horse's domain.

By the day's end, Dan was frustrated and tense. He slept poorly filled with dread that, if they merely relied on everyday child rearing techniques, his firstborn son would wind up in a crippling or fatal accident. In the morning with Sue recovered, he offered, half seriously, "Honey, you think I ought to build a cage for Gerald? However do you keep track of him?" His hands thrust deep in his pockets, the father's troubled eyes searched his wife's serene ones.

"Jodi helps me," she replied with a nonchalant wave of her hand as if her response somehow resolved their predicament.

Her husband worried that perhaps she was still feverish, "Jodi?"

"Yes. Jodi. Gerald's Guardian Angel." And she proceeded to recount examples of her accumulating adventures with Jodi and Gerald. Dan, if not persuaded, appreciated the assurance Sue derived from her belief that she received celestial assistance with their little character. Otherwise she'd have to relent to his more drastic solution. It was another year before Gerald met Jodi.

One of the tasks Sue most dreaded was shampooing her son's hair and she did put that chore off if she could. But that evening Sue knew she had to face the task.

"Gerald, you're making this worse." Sue gritted her teeth as she lathered his head. The expected struggle commenced with head-tossing; soapsuds and water flew in all directions. A tickly cluster of bubbles landed on her nose. She sneezed; Gerald giggled. Her well-worn shirtwaist, saved from the rag bag for this purpose, draped her body in drenched, sagging heaviness. Her hair, pulled back into a tight bun, escaped most of the deluge. She felt mighty disgusted. This did not fit her view of fun even though her wildly splashing son found it hilarious. "Ger, stop it right now. You're behaving ridiculously!"

"Soap's in my eyes," screamed Gerald who'd been merrily racing two pieces of wood that substituted for boats across the tub before his mother tackled his shaggy curls. Although she kept his locks short to facilitate cleaning, he nevertheless objected vociferously. Hair-washing went beyond the inconveniences mothers dictate: he protested that it was hazardous for his eyes. He secretly hoped she'd yield if he set up enough obstacles. He was four, after all, and big enough for dirty hair if he fancied it.

He created a mammoth wave. Much to his surprise, he lost his balance and slid under. His feet and hands slipped on the soap-filmed porcelain: he couldn't push himself off to reach the surface. A foot of water separated him from the air. This unexpected peril panicked him; he accidentally inhaled water and choked.

Next thing he knew he stood on the tile, dripping puddles, sputtering and coughing. He barely realized his mother had yanked him out. She snatched the towel; her vigorous strokes stung. Aware he'd been naughty, he meekly submitted to her roughness and figured she should swat him. How come she didn't?

And, she didn't even scold. Her ominous silence instilled more dread than a harsh lecture. He dared glance up from the floor and trembled when he saw her lips tightly pressed together. Although subdued, a new panic overwhelmed Gerald, *Will she ever love me again?*

After Sue pulled his crimson nightshirt over his head, she placed her palms firmly on his cheeks and turned his head to gaze directly into his eyes. He stared back, frightened, no longer the least bit defiant. "Sorry, Mamma," he mumbled. What she said next forever changed his life.

"Ger, when are you going to desist with this wildness? Not even Jodi can protect you from that kind of nonsense in the tub."

"M-Mamma, I w-won't be so bad. Never again. I'm …." He froze in mid-sentence: his mother's words finally penetrated his guilt-clouded consciousness; he gaped up at her. His demeanor flipped from shame to curiosity. "Who's J-Jodi, Mamma?"

"Oh, she's your Guardian Angel," his mother used the off-handed manner she might employ to tell him Aunt Jean was coming for dinner.

Gerald's apprehension resurfaced. Was a Guardian Angel a monster that would eat him if he acted too naughty? Voice breaking, he murmured, "What's a Guardian Angel?"

"Someone who stays with you. Keeps you safe," she rose from her crouched position and gently pushed him toward his bedroom. "Now it's time for prayers and sleep." Beside his trundle bed the two rested their forearms on the red-and-white quilt. Gerald adored the scarlet rug on which they knelt. Red was his favorite color. Sue rejected his choice of wall paint but consented to sew curtains with the apple-decorated remnants from a quilt she'd done last winter. The small room contained a tiny chest in the corner for toy trucks and balls. Gerald could put his folded underwear and socks in the correct drawers of his little bureau, built by his father.

Together they prayed, "Now I lay me down to sleep…" then Gerald cycled through his "God Bless Mamma, Papa, Sally, baby Jimmy, Grandma…."

Then, he climbed into bed and received his mother's goodnight kiss; but, while she tucked him under his quilt, questions bubbled out: "What's Jodi look like? Is her hair brown like yours, Mamma? What's the color of her eyes? And where is she? Can I see her?"

His mother's only response, "Ask Jodi to chat with you, Ger."

He commanded, "Jodi, talk to me!" Although Jodi did in fact speak, her voice blended in with the cacophony of his inner excitement. There was nothing his mother couldn't do, he believed, so, sitting up straight and in his most grown-up, authoritative voice, he declared, "Mamma, Jodi won't say nothing to me. Make her, Mamma. Make her!"

Sue, near the threshold, gently whispered, "You need to listen carefully, Ger." At that moment Dan walked in. Gerald figured he should hear what his father thought about this Jodi idea.

"You gotta angel, Papa? Mamma says mine's named Jodi. You know about Jodi, too?"

Dan was prepared for that question since he and Sue had mulled over the appropriate time to tell Gerald. They'd concluded that it couldn't hurt for the child to communicate with his angel. Therefore, without hesitation, his father responded, "Sure, son. Everyone has an angel."

To Gerald his father's solemn tones, delivered as he leaned comfortably against the door frame, conveyed the belief that what seemed an outlandish theory was actually an everyday topic. Gerald peered into Dan's serious face and saw truth written on it. "What's the name of your angel, Papa?"

"Why – uh, er? Guess I don't know." Dan appeared a trifle flustered. Shuffling his feet a little, he shot his wife a glance that pleaded for her to bail him out. Sue merely grinned. He inferred this was her retaliation for Gerald so thoroughly drenching her. He was dry; she was soaked. He moved back a step. *Don't need both of us wet.*

"So what's the matter, Papa? Can't take a little water?" Sue cuddled up to her husband, determined that he should share, if only vicariously, in the storm she recently endured. Sensing the inevitable, he put his arm around her shoulder.

Gerald, oblivious to the adults' behavior, persisted in exploring his own quandary. "Mamma, what's Papa's angel's name?" Curiosity consumed him.

"Better ask Grandma, Ger." Dan was intrigued by the purposeful evasiveness of his usually informative wife then recognized the former teacher's device: Sue was forcing their young scalawag to think before rushing headlong into his world. Once again, Dan appreciated her wisdom. He drew her closer and ignored the wetness seeping through his denims. If anyone could handle their impulse-ridden boy, the mother with whom the lad had been provided was the best equipped. Holding her to him, dazzled by her performance, Dan smiled fondly at that amazing woman he'd married.

"Who's your angel, Mamma?" came the next demand. The bewildered four year old sat with legs crossed, hands in front of him, palms down on his sheet, and stared at his mother. Not in the least sleepy, Gerald obsessed on this wondrous idea.

"Gerald, why don't you ask Jodi?"

Thanks a lot, Mamma, Jodi transmitted to Sue.

Well, you might as well join the action, Sue laughed, with a tinge of malice. She'd resolved to encourage Gerald in actively attending to his angel.

"What's Sally's angel called, Mamma?"

Jack, Jodi's alto sounded in Sue's head.

"Jack," the mother mimicked the angel's sure riposte.

Jealousy flooded Gerald. He yearned for a male playmate right under their own roof. Jimmy was only a baby and his best friend Teddy lived so far away that Papa or Mamma hitched the horse to the cart and drove forever for the two to play. "How come she has a boy angel to play with? Why can't I have a boy? Can I trade my girl one for her boy one?"

You field that one, Sue communicated to Jodi. Although neither father nor son could perceive the inaudible exchange, Dan had previously witnessed his wife display this same introverted, meditative expression. At such times, when she seemed to focus on some inner voice, she would meet his concern with, "Chatting with Jodi."

Jodi giggled at the notion of switching angels and teased, "You should ask Jack."

A jolly banter ensued between Gerald's mother and angel — like two school girls. Sue, in her bathing-Gerald rags, leaned against her husband; Jodi perched on the bookcase. But, ever the responsible mother, Sue cut short the dialogue with her unseen pal and approached her son. Gently, she pushed him back into his pillows and tucked him in once more. "To sleep now. Morning's time enough for these questions," and she kissed his cheek.

Dan walked over to Gerald and, bending, planted a kiss on his son's forehead. Then spontaneously the man gathered his boy to his heart and gave an enormous hug to this child he loved fiercely but found near impossible to cope with. Laying the startled child back into his bed, he tautly arranged the covers and gruffly stated, "Time to sleep, son."

Gerald's parents snuffed out the oil lamps and headed toward their bedroom, peeking in on Sally and Baby Jimmy as they passed through the hall. Sue reviewed the last hour as she took off her damp clothes. Although mentally as well as physically fatigued, exhilaration energized her. *Oh God, please teach Gerald to stop and think. And please assist Jodi in guiding him.*

Jodi definitely yearned for a reciprocal relationship with Gerald. Therefore she opted to manipulate his dreams since that method had worked so well during her introduction to Sue. The minute he fell soundly asleep, she flew into his dream and announced, "Hi, I'm Jodi." The young woman with sandy hair, twinkling blue eyes, and dressed in a white gown sprinkled with gold stars, awed the child. She'd added a pair of wings and halo to resemble the angel in Gerald's storybook. Initially in the dream, he was timid; however, when Jodi produced a bright red ball and tossed it to him, he played catch with her. That game, including his leap and perfect retrieval when the missile flew high overhead, established their friendship.

But this action of Jodi's echoed throughout Heaven. A moment after she departed from Gerald's dream, Jeff arrived for a supervisory session with his impetuous trainee. Together the two angels exited Gerald's room to materialize in a clearing in the woods. An owl screeched. Jeff, as usual, selected a steely gray for his curly hair that contrasted sharply with his chocolate-hued skin, an appearance that impressed his subordinate as mature.

"Jodi, you know we never, ever introduce ourselves to our humans. It's not part of the tradition." He frowned and glared at her. Jeff epitomized the officious supervisor: his white robe was decorated with the golden sash of his rank and he carried a gilded staff to symbolize the celestial hierarchy and its regulations. Jodi, unimpressed by his embellishments, did not waver in her rebellion. Jeff sighed, "Certainly, I can see you're communicating with Sue — and plenty of mothers put trust in their children's Guardian Angels. But, Jodi, not the child. You do not communicate with the child."

"Why not? Why these stupid rules!" Despite her use of telepathic speech, Jodi's retort resounded in no weaker or less challenging a timbre than would such a human outburst. As she argued, the elegant angelic garment she'd donned for Gerald's dream transformed into a defiant military uniform similar to the silvery gray one in which Joan of Arc has been painted. Jodi added the lance, but no horse.

"Humans are supposed to discern their own talents and devise their own solutions." Jeff scowled and thumped his staff on the dirt for emphasis. "We participate in extreme emergencies and supply assistance when required." He continued, in a less domineering, more instructive tone, "If Gerald elected to study metaphysics, exhaustively researched Guardian Angels, and deduced how to cooperate directly with you — that would be a free choice and therefore acceptable. But you! You forced the knowledge on him." Jeff frowned, his shoulders slumped, his voice lowered in resignation, "Now he no longer has a choice; he has been forced to learn about spiritual beings at an incredibly young age."

"But Sue told him about me and he insisted I speak to him. He wanted me to be his friend." Jodi stamped her foot and clutched her lance, hilt on the ground, sharp point toward the sky. Her eyes narrowed with fury.

"He's. Only. Four. You have set his entire life on a track that perhaps he wouldn't choose."

"Don't you see?" Jodi pleaded, suddenly craving approval from her supervisor in guardian affairs. Her body slackened, her hand reached out toward Jeff. "Don't you see?" she repeated. "What else could I do? I'm expected to respect my charge's wishes no matter what his age. That is also part of my duty." Her body straightened up as she quoted from the Handbook for Guardian Angels she'd been required to memorize prior to her apprenticeship as a Guardian. "To be available to my human in the way they request, if it is spiritually appropriate." Jodi felt proud, pleased at her ability to support her action with the word of angelic law. Certain she'd prevailed, she wanted to smirk.

Her supervisor refused to acquiesce. "Jodi, you sought neither advice nor permission." Jeff relinquished the mentoring mode because he was on the verge of losing self-control. Rage welled up at this recalcitrant neophyte; his right hand clenched his staff; his left fist accentuated his every syllable. His black eyes flashed. His tones surged forth, cold and brittle. "You must permit your supervisors to interpret what's 'spiritually appropriate.' You sometimes are as headstrong as Gerald. And, you're not a four-year-old human."

"Someday, far in the future, it will dawn on Gerald that he's never walked through life without angels. He'll discern an incompleteness. He will insist on walking alone. Intimately familiar with life with angels, it will be doubly difficult for him."

Terror struck Jodi as she assimilated Jeff's summary, presented in such ominous tones. She paled, looked at the ground and gulped. Her attire switched into the ankle-length robes of a novice in early training; her head was bared.

By her shift in appearance and body language, Jeff ascertained that he'd made himself clear. The supervisor, released his tense pose and switched to a compassionate tone, "Guardian Angels don't always follow the law precisely.

It's a guide. There can be extenuating circumstances. God's available to provide advice – but, Jodi, you didn't ask. Yet, you want Gerald to listen to God, you and his own conscience. What kind of a role model are you?"

Finally Jodi fathomed the extent of her mistake. A significant part of her assignment as a Guardian Angel — to teach Gerald to listen for divine guidance –she herself failed to do. She recognized that she'd presumptuously put herself in the role of Divine Guidance. "I'm sorry, Jeff. I've behaved arrogantly. Thank you for your patience with me." Jodi's voice shook with contrition.

Nonetheless, although she admitted she'd goofed in not petitioning for her Father's approval, she secretly delighted in the realization that she and Gerald would have an actual relationship. That is what she'd longed for over the centuries — a friendship with a human. *Please, God, forgive me and don't let anything ever intrude between Gerald and me*, she earnestly prayed.

Chapter 2

No birds sang; no humans settled in this desolate part of the planet. High over-head, the tips of the Himalayas pierced the clouds in their cold stillness. Hav-ing elected to pilgrimage on foot from the village many miles below, Jodi trudged up the rocky path, buffeted by gusting winds. This journey was a sym-bolic walking away from the last eighty-some years and the people with whom she'd intertwined her life; she was hopeful it would rejuvenate her. As she climbed steadily upward, she replayed scenes from those early years of Ger-ald's life. She missed Gerald so dreadfully: a human whose life had ended while hers continued – after all, she was an angel.

During the hike, she sometimes reminisced, sometimes mourned, some-times just gazed at the majestic beauty of the mountains and reveled in the glo-ries shaped by God eons ago. She had reached the timberline: trees were rare, only an occasional straggling pine. Mostly she saw rock, ice, and snow on these windswept peaks, ridges and valleys. The stunning but arduous trek to the Li-brary of the Angels served a purifying function; as her grief slowly dissipated, the events of Gerald's life assumed their proper niches in her memories.

Few humans tackled these paths formed by mountain goats over the cen-turies. In this remote land many, many lifetimes ago, angelic scholars elected to situate their library. From where she last rested, Jodi had glimpsed a flash of the extraordinary alabaster structure, her destination. Its height, stretching toward the mountain summits, surpassed that of any contemporary sky-scraper. As she drew closer, she gradually distinguished the building's turrets, tall narrow windows crowned by tiled roofs.

Gothic marble columns, each topped by the statue of an angel were evenly spaced every six feet along the sides of the porch which extended around the front of the building. A slender golden bridge arched down to intersect the path on which Jodi trod to provide a walkway to the library's main entrance. Jodi knew that, when she was closer, she would be able to see the gently curved railing of gold, inlaid with emeralds and diamonds that traced the length of the span. It served as decoration and handrail for angels who preferred to walk, rather than fly, to the portal at which the archway terminated.

Vibrating at a frequency too high for human perception, this magnificent construction could have been positioned anywhere. When an explorer or shepherd wound his way through these parts, he tramped right through volumes upon volumes of treatises on angelic lore, law, customs, and how-to skills. Perhaps an occasional traveler discerned an unparalleled peace but most trudged through the invisible edifice totally unaware.

Jodi paused to admire the sunbeams dancing around the stone-like edges and reflecting off the stained glass windows. She understood the library was pure energy. Nevertheless those ancient architects opted to manufacture its components to resemble materials God created for humans to use. Jodi marveled at the elegant artistry as she leaned back against the mountainside to survey the uppermost tower.

Of the cloud-touching castle's many floors, whole levels were devoted to literature on each subcategory of angels. After Jodi was accepted as a trainee but prior to the assignment with Gerald, Mariah, her mentor in guardian affairs, had given her a tour of the Guardian Division's section of the library; two levels exclusively contained books on Guardians. "Jodi, God created we Guardians for the purpose of guiding individuals to belief in Him," Mariah pointed to such titles as <u>The Role of the Guardian in Human Spiritual Development.</u>

"Our Father also dedicated us to be the primary spiritual protector for our charges. We can call on Special Forces Angels to help in dire emergencies. But we are the first line of defense." Mariah had taken Jodi to another section where she noted <u>How to Attract a Human's Attention.</u> "An extensive set of techniques have been devised over the years on how to guard humans." Her instructor handed her a manual, "Read this carefully; it contains the basic rules you must follow."

Next Mariah motioned toward a shelf full of volumes that covered social interactions. "Jodi during your ward's life you must not socialize with other angels – even those who guard the family members of your charge." The teacher observed Jodi's perplexed frown and elaborated on this policy and its basis in the theory that socialization leads to a loss of focus and thus to neglect of the ward; injury or death could result. Mariah warmly encouraged her student to visit the library to reestablish ties with other angels after the death of her human charge. "But you must never leave your ward without an official summons during his lifetime."

As she stood on the mountainside and gazed at the library ahead, Jodi pondered Mariah's stern admonitions given eighty-some years previously. *So what that I broke almost every rule in that stupid manual? Gerald knew God. Gerald lived his full life. What was so wrong with the way I guarded him?* Jodi's breath quickened; her face flushed; she tugged on her hood's fur trim in lieu of the strand of hair she fiddled with in warmer climates. *What will be the verdict of the board?*

Jodi wrapped her cloak more tightly; shivers from the frigid mountain air were accentuated with tremors of anxiety. *Will I be granted permanent licensure as a Guardian?* The angel tilted her head and once more studied the edifice rising above her: the symbol of antiquity, of the whole of traditions that govern the angelic realm. Would her experiment be extended? Would a new tradition for guarding be encouraged? Her proposal to the Board of Guardian Affairs must cogently delineate the merits of reciprocal relationships between humans and angels. *I just have to make them see.* She tightened then relaxed her muscles.

The library's ephemeral quality struck Jodi with vivid clarity when she observed the solid body of a snow leopard traipse through a wall as if merely through a stretch of mist. Yet, when Jodi dematerialized from the human form with which she chose to climb this mountain, the library would be firm to her angelic body of pure energy.

During Gerald's lifetime she had existed as pure energy. Mariah explained that Guardians never materialized during their assignment. They communicated with their humans through the intuitive ability of the brain. Other types of angels, like Special Forces and Messengers, usually worked in a tangible humanoid form similar to the one Jodi had assumed for her trek. She appraised her appearance, bundled in layers of mountaineering garb. In memory of Gerald, she'd trimmed her boots, leggings and hat with bright scarlet braid matching her gloves. Even though it felt good to resume the human body, she desperately hoped to guard another lifetime.

Jodi's original appointment had been to the Special Forces, a unit established by God to respond to human crises. As an angel of that division, she'd sped quickly to an emergency or materialized on the spot to provide angelic assistance. Her bubbling creative personality, her impulsivity, and her keen sensitivity to her environment helped her determine and implement solutions. She excelled in Special Forces for the precise reasons that she didn't fit as comfortably into the role of Guardian. As she contemplated her struggle to remain focused exclusively on a single individual, she sighed.

Jodi resumed her deliberate ascent; the path twisted back so that the library was hidden by an intervening ridge. As she looked at the barren and forlorn landscape, she recalled how barren and forlorn those centuries in Special Forces became. Yes, she relished the excitement of the myriad transient situations in which she aided humans confronted by tremendous obstacles. In response to an individual's prayer or a summons from a Guardian, she was dispatched to jump in and then out of each life. However, each time she transferred to the next crisis, she wondered how the preceding life played out and what circumstances led to the condition in which she'd found the person. Over the years Jodi gradually perceived within herself a desire for participation in the entire life of one human; over time the yearning enlarged into an obsession.

Jodi drank in the panoramic view, wishing to erase the past from her mind. A pair of eagles perched by their aerie far below and farther down tiny specks marked the houses of the village from which she ventured forth earlier that morning. Once again distant memories overwhelmed her as she rested on a large boulder and picked up a pebble to rub.

Her initial prayer, "Please, Father, let me be a Guardian Angel," had surged from the depth of her being. She had flown to Rome to plead her request in a medieval cathedral with intricately designed windows, carvings, and frescoes. During those pre-dawn hours, flickering candles provided a dim glow; no one else worshiped among the pews. Jodi knelt reverently in one of the middle rows; humbly attired in a dark peasant dress, her head and shoulders covered by the traditional black shawl.

God's objections penetrated her soul, "Jodi, you're highly specialized. I depend on you in Special Forces. You rush to a crisis and resolve it expeditiously. I rely on you when I require quick innovations and genuine compassion." His empathetic voice, full of love and concern, reverberated through her spirit; the crushing weight of disappointment blackened her mood and she hung her head under the burden of a life that had grown onerous. Yet Jodi appreciated that granting her petition would detach her from the discipline for which He'd molded her talents.

"But, I do ache to guard a human, so very, very much!" Jodi beseeched Him yet again. His benevolent, yet firm, denial did not waver. Obediently submitting to His refusal but feeling there was no longer a sun in the sky, she rose, and with hands clasped at her waist, she moved down the aisle and out into the night. She despairingly obsessed on her longing — no, her *need* — to be a Guardian Angel.

Jodi still sensed that intense compulsion as she recalled the day she adorned herself in a sea-green sarong and materialized on the sandy beach of a South Pacific Island. Pacing the shore, she concentrated on the delicate shells and often stooped to examine an especially radiant one. She wanted to divert her mind and block out, if only temporarily, her craving to join the Guardian Division. She'd hoped the beauty of the beach would restore sunlight to her inner self. But instead of achieving serenity, she found herself scheming how to persuade God to grant her a chance.

Jodi shook herself out of her memory, *I'll never reach the library sitting here.* She stretched, then picked up the stick she'd found beside the path as she departed the village that morning. *Thank goodness I picked you up,* she balanced it appreciatively. *Up here there's nothing.* She started up another twist in the ascending route. *The landscape is so very dreary*, she repeated to herself. *So like I feel right now. Only the whistles of the wind for company.*

With her natural mental agility, Jodi pulled out of her depression by reliving a task that began with a typical brief message from the Special Force's Dispatcher: *South Africa. Vessel sunk. Family praying for assistance.* Jodi located three young children and their mother afloat in the turbulent waves. A swift, sudden gale had swept the ship onto the rocks. The family clung to ballast formed by shards torn from the vessel by the storm and waves. The surviving crew made a cursory scan for passengers then swam to safety.

They must have believed all were lost, thought Jodi putting a charitable connotation on what looked to be abandonment. One of the sailors had lit a fire on the beach so Jodi urged her group to face the distant flame; that action caused their kicks to propel them toward shore. Easily visible in bright orange, she swam back and forth between the older two children; each time the girl or boy faltered, she supported their bodies and encouraged, "Kick hard."

Their mother had propped her two-year-old daughter on a bit of debris. Her struggles to keep the toddler's head out of the water prevented her pro-gressing toward shore. "What's her name?" Jodi asked.

"Susie," the woman panted.

"May I help by carrying her? I'm a good swimmer and not as exhausted as you," Jodi's eyes exuded sympathy. The mother felt her love and let Jodi take the terrified child. Balancing the girl with the use of psychic energy, the angel lullabied her to sleep while continuing to urge on and shore up the others.

Jodi heard a crew member holler. "He must've spied us," she encouraged her group. "Look several men just dived into the spray. It will only be a minute or two and we'll have help." Before those rescuers swam close enough to see her, Jodi handed the sleeping girl to her mother and faded from view.

Decades later the boy, who matured into a prolific author, speculated on the identity of the mysterious woman, clearly visible to his family with her glowing golden hair. As he chronicled the dramatic childhood event, he re-counted how untiringly and swiftly she swam through the salty sea. He cred-ited their survival to her calm yet energetic encouragement. And her disappearance as the sailors arrived formed the basis of his conclusion that she must have been an angel.

Once her mission was accomplished, Jodi pondered how the lives of those children would develop. They had been so trusting. She had felt pulls of love and caring – not the mere excitement of a challenging rescue. And then, just as abruptly, they were out of her life. Gone. Why couldn't God understand how unsatisfying her life was becoming.

Since no news of an immediate job intruded into her consciousness, she flew over to a jungle and tramped among the vine-coated trees. For her safari she wore the typical costume of expeditions conducted in the early 1800's: tan jacket and matching skirt, with the customary, square hat to provide shade, secured under her chin with a scarf. Stumbling upon a pride of lions, she watched the mother return with meat for her cubs.

On that sweltering afternoon, Jodi pretended she had a charge named Mary and mentally created scenes of guarding the baby. While the infant napped, Jodi rehearsed the action of maintaining a vigilant lookout for in-truders, evidence of a fire, or attack of a jealous sibling analogous to the adult members of the pride protecting the cubs. She practiced inserting warning messages into the dreams or consciousness of Mary's pretend par-ents when danger emerged. And she sensed the stirrings of affection for this little imaginary human. It was a warm glow that filled her being – and felt so good.

On the mountainside, Jodi exhaled and watched her breath form cloudy vapor as the moisture condensed in the freezing air. She smiled fondly as she recalled the Mary she'd fashioned so many years ago. How dissimilar was that quiet, obedient child from the impulsive Gerald whom she'd ultimately been assigned. Although it was a clear day, at that altitude the brilliantly shining sun couldn't heat the towering bluff which she had reached. Her mind strayed — maybe to the 1850's? – when she reviewed the summons that had penetrated into her awareness: *London. Fire. Sarah and Jeffrey are your mission.*

Jodi sped to London where the tenement inferno dominated the sooty skyline. She immediately visualized the two children, about three and four years old she guessed. Materializing by their door, she walked over to the bed where the pair huddled in their second-floor flat. Mesmerized by the conflagration, they had not ventured to flee for safety. "Hi, I'm Jodi. I'm to fetch you for your mummy who's waiting outside. She can't come in with all these flames now, can she?" Two heads nodded in solemn accord; four eyes fixed on Jodi. "Let's pretend we're dogs. Do you ever play you're a puppy?"

"No," Jeffrey shook his head emphatically. "That's silly."

"Aw, c'mon. I'll be the mummy dog," and Jodi, squatting down to their level, licked Sarah's cheek making her giggle. "Arf...arf," Jodi barked. "Come to the floor with me little puppies! Arf. Arf."

Sarah laughed. Delight shoved aside her fear of strangers so she could allow Jodi to lift her from the bed. She found herself on the floor, under Jodi's body where the cooler air smelled clean. Jodi emitted psychic energy around herself to shield the child from the overpowering smoke and heat.

"Come, 'eff'ey. Nice here," begged his little sister.

Jeffrey, whose instinct was to protect his sister from this stranger, jumped off the bed and scampered to Sarah. Jodi explained, "See, I'll stay over you; you can crawl under me. We need to pass through those flames."

She urged the children to move rapidly. The building would soon collapse and she wasn't certain she was strong enough to block the inevitable explosion of burning debris from their bodies. Jodi reasoned that she must extricate them before the wooden structure crumbled.

Jodi's body formed a mobile tunnel as she bent over the children and extended psychic shields to the floor. Together they proceeded into the hallway and down the stairs; it seemed to take forever but at last she distinguished the exit. Although she was tempted to grab the two youngsters and sprint for the door, she restrained herself. Their lungs might be damaged by the toxic smoke even if exposed for a couple of seconds. Such young children could not be relied on to hold their breaths for a single frantic dash. Perhaps as important, her body prevented them from seeing the horrific destruction surrounding them.

Finally she got them out the door and onto the dirt of the dilapidated tenement's yard. As the three reached safety and, as if a divine hand had been restraining the explosion, the structure blew up with a roar. Sarah's and Jeffrey's mother, who'd been hurrying home from the market with their bread and cheese supper, heard the bells of the fire engines and saw smoke and flames overhead; she ran. Arriving on the block, she screamed when she saw the conflagration of what was left of the building.

Then the anguished mother spotted her children; she raced toward them, dropped to her knees, and smothered them with hugs and kisses. Over the next few weeks the boy and girl repetitively played at being puppies and chatted about crawling underneath a beautiful woman; their tale gained credibility because as she rushed to take possession of her children the mother had glimpsed Jodi. The stranger had vanished into the crowd before the grateful woman could thank her.

After rescuing two youngsters whom she'd never again see, Jodi decided to meander the streets of London. Little Sarah had been so sweet. She could envision spending a lifetime with the child, loving her and caring for her. And Jeffrey so conscientious. How much fun to work with him! The children's guardians were so blessed and her life so drab. Jodi's entire being slumped in the hopelessness of her situation.

Well I can imagine, can't I? No one can prevent me using make-believe. She outfitted herself as a mid-1800's nanny: black dress, white apron, black cap. While strolling through Hyde Park, she pretended a preschool Mary frolicked by her side. The child, whose cylindrical curls had been arranged by her adoring mother, pointed out a bunny peeking from behind the bushes and giggled. Then she darted into the formal garden they were passing to smell the gardenias but immediately returned to the path when Jodi called.

While she savored this reminiscence of the merry girl who exemplified obedience and on whom she had poured her love so many years ago, Jodi rounded a switchback of the trail and the clearly visible skywalk sprang into view again. She should reach it in perhaps another hour when she must dematerialize in order to step onto that ethereal bridge.

But, for now, her mind could drift through other Special Forces experiences. The recollections helped push aside the grief of Gerald's death, a black void within her very essence. The case of six lost hikers stranded in the Rocky Mountains during a raging blizzard popped into her head. One of the young men's Guardians had requested assistance from a Special Forces angel. Hopelessly off-course and fatigued, these lads couldn't perceive the intuitive suggestions their angels transmitted.

Jodi manifested as a mountain crone, walking with a stick. "C'mon, boys, I'll guide you down. You're a long way from nowhere," she made her voice crackle like an old woman's.

"Live nearby?" one of the youths asked curiously.

"Over yonder," she waved vaguely. "Can get you to a farmhouse about a quarter mile along." They tramped through deep snow, stung by the winds, unable to see more than a foot ahead until a slight outline solidified into a building. A startled woman opened her door and welcomed the wanderers into her home.

"I'm traveling farther tonight," Jodi mumbled and vanished back into the blizzard.

Concerned about their reception, Jodi lingered out of sight and overheard the farm woman's perplexed query. "Who's she?"

"Our angel," one of the fellows chuckled and they described the mountain hermit who'd saved their lives. Their words, though muffled by the closed door, were easily audible to the eavesdropping angel.

Jodi continued on the winding paths of the Rocky Mountains unhampered by the blizzard but once again excluded from the ongoing lives. Yet it had been fun to invent the crone persona and play it out. Yes, maybe she could create unusual characters to play. That might make Special Forces life more stimulating.

But she also sought respite from her dull existence by fixating on Mary, the pretend child no one could prevent her loving and cherishing. Mary, she imagined, was on the trails, lost in the mountains. Jodi stooped down to Mary's ear level, and whispered into her charge's thoughts the advice that would influence her to switch directions toward her tribe. Acting as a Guardian, imaginary or otherwise, she couldn't materialize for Mary as she did for the hikers. If she desperately needed a guide for Mary, she'd call for a Special Forces Angel.

Jodi's lips curved in self-deprecation. She'd deemed herself thoroughly trained thanks to her practice with the make-believe Mary. How Gerald had proved her wrong!

The past flowed on as Jodi plodded forward. Another Mary, whose family had recently been released from slavery by the war, looked after her younger siblings while her mother worked in the big white plantation home not demolished during the battles. Jodi sent psychic warnings as intuitions if one of the little ones wandered too far and needed retrieving.

Once she placed an older Mary in Baghdad. While Jodi aided Mary when necessary, she mostly acted as an observer, appreciating the Muslim girl's wise choices while maturing with her friends.

Thus Jodi continued her ascent to the Angelic Library, reliving the days before Gerald.

Chapter 3

The summer he turned six, Gerald ventured from the relative shelter of home and mother to spend many an hour in the fields with Dan. Riding the plow on his father's lap, he helped steer Blackie and Butterball; Butterball was Gerald's favorite. She nuzzled him as a way to ask for an apple. Blackie, however, had always stood huge and forbidding.

With his sized-down hoe, he toiled alongside his father readying the crumbly loam. He tossed handfuls of seeds, watched them fall into the furrows and pulled extra dirt across them.

Gerald adored his farmer clothes. His mother had sewn overalls identical to his father's and she made a brown-and-red checked shirt from the same bolt of fabric as Dan's. In addition, his boots tied up like other farmers'. But the straw hat his parents insisted he wear in the sun irritated his scalp; Gerald never could bear anything scratchy.

The little beets were the first plants to grow sturdy enough to hoe and weeds intruded on their space. Gerald conscientiously dug out weeds missed during his father's scrupulous first pass. "The durn varmits eat the baby plants' food," Dan had explained. "And, too, when we hoe, we loosen the soil so that air and water can reach their roots." Gerald watched as his father crouched down and delicately extracted one baby beet. "When they're this tiny, they're called seedlings." Gerald gazed in amazement at the fine white threads extending down from the stem of the miniature plant. "See how fragile it is?"

"I must be careful of it just like I am with Johnny when I help Mamma during his bath, right Papa?" Dan nodded as he patted Gerald's head. The farmer treasured each potential flower or vegetable as a living entity and was pleased to observe his son developing the same sentiment.

Gerald beamed that evening as he listened to Dan tell Sue how much he'd helped. He felt grown up when his mother answered Jimmy's entreaties, "You must be as big as Gerald before you can help Papa in the fields." The youngest boy pouted and kicked Gerald so their mother made Jimmy sit in the corner. Gerald felt so good when his mother hugged him for not hitting his brother back.

One morning Gerald helped his mother by playing catch, tag, then hide-and-seek with Jimmy and Janie while his mother did the laundry; Sally helped her hang the clean clothes on the lines. At lunch Gerald begged to join his father in the fields; he was tired of playing with his younger siblings. But his father argued that Gerald wouldn't feel comfortable in the sizzling heat and explained that during the morning shimmering waves of heat rose from the ground. As soon as the words slipped out, Dan mentally punched himself for the mistake.

Gerald's imagination spun out of control. *What's he mean? What're "shim-mering clouds of heat?" What do they look like? Is he joshing.* He jumped up and down. "Please Papa, please. Please let me go. I've just gotta see them."

His father gave in after much pestering and filled extra jugs of drinking water. "But," he admonished, "you can't come to the fields without your straw hat." To see the heat waves was the one thing Gerald wanted in the whole world; he put on the hat.

Gerald initially gaped at the clouds rising from the fields. His father hadn't been joshing. The etherealness of this spectacle intrigued him. But as he grew hot and itchy from salty perspiration, his enthusiasm faded. He was certain they'd been hoeing for hours when he asked, "Papa, almost quitting time?"

Dan checked the position of the sun, "No, Ger, only been here about half an hour. See, the sun's still right over us. Sun'll be yonder come time to go home." Wiping his forehead with his sleeve, he suggested, "Get a drink, son. Water's over there."

A few minutes more and Gerald's distress overwhelmed him. *Papa was right – I shoulda stayed home — I'm so hot – it's no fun.* The buzzing of the mos-quitoes seemed amplified in the still air. His brow and palms were sweaty and black from the soil. The air even smelled dusty. All he desired was to cool off; "Papa, please let me go play by the river, please? I'm too hot to hoe any more."

Dan saw the child's stringy mop of hair and his shirt drenched with sweat. He regretted having yielded to Gerald's entreaties. A sun-baked field was no place for a youngster; the father laid down his hoe and squatted in front of his son. "You mustn't enter the water," his voice was stern and his eyes peered di-rectly into Gerald's, "You understand? Not at all. Never."

Dan and Sue had drilled in the family rule: Children may only enter the river if accompanied by an adult who can swim. The boy nodded vigorously and pledged, "I'll stay on the bank, Papa. Promise."

And he dashed off. Gerald was aware that the river ran deep and wide and possessed a powerful current whose dangers his parents reiterated over and over. On many a Sunday afternoon the family strolled along the bank, ad-miring the white foam as the water crashed against rocks and dropped sev-eral feet on its inexorable flow to the Mississippi. Dan often tossed in a twig for the children to observe as the current snatched and threw it on the rocks. Sue used the example to explain how badly they'd be injured if they lost their footing and the waves tossed them on those boulders. Gerald pictured Jimmy or Sally or Janie sprawled out there, and vowed to guard his siblings because he was the big brother. He wasn't yet worried about Johnny since the baby couldn't even crawl but he supposed some day he'd have to keep an eye on him too.

At the river's edge, Gerald plunked himself down to undo the knots Sue had tied into his bootlaces: once liberated from the confining footwear, his left foot found itself inching toward the enticing water. Jodi warned, *No more than your toes, Ger!*

"I'll be fine, Jodi. See. Just stickin' in the tips. This whole foot's out of the water." To prove it, he stood with his right heel dug into the sand while his left toes got wet.

Oh, it felt wonderful. *Can't hurt to step in just a little bit.*

Don't, Jodi cautioned. *You've been told not to go in alone. It's not safe! Remember, the current runs strong.*

The refreshing chill of the river tickled his ankles; he closed his mind to his angel's objections. His toes blithely pushed stones here and there on the riverbed and traced lines in the sand. He spotted an eagle and imagined he could soar as high, swoop down and grab a fish, then fly away. Soon the delightful coolness enticed him to step in a bit further – *What's the harm?* he reasoned. The water spun eddies around his calves. He stooped and dipped in his hands. Shivering tingled through his hot body.

In his head Jodi was screaming, *Stop! You're too deep! The current! Gerald, Don't!*

The boy needed to choose between his desire to immerse himself in this alluring medium and Jodi's demand to obey. Although he'd intended to keep his promise, the delicious sensations shoved his father's admonitions from his mind. No one would ever know. He'd be fine. After all, he was big; he'd go to school in a month or two.

Gerald took another two steps; his knees were immersed. "See, it's safe Jodi," he confidently told his angel and mentor. "I'm strong. I'm six. See, I can swim." He defended his actions while he flattened himself on the surface of the river, dug his fingers into the bottom silt and kicked his feet like Dan had him practice during swimming lessons.

But Dan pointed him toward shore and stood behind him. This time Gerald faced the open river so his sturdy kicks propelled him past the depth where his fingers could touch the bottom. He tried to get footing, but couldn't. The current snatched him and swept him away.

When he gasped for breath, water rushed into his throat and he sputtered and coughed. He hadn't yet learned the arm motions for swimming so his head kept bobbing under. He kicked his legs the way his father taught but those thrusts sent him further into the middle of the river. His body stiffened with panic; he shrieked, "Jodi!"

His guardian angel was equally scared. When the wave ensnared him, Jodi nestled on his shoulder. If only she could materialize and provide concrete assistance as she did in Special Forces! She felt helpless with nothing but intuition and thought-wave commands as her tools. Over the years of shepherding this child, she appreciated the stress under which Guardians live. It had been much easier when she could take control. As a guardian actions must be initiated by Gerald; she could only supply encouragement, insights and warnings.

Moreover, right at that minute, she had no idea what to suggest. Yet, with Gerald crying out to her, he would perhaps heed her advice regardless of his fright. Peering ahead, she spied a log that the current had driven from the upstream fields. *Maybe he can kick over to it. It might act as a buoy,* she reckoned in desperation. *Gerald, look toward the bank. See that log?* As she hoped, her psychic command broke through his inner turmoil. The process of looking for the log reoriented his body. A few strong kicks sent him to it.

Now, hold on! she shouted into his fear. *Hold on tight!* Gerald grabbed the floating wood, a piece large enough to lift his head above the surface but not so big his short arms couldn't reach over it. After his head popped up out of the water, he could breathe. Jodi exhaled a sigh of relief. *Safe.*

But in another instant, she gulped, *No!* The log was headed straight for churning rapids. Sunbeams highlighted water droplets flung into the air as the river tumbled over boulders. Although the silvery spume would have been a captivating phenomenon under other circumstances, it caused Jodi's anxiety to redouble. *If he's flung on those rocks, we might be out of the rapids but he might be battered. His muscles will soon get tired. How much longer can he clutch that log? It's huge for such short arms.*

Jodi perceived that Gerald had grown as passive as a puppet; terrified, he had abandoned conscious participation and merely allowed his limbs to function at his angel's direction. She poured the extra energy of encouraging images into Gerald and issued clear *kick now* orders to move him toward any slower currents she saw on their tumultuous transit. She could tell that her messages reassured him and urged him on, even as such efforts weakened him.

Meanwhile, Dan, oblivious to his son's misadventure, continued to work the rows as he envisioned the corn rising and the beans that soon should be staked. His Guardian angel, Josie, picked up Jodi's telepathic anxiety and transmitted pictures of Gerald into Dan's mind hoping to attract his attention. Josie, as well as Jacob, Sue's angel, habitually resisted the rookie's attempts to engage them. Long-term Guardians, they possessed no concept of socialization or collaboration.

Nonetheless, Josie had witnessed a few of Jodi's unusual methods with Gerald, especially when Jodi tried to enter Dan's awareness. The novice's style proved interesting to observe during that boy's assorted crises. This day's events certainly constituted an emergency. Josie's duty was to protect Dan and lead him to God. Dan, her charge, would never be as adequate a father if Gerald drowned. He might not forgive God. Sometimes, she speculated, unusual situations dictated a deviation from usual methods.

So she listened to Jodi's request and sent Dan images of Gerald; but the first psychic messages resembled daydreams and evoked pleasant reminiscences on father-and-son times. It gratified him that Gerald had grown somewhat easier to keep track of. The pictures of his son thrashing about in the river elicited cheerful recollections of swimming lessons and fantasies of an adolescent Gerald testing his own strength against the river as Dan himself did.

Josie next received a telepathic image of events transpiring from Jodi's vantage point, similar to how, a half-century later, cameras would radiate live events to television screens. Josie passed along the scenes to Dan who saw, as in a vivid dream, the river in all its primitive grandeur: fearsome waves pounded rocks and hurled branches.

After the depiction of a panoramic view of the erratic water rushing on toward the wider rivers downstream, Jodi shifted to a close-up view of the desperate Gerald hanging onto his log. His legs barely kicked; his eyes were glazed.

Dan remembered Sue's descriptions of Jodi's use of visions when Gerald was in danger. The father grew uneasy and, after what seemed like eons to the angels, decided to take a break from his labor to check on his son. As Dan neared the river, he discovered two familiar boots...but no Gerald. His throat tightened; he called out; he searched the shore upstream and then down. Had Gerald truly been in the midst of that daydream of rushing water? Tense he scanned the raging aqueous monster, swollen by heavy early summer rains.

If Gerald's in the river, he's traveling downstream. Dan jogged along the bank to the west. As he neared the rapids, his eyes skimmed over the rocks. Something red snagged his peripheral vision; Gerald's shirts always contained some red. Crazed by the implication, Dan hopped across to the boulders where ... he found a stray red towel wrapped around a child-size rock.

Relief intoxicated him, briefly, then anxiety returned with ferocity. His impetuous son's little body could be tossed onto one of these menacing boulders. He kept hunting. Shoulders sagging, the father forced himself to methodically search. Out of the river, a sandbar loomed into sight. *That a body? In the hollow of the bar? Is it alive? Is that brown coveralls — or a grain sack?* Dan plunged into the river, not wasting a second to remove his boots and shirt, and swam toward it.

In the interval between Dan's walk toward the river from the fields and before he spotted Gerald's boots, Jodi had spied a streamlet that split off toward a sandbar. *Ger, kick your hardest! Right now!* When the child reached the sandy bar, she screamed, *Let go,* and, because he was startled by her shout, he did – and rolled onto the beach. *Get up! Get up!* Her words pierced through the fog that addled his thinking and the boy scrambled to his hands and knees. He crawled out of the water onto the solid surface and collapsed, panting, whimpering, utterly exhausted. Immediately the angel induced a sound sleep with her hypnotic hum. Finally, Jodi collapsed beside him.

Thus Dan found his boy, asleep, on the warm, sun-baked sand. He hugged his miraculously alive son, then the energy of Dan's terror flipped to fury. "Why are you here?" He barked. "What happened? You went in the river without permission! You disobeyed! You could be dead!"

Gerald believed he deserved the whipping he got that night. He vowed he'd never, ever, disobey again, aloud to his parents, and privately inside himself to his whole being. On his knees that night, he turned to his mother, "Can I ask God to help me keep my promise to be good?"

He couldn't comprehend why his mother grabbed him and cried in sobs that wrenched her entire body; she managed to squeeze out, "Yes, Gerald, we'll both pray for that." And they all did: Jodi's well-known thought-waves mingled with their oral prayers.

A scant six weeks later at the church picnic, Gerald again confronted the dilemma of obeying rules. He and his friend Teddy felt belittled during the ball game. Not only were the six year olds not allowed to bat but the older youths reached over their heads to intercept each potential catch. Finally the softball was flying straight toward Gerald, he excitedly leapt as high as he could; he would catch this one and show those dratted fellows.

His red-and-yellow plaid shirt flashed against the green of the nearby maple's lower limbs – in a flash the ball would reach his fingers. His father beamed with pride at his son's athletic development. Dan turned his head to hear Paul's remark about the upcoming haying and missed seeing the mean-spirited Joel swipe the ball from Gerald.

Gerald screamed in frustration as the bully easily nabbed the flying sphere from the highest point Gerald's fingers could stretch. "Snippet, you couldn't field it if you caught it," his tormentor jeered and mumbled about pests who insist on playing only to mess up a decent game.

Glowering, fury rising in his diminutive chest, Gerald proposed to Teddy a more profitable enterprise, "Let's stalk deer."

"Where?" asked Teddy, pragmatically. The stocky little fellow, blond and blue-eyed, was quite sensible.

"Deer'll be in the meadow down by ol' Jude's place." So the pair set off into the woods.

Jodi reminded, *You're supposed to obtain permission to explore.* Gerald cockily rationalized, *It's just after lunch. We aren't going far. Mamma'd say, "No, dinner time'll be soon." But it'll be forever until we eat.* He jumped up and grabbed a leaf replaying his memory of his near-catch of the ball. *Everyone's playing or watching the game. We won't be missed.*

The tall straight oaks and walnuts were interspersed with hemlock and cedar. Last fall's crunchy leaves and pine needles allowed their feet to sink deeply into the natural carpet, deliciously cool to their soles. Fragrances from the flowers and pines filled the atmosphere. Occasionally, a squirrel or chipmunk scooted on ahead of them; rustlings sounded in the brush; birds chirped overhead. Dense foliage shortened the distance they could see.

The two inseparable chums had played together since infancy while their mothers participated in community projects. Folks in town said the friends represented Christmas when together, what with Gerald invariably decked out in red and Teddy in green. Teddy even wore chartreuse suspenders to the picnic and both pranced around on bare feet during that splendid summer day.

Jodi enjoyed comparing and contrasting the children. Teddy's husky and sturdy body differed markedly from the lithe, wiry Gerald. Her charge's eyes perpetually darted about checking out his surroundings; his friend's maintained a steady gaze. Teddy's natural caution balanced Gerald's impulsive quickness. Already at six Ted reasoned out problems and arrived at logical conclusions. He would never have waded into the river — less out of obedience than because he understood the inherent dangers and foresaw the dire consequences.

Soon after entering the woods, Teddy hesitated, "What if there's bear in here?"

"Papa said there are no bears round these parts no more. Wish there were. I sure'd like a cub." Jodi grinned at the boy's naive confidence.

"Would your mamma letcha keep one?" Teddy wondered incredulously. His mother would never permit such a pet.

"Why not? I'd take care of him," Gerald nonchalantly picked up a twig. With stroking motions he explained, "I'd brush him." Then he pretended to pull on a well rope, "I'd water my cub. And I'd feed him." He completed his fantasy by putting imaginary food into an invisible bowl that he set on the ground for his cub.

Although tempted, Jodi did not project her sarcastic reaction, *Oh, yeah, you can't take care of yourself.* Instead she suggested, *But the cub would miss its mamma.*

The small boy pictured his cub crying unconsolably, and replied, "You're right. I'd better not take any cub from its mamma."

"Huh? Who's right? Who're you talking to?" Teddy pivoted and gaped.

"Just Jodi." Gerald spoke in childish innocence. He presumed all people were acquainted with their Guardian Angels so he'd never before bothered to bring up the subject with Teddy.

"Who's Jodi?"

"My angel. What's yours called?"

"Your angel! What? Where's it?" The child glanced up in the trees and around at the bushes. "And whacha mean, 'What's yours called?' You're crazy!" Teddy guessed his buddy was joshing – and he got enough teasing from his older brothers.

"Jodi's not an 'it'. She's my angel. So who's yours?" Gerald's perplexed expression conveyed honesty. A typical self-centered lad, he'd never reflected on his pal's angel. "I don't have an angel," Teddy pouted. Then he scowled; his eyes squinted, "You're lying!" His knuckles rested on his hips like his mother's did when she confronted one of his older brothers about an unbelievable half-truth. His foot tapped like hers. "So, lemme see your angel. That is, if you've got one."

"Okay. Jodi, talk to Teddy," commanded Gerald. He must prove he wasn't lying.

Teddy paused, his eyes glazing over for at least a minute; he did possess an inordinate level of patience for a boy his age. "Nope. Nothing," he proclaimed, disgusted that his friend would fib to him.

"C'mon, Jodi. Please talk to Teddy," Gerald begged. "Please." His angel empathized and didn't want her precious ward to lose face. This was his dearest friend, aside from her that is, and Teddy could even physically play ball with him.

Utterly frustrated, Jodi struggled to figure this out. Already in plenty of trouble with Jeff for introducing herself to Gerald, she knew the proper response: *Ger, I mustn't. Teddy isn't aware of his angel. You weren't supposed to meet me.* She stretched out her open hands in a plea for understanding. She pictured herself in his mind with wrinkled brow, tightened lips, fingers of one hand tugged on a strand of hair that dangled by her ear: the visualization she employed to convey the message, "I'm confused: don't know what to do."

"But you talk to me. C'mon, Jodi. How can it hurt? If Teddy listens to you, maybe he'll hear his angel. Please, Jodi, Please!" Gerald's sweet persistence made it nearly impossible to deny his request.

Conflicting thoughts crashed together in Jodi's mind: *Humans aren't to actually meet their angels. If Teddy doesn't participate in Gerald's life with me, can the two boys remain chums?* Jodi avoided Gerald's eyes and instead stared at the wistful expression on Teddy's face. *Can the boys remain close friends if Gerald has a secret life Teddy can't share? My friendship with Gerald feels marvelous and correct. Teddy is a special child.* Jodi flitted off to a tree branch to distance herself, if ever so slightly, from the concrete source of her distress. *Teddy would benefit from a reciprocal partnership with his angel. It would be such fun to work together with Teddy's guardian. We could keep the boys safer if we collaborated.*

Through this inner turmoil, Gerald's plea pierced, "Jodi, please, please, please." She projected herself compulsively pulling at that lock of hair; she leapt to the ground and paced, swishing the red skirts that draped to her ankles. She wished for a miracle to escape this mess. *What to do?*

"Yes, please talk to me, Jodi," Teddy listened to Gerald's attempts to persuade Jodi; his friend had never lied before. If Gerald declared something true, he should be believed. And Gerald seemed so very certain. Like any child his age, Teddy coveted what his buddy had. So he desperately wanted to meet Jodi. *Maybe she'll be my angel, too.* Teddy's poignant entreaties compounded Jodi's ambivalence.

Jodi could not resist. *What harm is there? If Teddy isn't supposed to communicate with his angel, he'll never meet him.* She justified her wayward decision: *After all, his angel will seek permission. If I ask, the answer will definitely be, "No."* And without further thought, Jodi sent a fresh image of herself, dressed in green with silvery wings and halo set upon hair sparkling with stardust, into the minds of both children. Her, "Hello," sounded audible to both.

Teddy, mouth agog, was permeated with awe. The boys could not have known it, but Teddy's future, his whole life changed course at that second. God had intended he be a builder. Instead he would become a seeker after truth — a profession ill-suited to the talents with which he was born. He would explore writing, art, philosophy and wander his physical world, always searching the spiritual realm, never quite finding the divine within his everyday life. His fate had been to construct solid foundations with bricks and mortar, not to construct within the world of metaphysical ideas.

Swept up in that moment in the woods, neither he nor Gerald, not even Jodi, realized the consequences of her choice to act on her own inclination rather than follow the angelic laws. Teddy somersaulted in glee. He pleaded for his angel to introduce himself. His angel, Miguel, sought guidance. God, aware of the future, anticipated that Miguel could provide the grounding Teddy required for the life he would embark. God granted Miguel permission.

Miguel fashioned a humanoid facsimile of himself with whom Teddy could relate, a young, clean-shaven man who wore the typical costume of male angels: a green hunting outfit, pointed hat and shoes, similar to the elf in Teddy's storybook. "Hello, Teddy, my name is Miguel. I'm your angel." His greeting mesmerized the child who stared at the portrait Miguel inserted into his mind.

Jodi's supervisor, Jeff, who was notified almost instantly by the Guardian Overseer, sputtered and fumed. *"Oh Jodi!" What a day in the history of mankind: two human children in direct contact with their angels! And on my watch! Where have I gone wrong? What eventual consequences should I anticipate? How do I get Jodi to stop acting on her own initiative and to obey established angelic protocol?* And he flew off to consult the Guardian Overseer.

After meeting Miguel, the boys, with Teddy in a bit of a daze, resumed their trek and penetrated ever deeper into the woods. The path narrowed from encroaching weeds. Squirrels chattered. A red fox peered down the trail at them. Gerald pointed; both boys froze. The fox soon tired of watching these two-legged oddities and scampered off into the brush. But no deer, the object of their expedition, startled into flight.

Mosquitoes bit. "Ow!" yelped Teddy, pulling back his sleeve to see what caused the sharp pain. A thorn. Drawing it out slowly so it wouldn't break, Teddy then rubbed the spot and turned to Gerald, "You sure this is the right way?"

"Yeah, well, uh — sorta sure." However, as Gerald surveyed the scene, his skin itchy and his throat dry, the darkness disoriented him. Last spring, when he and his father hiked through the woods, the path had been much brighter. The season's thick foliage dimmed the light so much that it seemed almost like the hour when his mother called him and Jimmy inside from play.

Also the last time he covered this route he could see farther. Now, with the summer overgrowth, he could barely see past the edge of the trail. Before the walk to ol' Jude's place had been short. Since Gerald hadn't noticed the fork where his father and he jogged onto a side path, the six year olds had trekked much deeper into the woods.

Wiping the sweat from his forehead with the back of his hand, Teddy rebelled. Even the excitement of meeting his angel no longer sustained him. "I wanna go back right now," he snapped at Gerald. He refused to take one more step and was prepared to fight if Gerald didn't agree to abandon their pursuit of deer. His fists balled and his lips puckered.

Gerald's tummy growled; his throat felt parched. The ground was packed dry and no sounds of running water beckoned from a nearby spring or stream. Glancing around, scuffing his toes through the pine needles and scratching his bites, he reluctantly concurred, "You're right." A slug-it-out prevented, they turned to retrace their route. All too soon the adversity resumed when in a few yards, they arrived at a fork.

Nothing looked familiar. Gerald panicked. He nervously scanned both branches with a saluting gesture like his father used when he scrutinized the distance. His forehead creased in worry lines. "Teddy, you know which way?" a slight catch in his high-pitched voice betrayed his anxiety.

"Doncha know?" Teddy sounded annoyed. He too checked their options. Since the intersection came together in a tight angle, it seemed they must have continued ahead when they hiked through this Y a few minutes before.

A fallen tree distracted Gerald and provided relief from the serious business at hand. Ants marched out from under the rotting bark and a green caterpillar wound down a vine twisting around the desiccated roots.

Gerald managed to engage his impatient friend in the wonders of the dead pine. They watched a grasshopper jump from leaf to leaf on the surrounding plants. Teddy stuck out his finger to seduce the caterpillar and the furry creature slithered along toward his wrist. After a few minutes Gerald thought to seek Jodi's advice about the fork.

"The one on the right," she replied. Of course Gerald headed left. Hadn't yet figured out left from right. Jodi screamed, "No!" But the child, believing himself to be safely on the route, was again focused on stalking deer and ignored her attempts to snag his attention. After all hunters don't talk to their angels when on the track of big game. His trepidation subsided — Jodi always provided the solution. Teddy, a newcomer to angelic assistance, relied on his more knowledgeable pal.

Oblivious to time and surroundings, the pair pretended to hunt wild animals, secure in the belief they would soon be at the picnic. Hills rose on each side forming a winding valley. In some spots the children needed to skirt or climb gigantic boulders. Finally, Teddy, slightly more experienced a tracker, realized he was in a place he'd never before visited. Sounds of rapids echoed off the far side of the hills.

When he sensed that something was terribly wrong, Teddy emphatically quit playing; hands on hips, he surveyed the landscape, "Ger, I've never ever been here before. I'm hungry. Where are we?" Although Gerald had been wondering the same thing, he wasn't worried since Jodi had told him which fork to take. While the boys stalked imaginary beasts, Jodi berated herself for forgetting Gerald's tendency to confuse left and right. When he was ready to listen, the two had traveled miles from their parents. Evening clouds were closing in; they could never reach the picnic grounds in daylight. If they trudged, tired and without a lantern, through the forest after dark, one or the other could be injured.

Miguel, in his first stab at guardian teamwork, suggested, "Let's recommend they stay in the cave over there under the trees. No snakes are in it." He pointed out a shallow plateau on the hillside. A clump of trees marked the center of the clearing and, behind it, a dark hole opened into the hill. The cave would be one of the many created millennia ago by the river and its tributaries as the water etched out the valley before the river evolved to its current route.

Jodi agreed and beamed the directions to Gerald since he was more accustomed to human-angelic exchanges. "C'mon, Teddy. Jodi says there's a cave. See, behind those hemlock. We're to stay because it's so late and it'll be dark soon. See it?" Elated, Gerald galloped forward; a rabbit munching on leaves nervously jumped then hopped into the bushes.

"Hey! A stream," shouted Teddy. "I'm so thirsty!" The sturdy boy raced toward the rivulet. His mouth seemed stuffed with cotton. That water, miles from the big river, was certainly safe to wade. Without hesitation, he plunged into the cold, clear liquid; Gerald ran close behind him. On hands and knees, the boys dunked their mosquito-bitten faces under the surface and lapped up greedy gulps; then, splashing noisily, they threw handfuls at each other. The giggling water fight that ensued proved such fun they forgot briefly that they were far from home and extremely hungry.

Teddy first spied the wild raspberries next to the stream. The berries, ripe and plenteous, made the bushes more red than green. "Look!" he cried out and both sprinted over and shoveled handfuls of the sweet fruit into their mouths. Tummies full, chins dripping rosy juice, bodies cool and wet after their water play, the youngsters were satisfied and energized.

Teddy preferred to resume the task of locating their families. The black opening of the cavern frightened him. "What if there're bear in there," his words quavered.

"There're no bear here. Jodi'd warn us," Gerald's confidence remained unwavering. His guardian's presence meant he was secure.

However Teddy, without enough opportunity to assimilate Miguel as an adult companion, missed his parents. As the shadows from the surrounding trees lengthened, he whimpered, "But…I want Mamma and Papa. I wanna go home." his persona reverted to that of the youngest brother who, although teased mercilessly, was lovingly protected by his entire family.

"Can't Teddy. It's too late." Gerald's carefree attitude exuded the expectation of a fun night in the cave – a true adventure. Not only was Gerald devoid of common childhood caution, he was seasoned in angelic companionship. He couldn't be lonely. In fact, he didn't understand Teddy's angst. "C'mon. Don't be scared," he tugged at Teddy's sleeve before he crawled into the hole then down the tunnel to the cave floor. "Jodi and Miguel are with us."

Fighting back tears, Teddy tagged behind. The faint light creeping through the opening revealed a roomy cavern. Its depths were pitch black: there was no sign of a second opening or side tunnels. The place would have been terrific to explore under more favorable circumstances.

The natural wonder intrigued Gerald but he needed to help Teddy feel safe. The night would be a lot more fun if Teddy weren't so sad. Miguel endeavored to speak into his charge's thoughts but the boy's fear and loneliness prevented him from hearing the angel.

Gerald was confident that Jodi would fetch his mother and father. Yet his conscience accused him of once again disobeying. He took off on his adventure without permission and ended up in trouble. Teddy was so unhappy and Gerald grew miserable in the waves of guilt.

Abruptly the wind picked up and started to howl; rain pelted; a freak storm erupted. Peals of thunder and flashes of lightning interrupted the quiet and terrified Teddy. A huge tree cracked loudly, then crashed. As it toppled, a substantial section of its root structure ripped from the ground. Loss of stability in that sandy soil triggered a rumbling landslide that blocked the entrance to their cave. Instantly it was black: not a thing could be seen.

Jodi had already flown off to notify Sue and Dan. The children were alone except for Miguel. Teddy trembled. Gerald was truly afraid. What if Jodi couldn't find the cave with its entrance sealed shut?

Miguel longed to comfort the children. When he tried to engage Teddy, he found the lad couldn't perceive him through his fright. *We'll need to work on our communication skills;* he pictured himself ruefully rubbing his nose with his index finger. This condition was brand new for him. He'd never before related directly with humans although he'd acquired eons of experience with intuitive directions to guide his charges.

He admired Jodi's finesse with Gerald, but he had just witnessed today that even she couldn't achieve one hundred percent accuracy. *I wonder how she was able to broadcast her message to both boys at once. I must learn that skill. It would be useful tonight. Gerald would probably hear me.* But, try as he might, he couldn't figure out how Jodi had done it. *I have lots to learn,* he mused as he failed the third time.

Miguel pondered his oblivion to that previously unique partnership. Certainly he and Teddy had frequently accompanied Jodi and Gerald. *We Guardians really do focus on one individual; we notice little else*, he admitted. Acquainting himself with Jodi could prove as novel as participating in her method of easy conversation with humans. One of his talents as a Guardian was his introversion: he could be happy without socialization. Special Forces angels, in contrast, were extremely gregarious. Would he fit into this new world where he would be expected to share comfortably with that trainee? He alit on Teddy's shoulder. Maybe the boy would sense his presence and be soothed. *Are her ideas a fresh, better approach to guarding? Will there be unforeseen disasters?* Teddy did seem to relax a little. *Should be an interesting lifetime*, Miguel concluded.

The friends clung to each other. Miguel deduced that Gerald had been assured he was safe because of Jodi. What with the landslide and her off to fetch his parents, Gerald's face was screwed up and he wiped the occasional tear trickling out the corner of his eye. *At least,* Miguel conjectured, *maybe this will teach him to make wiser choices.* He tried another time to insert a thought into Teddy's mind and to broadcast one to Gerald. *How can I let them know that I sent that telepathic message to Jodi about the slide? If only I could reach into Gerald's thoughts. Teddy's mind is closed tight.* He rubbed his nose with his imaginary finger. *And how did she communicate with the two at once?*

At the picnic grounds the sudden summer downpour brought chaos. No one missed the boys — each set of parents assumed they played in the other's family group. People ducked under tables, into buggies, wherever they found shelter. Later, in the confusion of gathering drenched and wind-blown clothing, playthings, baskets, and blankets, Sue and Emma still didn't worry about their six year olds.

Not until she was about ready to leave did Sue feel uneasy. She counted heads a second time: four-year-old Sally, three-year-old Jimmy, 15-month Janie, and baby Johnny in the bassinet. *Where's Gerald?* Emma rushed over to her and gasped, "Is Teddy here?"

"I think the boys wandered off," Sue informed her friend; she breathed slowly to maintain her serenity but sensed something wrong. She replayed recent events: *When did she last see Gerald?* As her inner self opened into her conscious awareness, she detected Jodi's presence. *Why's Jodi here if Gerald isn't?* She squelched her panic so she could distinguish the angelic voice. Tucking a strand of hair back in place, she concentrated, *Jodi? Where are they*?

Several miles away, the angel responded. Sue's initially mild anxiety mounted and nearly overwhelmed her as Jodi explained. *They're stuck in a cave along the old riverbed. Lightning struck a large oak during the storm; the entrance has been sealed by a landslide caused by its fall.* Genuine horror washed over Sue: she gulped, her hands covered her mouth, her eyes widened while the implications registered.

Emma, reading her friend's demeanor, asked desperately, "Sue, what is it?" Grabbing Sue's shoulders, she gently shook her. "Honey, tell me what's wrong!"

Sue, with an abrupt twist, freed herself from Emma and ran toward the men harnessing the horses to the carts and buggies. "Dan…. Dan!" she screamed. He came running. Her agitation ignited his. Other men turned and stared; a few gradually approached them.

Breathlessly Sue repeated Jodi's summary to her husband while Emma, listening in, stiffened and clutched her skirts, nervous about her friend. Teddy's mother forced herself to remain composed as the unbelievable words Sue relayed to Dan echoed through her consciousness.

Emma considered, *Dan's grave, not anxious. He's not shaking her back to sanity. She must've acted this way before.* She shifted her weight from one foot to the other and fingered her apron as she observed, *He's clenching and unclenching his hands; his lips are taut. Seems more angered by Gerald's latest escapade than fretful about Sue's state of mind.*

The man's unfaltering voice directed, "Take the others home. We'll go get the boys." He appended a bit of humor, "And when I find him, I'll strap a harness on him until he turns twenty."

Obviously he's used to this behavior. Emma's posture slackened. *I'd be a perpetual hysteric if I'd a child who took as many risks as Gerald does.* Emma empathized with her friend who was insisting, "I must go, Dan. I can identify Jodi's messages more easily."

What is she saying? Sue's desperate. Poor dear is deranged; she wants to coerce Dan into letting her join the search party. "Sue, c'mon!" Emma took hold of her friend's arm. "Let's go home." But the anguished mother furiously shook her off.

"I'm okay, Emma, but I must go." Sue's tone reverberated harshly.

She's obviously consumed by her fantasy, observed Emma, who strove to mimic Dan and act calm so her friend might regain her stability.

With equal assertiveness, Dan declared, "Sue, You've got to trust me. Emma will stay with you." His wife had no choice but to accompany her friend. The women woke the younger children who were sleeping on the single blanket that had remained dry during the storm and headed toward the buggy to which Jenny, one of Sue's and Dan's mares, was harnessed.

"Where's Ger?" Sally looked around anxiously for her big brother.

"He's with Papa. They'll be home soon, sweetheart," Sue hugged her reassuringly as she lifted the girl into the back of the buggy.

"I wanna stay with Ger," whined Jimmy.

"You can't keep your eyes open," his mother grinned. She tickled the little boy's chin and he giggled.

Since Emma's older sons would join Dan and their father for the rescue, by unspoken concurrence, Emma joined Sue on the ride home with baby Johnny on her lap.

Emma tentatively inquired, "Honey, you feeling all right?" With no immediate reply, she bit her lip, fingered the edge of the infant's bonnet, then lay a hand on her friend's shoulder, "Are you okay, Sue?"

Sue sighed deeply, gripped the reins more tightly and, with a leap of faith, elected to share the story of Jodi. Her childhood buddy, whose emotions were inwardly taut as strung wire, attempted to display outward relaxation as she listened, incredulous, to Sue.

A typical farmwife, Emma had an ample lap for infants and toddlers. Her black hair sprinkled with gray was drawn into a handy bun, and she wore sensible attire. She managed any chore efficiently and capably — but this mad tale of Sue's strayed beyond her expertise. As she gently soothed the baby, cuddled close to her body, Emma studied Sue's profile which came in and out of focus as the moon played peek-a-boo with lingering clouds. Unwilling to believe her ears, she nevertheless felt inclined to give credence to Sue's words, so impressed was she by the sincerity.

Sue recounted several Jodi anecdotes that Emma absorbed as if hypnotized. Once or twice she turned around to check on the three sleepers, curled up on the buggy's back seat, wrapped in the dry blanket. Emma considered Gerald. She had witnessed the paucity of caution, the pell-mell sprint through life of her best friend's firstborn; she'd often questioned how Sue and Dan coped.

The angel stories started to sound plausible in light of Gerald's astonishingly lucky escapes which Sue had previously shared when the two sipped tea while their children played. Emma seldom had any advice for Sue despite her guidance of three older boys through childhood without incident. Her husband, Ryan, tended to agree with Dan's repeated, only half-joking, option to harness the boy. Ryan commented to Emma that at least their six year old was cautious enough to curb his wild friend's exuberance and be safe when with him.

Well, maybe Jodi existed, or, maybe she was a whimsy that permitted Sue a tolerable life with her impulse-ridden child. Emma would indulge her friend's belief in this guardian angel and not argue.

Teddy's mother wished to furnish her friend with an indication she was mulling over this peculiar possibility but without committing herself, "Gerald has indeed been a trial for you. You've needed lots of assistance, uh, to just keep him alive and, well, uh, yourself from going mad." Emma reached across the sleeping Johnny and put a hand on Sue's. "Tell me if there's anything I can do," she appealed, scanning the woman's disquieted countenance.

Sue swiveled toward her passenger. "Thanks, best friend." She switched the reins to her left hand, and stretching her arm around Emma's shoulders, hugged tightly. The horse plodded on along the well-traveled road while the old pals sat close against each other; the peacefully dozing baby boy wrapped snuggly in his blue and white blanket. Emma relaxed as she sensed the return of her valiant buddy's normal steadiness.

The boys' spending a night in the woods didn't much distress Emma: Teddy camped out frequently with his father and brothers. She'd lived through numerous such episodes with his older brothers. Moreover, she doubted that they were actually trapped in a cave. She chatted animatedly to boost Sue's spirits, "It's warm tonight despite that storm. They'll be safe, even if it's all night. Teddy's spent many a night under the stars with Ryan and his brothers. He'll know what to do."

Sue thereby inferred that her friend neither believed her about Jodi nor the cave. *That's best,* she reassured herself. *Emma isn't as alarmed as I am. She doesn't share my dread. That's best.* But the wistful thought flitted through her head: *Yet it would be nicer if she believed me.*

As she glanced over at her Johnny, she projected many worries into the night enveloping them. *Will Dan be able to communicate with Jodi, what with his anxiety, that noisy search group, his anger? Oh, God, Please bestow trust on him so he can discern her promptings.*

"Emma, what should I do?" Sue blurted out as tears rolled down her cheeks. "Just six weeks ago – the river, remember? Gerald promised to always obey. We told him over and over not to enter the woods without permission.

Where am I going wrong? I've gotta be the lousiest mother that ever lived!" As the self-blame gushed out, her tears became sobs. Emma slid little Johnny into the crook of one arm and embraced Sue with the other.

"We always accuse ourselves. I do it all the time. Whenever a kid gets into a scrape, I'm positive it's my fault." She chuckled, "and, to think of how my poor mother must've blamed herself during my escapades." Sue began to laugh at herself. Soon the two giggled as each recounted childhood incidents when their mothers probably pulled out their own hair while probably wishing to wrench out their daughters'.

Jenny veered onto the driveway to her home and halted at the kitchen porch; Sue and Emma carried the children to their beds. Barney barked and whined; he missed his pal, Gerald, who could be counted on to throw him some sticks. Jenny would wait patiently until an adult returned to unharness, rub and feed her. Emma and Sue tucked the four young ones into bed then Emma brewed tea while Sue tended to the faithful mare.

As she rubbed and brushed Jenny, Sue prayed and cried. Regardless of Emma's encouragement, she felt a failure as a mother. Emma imbued her sons with discipline and obedience while she couldn't even teach Gerald the most basic rules. He always acted so sure of himself. Tears flowed, "He's yours too, God. Please help us. We're trying. But it's not working." Barney, alert to her distress, gently licked her arm and whined; she caressed him.

Meanwhile the men followed Dan deep into the woods. The moon, often a beacon in the night sky, blinked off and on that evening as clouds intercepted its light before it reached the forest paths. Ryan and his sons, excellent trackers, carried torches to check crossways for telltale signs. However, the heavy rain had washed away any traces of the boys' passage. Sue, via Jodi, had reported them trapped in a cave along the old riverbed. How to lead the group in that direction without revealing the source of his information presented a quandary.

In fact, the first intersection brought the a debate over which way the children would logically have proceeded. With his feet widespread at the fork and gesturing sharply toward one branch and then the other, Jim Green, the town barber, argued for an equal number to explore each. "Doing that, enough will be available to cover each trail."

Jake Robins, the blacksmith, objected; his bass tones resonated with a timbre and depth that matched his massive hulk. "My lads tend to follow the obvious trail unless they know the area. Either of them been along here much?" he turned toward Dan and Ryan.

Both fathers recalled that they each had hiked with their sons in these parts, but neither deemed the boys familiar enough to deviate for side explorations. Dan breathed a quiet sigh of relief when the men concluded they'd send out two men at each intersection and the rest would keep to the main route. Thus, the majority were available as the party approached the old riverbed.

At this point, however, Dan realized that a considerable amount of exploration still lay ahead. In the dark, identification of a particular clump of trees in a specific clearing might prove impossible unless the moon cooperated. They could hardly see each other. Those with whom he searched appeared merely as black silhouettes against the night sky. When clouds covered the moon, a sprain or worse, a broken bone, was possible. He rubbed his fingers through his hair, drew a kerchief from his pocket and mopped his face. As he did so, he consciously tensed then released his muscles, *Jodi, I'm trying to heed you.* And, he prayed, *Jesus, please quiet my fears so I can hear her.*

He could sense Jodi's attempt to transmit which direction the children wandered but the voice was muddled by his own anger and misgivings. The urgency also affected his concentration. Some of the men counseled halting through the night and starting again at daylight. Although the men called, "Gerald," or, "Teddy," every few feet, they apparently were not near enough for the children to hear. "Hey," asked Joe Miller, one of the younger searchers, "are we sure this is the right way?"

Dan couldn't announce, "It is." The group would demand the search be abandoned for the night if they judged him a little crazy, with anxiety overwhelming his reason. He was determined to keep as many with him as possible for the dig they would confront at the end of their hunt.

He soldiered on, unable to control the turmoil that ravaged him internally. Recriminations rose through his fury. *What's wrong with me? Why can't I teach him to listen? And what if I can't rescue him tonight? Can we find them in time?* Alarm began to usurp anger. Through the emotional maelstrom, angelic guidance was impossible to detect.

In addition, the night deepened. When the dark clouds moved, stars twinkled and decorated the sky overhead. Underfoot twigs and leaves lay helter skelter in the mud. Owls hooted. A red fox dashed across the path. A wolf howled in the distance. A dank odor hung in the air. Ryan burst out, "How many times have I told the boys to leave traces to mark the way home? Why didn't Teddy obey simple hiking rules? 'Cause he's always sure his brothers or I will protect him so he never troubles himself. This will sure change. He's gonna be the family's trailblazer from now on."

Dan recognized that he wasn't the only father berating himself for a laggard son but received scant consolation: the awareness didn't erase his shame at his monumental failure. He trudged on, lost in self-accusations. He knew whose boy was responsible for that night's dilemma.

The searchers covered numerous divergences off the main riverbed. Warned by Jodi's message to Sue that the children had traveled quite a ways, Dan urged an investigation some distance along each. But he figured he'd soon be vetoed because more were demanding a halt for the night.

A newly fallen tree! The marker he sought — but the dark spawned innumerable shadows. Would identification be possible? A fresh wave of desperation overcame Dan: the boys were in a sealed cave — *is there enough air?* Without his extra knowledge, no one else appreciated how abysmal the situation was. He regretted his decision to leave Sue behind. *Will she ever forgive me if we're too late, if Gerald...?* He paused and wiped his forehead once more.

Blaming myself isn't helping. Can't hear Jodi's hints. Have to trust. Dan prayed and pictured Jesus sitting with the boys. And he believed.

As he admitted faith, his mind emptied. Jodi's voice came through so loudly he instantly pinpointed her location. *Dan, over here!* He followed that clear, inner voice.

The others reluctantly trailed behind; he inferred that the increasing consensus to desist until daybreak would soon be irresistible. He became aware of Bob Stranton, their town cobbler. Strongly critical of the wild nighttime foray, his sharp words sliced through the air, "After some shuteye, we'll be much better trackers. We ain't gonna find nothing in these durn woods in this @#!! dark." The men assented, not all as vocally.

Ryan tried to persuade Dan. "The boys will be fine. I've had Ted out camping and he can find shelter —isn't afraid of the dark. They'll sleep tonight and we'll find them tomorrow. It's warm. They'll be fine."

Dan figured the party chalked up his persistence to an exaggerated paternal-duty compulsion. He'd long been kidded about stubbornness, but this time was different. Worse, he couldn't explain why. He stared ahead fixedly; he shut out their arguments, and he focused on Jodi. Striding forward, his body tense, he prayed. *If the men leave...O God, please keep them with me until we find the boys. I can't dig them out alone. Please, Father.*

"Dan, this is ridiculous. The boys are sound asleep," Pastor Drake reasoned with him.

If they call a halt, do I dare tell them about Jodi? The other men's concerns were growing louder. They doubted that the boys were in that vicinity because they weren't responding to calls of their names.

Ryan turned to him a final time, "Dan, we have to stop."

But at that very moment, Dan spotted the freshly fallen tree with the huge mound of mud its roots had heaved up. *The cave must be behind that loose debris. Is that Gerald's scream?* He cupped his hand around his ear. *Yes, it's him. Jodi must've told him to cry out.* "Men, listen." he yelled, his voice jubilant. "Gerald's voice!"

And they all heard, ran to the landslide and dug with their hands. Because the newly formed barrier was composed of soft silt — not firmly packed, dirt showered down the tunnel onto the boys. Jodi screamed, *No! They'll suffocate!*

Gerald and Teddy scooted to the rear of the cave, but the sand raining down began to fill the air. They coughed. Jodi, reinforced by Miguel, sent psychic messages of impending disaster to the men. Couldn't one of them foresee that danger? Finally Teddy's father shouted, "Stop! Stop, I tell you! Maybe we're causing sand to dump into the cave. We may be smothering them. This isn't packed; there's no clay in it."

When his friend's words registered, Dan froze in his frenzied attack. Then Jodi could successfully penetrate his mind, *Please, Dan! You'll kill them. Find another method!*

"Let's ask the children," Dan held up his hand, effectively silencing the diggers. "Gerald! You hear me?"

A barely audible "Yes" came back.

"Is dirt falling in?"

"Yes."

While the others headed home for shovels, Dan and Ryan stayed to reassure their children. Jodi advised Dan she should put the boys to sleep and avoid wasting oxygen. *It's not a good time to tell him about Miguel,* she decided. *That would be too confusing.*

The air in here is stale, she explained. Dan suggested to Ryan they tell their sons to sleep in order to use less of the precious air. The angels hummed favorite lullabies; the children slept; the two fathers clasped hands and, kneeling in the mud, prayed together.

Eventually buckets and shovels arrived. About ten yards from the cave the men dug to its estimated depth; they planned to tunnel toward it. Someone recommended the creation of a bucket brigade to remove the loosened dirt. That did make the excavation proceed faster.

John Green returned from his grocery store with a loaded mule. He lit a fire, made coffee, then grilled bacon and eggs which he slapped between bread to form sandwiches to feed the men as they took turns resting. Only Dan and Ryan, at the head of the tunnel, wouldn't pause. Finally Pastor Drake passed sandwiches and cups of coffee up the line to encourage them to take a brief respite. "You need your strength," Doc MacNamara urged them both.

During the several hours necessary to break through the rocky riverbed, Dan and Ryan, anxious about their children's conditions, still refrained from calling out to them. By the time the men penetrated the last layer of rock, the sun was at its zenith. Physical labor had dissipated anger. Dreading they would find a pair of unconscious bodies, the fathers crawled into the cave proper through the carved-out hole. The two deeply asleep boys, evidently none the worse for their ordeal, were easily roused. *Thank you, Jodi,* was all Dan could muster.

And, Jodi? She just sighed.

Chapter 4

That evening, the boys safely home and everyone securely asleep in their beds, Jodi received a summons which couldn't be ignored. All available angels were to gather for a crisis-resolving session. Jodi had witnessed previous such meetings during her years in Special Forces and knew that the councils were held in a circular arena, which enlarged or shrank, depending on the number of participants. The Central Chamber, like the Angelic Library, was invisible to any human beings because its vibratory wavelength exceeded the range the human retina can encode.

During that night's session Jodi would be more than a passive member of the audience; she had never before participated at such a gathering, let alone been called to justify her actions. On her arrival she perceived herself in a mammoth room that measured perhaps a half mile across. Opaque energy fields of blue and white light created the perimeter walls; cloud mounds provided both flooring and fleecy cushions that served as seats; open skies roofed the enclosure.

Angels lounged on the clouds, floated in the air, and congregated in small and large groups. Most Guardian Angels, male and female, appeared the way humans have envisioned them over centuries of frescoes and oil paintings: platinum hair and dazzling white robes with silvery wings and halos. Many of these angels carried opal wands with a golden star at the tip. Several male angels did prefer elf-like outfits similar to Miguel's.

Special Forces and Messenger Angels materialized in more individualized apparel; ethereal gowns in radiant pastel hues were scattered throughout the crowd. Quite a few remained dressed however in the costume required by a recent assignment. A spectator would see a multitude of cultures, various occupations, and a variety of social strata represented among those gathered.

Jodi marveled at the myriad angels. How she wished she could read the minds of these beings, as she could Gerald's; she looked hopefully for even one friendly smile. It seemed every angel of the universe was present. But, if that were so, …no, she chuckled at her silliness. Only off-duty angels would be in attendance and a dispatch could instantly summon any or all present in the event of a catastrophe. Yet, the congregation was so enormous! *How many angels are there?* Jodi looked around then grinned. *Too many to count and this is but a fraction of the total.* She grimaced, *I'd have to research the latest angelic census to figure out our population.*

The chamber, conceived ages ago by the Archangels, enabled the debate of complex issues. Of course members of the angelic realm could easily communicate across continents via telepathic skills but convening in a single location added focus. Jodi curiously speculated why such a huge crowd chose to attend that night's assembly. *Oh, please God, please convince them to allow me to continue guarding Gerald.*

Jodi's anxiety, while waiting for the conference to begin, triggered the memory of when she approached God the second time to request reassignment to the Guardian Division. After a half-century of fantasizing about her imaginary charge Mary, the Special Forces Angel felt compelled to act. She mustered the courage she would need and materialized in a meadow, surrounded by an array of motley wildflowers. Her dress was a flowing gown dyed to simulate the cloudless autumn sky; ebony tresses cascaded to her waist. A family of grazing deer and a couple of frolicking bunnies kept her company while a chorus of canaries supplied music for the occasion.

To reach the quiet field, she had strolled along woodland paths scented with wild roses and gardenias; she felt serene, at peace. That is, until she initiated her plea. Brow furrowed, posture tense, hands squeezing a floral bouquet in her lap, she struggled to compose ideal replies to His queries.

"Why do you persist in this petition, Jodi?" Her Father in Heaven spoke with kindly concern in the manner of an empathetic supervisor, His tone non-judgmental. Although she could have prayed as a vibrating spirit to an unseen force, Jodi related more easily by shaping a mental portrait of God.

So she envisioned Him, settled in an oversized chair behind a massive desk. In front of Him lay parchment, quills, and an ornate ink stand. In addition, He held an onyx cup on which some impish angel had inscribed in gold, "My Lord is CEO of the Universe." Jodi's image portrayed Him in a dark Western-style suit and tie; a gold watch chain dangled from His vest pocket and diamond cufflinks were at His wrists. She imagined the bustle of secretaries and aides around Him while they waited for directives to carry to residents on Earth and in heaven.

Thick gray hair, trimmed above the neckline and ears, framed His genial mien. From under shaggy gray brows his deep brown eyes were filled with compassion, clarity and insight. Jodi knew that countenance could be fiery and stern. But on that particular day He listened to her, one of his petitioners, calling his wisdom to bear on one minor detail in the management of his infinitely vast organization, she pictured a grandfatherly demeanor.

She slowly inhaled, then exhaled. Here was her chance. "Please inspire me with the words," she prayed. In her nervousness she didn't pause to consider the paradox: she was requesting help to formulate her plea from The Very One whom she petitioned.

"To become a Guardian for a human, uh…, would be an integrated task, from start to finish, er…, not a piecemeal assignment," her words became more confident, "As a Special Forces Angel, I rush to the scene, often at the call of a Guardian. I provide the necessary assistance, then, off I go." She flicked her wrist, "It's over. Done." Leaning forward, peering into the depths of his wondrous eyes, "I yearn to devote myself to one person over his or her lifetime."

"Jodi, Guardians require special talents," God responded in His rich baritone. She pictured him scratching His chin; His visage serious; His brows crinkling. He continued in the benign, but firm, tones of absolute authority, "You'd be committed to the task for years, for decades, and never, ever, could your attention wander. Jodi, your skills are highly developed for emergency reactions. I expect you'd be bored quickly: you're in perpetual motion. It's difficult to think of you, Jodi, sitting silently for hours, hovering over a sleeping child."

She cringed with dismay. It was true; she rarely sat still. However, she had been sure of her ability to perform the requisite demands. Sadness filled her. It seemed He would deny her a second time. As she panicked, impetuous words spewed out of her lips, "You have to grant me this chance. You just have to!" She saw herself jumping up from the grass, stamping her foot and waving her arms. Her behavior appalled her. How could she be so disrespectful?

But she brightened at the sound of his chuckle, "On the other hand, you know, sometimes it's interesting to shake things up a bit." His eyes twinkled, "Angels and humans get stuck in the way-it's-always-been." He hesitated, frowned, picked up His cup and rubbed the handle. "I'll grant your petition, Jodi, but be warned, each individual is crucial. No matter what is happening in the larger world, you are committed to your human. And that's all. You may be unable to participate in major events. You will be bound by your charge's destiny and his or her life choices."

More than once during the past six years, Jodi speculated that God, in His omniscience, knew Gerald would need an atypical Guardian and decided Jodi fit Gerald's specifications. For Gerald was the opposite of a temperate child.

Abruptly the auditorium's low hum and murmurs ceased. Jodi's concentration snapped back to the present. She realized she must have missed the opening phrases of her supervisor, Jeff, who was standing before her on the raised podium, in his traditional robes and holding his scepter. The first words that registered were, "I hope you understand, Jodi, that some of the troubles you're encountering with Gerald are precisely because he knows he's safe. He relies on you to rescue him no matter what he gets into."

Jodi's heart pounded; her knees grew weak. She found it difficult to concentrate on Jeff, "Gerald is failing to learn responsibility. He's certain you're omnipotent." Jodi bowed her head in agreement. "Whether or not he stops to think, he inevitably ends up doing what he chooses. He rarely pauses long enough to discern you — or anything else for that matter — including his innate sense of right and wrong."

Engulfed in shame, hands intertwined in front of her, gaze downward, Jodi's gown transformed into her trainee shift, belted with a rope. Her feet were bare; her hair fell in tangled strands. Her physical presentation matched her mood of self- recrimination because Gerald definitely experienced more mishaps than any other child in the community.

Miguel, arms crossed over his chest and still attired as when he met Teddy, complained, "Now I'll need to contend with the same dilemmas with Teddy." Other angels throughout the vast hall nodded in concurrence with Jeff and Miguel.

"The job of children is to accumulate skills that foster self-accountability." Jeff cleared his throat, "You've so far totally deprived Gerald of opportunities to acquire such abilities, Jodi. He has faith you will protect him — even from himself."

He's obviously frustrated. Probably, feels a failure as my supervisor, Jodi contritely regretted the complications of her rebelliousness.

"Guardians react to genuine emergencies and danger," declared Jeff, pounding his staff on the cloud floor, his expression intense. "Humans are supposed to use their own skills – at least to some degree." Jodi sank into deeper humiliation; her cheeks flushed; her muscles tightened.

Johan, a tall, darkly clad Messenger Angel, stood and waved for recognition. Jodi cringed at his proposal, "Maybe we should pull Jodi and Miguel from their assignments. Force those children to learn common sense."

"Gerald wouldn't believe she was gone," Gillian chimed in sharply as she leapt to the podium. A good friend of Jodi's, she intended to do all in her power so that Jodi retained her post. "Gerald wouldn't survive a week." Jodi appreciated the intervention on her behalf.

The cold harsh tones of a Guardian Angel, in the midst of the throngs, penetrated the ambience, "Maybe we should permit a severe injury; the humans, if crippled, couldn't incur further harm."

"Oh no! You can't! Please! No!" Jodi interrupted frantically. She couldn't suppress the horror exploding in her heart.

"What's your advice, Jesus?" Archangel Michael unexpectedly entered the fray. Jodi listened intently to His words. Her breathing was shallow, alarm evident in her rigid posture. Her knuckles blanched from the grip of her hands on each other; her legs trembled.

"Let's allow the experiment to continue without change. Since the young humans possess first-hand knowledge of Miguel and Jodi, let's play this out and investigate what happens when humans develop while in direct contact with their angels. So far the situation has caused some consternation, but not much else that I see. Look, for example, how Dan is learning to quiet his mind. This experiment might result in a variety of benefits." Jodi could hardly believe what Jesus recommended. She relaxed a little and dared to look at the wise, kindly countenance of her beloved Lord. After He addressed the assembly, Jodi did a double take: *Did He really wink at me?*

Jodi's whole body was on the verge of collapse after the stress of those few hours. She was exhausted — but the session wasn't over. The angels prized their free will and weighed the advice of their Lord with other options. Finally, after careful deliberation, they concluded the only suitable decision would be to observe the course of events. The angelic host acknowledged that it shouldered extra responsibility with these two children who had an unprecedented awareness of the spiritual world.

Furthermore Jodi gained more appreciation of her friends and allies; in addition, she comprehended more clearly the significance of the Angelic Council. With countless angels collaborating on the wisest solution, the ideal became probable.

Chapter 5

"Get your socks and shoes, Ger," Sue lay his shirt and coveralls on the chair. Mother and son were working in the boys' recently enlarged room with bunk beds and throw rugs on which the brothers played trains and built magnificent structures with their blocks. Against the wall, shelves held boyish treasures: smooth river pebbles, an actual bird's nest with a pale blue shell, a rusty nail, the marbles Aunt Jean gave them for Christmas.

While passing the trophies, Gerald paused to examine a shard of yellow glass he'd found in the garden the day before. His mother, exasperated, scolded, "Gerald, your socks are in the chest not among the toys." He dashed to the bureau in the corner, pulled out his drawer, the third one up, and selected a pair from the neatly folded pile. Pretending to be a pony, he whinnied and pranced to the closet in the far wall; Barney trotted beside him and Mister Jack skedaddled out of the room. He'd remembered the shoes!

His mother kept the boys' room meticulously organized. That way her sons could find their things without much trouble. Although Gerald and Jimmy put toys and clothes in their proper places, Sue did the major straightening. Gerald protested that she nit-picked.

After dinner, the two had made a sandwich and chosen an unblemished apple to put in his lunchbox, the same one Sue had carried. Gerald closed the box. "What will school be like, Mamma?" He couldn't quell the butterflies in his stomach.

"You've visited the schoolhouse. Remember the desk? That's where you have to sit quietly and obey Miss Smith. She'll teach you your letters and how to cipher — like the big boys." Nervous about school and scared about a whole day away from home, Gerald for weeks had insisted she repeat those same reassurances several times a day.

His mother emphasized that he must hold still and focus. Although Gerald listened to her, he wasn't worried over that. *What's tough about sitting still? Anybody can do that!* He was oblivious to the fact that he never did.

Apprehension filled Sue. Over the summer she had become aware how rarely her eldest child sat – still or not — as she anticipated the start of school. The boy ran; he never walked. At home, he interrupted meals to dart off for an extra spoon or to fill the bread pan or fetch the milk, perpetually chattering as he did so. And outdoors, who knew where he'd wind up!

Dan told his wife to quit fretting. He assumed Gerald would settle when he needed to. Sue wasn't so certain. At church he busily assisted the younger ones, which meant he seldom sat quietly in the pew. She continually discussed keeping his body and mouth still in school. He promised her he would. *But, can he?* she wondered.

The big day had arrived; Gerald was so agitated he hardly ate a bite of porridge. While his father harnessed Jenny for the three-mile ride, Gerald re-played his questions; his mother obliged, determined that his day begin without friction.

Again she told him that thirty-one boys and girls attended the school, and, she named them; he was acquainted with all of the students either from church or from town meetings. Even though the older boys tended to tease, they also protected. Again she explained that he'd be in first grade that year and next year he'd be promoted to second. After he finished eighth, he'd move to the high school.

Gerald listened as he swirled his spoon in his porridge. *How come I'm not hungry today?* His mother's litany went on: Robin and Cindy Eldrick were in the first grade class, along with him and Teddy. Gerald had watched the twins at Sunday School ever since Sue mentioned they'd be in his class, but they were girls, so he wasn't very familiar with them.

While absorbing the familiar lecture, Gerald's frown lines softened. When his father summoned him, he jogged out of the house and climbed into the buggy in seemingly better spirits. Sue sent a *Please, Lord, help him today,* heavenward. Sally and Jimmy, envious that Gerald got to go to school, obediently stood on the porch and waved good-bye.

On the trip to the schoolhouse, he and his father passed other children on foot; some older boys galloped past them on horseback. With mounting unease, Gerald gawked at the shouting, laughing crowd headed toward the same destination.

Gerald spotted Teddy as Jenny pulled into the schoolyard. He leapt out and raced over to his buddy, who had hiked with his big brothers, Jed, Donald and David. Dan gave Gerald a hug and left him with Teddy in Jed's care. "Jodi's here," Gerald whispered. "Is Miguel?" Teddy nodded. Jed dropped off the boys with Miss Smith; the teacher welcomed her new pupils and gave them front-row seats next to the twins who'd already arrived with their older sister, Jill.

Gerald surveyed his surroundings, enthusiastically examining an object that caught his eye, then another and another. The wooden desks and benches lined up in straight rows that extended to the back. Letters and numbers he'd practiced printing at home with his mother decorated the walls. His pride got a boost when he identified every one. A large map and a smaller one were posted on the right side of the room. As Gerald grew more educated, he would recognize the big map as the United States, his country, and the other, his state. On each, a black star pinpointed his hometown.

A bookcase, its shelves piled high, stood between the windows. Along the back he noticed the hooks where coats would hang in winter when the wood stove in front would warm the class. That one single room, which served children from six to fourteen, contained a variety of playthings from bats and balls to rag dolls and blocks. The miniature farmyard animals impressed Gerald, but also the tiger; Gerald nudged Teddy and asked, "That a giraffe – that one, with the long neck?"

Miss Smith stepped up to the blackboard, "Welcome, boys and girls. Let's introduce ourselves and tell something you did this summer." Gerald gaped at his teacher's red hair and fell in love. How he wished he, too, had red hair!

The eighth graders, at the back, recited first. Gerald's gaze, incessantly darting about, soon abandoned its study of his beautiful teacher and looked out the window. A butterfly alighted on the ledge. The boy, filled with unsquashable curiosity, tiptoed over and hoisted himself onto the sill for a closer scrutiny of the delicate black creature with gold-tinged wings. Dan had taught Gerald how, when it emerged from its cocoon, the dainty creature only lived a short time. *Where's the cocoon?* He scanned the trees that abutted the playground.

Miss Smith's peripheral vision alerted her to his movement. Gerald had boosted himself up by pressing his feet against the wall. His hands gripped the outside edge. Startled to see a student hanging half out the window, she exclaimed, "Gerald Daniels!"

When his teacher called his name, Gerald casually twisted back from his perusal of the alluring outdoors, "Yes, ma'am?"

"Go back to your desk and stay there," she commanded, pointing at his chair; her stare directly met his eyes.

He complied and got down from the window, only then remembering his mother's admonition, "Sit quietly and pay attention." A number of the older pupils grinned and one chuckled until Miss Smith silenced him with a fierce glare.

By the day's end, Gerald successfully remained where he belonged ... for ten minutes, one time, while drawing a house. Drawing was fun!

Jodi, in a quandary, fidgeted. *What is a Guardian's responsibility at school? What should be left to Gerald and his teacher?* She fiddled with the lock of her hair. *How could he stay in his seat? How could she help?* She tried to snag his attention but the distractions were too great; she couldn't pierce through that mental muddle. Teddy heard Jodi and turned to look; Miss Smith scolded him and ordered Teddy to pay attention.

When Gerald saw his father arrive after school, he dashed toward him; the child bubbled over with exciting news to report about school — the drawing, his pretty teacher.... But Miss Smith intercepted Dan. Gerald observed as Dan's neck flushed while the teacher spoke; Gerald deduced he'd somehow embarrassed Papa. On the ride home, his father chided him for misbehavior, on his first day no less, and concluded his lecture with a stinging, "I'm right shamed."

His beloved father had never before condemned him in such terms. Gerald's enthusiasm evaporated. Defeat supplanted joy. Tears streamed down his cheeks. He wasn't any good at all. He'd failed.

Sue counseled him, too, though a bit less sternly. As did Jodi. Gerald fell asleep that night with plans and promises made to himself and the whole wide-world that, from that moment on, he would sit still.

The next morning he set out optimistically. "Now remember," Dan reminded, "you're to stay in your seat and pay attention."

"I promise I will. You'll see."

With a conscious effort to hold his muscles motionless, Gerald managed to remain at his desk for many minutes. Sometimes he held his breath. But, when Miss Smith called on him to identify the letter "A" written on the chalkboard, what with so much of his thought devoted to forcing himself to be still, he didn't hear her. "Gerald," her voice snapped, "you must pay attention!"

The only way he could focus on the board was to shift his concentration. Cindy identified the "A." And Gerald neglected to think about staying put. It wasn't three minutes before he went over to Teddy's desk to tell him about his new baby frog. "Gerald! Back in your seat, now! This is school."

By the end of day two, Gerald was convinced he was incapable of being good. He hated school. Gerald again witnessed his father receive the exasperated teacher's negative report and again felt shame as his father lectured him on the trip home. In the kitchen Dan informed Sue about the disgraceful behavior and Gerald thought his mother close to weeping as she said, "Oh Ger, not again."

After the reprimands, Gerald sneaked into the woods, huddled under a tall oak, and sobbed hopelessly. "I can't try harder," he announced to the world around him. "And there's no way to sit still and pay attention, not both, not at the same time. And no one understands that I can't."

When he heard the dinner bell, Gerald didn't react. *They don't want a bad boy like me in their house.* He headed deeper into the woods. *If I run away from home, I won't shame them anymore.*

Jodi was beside herself. What was a Guardian supposed to do? During the day, she had taken a stab at keeping him on task. But the countless distractions barred her from breaking through. What with eight age-grouped classes — even though Miss Smith combined several classes for geography and history — a lot of disparate activity filled the room. When Teddy whispered, "Get busy, Ger," their teacher rebuked Teddy and warned him not to chatter.

So Gerald plodded farther and farther from home. Since he reckoned that Jodi was as disappointed as were his parents, he shut out her voice. With the forest thickening and with evening limiting his visibility, Gerald couldn't allow himself to admit fear. He needed courage; after all, he'd be on his own from that day on. He'd need to find a place to live and food to eat. *I'll miss Mamma, Papa, Sally, Jimmy, Janie and Johnny.* He rubbed off a fresh batch of tears with his sleeve.

Ger, Jodi nearly shouted to penetrate the haze when he dropped his barrier against her messages for a second, *You tried as hard as you could. I saw you. I don't think anyone who's really trying is "bad."*

When her words broke through the inner turbulence, Gerald retorted. "Then y-you're the only one who d-doesn't think I'm a-aw-awful," he shuddered. "M-Mamma and P-Papa are m-mad at m-me. I-I'm so bad." He wailed. "What c-can I do, Jodi?"

"Let's ask Jesus to solve this problem."

"Think He would?" Gerald froze in his headlong plunge, afraid to trust. Right then he feared absolutely everything.

"Of course He will." Jodi's voice radiated the utter faith instilled by centuries of working with God. Since Teddy met Miguel, their angels had broadcast their voices to both boys in order that all four could participate in any general conversation. Jodi had started to use this method with Gerald when they were simply chatting; their reciprocal relationship seemed more interactive using this device. It is true that when she needed to break through Gerald's stormy maelstrom of emotions, the thought-intrusion method worked best.

Without prompting Gerald slid to his knees, bowed his head, folded his hands. He shut his eyes like he did at bedtime prayers with his mother. Despite this preparation, he had no idea what to say. "—uh, you go first, Jodi."

Jodi provided Gerald a portrait of herself kneeling beside him, with folded hands and bowed head. "Jesus, please assist Gerald. He's doing his best, but it isn't working. We need your miracles."

"Yes, Jesus," the shrill young voice chimed in. "I can't do it. Please help me sit still and pay attention like Teddy does."

When the prayers were completed, Gerald lifted himself up on all-fours with bottom sticking straight up, "How do I know He heard?"

"He did. He always does. He'll take care of it," Jodi sprang up with a quick twist of her body.

"It's hard to believe." His eyes were red and puffy; his lips puckered into a scowl. His foot kicked at a stone, "God's so busy. It's tough to suppose He'll have time."

"He's very busy! However, we can trust Him." Eager that Gerald reach home before nightfall, she advocated their immediate return. "Now, c'mon! Let's go home."

"Okay, I guess." Gerald was skeptical but, maybe, just maybe, Jesus could help. He didn't dare get his hopes up too high. It seemed an impossible puzzle — even for Jesus.

As they hurried, Gerald followed the plan the two of them had devised for finding his way if he got lost again. He both listened for her direction and checked his understanding. If she ordered, "Go right," he'd pretend to eat and see which hand held the spoon. That one was his right. Although he'd practiced diligently, this was a test. He listened, deliberated and turned correctly. Jodi glowed. "See how much progress you've made, Ger?" Jodi sent him a mental hug. "That's perfect."

Gerald grinned, performed a somersault, and relished the first praise he'd received in quite a few days – or that's how it seemed to him. In reality, it'd been two.

In the distance his father's voice echoed, "Gerald."

"Here, Papa. With Jodi." He dashed to his father, who stooped and seized him. "Papa, I'm sorry I've been bad. I didn't think I could ever be good. I thought I'd have to live by myself in the woods. But Jodi and I asked Jesus and she says I can trust He heard me."

A lump formed in the man's throat. With husky voice, his father responded fervently, "Oh, son, He will." Dan gave his child an extra-reassuring hug, before hoisting him to his shoulders where Gerald rode the last mile home.

His sisters and brothers were snuggled in bed though it had taken some time to settle Sally; Sue had to rock her five year old to induce sleep. Sue was frantic; it was much easier to soothe her daughter than herself. As soon as she heard Dan's step, she raced out the door and lifted her son from his father's shoulders; she stooped to the boy's level, for an extended, warm embrace. Gerald felt loved again.

Gerald plopped between his parents on their big sofa and babbled on about school and how hard he tried and what happened when he ceased concentrating on sitting still and tried to pay attention and how he couldn't figure out how to do both simultaneously and how afraid he'd been that they'd stopped loving him and would never again because he'd proven himself such a failure.

"Oh, Ger," his mother choked out, "I didn't realize how hard you've been trying." Her voice contrite, she gathered him close, "Please, please, forgive me. I'm sorry I didn't let you explain what was happening."

While she fed and put him to bed, his father turned over a variety of ideas in his head. Late into the night his parents discussed possible solutions but judged none viable. Next morning they'd confer with Miss Smith before school. Regardless of that decision, they spent a restless night.

In the morning Sue and Dan woke the children early, fed and dressed them, and piled everyone in the wagon. First they stopped at Teddy's house to drop off the little ones. Teddy, terribly upset about Gerald, had lingered at home; he felt unable to face another day of his chum's castigation. Emma had yet to decide whether to shoo him off to school or walk with him.

When the Daniels arrived, he tentatively hopped into the buggy beside his buddy; he was nervous about why both of Gerald's parents were coming to school. Were they going to yell at him in front of everyone? Gerald scooted over and whispered, "It's going to be all right. Jodi and I asked Jesus to help and Mamma and Papa are speaking to Miss Smith."

Teddy grinned and gave Gerald a knock on the arm. "I prayed, too, and so did Mamma and Miguel. Mamma says we've gotta trust now." Teddy looked at Gerald's parents in awe, "Ger, Jesus did answer my prayers—your mamma and papa are here, sure enough." That evidence of how much other people can care startled Gerald.

School started late that day because of the impromptu parent-teacher conference. Miss Smith also had contemplated the situation overnight. She dreamed that Jill, who enjoyed teaching younger children, sat next to Gerald. The older girl gently prodded the little boy to task each time his focus strayed and reminded him to stay seated each time he stood. The dream's schoolroom was rearranged: pupils were paired in ways to assist each other. Therefore, when Gerald's parents entered the schoolhouse, they found the teacher busily pushing and pulling desks as she positioned the furniture to match the room in her dream.

Dan and Sue helped her and simultaneously recounted the previous evening's events. Miss Smith fingered the cross she wore at her neckline. "Oh, I never realized that he was trying hard. I'm sorry," she murmured. "Let's call him."

Teddy accompanied Gerald into the room. He was determined to prevent anyone from berating his friend again. Tentatively he watched as Miss Smith squatted to Gerald's height. Wearing a bright red dress with a green rickrack trim and displaying a warm smile, she appeared nicer; she no longer resembled the witch he had perceived when she was irritated with his chum.

As his teacher hugged Gerald and apologized for her lack of awareness of how hard he'd been trying, Teddy skipped and jumped; he added a somersault when she suggested Jill, their Sunday School teacher, sit beside Gerald. Teddy liked her. Ger would be okay.

Jill was ecstatic when Miss Smith inquired if she would be willing to work with the child. Jill assumed this the answer to her own prayer for the first grader. Gerald settled in for a new and easier day.

And, though the impulsive boy never found it simple to sit still and pay attention, prayer and improvisation made the chore attainable from that day forward.

Chapter 6

Jodi snapped out of her memories of Gerald's childhood and glanced around. Angels were everywhere. Lost in thought, she had been scarcely mindful of the mounting congestion. Numerous colleagues were hiking the path in one direction or the other: she wasn't the only one who had stolen a moment to walk instead of fly to and from the magnificent library that nearly filled the sky ahead. In addition to those that had found the leisure to appear at the foot of the bridge and trudge its span, angelic figures glided through the sky to land on the porch and Jodi knew that still others would materialize in the building's vast interior.

In this palatial structure angels could review all that had been written by humans or angels on any topic imaginable. Writings from the earliest times, when only a handful of archangels acted as God's messengers, were stored in the archives along with the volumes accumulated as the angelic realm developed into its current hierarchy of trainees, agents, support staff, supervisors, administrators, liaison and coordination specialists. Among those tomes Jodi intended to research arguments to support her contention that personal relationships between Guardian Angels and humans should be acceptable and even encouraged. She trembled as she contemplated the significant changes in the laws of the realm she was advocating.

Jodi had reached the intersection of the slender golden bridge with her path. Before she dematerialized and stepped onto the archway, Jodi gazed back over the distance she'd climbed: she felt compelled to say farewell one last time to the rocks, the solid stuff of planet Earth. Then she thrust her apprehension aside and changed to her spirit form. If her body remained solid, she would pass through the ethereal substance and continue up the mountain.

In spirit form angels exist as rapidly vibrating pure energy, yet etiquette mandated creation of a humanoid figure from that energy for visits to the library. Jodi had no desire to attract attention or condemnation from her superiors or peers for breaking more traditions; besides, one of her favorite hobbies was the invention of novel appearances. So she donned a red tunic covering cream-colored britches; after all, this endeavor should memorialize Gerald. In spirit form, clothing wasn't required for warmth; thus she shed the gloves, coat and hat and slipped into soft sandals. She did keep sandy curls that she elected to braid and tie with a ribbon woven from the material of her tunic. A few strands dangled on either side; something to fiddle with certainly helped when she was frustrated. Satisfied with her appearance, she began to cross the bridge, solid under her dematerialized feet.

Even though no longer in human form, Jodi felt like her heart was fluttering as she continued toward the knowledge she prayed would add cogency to her presentation to the Angelic Council. *What should I include? How can I earn their approval of my tenure with Gerald? Will I be licensed?*

Jodi paused and clutched the golden railing with both hands. She studied the view. At this altitude, she could distinguish neither the eagle's aerie nor the village far below. She was about to enter condensation that from the ground below had appeared as clouds.

"Hey, Jodi. Wait up."

The sound startled Jodi after her hours of solitude. Her long-time pal Rachel rushed toward her. "Jodi. Why are you here? You seldom play the scholarly role." Rachel's eyes softened, "Sorry about Gerald. You must miss him terribly." She grabbed Jodi in a tight hug; their spirits intertwined briefly.

"Thanks, Rachel, I do miss him," Jodi gulped. "That's the worst part of an intimate relationship with a human. Now I'm here to prepare my presentation of his life and my plea for Guardian Licensure. Uh...Oh, Rachel, I so hope I'll be accepted as a permanent, qualified Guardian." She loosened her grip on Rachel and squeezed her hands together, "On the trek up the mountain, I've been reliving my obsession to guard one human for a lifetime. It was awesome – guarding Gerald that is. But, it will be dreadful if my plea to continue is denied." A wry smile played across her lips. "Guess I guarded a little oddly...."

Rachel nudged her and gave a conspiratorial wink, "Yeah, you sort of set your corner of the world upside down."

"What are the rumors? Is there gossip about me?" Jodi clutched Rachel's wrist. "Please. Be honest."

Rachel hesitated. How should she reply? She gazed at her toe, drew a circle on the bridge with it, straightened her shoulders, and plunged into an earnest response, "You're controversial. While many respect you for what you did, others are appalled. I can report that you're the main topic discussed among Guardians. And we in Special Forces are bragging, 'What did you expect from our Jodi? She sure stirs up the soup and adds the spice.'"

The friends giggled at Rachel's apt representation of Jodi's livening up the universe. Her high-spirited, creative, impulsive and headstrong personality attracted attention wherever she labored.

An angel robed as a bearded Arabic scholar, jogged up the span only to be abruptly halted by the barrier which the two chatting friends caused. He burst out irritably, "You gals are impeding the way." Then he recognized Jodi. "Hey," his expression changed. "How are you, Jodi? I saw Jeff yesterday and he's as agitated as I've ever seen him. Not sure if he'll ever recover from supervising you. You do have that effect on your superiors."

He gave her shoulder an affectionate squeeze, "Will you return to Special Forces now that your experiment is over?" Pouting, he muttered, "Sure have missed you these last eighty years. Seems like forever."

"I hope not Jack." Jodi grinned at her old friend as she grabbed his hands. "I mean, about returning to Special Forces. I pray they'll license me in the Guardian Division...." Jodi's words faded. She spontaneously touched his upper arm, "Oh, I loved serving with you but I yearn for a second relationship with a human. For me, a guardianship is much more fulfilling than my experiences in Special Forces."

Jack picked up on the intensity of Jodi's longing yet he knew that her guardianship had shaken the very foundation of the hierarchy. "Uh, okay, I guess. Would sure like to have you back with us. So why are you here?"

Jodi laughed with a wave of her hand, "Not you, too? Does no one think me capable of quiet study in a library?"

Jack roared. "So, when did you become a bookworm? How will you hold still?" He mocked her with a teasing two-step, which set the bridge to swaying and jiggling and resulted in glares from others.

The girls chuckled. "Well, if you're acquainted with an academic angel who can facilitate my research, I'd certainly rather chat than read." Jodi's eyes danced. "But I've got to admit that I'm not familiar with many of the studious types."

"Hey," Jack clapped his hands at his sudden inspiration. "I spotted Archangel Michael in the halls. Since he participated in assembling the structure of the realms, I mean, he's a member of the founding force of angels, anyway, I bet he has loads of wisdom you could use." Jack yanked her hand and pulled her forward. "C'mon, I'll introduce you."

Jodi's excitement at her good fortune mixed with reluctance; she resisted Jack's attempt to drag her along. "Sure he'll spend time with me? I'm only ...."

"Never hurts to ask," Jack interrupted impatiently. "C'mon." So the pair sprinted for the porch, closely pursued by Rachel who wouldn't miss this adventure. Free for a while, she had intended to indulge her hobby of combining different textures of food and seasonings to produce innovative concoctions. She planned to research West Indian curries that day; but she couldn't resist the opportunity to join in a conversation with Archangel Michael.

The trio entered the mammoth oaken doors carved with angelic figures by ancient artists. Reflexively, Jodi, Jack and Rachel hushed as they crossed the gigantic foyer where angels silently glided toward branching corridors. No perceptible noise was heard as associates conversed telepathically. All respected the library's rigidly enforced decorum.

Jack proceeded to the spiral staircase that rose from the ground level hundreds, maybe thousands, of yards up and every dozen feet intersected with more hallways to more rooms and floors. Jodi gazed up. Intricately sculpted cherubs functioned as struts between sections of the smooth, gleaming railing. Jodi had always marveled at the six crystalline chandeliers suspended through the open space at the spiral's center. The flickering effect simulated candlelight and illuminated the area, yet these "candles" of pure energy never melted away.

On each floor, four or five departments were accessed via archways labeled with pictographs from the ancient angelic language. The threesome soon ascended beyond the departments that Jodi had encountered on past visits as they entered the more technical arenas. One level, Jodi noted with fascination, was entirely devoted to the care of the Earth and its four arches were designated by symbols for forest, oceans, mountains, and plains. The next landing's symbols showed fish; and immediately above came birds, then mammals. As they climbed, she noticed icons for political science, war, education, human psychology, human sociology; multiple stories dealt with mathematics and physics. Foot traffic was heavy: angels stepped off the stairway and ducked through arches while others exited the chambers to ascend or descend.

At last they arrived at a series of smaller quarters. Jodi noticed the turrets with narrower dimensions. There, Jack abandoned the stairs, veered to the left, then up a ramp and into a tower adjacent to the main one. He approached a door and rapped its glistening brass knocker.

A baritone "Enter" resonated. Jodi and her friends stepped into a homey scene: a sitting room with the fragrance of vanilla-scented tobacco in the air. On a desk several leather bound books seized her interest until she caught sight of the tall wiry youth seated there. The young man, who had closely cropped curls and a clean-shaven face, was resplendent in pale garments which complemented his dark skin. But it was his eyes! When he glanced up from the manuscript he was perusing, Jodi felt enveloped in their depths. Awestruck, she realized she was in the presence of one of the original ancients, regardless of whatever bodily form the Archangel assumed.

"I've been expecting you, Jodi." He rose to greet them. "And you'd be Rachel." Rachel, nodded and reddened. "Come, let's be comfortable." He motioned them toward the cushioned chairs by the fireplace with its crackling logs. Bookcases lined the walls. With a flick of his wrist, a tea pot and four cups materialized.

Jodi couldn't believe his informality. For once the chatterbox discovered herself tongue-tied! "I, uh, presumed we'd be bothering you. We aren't, are we? I, er, I mean, thank you for your welcome." She received the teacup he proffered with both hands; Jodi would be mortified if she spilt tea in that gorgeous room.

Jack teased, "Don't let his fame get to you, girls. When a being has been around as long as Archangel Michael," and Jack gave their host a mischievous bow, "my impression is that he's able to predict what will happen on any given day."

The Archangel smirked at his impudent young friend. Then, seeking to ease Jodi's tension, he feigned a lack of such foresight. "And so, Jack, what did lead you to bring these two lovely angels to my office today?"

"How about answering questions for Jodi, save her some of the trouble of digging through those tomes in 7C?"

"Oh would you, please," Jodi bent forward, her hands on her knees.

"Yes. Yes, of course," Archangel Michael assented. "I'm eager for you, Jodi, to obtain the necessary data. That ripple you made in the flow of the universe has swollen into waves: it needs analysis."

"Do you, uh, condone what I did, Archangel? Do you think, uh, it's a wise innovation?" Jodi's tones were muted.

Archangel Michael, relaxed back into his chair, materialized a pipe and an ottoman then propped up his sandaled feet. He carefully contemplated his response. Jodi busied her fidgety fingers by taking out a notebook and pencil from her backpack. Her friends, curious spectators, also tensed as they awaited the authority figure's judgment.

Michael reached into the drawer of a nearby table for matches. He manually struck one and drew on the lighted pipe between his full lips. Once lit to his satisfaction, he continued, "Fascinating question, Jodi. Not sure where I stand. Your actions did open up possibilities."

"Has anyone else attempted to switch from Special Forces to the Guardian Division?" Jodi nibbled on the eraser of her pencil.

"Now, that I can answer." Jodi speculated on what he'd say next, but guessed wrong. "Definitely not. The divisions are too dissimilar."

The two Special Forces angels nodded; Rachel interjected, "I'd resist becoming a Guardian." She shuddered dramatically, "I'd get bored."

Jack's scrutiny bounced to Jodi, "Wasn't the job awfully tedious those first couple years before you established a relationship with Gerald's mother?"

Jodi stared at the three in disbelief. She couldn't fathom what her friends meant. Each new evidence of Gerald's developing personality and skills had enchanted her. However, she was all too aware she'd not been a customary Guardian.

She shook her head vigorously. Archangel Michael empathized, "Your utilization of your Special Forces talents mitigated the inevitable monotony."

Jodi blushed and twitched as she reflected on the magnitude of her transgressions. *Why do the rules exist?*

"It's hardly your fault," the archangel's compassionate glance met her anxious one. "Nobody anticipated an angel would request a transfer. Until your experiment, no one conceived such a radical shift in duties."

"God did throw a monkey wrench into the system," remarked Jack. At that comment, Archangel Michael belly-laughed.

Twisting the dangling strand of hair, sitting forward on the edge of her chair, pleading through her facial expression, Jodi blurted out, "Why, Sir, must those particular regulations be in place? Why can't there be more of a mutual relationship between humans and their Guardians, and communication and reciprocity among various Guardians and approvals of angelic job transfers and opportunities to apply for trainee status and…."

Archangel Michael's half-raised hand halted her midstream as he studied her. *Without a doubt, she'd stirred up the realms. What will be the outcome?* After a pensive moment, he spoke, "There are seldom deviations from the original design. When a slight change occurs, the imperceptible wrinkle barely creases our tightly knit fabric." He tapped his pipe with his finger and gazed into its bowl. "But your actions, over the last eighty years, rewove a major part of the pattern – at least in your miniscule section of the overall design." He winked at her, "Now we must decide if a larger piece should be rewoven in similar fashion or if the existing bit of change should be allowed to extinguish itself by adding no new angel-human pairs." He tamped and relit his pipe, "The council meeting will be interesting."

Jodi wanted to be circumspect in the presence of this wise ancient but inevitably her innate impulsiveness took charge of her tongue, "So, what should be the decision, Archangel Michael?"

"I'm not certain, Jodi. I'm waiting to hear your defense." He scrutinized her, not unkindly, as he added, "You created an intriguing dilemma for the governing body."

"What should I definitely include?" She pressed her chance for some assistance.

He puffed on his ebony pipe, then walked to his desk and picked up a piece of paper. "I wrote down the items I'll pose at your defense." He smoothed out the rather crumpled sheet, "I'll read them for you to consider: What were the advantages in a reciprocal relationship? What problems arose? What was the most significant accomplishment from this unusual guardianship? How did Gerald's life, as a result of his angelic companion, affect humans, affect angels? What are the implications for the future?"

A rap at the door punctuated the last.

"Come in." All eyes turned toward the entrance, "Oh, hello, Gabe. Meet Jodi, Rachel and Jack."

"The Jodi," grinned the lanky Semitic angel at the threshold.

"Yes. This is the one."

"Folks, meet Archangel Gabriel," and they shook hands.

"Are you about finished, Mike? We've got matters that require urgent dispatch. I have a special message He requested me deliver personally."

Archangel Michael sighed, "Must return to my work, friends, but this has been a stimulating respite." As he escorted them to the door, the angelic statesman put an arm on Jodi's shoulders and whispered, "Prepare well, Jodi, I'll see you at the council next week."

She stepped out and headed to the staircase with Jack and Rachel, "Thanks, Jack. What an opportunity!" He acknowledged her sincere gratitude and the three intermingled energies before Jack and Rachel teleported to their individual research sections. Jodi, however, opted to descend on foot to the seventh floor where the Guardian Division housed its extensive collection; in that hall she would settle into a cubicle where she could map out her defense. But, first, she needed this solitary walk to think through her interview with the Archangel. Within the hierarchy she could find no better consultant. *Was her perception of him accurate? Did he more or less advocate her positions?*

Chapter 7

Jodi smiled; the pictograph on the entrance archway over the guardian section seemed apropos: a hand resting on a shoulder. She paced up the ramp that passed under the symbol into an entryway where she met the reserved, non-descript angel who monitored the section. That librarian assigned Jodi one of the perhaps fifty cubicles that jutted off from the foyer; she pointed out both the supply cabinet where writing paraphernalia was stored and the location of the index card catalogue for the volumes in that section.

Jodi chose a yellow-lined pad along with a set of pencils before she settled at her desk to outline Gerald's biography as it intertwined with hers. She scribbled down the circumstances of her meeting Gerald's parents, Gerald, Teddy and Miguel. Then she mused, *There really isn't much in the first few years that will be relevant for the Council. It was really during Gerald's eighth grade year that the first event occurred that should be included in the presentation.* But she doodled in the margins as her mind searched the earlier years to ensure she wasn't missing anything. Gerald and Teddy did develop a close foursome with their classmates, Robin and Cindy. Together and separately, they had each grown in worldly knowledge, in friendships, and in skills although the boys kept their experiences with their angels private.

Jodi grinned: how frustrated she and Miguel were with six-year-old Gerald's and Teddy's apparent inability to remember to converse at the thought level when playing with other children. Miguel and she decided to refuse to respond unless the child dialogued inaudibly. She chuckled as she recalled Gerald's irritation when she wouldn't answer him. Once he stamped his foot and yelled out loud at Jodi which caused his classmates to stare; he pretended he'd been bitten by a mosquito. Soon telepathy became a habit.

Miguel was amused by her astonishment at the rapid development of a human child. Thoroughly accustomed to the phenomenon, he had forgotten the thrill of the first tying of a shoelace or reading of a word. Moreover everyday sadnesses, losses, deaths — the stuff of which life is made — were raw, novel crises to the first-timer. But Miguel lived through new and unusual experiences during this guardianship as he learned to coordinate his efforts with Jodi; such collaboration had been common for her as a member of the Special Forces Division.

But, after running through her recollections of the first few years, Jodi decided, *If this paper opens with the eighth grade year, I still can bring in some earlier times if necessary.* And so, now that she had decided where to start, Jodi wrote in earnest. In early adolescence, the robust, athletic Teddy, although only fourteen, thought out topics thoroughly and produced surprisingly insightful commentary on the human scene. Gerald, in contrast, exhibited a keen appreciation for the tantalizing and unusual; his mind jumped from issue to issue. Gerald's lean physique seemed tailored for the quick, perpetual movement needed to follow his every perception. He was often teased for dashing "fast as sunbeams" when he pursued an idea. In the initial phase of puberty, he hadn't then reached Teddy's clumsy, gangling stage.

Cindy had developed into a conscientious and practical but, occasionally, rather dictatorial early adolescent. Her sister, Robin, on the other hand, proved spontaneous, joyful and filled with awe at life's eccentricities. No one would guess them twins: Cindy stood tall and sturdy. She kept her straight hair in an easy-to-care-for bob. Her favorite clothes were simple jumpers of earthen hues. Robin, on the contrary, was petite and lithe. Her sandy hair curled naturally and her blue eyes twinkled unlike her sister's unwavering brown ones. Robin's wardrobe consisted of light pastels, yellows and pinks. Even when she was little and difficult to keep clean, her mother had abandoned the dark fabrics common for young children. They didn't suit Robin and Robin detested them.

The four friends had been blessed with basically innocuous childhoods. Although Sue and Dan might dispute that observation, Gerald had survived his perils — all of which were of his own manufacture. Perennial concerns of such a farming community, besides new babies, were the crops — but through the last few years excellent harvests had been the norm. The men remained devout and stable; the women, pragmatic, energetic, and wholesome fulfilled by their love of husbands, children and homes.

On the cusp of adolescence, the foursome were quite typical self-assured youths; other people's troubles could not truly register in their consciousnesses. Jodi did remember that when they attended the funeral of a schoolmate's father who was killed during a tree felling, they vicariously grieved with their bereaved peer. Yet, common to their age, the four quickly flipped aside their sorrow and deemed their own families impervious to tragedy.

They had been exposed to the ugliness of human behavior. Along with their classmates they had noticed bruises on nine-year- old Jeremy and his younger sister, Sherry. The beatings by the siblings' alcoholic father sometimes left such welts that it was tough for the pair to sit down. The foursome fed them from their lunchboxes when the unfortunate boy and girl had no food.

The chums couldn't fathom how a person could be so cruel as to harm his children: such actions didn't mesh with their peaceful view of the world. All sought reasons why the two would be so badly treated by their own parents but the foursome's parents also seemed unable to comprehend such conduct. Their mothers did encourage their sharing lunches and packed extra food.

The beginning of that last year in the one-room school held no hint of coming sorrows. Since the week of Thanksgiving, several heavy snowfalls had occurred, atypical for the time of year. Each added inches atop the existing blanket; no thaw reduced the drifts. Most mornings Gerald needed to perform his assigned chore of shoveling the path from the house to the barn and stable.

The abundance of snow heightened spirits as the community approached the Christmas season. That much, that early, was a rare treat. Jodi remembered with delight how the inseparable quartet planned and guided the school's holiday festivities. The obligation for organizing the celebrations traditionally fell to the oldest class. Predictably, most of the responsibility became Cindy's. Robin helped but refused to worry. The boys, exhilarated by conditions ideal for sledding, skiing and snowball fights, neglected their part of the project. Jodi sympathized with Robin and the boys; she too was unable to resist that marvelous winter when Nature seemed determined to celebrate the holidays.

The morning of the Christmas party exemplified the difference between Cindy and her pals. The boys dawdled on their trek to school, stooping to gather a handful, mold a sphere, and engage in one more round of the snow battle. Trees weighted with the night's fresh fall glistened in the sun; a shake of a branch would send a clump of the white stuff onto someone's head. The boys zinged snowballs at heavily laden limbs to dislodge huge showers. Rays of sunlight sparkled on the distant hills and ice crystals danced in the air around them. In the fairyland wonder they entirely forgot the school Christmas tree.

While the boys frolicked, Cindy, with Robin's aid, busily orchestrated the decorating. Ronnie, their brother, did what he could, but mostly just drank in the comradely scene. His asthma often precluded fun – most winters he had to stay home, out of the chill, to protect his lungs. That year, much improved, he eagerly wished to participate.

Everyone admired Ronnie's mysterious ability to intuit how to help each of them. Despite his having the diminutive size and pasty mien of the chronically ill, he lacked the bitterness that often shows in people with similar disabilities. His sanguinity impressed his healthy peers who appreciated the way he detected humor in the little things. And, on that party day, with his impish grin and favorite green pants and sweater, he personified a Christmas elf.

Ronnie noted how harried Cindy appeared. If only he could lessen her distress! "Where *are* those boys?" She again repeated as she took a snowflake he held up to her and fastened it to a streamer. She glanced out the window.

"Can I have another one, Ronnie?" Robin reached for one of the white cutouts he had helped the first and second graders make; she giggled as streamers entangled or when an occasional snowflake tore. Not Cindy. No laughter or merriment for her until all the preparations were completed. Ronnie admired her expeditious management as she simultaneously monitored the younger children who strung silver ribbon into the white cutouts and directed the sixth and seventh graders who crisscrossed the room with the garlands. Cindy was supervising so that everything ran efficiently just like she did at home when their mother was busy. While his sisters complained about Cindy's bossiness, he realized that she was only ensuring all went well.

Ronnie had been disappointed the day before when the older boys wouldn't let him help cut the tree. "I can breathe through my scarf. I'll be fine," he'd protested.

"Tell you what," Teddy had said. "You can help me secure it in the stand." Johnny, Gerald's youngest brother and Ronnie's best friend, had stayed behind to play checkers while the others tramped off to cut the tree. And so Ronnie, with Johnny's help, had been chief-in-charge of screwing in the bolts. That had been fun and didn't make him wheeze. *Maybe someday I can be a builder like Teddy. But, no, I can't go into the woodshop 'cause of the sawdust. Durn this asthma.*

There hadn't been enough time to properly secure the tree. Teddy wouldn't be satisfied with any tilt. Nothing met his approval. *He sure is a – what does Papa call Cindy — perfectionist,* Ronnie had hoped the older boys would arrive early that morning so he, Johnny and Teddy could get the tree up before Cindy found time to worry. *But she'll fret no matter what we do. She's always nervous when there's a project to finish. She never plays when there's work to do. She's like Mamma. Neither of them rest until everything is finished.* How he wished he dared say, *Cindy, can I help? Please don't bite your fingernails. There's nothing left of them.* But those words might make her more irritable.

Startled by his sister's leap down off the chair on which she had been standing to fasten red berries to the wreaths, he glanced out the window and spotted the older boys. Teddy had dodged a well-aimed missile and was scurrying to form one with which to retaliate. Johnny and his brother, Jimmy, were wrestling in a snowbank. If only he could join them but that chill air made him wheeze just walking to school.

Cindy ran to the door and scolded, "Hurry! The tree must be up before school starts." He grinned when Robin winked at him. "I can't believe you! Playing when the tree isn't ready!" Cindy's caustic tone made Ronnie cringe.

"Sorry, Cindy," Teddy apologized. "Guess we aren't setting a good example, are we?"

"But how can anyone resist this tempting snow?" chuckled the irrepressible Gerald.

Ronnie sighed and smiled when Teddy, Johnny and he finished assembling the tree stand before the school bell clanged. He nodded enthusiastically as he heard Gerald proclaim, "Ted, you're going to grow up to construct the most incredible buildings — they'll be solid and objects of art, all at the same time."

Cindy concurred, "I'm hiring you for my house right now. It must be three stories high, and contain bedrooms for ten children, and a sitting room and a ..."

Ronnie flinched as he saw Robin shoot her twin a wicked gleam and tack on "and a room for you and Gerald, alone."

Cindy turned tomato red. Gerald paled and almost fled. Thankfully, Teddy interrupted, "And I'll build one for me and Robin that is six stories tall; we can spy on you from the top of a turret." Onlookers roared.

The bell rang. Johnny made a face, "Yuck, come on Ronnie, let's sit down. And the two pals raced to their desks.

A bit later that winter, influenza hit the village and killed some children's grandmas and grandpas, as well as the Weber's newborn baby. Cindy and Robin came to school one February morning distraught. Their mother had insisted they attend school although Ronnie lay in bed, propped by pillows to facilitate breathing, extremely ill; he looked and sounded worse than he ever had. Even Robin couldn't muster her cheerful optimism. Instead, dread pervaded her spirit. *What if Ronnie dies? He can't die!*

Miss Jones, their teacher for the last three years, was acutely aware of the eighth-grade girls' despair. She squatted beside the twins' desks. "How is he today?" she asked. Tears flowed down Robin's cheeks; Cindy gulped and couldn't speak; the woman lightly squeezed each of their shoulders then walked to the front of the room. "Boys and girls, Ronnie is very ill. Let's pray for him." With bowed heads and folded hands, all did. Sally noticed the terrified expression on Johnny's face and left her chair to comfort him. Soon Jimmy and Janie huddled around their older sister.

The whole school adored Ronnie, with his sense of humor and jolly kindness. He was so caring. Six-year-old Sammy's mind wandered to the first day of school when Ronnie noticed his homesickness and silently scooted over to sit next to him; Ronnie taught him how to draw a picture of a horse. As he remembered, the little boy sketched out such creatures on the paper in front of him. Nine-year-old Deborah recalled Ronnie's drilling her on her multiplication tables. None of the students could work. Gerald and Teddy had no clue how to ameliorate Cindy's and Robin's distress, unaware that merely being with them was sufficient.

Pragmatic Teddy assumed Miguel had a solution. But the boy learned that even angels can't affect the natural laws. *He's very sick — there isn't much we can offer.* Miguel's characteristic stoicism aggravated his charge.

But his Guardian Angel should help. Teddy persistently, helplessly probed. *Who is he?* He stood up from his place by the wood stove and paced; he pivoted toward the opposite direction at Miguel's unwelcome words.

Guardian Angels can't prevent death, Teddy. That's God's decision; He has His reason. Maybe He needs Ronnie elsewhere. Miguel, cognizant that his understanding of death exceeded the lad's, desired to facilitate Teddy's acceptance of the inevitable. He rubbed his worry stone formed from a bit of psychic energy. He'd picked up the habit from a child for whom he cared in the Philippines. At the age of 12, Filipinos receive pebbles from the beach and are taught to rub them when nervous. By the time a person reaches middle age, the piece of rock is translucent from the years of pressure.

Miguel, there must be cures for ailments like Ronnie's. Fists balled, with an intense scowl, Teddy continued his firm, no-nonsense attitude. *If there are angels like you, there must be other mystical powers – perhaps things no one has yet discovered. Prayer isn't enough — but I bet something else is.* Teddy furiously hammered at Miguel's apparent nonchalance about this lovely child's imminent death. He vowed he would never be so cavalier.

Later, when Teddy and the weeping Robin warmed themselves by the wood stove, he felt powerless and awkward. He despised his inadequacy in the presence of his friend's misery, and, at that moment, Ted determined to dedicate his life for unraveling the mysteries of illness and death. That Friday afternoon he committed himself, "Robin, the truths to heal Ronnie are unknown. Yet there are awesome secrets in the spiritual world. I promise you that I'll find those hidden remedies; no one else should be sick like Ronnie and die when they are only eight years old."

"Thanks, Ted. But, don't be silly. There're no cures, not for Ronnie." Her natural exuberance lost, Robin snapped irritably at his lack of realism. His first love's abrasive response stung, as did her failure to comprehend that he understood that Ronnie couldn't be saved: it was for people in the future that he meant to serve. It would be decades later before he would grasp that Robin could be sharp with him precisely because she trusted him absolutely.

At the funeral, Ted and Gerald acted as pallbearers; the boys' emotions were a muddle of anger and sadness. The twins huddled in a pew with their family. Ted noted the glazed looks in their eyes and wondered if they fathomed what was happening; he suspected the reality was too vast to accept. The youth absorbed the pastor's eulogy of Ronnie's abbreviated life and his sermon on death and heaven. Teddy's adamant vow redoubled. What a waste: sick for his entire tiny scrap of life. And, Ronnie lived as such a beautiful person.

At the wake, organized in the church fellowship hall by the Women's Circle, mourners ate tea sandwiches as Ted shared with his best pal his belief that better remedies must exist. "Ger, our relationship with Miguel and Jodi proves to us that spiritual beings exist. I bet lots of mysteries are there, available for the seeker – even like answers to the questions Ronnie's death poses."

"Certainly must be, Ted," Gerald agreed as they climbed the stairs for a stroll through the field behind the church, unable to remain in the midst of the grief.

"As soon as I finish school, I'll dedicate my life to uncovering such mysteries," announced Ted as he stared in stubborn determination at a surrounding thicket as if willing wisdom to pop out from the bushes. As predicted that summer day when he first met Jodi, Ted started toward the world of psychic phenomena to solve life's difficulties and left the building of earthly structures to others.

Gerald followed Ted's reasoning eagerly. But he couldn't procrastinate until adulthood. As usual, his active mind leapt from scheme to scheme. "Hey, we could start at the town library. And Jodi and Miguel will definitely propose ideas to pursue. Jodi told me there's an Angelic Library. Maybe she'll check into the knowledge stored there."

Jodi sided with Ted. During her service in Special Forces, she had learned to have faith that each dilemma has a solution. She found herself less ready than Miguel to concede the inevitability of illness and death.

Gerald refused to allow Ronnie to fade into anonymity. Whenever in a quandary, his mind incessantly unraveled, twisted, and reconstituted the facts. Finally it occurred to him: a newspaper to memorialize Ronnie. As soon as the inspiration struck, he assigned classmates to write stories about the boy. The first graders drew sketches and dictated accompanying words. Johnny, with Sally's and Sue's help, wrote about having a best friend. Gerald composed a biography for the front page after interviewing Ronnie's parents, siblings, some aunts and uncles for details. Cindy managed the ultimate organization. Gerald always did have such trouble figuring out how to fit things together!

With the children's masterpiece assembled, Gerald mustered the courage to request an appointment with Tom Walthers, the village paper's editor. Apprehension flooded Gerald. *Will Mr. Walthers bother with me? Will he be annoyed?* The youth's preparations were meticulous: freshly pressed Sunday best, hair carefully combed in front of the bureau mirror, polished shoes. When he consulted his mother about his grooming, she fussed a little with his collar, swallowed and commented, "Ger, you look right grown-up." Although nervous that his acne might detract from his professionalism, he carried the layout to his interview. A lump came into Tom's throat as he looked it over; after all, he was Ronnie's uncle.

Impressed by the work's quality, Tom offered to typeset it; he pulled an old shirt and pair of trousers from a closet and instructed Gerald to remove his fancy clothes so he could assist. "After all, ink would ruin your Sunday best and have your mother's ire on my head." As they worked, the boy's conscientiousness, lively conversation and quick mind impressed him. Moreover, recognizing genuine talent in the newspaper, he reflected on the lad's potential in journalism. And, so, as they bundled the finished newspapers, he offered, "I've need of a junior reporter, someone who can sense a story and ferret out information. Wanna try?"

"Oh, y-yes, Sir!" spluttered Gerald. "Oh, yes, I-I really do." Many people loved Gerald but no one, prior to that moment, regarded him as possessing special talent. His feet shuffled and he flushed as do boys his age when shockingly confronted with an adult believing in them. He swallowed, barely managing, "When c-can I start?"

"Right now if you'd like. Ten cents a story. Sometimes I'll supply suggestions. Other times you'll dig them up."

Gerald jogged the whole way home, eager to share his incredible news. Ronnie's newspapers, bundled and ready for delivery to neighbors and relatives, plus a paying job! *Wait until I tell Mom and Dad! They'll not believe it!*

Thus the death of one boy determined the lives of two others. One would become a journalist, following his talents to the stars. The other would follow a star, abandoning the skills he came to Earth to use. Alternatively, would he perhaps ascend on a different path? A bit like Jodi's deviation: interesting question for the muses to ponder.

Chapter 8

Archangel Michael recommended I include the most significant accomplishment? But which one would it be? Jodi nibbled the end of her pencil as she mulled over the list of achievements scribbled on the pad in front of her. For what seemed a decade she had been sitting in her cubicle in the Guardian research stacks diligently producing notes. She rather desperately needed a break so picked up her list and strolled over to a nearby window to gaze at the mountains. Some feathery clouds wound in and out of intricate formations; she realized that someone must be drawing a picture of angels in an intricate dance around the throne of God. *I'm not the only one who's a little tired of studying,* she mused. *Wonder if cloud-watchers on the ground ever realize that some of the more realistic pictures are drawn by angels taking a respite.*

Jodi wandered the perimeter of the room, stepped into the hall did some toe touches and yoga stretches. She meandered over to another window. No one seemed to be manipulating these clouds. Jodi pushed and pulled the mass of white into a scene of humans and angels lounging in a circle as her mind flashed over the items she had listed. *Confabs,* her face brightened as she considered the third item written on her paper. *They've gotta be the major achievement! But how do I describe them?* She tugged back and forth at her clouds. An angel or human stood, gestured, then sat and allowed another figure to take center stage. She grinned as she worked to sculpt the cloud mists to keep the drama solid. *Confabs were complex and I must be concise.* Her recollections flew back to Gerald's high school days. *Yes, that's a good choice,* she gave a final tug to one of her cloud creations, then turned back to her desk.

Jodi couldn't suppress a chuckle as she recalled the football games with Ted suited up on the field, Robin cheerleading, and Gerald and Cindy rooting from the bleachers. Even in ninth grade, Coach Davis noticed Ted's exceptional athletic talents and assigned him to first string by mid-season. Although Ted set rookie yardage records, he didn't actually cross the goal line until his sophomore year — much to the foursome's disappointment. By his senior year Ted had earned stardom at Central — gaining more yardage than any other player in their division. A husky six-foot three, who weighed in at two hundred thirty pounds, the tough tenacious halfback was nigh impossible to tackle once he got hold of the ball; he seldom charged fewer than five yards and routinely achieved ten.

He and Robin made quite the couple decked out on game nights: he, the giant, in his brown with gold trim uniform, and she standing a petite five-foot-two in gold trimmed with brown. Her pertness allowed her an obstinacy that rivaled Ted's determinedness. The two were a definite pair: her happy laughter tempered his staidness. By their senior year no one doubted their wedding would occur soon after graduation.

Jodi shook herself out of her reveries and back to work. It was ninth grade, not twelfth, where she planned to focus. During the first few days of high school, Gerald stumbled around feeling awkward as he tried to remember where his classrooms and locker were located and figure out how to keep track of his assignments. He was utterly frustrated by Thursday afternoon of that first week. The student bulletin board caught his eye and he paused from the arduous task of finding his way in these new environs to peruse the list of clubs and positions available for student participation. One posting lifted his spirits: Anyone wishing to work on the school paper, contact Jake Brewer.

The bulletin board was at the front entrance. Gerald spotted the office off to the side and dashed in; the secretary directed him to the room reserved for the school newspaper; the room even contained its own press. Jake warmly welcomed Gerald. Any warm body could help. Then he looked with genuine interest at Gerald's samples from The Eagle, more than thirty articles. "Okay, guess you have some experience and talent. We need a sportswriter since Don Kramer graduated last year. Want to try?"

"Oh, yes," gulped the lowly freshman who had expected to shadow an older writer as an errand boy. He was later to learn that the newspaper always lacked actual reporters; few students clamored for such opportunities. That day his enthusiasm knew no bounds. Tall and lanky, Gerald jogged rather than strolled through the corridors, ever in quest of a story. Frequently he did short features on his peers' diverse hobbies for the school paper, The Central Report, or The Eagle. Students appreciated his personable style and avid interest in their affairs. Mentored by none other than Tom Walthers, his clever articles were consistently excellent.

But, as sportswriter, Gerald's objectivity came into question that first semester. Some students complained that Ted, a freshman, received unfair coverage because of his close friendship with the reporter. One or two even griped that Ted's rapid promotion to first string was due to the repeated mention of his name in print. However, as Ted's innate talent unfolded over the season, critics were forced to retract their gibes. By the end of that year the team's high scoring games eliminated every bit of criticism. Ted's ability and Gerald's integrity remained intact.

Jodi admired how Cindy both applied her talents and accepted her limitations. Although she wanted to act, the girl recognized her paucity of dramatic gifts. Undaunted, she analyzed her strengths and volunteered to organize the design and construction of scenery for school plays. Since Ted relished spending his spare moments in the woodshop, Cindy enlisted him in assembling stage sets.

Mostly Jodi enjoyed watching the four interact. Although they socialized with peers from outside their sheltered childhood community, they always shared their varied interests and new friends with each other. Together, with each employing his or her talents, the quartet contributed to their high school in countless ways — even from the opening days of ninth grade.

Jodi's reveries about that distant past paused on those first months: Gerald was bogged down in details. Instead of a single teacher, he had six to satisfy. He needed to schedule homework assignments, determine what books and papers to carry home, and remember what to complete in six classes and by when. He was overwhelmed; techniques effective in the one-room schoolhouse proved inadequate. A half year ago, everything he needed had been in his desk. He could reach in and grab any item. In the high school, his locker contributed to the chaos: papers disappeared in its recesses; books required in classes remained on its shelf.

Several times he finished an assignment, only to lose it, somehow, somewhere, between home and school. Often he would turn up in algebra without pencils for the practice problems or bring pencils to grammar but forget the required pen and ink. Frustrated, toward the end of the first quarter, he realized he should withdraw from school and help his father — a fairly common decision for boys in farming communities. But he wanted to be a journalist and he did enjoy socializing. Jodi couldn't figure out how to cue him. His discouragement intense, he angrily ordered his angel, "Leave me alone! Lemme flunk. Go away!"

His friends felt weighed down by his increasing gloominess: it seemed to permeate the atmosphere around him. One October afternoon the foursome were enjoying a late fall picnic under a willow during the lunch hour. Gerald was hunched over his crossed legs studying the blades of grass. Even Robin's optimistic, cheerful disposition disappeared when near him those days. She resolved to uncover the truth, squatted in front of him and intruded by putting her hands on his shoulders. "What's wrong, Ger? I'm sick and tired of your saying, 'Nothing's wrong, leave me alone.' So, out with it!"

Brava, Jodi clapped her hands; her spirit jumped up and down with glee. *Maybe we'll get some place now.*

"I'm flunking ninth grade." Gerald muttered morosely. His guardian remembered the scene vividly: he picked at a hangnail till it bled. Then he swished his fingers through the nearby red and gold leaves and snapped dead twigs. His sandwich lay forgotten on his lap. "Mom and Dad will never, ever, understand. I can't do anything right." He gathered a handful of the exquisite dry leaves and pulverized them, tossing the bits into the wind. "If there's math to study, you can bet I'll leave my book at school. And if my English report's due, I'll leave it on the desk at home."

Cindy's practical suggestions echoed in Jodi's mind, "Why not make lists? You can enter 'algebra test' and leave three spaces: one to check off when you put your book in the pile to go home, another when you complete the studying, then one for returning the book to school." Cindy knew her boyfriend well and sensed her recitation was baffling him. If he could just visualize her scheme... she opened her notebook, found a blank lined page and drew columns on it. She headed the first, four-inch column, "Assignment", then, in a narrow one next to it, printed "B in P". The third she labeled, "Completed," and made another "B in P" in the fourth. "See how it works? And you can make a fifth, 'Turned In.'"

Although Gerald peeked at her sketch briefly as she worked, he mostly examined the leaves until she handed the sheet to him for his scrutiny. Robin and Ted relaxed. Cindy would win any award for pragmatism.

An appreciative half-smile twitched at the corners of Gerald's lips as he scrutinized her handiwork. "So what is 'B in P?'" he inquired after a pensive silence.

"'Book in Pile.' It's abbreviated." Cindy shrugged. "It would be tiresome spelling it out."

Then Robin, having scooted back to her original place in the circle of friends and picked up her sandwich, piped in with a full mouth, "We've lots of the same classes – at least one of us is in each of yours. We can make sure you've got what you'll need." She glanced around at the group, "Can't we?"

"Yes," was the simultaneous response of Cindy and Ted.

That's when Jodi spotted Ted's mischievous smirk, "And maybe if we forget something, your Guardian Angel will provide a little nudge." She and Miguel both laughed. Obviously, his addition was for her benefit. The girls were predictably amused by his wit.

Gerald sat dumbstruck. He hadn't supposed anyone, even his friends, was able to help him. His spine straightened. He meditated further on the suggestions. Life flowed back into his deadened eyes. "Gee. Gosh, guys, I couldn't survive without you." And the weight of the world lifted from his shoulders, identical to the release he'd experienced when rescued from first-grade failure.

How well the group solved Gerald's predicament: each made it his or her own! Jodi marveled at how they utilized their distinct expertise.

Jodi squirmed on her wooden library chair while she recalled the first confab –*occurred when they were eight. At school. Third grade, maybe*. She'd sure felt inadequate as she struggled to help Gerald remember the steps for assembling the paper trains. The first fold and often the second seemed easy. But then, at some step before the final fold, the whole thing always fell apart. The rest of the class showed off their creations; Gerald couldn't do it. When his fifth attempt failed, he threw his crumpled paper on the floor and ran outside. Gerald knew himself hopeless, worthless in fact.

While Gerald stomped around the playground, Jodi suggested, "What if I prompt you?"

She would never forget the sting of his vehement refusal. "That's cheating!" He balled his hands into fists, "What should I say? 'uh, my angel, Jodi, did it?'"

Although Jodi wondered what harm would occur if she got a little credit, she appreciated how much he craved to function exactly like his classmates. Through the years together, he occasionally assumed that a competent human accomplished tasks without angelic prompts and refused her aid.

Both of them stewed as they marched around the schoolyard's perimeter. Jodi represented herself as striding beside him, hands behind her back. Gerald trudged along kicking at clods of dirt. Sequences of directions defeated him every time. The eight-year-old child alternately berated himself and devised potential solutions. No way would he ask his peers, imitate their steps, or expose his incompetence. Independently, Jodi had similar musings. Her inability to find a solution was causing her, too, to feel a failure. It didn't dawn on her that her behavior mirrored his. To disclose her inadequacy to a fellow angel might discredit her as a Guardian – she was, after all, a trainee.

Along with the rest of the pupils, Teddy saw his pal flee and assumed him on his way to the outhouse, but he became troubled when Gerald didn't return. *Maybe he's sick?* He approached Miss Smith for permission to check; the teacher, distracted by the first-grade reading lesson, simply nodded.

Once outdoors, Teddy spotted his buddy and Jodi rounding the far corner and ran over to fall into step beside them. Gusty breezes swirled maple and oak leaves on their descent through the brisk autumn air. "What's wrong?" Teddy pressed.

"Nothing. Leave me alone," Gerald growled. So they plodded side by side crunching the fall carpeting.

Miguel pulled Jodi aside, "What's the matter?"

"He can't remember the sequence of directions for that train project, and, he's convinced it's cheating if I make suggestions." She tugged that lock of her hair. "He's proud. He wants to succeed without my aid." Jodi mimicked the childish voice with all its petulance, "No one else needs an angel to show the next fold."

Miguel sympathized, "You haven't an answer, correct?"

Jodi blushed; she stared at the ground. "Why is it that you are supposed to have a response?" Jodi gaped. She stared at her companion. His expression exuded compassion, not jeering. Teddy's angel never teased.

Jodi bristled as she thought. *He considers me an inferior Guardian for Gerald.* Her shoulders slumped. *And he's probably right. Gerald is my first charge.*

She huffed at Miguel, "So what would you do?"

"Probably seek advice," sincerity imbued the words of the experienced Guardian. "You've the same problem as Gerald. You won't ask for advice. And, you could, you know."

Abashed, she contemplated his eyes. "So what would you suggest?"

"I'm not sure. How about a confab?" Miguel's voice trickled off as they watched the schoolhouse empty for recess; fortunately only Miss Smith approached the angels' charges. Alert for trouble, they observed her ascertain that adult interference was unnecessary; she summoned the other children to a different area of the playground where she initiated a game of catch. They noticed she hugged Sally, apparently reassuring her that her big brother was fine.

Jodi turned to stare at Miguel, "So, what is a confab?" The odd word underscored her realization she had much to learn. Impatiently, she kicked at a twig. Why hadn't her mentors taught her about "confab", whatever it was, when preparing her for guardianship. How much more knowledge existed out there that she lacked?

However Miguel remained serene; he showed no sign of any reaction to her mood. How could he be so tranquil when he had to work with a Guardian Angel who didn't even know about this confab thing?

"A confab," he explained, "occurs when we all put our heads together: you, me, Gerald and Teddy. An inkling of an inspiration will come to one of us and another will elaborate, then another. Eventually the idea will expand into an ideal solution." He paused to check on the boys, "So, shall we recommend one?"

"—uh, sure." Secretly she took pleasure that Miguel couldn't conjure an instant answer. A bit of worry abated: perhaps she wasn't such a poor excuse for a Guardian Angel.

While their angels consulted, the boys played catch. Gerald, normally incessantly informative, remained strangely silent. Intuitively, Teddy stopped fishing for explanations and instead flipped his new green ball at Gerald. "See what I got yesterday?" Glad for the distraction, his friend flipped it back. By the time Miguel and Jodi finished their discussion, Gerald had experimented with a backward toss from beneath his legs and Teddy with a quick return over his left shoulder.

Gerald ignored Jodi when she spoke. But, Teddy, eager to understand Gerald's strange behavior, held the ball while he listened to Miguel. Once the children stopped their game, Jodi requested gently, but firmly, "Gerald, let's share with Teddy and Miguel. More heads collaborating can untangle really worrisome knots."

Gerald blushed. "You didn't tell Miguel, didja?" He confronted her angrily and kicked at a pile of stones. Miss Smith glanced across the playground, tensed, but relaxed as the scene unfolded.

"Please, let's risk it," Jodi pleaded, "Let's see – maybe they'll have suggestions." Finally Gerald loosened his posture and dutifully related his difficulty to his chum.

Jodi was stunned by little Teddy's ability to put two and two together with precocious logic. "Sort of part of the trouble you have paying attention, isn't it?" Teddy thought aloud.

"Yeah, guess so," Gerald gazed forlornly at the ground, kicking up dust.

"Wonder if it's a little like me and those durn spelling words," Teddy offered.

Teddy's comment triggered Gerald's memory of a previous conversation with Jodi about Teddy's poor spelling. Gerald had supposed that his friend wasn't studying the word list like he did. Routinely, after he and Sally dried the supper dishes, Sue sat at the kitchen table and recited each word aloud for Gerald to spell; she did the same for Sally with her list. When talking with Jodi about Teddy's difficulty, Gerald had wondered if Teddy's mother didn't have time to help him. But Jodi had posited that perhaps Teddy's difficulty involved more than a lack of practice. Gerald stared at Teddy with narrowed eyes, "—uh, whaddya mean?"

The web that unraveled during that nascent confab, proved Jodi's theory. Teddy shoved his hands deep into his pockets, glared at his dusty shoes, and whispered through clenched teeth, "Mamma and I go over the words every single night. She drills me and drills me and I still forget them for the test. I never get them right in my sentences. Spelling won't stick in my head."

Gerald blurted out with an eight year old's honesty, "You said you didn't bother studying them."

"I lied so you'd think I'm lazy, not dumb. Now you know I'm stupid." Astounded, Jodi absorbed how succinctly Teddy phrased the inadequacy she had felt with Miguel.

"Aw, c'mon, Teddy. You're not dumb. Heck, you figure out too many puzzles. You just can't remember your spelling words."

How wise a child can be! Jodi marveled to herself.

"Ya think so?" Teddy looked up from the stones he was inspecting and sought confirmation in Gerald's demeanor. His face brightened and he leapt into the air. A colossal load evaporated as he absorbed his friend's matter-of-fact analysis of his weakness.

Gerald couldn't believe that his pal Teddy would think himself dumb. Not in spelling or anything else. "Teddy, you reckon everyone feels stupid once in a while?"

Decades later Jodi chuckled when she replayed the reply, "Dunno. Probably not Cindy and Robin."

"Yup." Gerald supplied the explanation. "They're girls. Meant to say, do all us boys feel stupid about something?"

At that, the two angels howled.

"Oh, you two," burst out Jodi. "Thinking us girls never feel dumb. Everyone feels stupid sometimes. Huh, Miguel?" Her angelic comrade chuckled.

"Teddy," Gerald ignored their angels' silliness, "What if we invent tricks to remember words? Like for "beet" draw a bee on a beet."

"Hey. Maybe that'd work!" Teddy brightened. "—and, uh, you know how to make the train? We could make a model and number each fold."

"And I could follow the numbers," Gerald danced up and down, snatched the ball from Teddy, and returned it with an underhand toss. Teddy, catching his ball, nearly ran home to tell his mother the plan. Sally, finger in mouth, had been surreptitiously observing. Seeing that her brother was okay, she joined the game of tag.

Engrossed in their ideas, the boys almost didn't hear Miss Smith ring the end-of-recess bell. Jodi learned a lot as she observed how the confab proceeded that day.

Over time confabs became potent tools with the humans and their angels contributing equally. In future years those sessions continued to be Jodi's favorite interactions: she loved the intimacy that resulted when beings of both realms collaborated to form an incredibly powerful coalition. Jodi, the trainee, prayed the tested outcomes of those close alliances would win a permanent position for her as a Guardian Angel.

Chapter 9

Jodi rose and stretched – *five more days – that will have to be enough on the confabs.* Twisting her neck, bending down, arching her back, thinking, thinking – *Must include effect of World War I. Let's see.* She returned to her outline and printed: "1. Importance of each life. 2. Power of group prayer." *Wonder — was it partly because of their relationships with angels that Gerald and Teddy realized such spiritual mysteries while still so young? Maybe, maybe not.*

Jodi's muscles felt cramped; a reference on the war would help with this section of her presentation. The Guardian Division librarian told her that the History Department was located on floors seventy-five through ninety-three. The woman checked her catalogue; references for the Great War were shelved in the section on modern warfare on the eighty-third floor. Jodi grinned – that climb would energize her: she did need a change of scene. Jodi grabbed an empty tablet and a couple of pencils so she could write this chapter in the History Department.

During her ascent of the spiral staircase, she at times skipped a few steps when no one was immediately ahead of her. How good to be moving again! On the forty-third floor landing she almost did a handspring – but bowed to the decorum of the library, even with no one around to notice. At the designated level, she saw a pictograph of an early airplane with a couple of small eruptions exploding beneath it: the symbol for the Great War was an airplane dropping bombs. The archway next to it could not be mistaken: the exploding atom bomb being the symbol.

Jodi pulled a reference from the shelf, selected an empty chair at one of the tables, and spread out her materials. During the spring of 1917, on the cusp of the boys' junior year, the U.S. joined the allied efforts to battle the Central Powers. Gerald, Ted, and their male classmates expected to don uniforms after graduation. Robin and Cindy considered naval nursing careers. The town's entire populace, along with the rest of the country, immersed themselves in war news.

Apprehension filled the foursome as they scrutinized the lists of the brave men who'd been killed on the battlefields published in the newspaper. Gerald, with pimples and glasses, occupied the positions of Editor-in-Chief of the school paper and Cub Reporter at <u>The Eagle</u>. He figured service during the war would provide life experiences, background he needed to accumulate for a successful journalism career. And, although he knew he stood no chance of joining the elite corps of war correspondents, he could send back feature articles to <u>The Eagle</u>. Jodi could not even imagine his exponentially worse near-misses which would require her intervention. She figured he could find plenty of opportunities to hone his writing skills and perhaps garner a bit of acclaim without participating in combat.

Ted hadn't deviated from his goal to pursue metaphysics instead of architecture — the consequence of Gerald exposing him to angels at age six. He exhausted the meager references on angelic sightings in the local and county libraries and searched the collections at the state university during a church youth rally. Battlefields historically had provided an arena where such visitations occurred according to his research and he grew fascinated by the possibilities for first-hand encounters with celestial beings. Participation in the war effort might provide him opportunities to observe spiritual events in action. Then he could learn more about the mysterious forces which interact with citizens on the planet.

But horror suddenly struck home. Jim Granger, three years ahead of the four, became the first soldier to die from their town. Gerald, Ted, Cindy and Robin reminisced about his basketball feats, jokes and pranks. In their pre-teen days, they had idolized him for his athletic prowess and his sense of humor. Sally, Gerald's sister, was best friends with Jim's sister, Sharon; Sally desperately wanted to help Sharon cope with her anger and grief. Remembering little Ronnie, Gerald suggested that the girls compose a memorial newspaper. The two girls wrote poems and, following Gerald's advice, interviewed family and friends for a commemoration of Jimmy's life. Gerald helped them typeset their production in the school newsroom; they distributed the special edition to all in the high school and Tom Walthers was so impressed with it that he included their work as a supplement to the next <u>The Eagle</u>. In the meantime, Gerald's eagerness to report from the war zones and Teddy's to encounter spiritual phenomena in that milieu faded with the abrupt equation of war and death.

The foursome worried about David, Ted's brother, and John, the twins' cousin. Both were fighting in the European theater. The entire town had gathered for their send-off; cheers rang out as the lads obeyed the train conductor's "All Aboard." That summer day of the recruits' departure, envious high-schoolers had begged to participate in the war effort and parents vigilantly kept an eye on their younger sons to prevent impetuous ones enlisting before graduation. However, the collective mood shattered with the death of someone they knew. Prior to Jim's funeral the war had remained a faraway abstraction; after, none felt in such a frenzy to finish school.

"Who's David's angel?" Ted asked Miguel one evening. Ted clutched his pencil so tightly that his knuckles were white; he'd written the name, David, repeatedly instead of the trigonometry functions he was supposedly memorizing. His mind, filled with apprehension, couldn't be forced to concentrate on mathematics. Haunted by fears of his brother's death on the battlefield, Ted even neglected to wash after barnyard chores; his cheek bore a grimy indentation from where his hand propped up his head. All he could do was obsess on his brother's safety.

Why do you ask? Miguel pictured himself lounging in the chair on the opposite side of the room clad in contemporary boots, shirt, and cap. He'd long ago discarded the elf-like costume worn for Teddy the child.

"Just wondered if you knew him?" Ted jabbed his pencil into the papers on which he'd been scribbling and wiped perspiration from his forehead, the back of his dirty hand leaving another streak. "I —umm — wonder if, uh, he's previously assumed wartime duties – and ...."

"Are you asking me if he – or she – can keep David alive?" Miguel interrupted.

"Yeah, whaddaya think?"

"I don't know, Ted," Miguel honored the young man's concern with cautious reason. "Even though the ultimate outcome partly depends on David's destiny and God's plan, there are situational factors... you know, time and place...." He scratched his chin. "You are accustomed to angels, how to converse with me, how to get advice and warnings – but you frequently ignore my expertise." He grinned. "You're aware that you and Ger take more risks than most since you know us so well." His expression became grave, "David will take fewer chances and may better protect himself; he might be safer, regardless of his inability to communicate with his Guardian. It's hard to tell."

Ted appreciated Miguel's reasoning, but his worries didn't abate. On the following day while he and Gerald hurried toward their first class, he shared his fears with Gerald and concluded with his chief worry, "What if David's angel can't protect him?"

Stopping in the middle of the hallway, Gerald stared at Ted; his eyes narrowed. He tugged at an idea teasing at the corner of his mind, trying to coax it into awareness; his hand fiddled with the strap of his book bag. Back in ninth grade Cindy had persuaded Robin that they purchase such a carrier for Gerald's Christmas gift. She reasoned that, if he lugged his entire day's necessities of books, papers, pens with him, he could be better prepared for classes. The twins found nothing but black leather satchels with handles, so Cindy personalized the one they chose by sewing on a red strap; she figured he'd be less likely to leave it somewhere if it stayed on his shoulder.

Finally Gerald's perplexed expression brightened; he'd retrieved the errant thought. Grabbing Ted's shoulders with both hands; his excited words ricocheted through the corridor, "Hey, let's get Jodi and Miguel to help David. He'll be lots safer with three angels!" Around them classmates had been sorting books and materials at their lockers, gossiping, teasing, shouting, laughing, and scurrying in both directions. All activity ceased when the proposal re-sounded as if given over a loud speaker; the drip of the faucet could be heard. Passers-by, impeded by the well known journalist's and football star's block-ade of the hall, stared.

Ted flooded with relief at the proposition, but, glancing around, noticed the crowd Gerald had attracted. "Ger, you know, as well as, everyone here," he pointedly glanced around at the incredulous onlookers, "that each of us has just one Guardian Angel." He added a dramatic chortle, "You'd better come up with something realistic, ol' man."

Gerald, alerted to the fact that he'd invited undesired attention, chuckled, "Just trying to cheer you up, buddy. Must be horrible worrying about your brother all the time." The two turned and headed on to class. Relief washed over Ted as he imaged three angels hovering over David. But that peace was short-lived. Over lunch Jodi informed them, *We can't just do that — go off and guard David. Miguel and I have lifetime assignments to you two.* The familiar voice shredded his hopes.

"But, this is different. You could kinda provide extra shielding. Do just a little guarding?" Ted on the bench beside Gerald, with no one within earshot, didn't mind his friend's agitated discussion. In fact, he liked this way of con-versing when together; by doing so, one youth could follow the other's current human-angel debate.

"That's not how angelic law works, Ger. It's impossible." Jodi had her charge's full attention despite the cafeteria noise and confusion.

"Jodi, this is crucial! David can't die. What would that do to Ted? Why are you refusing?" Gerald briskly rubbed his apple, pulled at its stem, took a bite. *How can I persuade her? My idea's perfect. These stupid angelic rules. Jodi's al-ready broken plenty of rules in the past.*

Miguel reinforced Jodi's argument, *Each human has his or her own Guardian Angel. I'm responsible for you, Ted; Jodi, for Gerald.* Teddy's expression became disconsolate as he accepted the futility of attempting to convince Miguel to reinforce David's angel. However, Gerald, arms tightly crossed over his chest, stubbornly persisted. The sandwich in front of him sat untouched.

"But, Jodi, you assist Ted at times and Miguel has watched both of us while you fetched human assistance. Anyway, we're older now. We don't need mon-itoring every minute."

"Yeah, sure," Jodi mocked her charge. "And just yesterday who raced the buggy down that steep trail where he couldn't see the cow rounding the curve?" Ted recognized she was correct; his dear, impulsive friend was her ex-clusive responsibility.

"Oh, Jodi — I wouldn't have hit Bessie!" Ted wasn't surprised at that either. Gerald had no clue how many gambles he blithely took and how frequently Jodi's intervention eliminated potential disaster.

"What!" Jodi's exasperation showed in a razor-sharp edge to her voice. She shoved into his skull a visualization of her wagging a finger at him, "You durn well knew I wasn't navigating that buggy. You refused to listen to me! I coerced ol' Bessie to sniff out some clover in the pasture. Now, who is it that can function without his Guardian Angel?"

"What if we promised to be extra cautious till you return?"

Gerald never does quit, Teddy simultaneously admired his friend's persistence and comprehended that the scatterbrained daredevilry couldn't be cooled by a mere promise. Such behavior was innate in Gerald and assimilated in both boys' lifestyles over the years of angelic shelter.

Miguel intervened with another perspective, "No human or angel knows what'll happen tomorrow: you could be in more danger than David. Each human is equally important. That's why each person is assigned an angel. God has dispatched a multitude of Special Forces Angels to the battlefields overseas to backup the Guardians." Miguel's serenity calmed Ted so that he could entertain his angel's explanations of how life works. The spiritually inclined lad appreciated the profound wisdom that underpinned his Guardian's words.

"So, uh, what can we do?" Ted reached for a pencil and paper to jot down any advice.

"Prayer," Jodi's one-word answer rang out forcefully. "It really helps. Lots more energy and safety will envelop David. Jesus is there anyway — but your prayers support Him immeasurably."

When they met up with the twins who had spent that lunch hour at French club, Gerald and Ted proposed prayer sessions in which they would pray for every soldier they knew at the front. "We could schedule them during the school lunch hour and invite others to participate," suggested Cindy. Soon the school cafeteria filled to standing room during the daily sessions. Each student brought a list of loved ones: all of whom received individual prayers.

For whatever reason, no additional deaths or serious casualties occurred among the soldiers from their community, but some extraordinary acts of heroism were reported. Once stateside, David recounted the uncanny sensation that his little brother and the other three fought right there alongside him in the tightest spots.

In November of their senior year, the war ended and the entire globe settled down. The friends finished high school in peacetime, relishing the regenerated world as they eagerly read the reports of the formation of the League of Nations.

Jodi's ecstasy knew no bounds: she'd shepherded Gerald successfully through childhood and adolescence without loss of life or limb. Heaving a sigh of relief, she knew she had completed the trickiest years of her fledgling guardianship. She'd proven her abilities: she would never be ordered back to Special Forces. Gerald would enter a newspaper career; his choice for his wife was sealed; he lived in a town where nothing particularly dangerous happened; and the Great War had been relegated to history books. Not naïve, Jodi anticipated a few crises down the line, but her training days were over and she could relax until her next assignment some day in the future.

As Miguel had clarified, even angels cannot foresee events! Yet, perhaps, if angels and humans knew the future, life would lose much of its adventure and joy.

PART II

Chapter 1

Jodi yawned. *If only writing could be as effortless for me as it was for Gerald* was her wistful thought as she strolled out of the department and toward the spiraling staircase. Peering up she couldn't even make out the top level where they'd branched off into Archangel Michael's domain – was that meeting only a couple of days ago? The fun-loving angel chuckled, *What a kick it would be to slide down that banister from the uppermost turrets! It's polished so smooth. Bet I'd be at mach speed by this point.*

The angel laughed aloud as she pictured her long hair flying. Her imagination brought back the wintry day Gerald and Ted, eager for an exhilarating sledding, climbed to the top of Steep Rock Hill, some two hundred yards high. *And what a ride that was!* Jodi unconsciously jerked her body leftward as she replayed their close call with a giant hemlock that they brushed on the right during their rapid descent. And leaning backward, she relived the thrill of skimming hundreds of feet across the snow-filled valley then halfway up the other side.

"Hi, Jodi, whacha doing? You, okay?" An angel skipped down the stairs; twinkles surrounded her head as light reflected off the tiny crystals beaded through her braids.

"Hey there, Dee. You startled me. Just re-enacted a particularly breathtaking bobsled run." The two angels mingled spirit bodies. "What you up to, Deanna?"

"Verifying a fact or two in the military section. Hans and I debated last night whether the Armed Forces Division merely battles Lucifer or has other purposes. I thought the unit had been formed after Lucifer's fall to vanquish him but George argued that it participates in various earth-side battles."

"So, what did you learn?" Jodi was curious but couldn't comprehend such a waste of time: a gorgeous day she could enjoy on a glorious, sunny beach instead voluntarily spent in a library. However, Jodi bit her impulsive tongue. She didn't wish to hurt Deanna's feelings,

"Oh, seems God did create that division after Lucifer's fall. Its mission was to battle the dark angels both at the time of their rebellion and in future angelic conflicts." Deanna gasped for a breath and her brow puckered, "I learned it definitely doesn't function in human wars; those come under the jurisdiction of Special Forces – and you know that we don't fight; we simply assist individuals during combat." She gestured toward Jodi as she babbled on, "Oh, you know — you and I have participated often enough — we lead 'em out of danger or apply first aid until medics arrive."

Apparently reminded of Jodi's plight, Deanna's words slowed as she gently touched her, "And how's your research progressing? The presentation's scheduled five days from now, right? Wouldn't miss it!" Deanna didn't pause but rushed on without hesitating for Jodi's reply. "I'm amazed at the myriads of angels talking about attending the session."

Jodi eventually managed to disrupt Deanna's torrent with a quick, "Be sure to pray for me, Dee. There's scads more I need to outline." And Jodi strode back to her cubicle where her paper and pencils waited. "Next...the development of his career and family," she whispered to herself.

The memory of his first day as an official reporter on <u>The Eagle</u> lightened her mood. Gerald had propped his bike against the brick building which housed the newspaper and was releasing the buckle on the bag fastened behind the seat. On that first day of work he planned to begin the feature series he'd been assigned last spring. But Tom Walthers stuck his head out the window the second he heard the bicycle clank the wall. The man bent forward, fixed his palms on the ledge, and griped, "Where you been?" Then, without a pause, "Got a hot tip for you to investigate. Well, what you waiting for? Get inside!"

Gerald raced into his editor's office where he found that Tom, who had swiveled back to his desk, was pulling a slip of paper off the top of the "hot leads" stack. His boss read aloud, "Jon Yonster, over in the Glen, found cash hidden among rocks near a cave downstream from his farm." The man looked up at Gerald over the edge of the paper, "Called the sheriff — but thought we might like a scoop." Putting down the note, he hunched his shoulders, "Well, what's holding you up, boy? You should have been half there by now!" but the man softened the implied criticism with a grin, "C'mon. Along with you." And, shooing Gerald out, he resumed the project that buried him again in stacks of newsprint.

Jodi could sense Gerald's rising excitement as the ramifications of his first professional story sunk in. Although he'd done a lot of reporting as student and cub reporter, he'd mostly covered school events or written features. This sounded like real action. She laughed to herself as he enthusiastically mounted his bicycle and sped down the road in a cloud of dust.

Gerald biked vigorously along the roadway that led toward the ravine shaped by the swiftly flowing river over the ages. He imagined what lay ahead on this his first day – a day he'd expected to spend hunched over a desk working on the feature article Tom had assigned him last spring. Action was much preferable. As he drew nearer, he had to dodge rocks thrown from numerous tumultuous spring floods that lay scattered at the base of the cliff which formed one wall of the valley where Sheriff Jenkins and Deputy Bob were stooped over the residue of a campfire, poking the blackened logs with sticks.

The rocky side of the ravine, Gerald estimated, rose ten feet to a stand of maples. The reporter figured it unlikely a camper along these widened banks, nicknamed "the glen", would be noticed from that farmland overhead. An observer would've needed to hike through those maples and peer straight down to witness activity on the river bank. Plus the roaring rapids and the whoosh of short falls created a cacophony over which no voices could carry to a farmer in those fields.

Perhaps three feet above the cliff's base, he spotted the dark entrance to a cavern; it must have been chiseled millennia ago into the boulders by this very river. An involuntary shudder coursed up his spine when it sparked memories of his and Ted's terrified stay so many years back in a similar cave.

"What's here, Sheriff Jenkins?" Gerald shouted over the din. A little nervous about intruding on the man, he clutched his reporter's notepad and pencil tightly.

"Understand you're official news now, huh, Gerald?" Sheriff, his thumbs tucked under his belt, looked at him benevolently even though from what seemed the height of authority.

"Yes sir," Gerald's lips simultaneously smiled and trembled: he definitely didn't want to mess up this assignment.

The lawman, a husky cowboy type, wore a pair of holstered six-shooters and a wide-brimmed tan hat. One of Jenkins' duties was to steer the town's adolescent mischief-makers into responsible citizens. Jodi appreciated his no-nonsense approach: the sheriff unhesitatingly gave them a day in the town jail if he deemed the shenanigans deserved it. Youth in their county proved more circumspect before any cut-up as a result and the citizenry only rarely needed to provide room and board for its rebellious teenaged miscreants. Jodi'd also witnessed his softer side when he guided a troubled lad or lass into after-school jobs to use idle moments wisely and supply a bit of pocket money. No one in town stood prouder than the sheriff when local children grew into meaningful occupations.

That included Gerald. Jenkins wanted the youth to succeed on his initial professional scoop and so painstakingly enumerated his preliminary findings: he pointed to the blackened logs on the riverbank, "Seems they built a campfire here, stayed a couple days – maybe a week." With a thrust of his hand, he gestured to large boulders beside the cave. "When they moved on, they buried a cache of loot over there. Looks like checks and cash from that St. Louis hold-up couple months back."

Jodi swelled with pride as she eavesdropped on Gerald's astute questioning of the investigator – this young man – once the toddler she'd rescued from Mister Jack — had grown up.

"So, who discovered the loot?" Gerald wanted to credit the finder in his yet-to-be-written story.

"Jon and his sons were trout fishing this morning. They'd been inching steadily downstream when Jon spied the residue of the campfire and explored the area. Guess they'd already quite a catch and were fixing to head home." The man grinned; he knew his fishing buddy would never have noticed a thing amiss if not done trolling for the day.

Gerald, after scribbling down the words, jumped to the "why" of his report. "Uh, why'd the thieves abandon such valuable stuff, you think?" On arriving, he'd sketched a brief description of the surroundings to add background color and satisfy the "where" of the article as Tom had taught him.

"Probably didn't expect it'd be unearthed; figured they'd return for it one of these days." Jenkins moseyed over to examine a footprint he spied on the edge of the search area. "Hey, Bob, trace this, huh. First track I've seen."

Finally the full weight of this real-life story hit Gerald: Vicious Criminals Camp Near Town...what a headline! With equal suddenness he feared for his community — *are we safe?* He gulped and drew a long breath, his knuckles whitened around his pencil. "Do, do — you think these men are dangerous?"

"Probably so." The sheriff heaved his large shoulders, "Understand they shot a couple of bystanders who interfered during the hold-up."

Gerald took down the direct quote. "And why'd they stop here, you think? If Jon fished the river earlier and spotted them, they might not have gotten away."

"Suspect them not being familiar with these parts, they probably thought this glen quite isolated." Jenkins squatted by a boulder intently inspecting its surface, "They'd be on the alert though and Jon and his sons, not expecting criminals along the river, wouldn't have carried weapons. Might not have suspected anything awry and never mentioned the campers or might not have been so lucky."

An inspiration struck Gerald: *We need photographs for The Eagle.* And he blurted out, "Is a wanted poster available?"

"Yep, on the Post Office's Board. Names are Jake and Bill. In their twenties. Ask Tom to print up a flyer to spread the word for folks to keep an eye out."

"Sure will. Any other facts for my article?" Gerald flipped the pages while skimming his notes.

"Probably the fellows traveled on a day or two ago, south I bet." The sheriff nodded toward a narrow trail leading into the hills on the opposite side of the river. His hands unconsciously touched his holsters as if to check on his arms. "On foot at this point. No droppings or hoof prints and, anyways, horses would have been seen by one of the farmers roundabouts." He beckoned Gerald over to the site he had been scrutinizing. "One of 'em may be injured – splotches on these rocks – looks like dried blood."

Gerald squatted close by the sheriff and examined the dark stain. He never would've noticed that clue, much less identified it. "How you going to hunt them, sir?"

"Telegraph our findings to towns bordering the other side of those hills; form a posse to scout the intervening terrain." Sheriff Jenkins sauntered toward his brown stallion and gripped the saddle horn in preparation to mount, when Gerald asked, "Can I go?"

"Would expect the town reporter to join any posse," His assent was accompanied by a broad smile as he swung up onto the patient steed accustomed to waiting for his partner who spent hours perusing various isolated locales. "After all, you have to bring in stories for that new daily Tom is printing. Heard he's hired a typesetter and a proof reader. What's this world coming to? And he chuckled as he turned his horse toward town.

Me in a posse! And on the first day of the job! Ted will want to go, too. Gotta get word to him. Dad's talked about riding with posses. What's going to happen? Real live killers. Wonder if we'll have a shoot out with them. Gerald's imagination raced through a hundred possibilities as he pedaled vigorously back to <u>The Eagle</u>'s headquarters: *would he earn a byline from today's adventure*?

Jodi noted the quotidian sights they passed – scenes to which Gerald paid no attention: the green trees of early summer; farmers plowing their fields; children tending to younger siblings or weeding the family gardens; mothers hanging out clothes to dry on the lines since Mondays were washdays.

Gerald rushed into the office and was spilling out his news before the door slammed behind him. After he'd rattled off a list of Sheriff Jenkins' findings, he hurried for the door, "I'm going to go check for posters."

"Hold on," called Tom. Seemingly unfazed by Gerald's breaking news, he had been nonchalantly sharpening a pencil with his penknife while Gerald informed him of the extraordinary events. The editor muttered "Already got 'em."

"What?" Gerald was baffled. How could Tom possibly deduce the evidence at the glen? "When — How...?"

"Figured that's what you'd discover when the first report crossed my desk. Fetched the posters while you investigated the scene."

Gerald's pride visibly dissipated. He'd read the reports of the St. Louis hold-up but hadn't connected the two events until the sheriff spelled it out for him. Then Gerald surmised that Tom must be teasing him. "So, Jon told you everything when he called in the tip this morning!" his neck flushed.

"Not at all. Heavens boy, I've been in this business a number of years. Gimme credit for a little savvy. Now, write your piece before you ride with the posse."

Tom knew he was being rough on the boy but believed it his obligation. For any novice, there was a lot to absorb and absorb quickly. Besides the basics, journalists must learn to avoid letting personal bias contaminate their writing.

Gerald staggered over to his typewriter, totally humbled, realizing he'd much to assimilate before he'd be able to anticipate news connections. He pecked away at the keys, handed his lines to Tom and headed toward the door.

"Hey, wait a minute! Where's that notebook and pencil?" Tom called brusquely. "Just because you're on the trail doesn't mean you won't need your materials."

"Oh...." Gerald's voice trickled off, *Boy not only do I have a lot to learn, I forgot one of his very first rules. What Mr. Walthers must think of me! How long before he fires me?* Gerald didn't see the seasoned editor grin as he watched his trainee shoot off toward home.

Gerald gulped down a sandwich and glass of milk then trotted out to the barn where his father already was readying his strong bay. Gerald retrieved his gear and saddled his gray stallion. While Dan worked, he lectured his son, "Now remember, boy, this, I admit, is an adventure. But it's also a disciplined posse. No heroics." Gerald nodded and appreciated the admonishment.

Both grabbed their canteens and the lightweight jackets that Sue collected for them. "It'll cool off in those hills as the afternoon draws on," his mother advised before kissing Gerald on the cheek, "Now you two *be careful.*" Grateful that her husband would participate in the posse, she calmed her inner unease about Gerald on his first such adventure. Although a farmer during the part of his life she shared, Dan had served in the infantry. He intended his boys to be skilled enough to handle their rifles by reflex alone and had drilled them over the years on gun safety. No son of his better blow off a foot or, worse, another's brains out.

Ted's father, Ryan, was a crack woodsman and tracker. Both fathers, plus the sheriff and his deputy, formed the core of most community posses; they knew the sheriff's expectations and style. Sue could relax in the knowledge that Gerald's initiation into criminal-chasing would be in the company of such capable citizens.

That afternoon, the posse was composed of nine men mounted on strong horses. Sheriff Jenkins had agreed to admit Ted, Joe, Harry and Buck – Gerald's recently graduated classmates. The group gathered along the road opposite Ted and Ryan's house, which, situated on the outskirts of town, provided a sensible assembly area.

Before the posse set out the lawman reviewed the day's mission in painstaking detail. The horses pawed the dirt and snorted as the humans listened. Tails swished at the annoying mosquitoes. Gerald also swatted at the pests; their irritating buzz occasionally marred his concentration.

Gerald consciously mustered his every drop of attention as Jenkins briefed them from atop his huge stallion. To his uniform of khaki pants and shirt, he had added a matching jacket and had slung his Springfield bolt action rifle across his back. The weapon would be instantly accessible. Gerald scanned the group: farmers in their overalls, long-sleeved shirts, high boots. Each carried a rifle in front and a jacket behind. As Gerald compared the men, he observed that the sheriff's clothing set him apart as the conspicuous leader. *Somehow I must portray in words this picture of the obvious leader contrasted with the others.* With his readers in mind, he took out the notebook from his hip pocket and jotted down a bit of description.

The sheriff had advised against saddlebags to avoid encumbering the horses. The plan was for an afternoon's outing: no camping in pitch-black terrain with killers afoot. "Our primary goal," the sheriff stressed, "is contact with remote farmsteads along the likely way the robbers traveled. We need to be certain that no one's injured." Astride his stallion, with his back to the big white farmhouse on Ryan's property, Jenkins faced the semicircle of men on horseback.

"We'll also seek any witnesses who saw a pair of men heading south so we can determine their route and condition." Sheriff Jenkins caught the eye of each of the rookies one-by-one as he emphasized, "No one's gonna try to play hero and wind up getting us ambushed. I've telegraphed the sheriffs up ahead. They've situated men on the other side of the hills waiting to trap the killers as they exit that wilderness." He stared from one set of eyes to the next, "Everyone comprehend?" And he paused to watch each nod.

On reaching the glen, the party veered off the well-trodden road. After fording the river, they traversed the stony trail up through the rock covered hills that rose on the southern boundary of the county. On the ride they passed occasional grassy leas where isolated small farms nestled in the woods.

At the first couple of homesteads, the inhabitants had neither heard nor seen strangers and no animals were missing. However, ten miles farther, after their horses had climbed the hill adjacent to Jim and Ellen Davidson's small, remote cottage, the posse spied the body of a man sprawled on the ground in the vegetable garden. The sheriff didn't need to announce that they were most definitely on the right track.

Quickly dismounting, Jenkins ordered Deputy Bob, Joe and Ted around to the back of the farmhouse and barn. Ryan, Buck and Harry, rifles cocked, were to cover them. Gerald's excitement rose when Jenkins chose him along with his father to join the front approach and briefly subdued his increasing horror at the sight of the possible corpse. Gerald crept through the thorny under-brush while on the lookout for any motion; the silent, lonely scene was filled with tension. He felt his heart thump and prepared to shoot instantly if nec-essary. But the landscape remained still — except for crows cawing rapa-ciously above the downed man.

Gerald battled against his compulsion to rush ahead to provide first aid for the downed man. It was eerie and too quiet – where was the Davidson's collie? Then Gerald saw the guard dog, apparently dead, slumped by the gate. Blanching with nausea that threatened to crescendo into vomit, he swallowed hard, acidic gulps to forestall such an embarrassment.

The older pair continued their cautious approach. Ever present Jodi flew ahead and discovered no lurking criminal on the premises. While that fact re-laxed her, she knew it was unwise to notify Gerald. She suspected he'd move too quickly and thereby lose credibility with the sheriff.

Ted recounted to Gerald days later, how, in his anxiety, he aimed toward a noise on the house's far side. "Thank goodness Deputy Bob warned me. It was you! Remember when you stumbled on those branches out front?" As the boys processed their experience, they became aware that the sheriff had as-signed a seasoned man to each party in order to prevent mishaps – and harm — caused by overly stimulated neophytes.

When the frontal party advanced to the edge of the clearing next to the whitewashed log cabin, Sheriff Jenkins waved his men back from lines of fire through door or windows. His emphatic gestures effectively communicated sheltered positions if a gun fight ensued. Their leader's ability to express instructions without uttering a single word awed Gerald.

Once the lawman had situated each individual, he and his deputy crept forward to peer through the kitchen window. Gerald was perfectly placed both to watch the events on the porch and to peek through the front room's window; he avidly absorbed each drop of action like a sponge, *What a location for a reporter!* Gerald observed Sheriff Jenkins ascertain that no one was in the cabin's main room, crouch beside the door and yank it wide.

Then, with the interior exposed, the man dropped flat to the porch with rifle cocked and body inching half-extended into the room. His gaze swept left to right, then left again before he sprang to his feet; no evidence of the outlaws were visible from his vantage point. The sheriff sprinted across the floor's wooden planks toward a door on the opposite wall; Deputy Bob was on his heels. Gerald, unconsciously holding his breath, drank in the scene.

Light from the windows illuminated the entire room. Tom's lessons on description were so engrained that, even in his agitated state, Gerald noted the hooked rugs on the floor; he prayed neither man would stumble. A wooden table, covered by a green and yellow oilcloth, stood on the opposite side of the room: Sheriff Jenkins ducked for a quick glance underneath as he passed. Meanwhile his deputy zigzagged to peek over the back of the blue upholstered couch; the sheriff checked behind the maple rocker. It was like a Zane Gray novel come to life. The swift crime fighters proceeded in precision as they inspected for signs of intruders. The sheriff pulled on the inner door as carefully as he had at the cabin's entrance. Again dropping to the floor, he scanned the interior room: it proved empty. Jenkins called out, "All's clear." Gerald drew in a breath and ran toward the man lying prone in the yard.

The ghastly sights would be forever etched in the new investigative reporter's memory. Jim, obviously seriously injured, lay in a pool of blood. Waves of queasiness overcame Gerald who tried to forestall his physical reaction. He wiped his face and breathed deeply as Jodi had taught him to do during anxiety-provoking events.

Dan, his fingers on Jim's neck, detected a heartbeat, albeit faint; the sheriff exited the house and joined the others beside the fallen body. After tearing open the downed man's shirt, he pointed to the chest wound encrusted with dried blood. Gerald, initially baffled that the wound wasn't hemorrhaging, consulted Doctor MacNamara for background material to supplement a follow-up piece. The doctor explained that the chest had sealed itself and thus stanched further blood. "That rare event saved his life," was how Gerald quoted the medical authority.

"Gerald, fetch a blanket," Dan's voice sliced through his son's mental fogginess; the youth jogged toward the cabin. At the threshold, however, a new appalling scene made his mission completely slip his mind. Deputy Bob and

Joe squatted next to Ellen, who lay on the floor, her dress and apron splattered with porridge. Apparently she was carrying the pot of food at the moment the heavy rock at her side struck her head. Gerald noticed blood and clumps of hair were attached to the stone; then he connected the weapon to the grotesque dent in Ellen's skull. Gerald forced down the rising bile. *At least she's breathing*, that slight relief helped as he leaned over the woman. A new noise distracted him: an infant's whimper from the nearby crib.

The sheriff, who had followed Gerald inside, barked, "Harry!" The veteran was scowling at the young man who stood next to Gerald. The youth was as pallid as alabaster. Harry's unfocused eyes sought the direction of the sound of his name. Gerald reached to grab him but the sheriff was quicker and grasped Harry's upper arm. A firm pinch brought color back to the lad's face. "You fetch Doc," Jenkins ordered sternly. Harry's resolve resurfaced once he was assigned a specific task. "Yessir," he said as he sprinted out to his horse. Gerald imagined Harry's relief to leave behind the horror while at the same time engaged in a vital errand.

Their sheriff then concentrated on Buck who hovered over Junior's crib. The oldest of twelve, Buck had tended babies as long as he could remember. Gerald watched him clean and diaper the infant. *How do we feed the little tyke?* Gerald speculated as he watched Buck cuddle the baby he'd swaddled in a blue blanket. "Buck," the sheriff commanded, "You take him down to Aunt Jean on that farm we passed two miles back." He pointed in the direction they'd ridden. "She'll know who's nursing: believe we have two or three women available in town. She may require transportation, a messenger, or supplies; you're relieved of duty here."

Gerald questioned if his former classmate would resent that his choice to comfort Junior pulled him off the chase. No, the sheriff had selected well. Buck's demeanor exhibited no trace of disappointment, only solicitude for the tiny boy, as he packed the requisite blankets, diapers, and clothing into the bag by the crib. Gerald watched his father step into the picture. Dan held the infant while Buck tossed the bag on the horse's back and leapt up.

Suddenly the internal haziness cleared, Gerald grabbed a quilt off the couch to accomplish the chore from which he'd been distracted. He observed that once Buck and the bag were securely on the horse, his dad tenderly lifted up the baby. Despite the distance, Gerald swore he saw his father swipe his face as if brushing away tears.

Joe and Ryan covered Ellen with a blanket. Joe sponged her brow gently while tears flowed down his cheeks. Finally Gerald did gather his wits and hurried outside to Jim. Ted joined him and Gerald noted he too was pale and shaken. The two, visibly trembling, took opposite corners of one edge of the blanket and together drew it over the man.

A moment before Ted slipped a pillow under Jim's head, Joe yelled, "No! Ted! Keep his head low. He's lost a lot of blood. Needs an easy flow to the brain." Gerald, chagrined at the near mistake, recognized that Joe had gained much more skill in medical techniques than high school first aid. Joe, who intended to enter medical school in the fall, had assisted Doc for the last several summers and eagerly learned every remedy. The sheriff instructed, "Joe, stay with Joe and Ellen. You're the best trained to provide care while awaiting Doc." Joe proudly stood taller when singled out for such responsibility.

Once the crime scene was organized, Jenkins strode briskly toward the door. "Ted, Gerald, ride with us," he gestured toward the older men. Gerald dashed off a quick sentence about the competent sheriff's familiarity with his men's talents. Of the community's young men, they had been the most thoroughly trained by their fathers in the requisite skills for a manhunt. The pair might prove an asset on this initial hunt and would constitute the core of future posses. The sheriff probably thought to use this event to begin deputy training.

Although Ryan's tracking and woodsman skills had impressed Gerald during hiking expeditions with Ted's family, he hadn't fully appreciated the knack required to trace such a poorly marked trail. As they left civilization and rode deeper into unmarked woods, the clues Ryan used to guide their progress proved remarkable. Dismounting at the first fork, Ted's father hiked a hundred yards down each branch. A recently snapped twig with no animal tracks nearby influenced his choice of direction; a bit farther along he validated his intuition upon spotting equally subtle evidence: a partial footprint where a heel had slipped off a rock into a patch of loose dirt. Another ten yards along, he pointed to a couple hairs snagged on a tree branch. Ryan was the natural leader for this phase as they pursued the route of the criminals. Because the trail branched away from the homes of rural folk, posse members prayed no more horrors lay ahead.

Jodi's warning, "Gerald, a gun to the right!" caused him to swivel; he spied a glint. She'd sensed an ominous force on that far ridge. Because of Jodi's warning, not because he recognized the sudden sparkle for the reflection of sun-on-metal, he yelled, "Gun on ridge!" and jumped his horse back into the woods along side the exposed path.

All were startled by Gerald's sudden movement into the trees and galloped into that thicket. Their haste was aided not a little by Jodi and Miguel psychically nudging each horse to veer off the trail. And, just in time! A bullet whizzed near them, creasing Ted's cheek. Gerald trotted his horse toward his chum but Ted pushed his kerchief against the wound to stanch the blood and motioned his buddy off. Gerald tugged on the reins and swung toward Jenkins. "Sheriff," he gasped, "Ted and I can circle around there." He pointed toward the back of the ridge. "If we follow the tree line, we'll be safe." He paused, glanced around, and added, "If you provide cover, they won't notice us, being as they're so far away."

"Good reasoning, son. But," the man scratched his neck, "think I'll add Ryan to your party. His tracking skills will locate the most secure trail."

When he later replayed that day, Gerald surmised that the sheriff did not mean to squash youthful enthusiasm but intended a seasoned adult supervise each group. He meant to bring his men home alive. And, Gerald acknowledged how likely he and Ted would have been to attempt heroics if left on their own, especially after the appalling sight left behind a couple hours earlier.

Thus Gerald, Ted and Ted's father, Ryan, silently trekked through the woods. Like a strategy out of a book, the rest kept the outlaw's attention on the woods in front with scattered shots and brief appearances. They wanted the bandits to deem them hapless amateurs. Ryan continued to astound the boys; he unearthed a credible path that wound to the hilltop and culminated to the rear of their would-be murderers.

Once on the ridge, Gerald absorbed the images of those evil killers in one glance – another impression that would remain with him for years. He didn't need to take notes. Crouched at the cliff's edge, the villains peered out from behind the trees and occasionally fired down toward the trail. Both wore filthy garments, with holes torn by the rough terrain they'd covered on foot. Long greasy hair dangled from under the wide brimmed hats that shielded them from the sun's glare.

Gerald inadvertently stepped on a dry twig; it cracked; the men turned their heads while their rifles remained aimed in the opposite direction. The two appeared almost alien with their cold eyes — beady black on one and steely gray on the other. The latter Gerald recognized as Jake from the poster although his hair and beard had grown scraggly over the last several days. Bill's curving mustache enhanced his sinister mien.

A third image never to be erased from Gerald's memories: the startled expressions of those brutal men when Ryan fired over their heads and coldly announced, "Got company, gentlemen! I suggest you drop your weapons." To complete the effect, Ryan shot a hole neatly through Jake's sombrero. Ted thought the world of his father that day.

That evening, an exhausted yet exhilarated, Gerald proudly presented his preliminary report to his editor. Instead of the anticipated accolade, Tom grunted, "So, how soon's that first feature article gonna be in?"

Chapter 2

Both angel and youth respected Tom. Gerald had apprenticed with him ever since his memorial paper for Ronnie. The newsman's gruff façade couldn't conceal the caring, sensitive person underneath. Soon after he offered Gerald the cub reporter position, it became apparent that Tom didn't intend to passively observe Gerald's development. Instead, the mentor recommended themes for papers, assigned books he believed a journalist must read and proofread his essays. And, Tom never let Gerald slip by with a sloppy or incomplete production but instead insisted on the perfection of each line — even sentences for history drills. By emphasizing word choice and sentence structure, he taught the importance of readability and colorful language.

Although of slight build and five feet four inches in his boots, Tom's self-confidence more than compensated. When deep in thought, his fingers habitually combed back the few strands of black hair that covered his balding scalp. Clean-shaven, with wire-rimmed glasses, his dark eyes seemed to penetrate through to the innermost secrets of any interviewee. Even though residents honored the man's discretion in revealing their personal foibles, they did wish he'd print more tidbits about their neighbors.

Town folklore had it that their editor slept in his clothes to avoid losing one minute after receiving a hot news tip. He never was seen without his calf-high, pull-on cowboy boots. Gerald, in imitation, wore similar boots his mother purchased from the Sears Catalogue for his sixteenth birthday. The other component of Tom's uniform was his headgear. When he left the newsroom, he snatched his blue visor off its hook and replaced it with the clear one worn inside. These indicated either 'Open for Business' or 'Out to Wherever'.

Part of his job, he reckoned, was teaching the next generation of journalists: he treasured the tutelage his father gave him more than 40 years back. Big city publishers were so impressed with his former apprentices that they surreptitiously contrived to lure his students. At least one metropolitan paper had tried to convince Tom to relocate and train its motley city room. But neither money nor prestige could entice Tom from his hometown and <u>The Eagle</u>.

From the outset, Tom assessed Gerald's strengths and weaknesses and soon identified Gerald's impulsiveness, distractibility and tendency to flit from one subject to another. Still, he valued the boy's conscientiousness and creativity. In order to channel that energy, maximize his talents and curtail his impulsivity, the editor assigned projects designed to foster scrupulous research. He appreciated that Gerald, left to his own devices, would be so distracted by tantalizing, sundry news threads that crossed his desk that he would bounce helter skelter from idea to idea and never achieve his potential for in-depth journalism.

Although Gerald had tried desperately to prove himself to Tom, he lived through a tense couple of days in the early spring of his senior year. One Wednesday evening when he stopped in the newsroom to check for assignments, he found a message in his cubbyhole: "Meet me, 2 pm Saturday, my office. Walthers."

Afraid that his boss might be irritated with him, Gerald ruminated for any clue as to what was amiss. Nothing came to mind. Gerald chose his red-and-green plaid shirt for the meeting even though he laughed at himself as he buttoned it. *Am I trying to bring a little of Ted with me? Keep me steady and focused?* He grinned at his reflection in the mirror. *What you think, shirt? Can you do that for me? Wish I dared bring Ted in person.*

It was time to go. He pedaled over to The Eagle's headquarters perspiring profusely in spite of the cool spring breeze. Normally a little over confident, on that particular day, he shuffled unobtrusively into the editor's sanctum. Clutching the notebook and pencil that Tom demanded he always carry, Gerald slid onto the wooden chair in front of the massive oak desk.

Jodi, also jittery, prayed that her charge wouldn't be the recipient of some pronouncement like, "I've changed my mind about hiring you." Yet Gerald had been conscientious and industrious: she couldn't conceive of that happening. To convey her confidence in him, she depicted herself sitting on the desk's edge since, if she were extremely worried, he knew she'd be flitting around the room.

Tom's entire desk, covered with a huge mound of newsprint, looked like a disaster area; but, in reality, the apparent mess was composed of many discreet overlapping piles from which Tom could extract a scrap relevant to any project. When Gerald entered, he observed that the editor was busily underlining, crossing out and circling a page. As soon as Gerald plunked himself down into the seat, Tom raised his visor and peered at Gerald through his glasses.

"We're a small community, Ger," Tom commenced without a greeting. "But we're a single part of an almost-limitless network. Our little village," he pointed to the wall map of the United States, "plus this group," he indicated hamlets familiar to Gerald, "feed into this larger town. The towns that surround a city send produce, ideas, people into its midst and receive back commodities necessary to each of them. And the cities interact in the same way with the metropolises." He noted the red circles around Chicago, New York, Atlanta, San Francisco.

In order to return his focus to Gerald, Tom placed his own hands flat on the surface and leaned forward to engage his full attention with that penetrating gaze. Gerald, biting his lower lip, fidgeted self-consciously. "Son, to be a reporter, you must appreciate how individuals and communities affect one another." He jabbed his index finger at Gerald who jumped, "So your first post-graduation assignment will be a series of feature articles detailing how our local tradesmen contribute to the larger community and are, in turn, affected by the outside world."

The man's posture and voice softened, "I'm impressed by you, son; one of my jobs is to furnish experiences you'll need for success in our profession. Heck, if the pieces are good enough, they might be picked up by one of the wire services. That means they could be printed almost anywhere. Might even carry your byline." Gerald's mentor surmised that the youth could accomplish much in an American small town whereas the big-city distractions would overwhelm him. Thus, The Eagle's publisher didn't intend to groom Gerald for one of the major publications where he'd sent others. Since his protégés were so prized, he reckoned that a one-sentence letter would place his student's work into syndication when Tom judged the work sufficiently refined.

When Jodi caught the gist of the proposal, she became enthusiastic about this project. Gerald, dazed, belatedly opened his notebook to take notes. He grew steadily more intrigued as the implication of this conference sank in. By the meeting's end, his eyes danced and his questions poured forth. On that momentous Saturday, Tom outlined for Gerald his first major post-graduate series. Gerald chose their grocer, John Green, for his first interviews: after all, food generates universal interest – everyone eats.

But, even with the research and interviews for his first article, after the excitement of participating in the posse, Gerald found that most days as a reporter were humdrum compared to his first. He gathered news of the comings and goings of the community members, of the decisions of the various committees in the small town assembly and of the local births, weddings and deaths. He wrote the news into reports and met the deadlines Tom dictated. But then his mother received a letter from her brother.

Gerald's life changed radically when she showed him the clipping his uncle had enclosed in the letter. The young reporter simply gaped at the three-column-inch version of his eyewitness account which had appeared in his uncle's Oregon newspaper – under Gerald's byline.

The thrill of achievement infused Gerald as he studied his very own words that were published in a newspaper across the continent. He had contributed to the national press. Intrigued, he traced his story on the map which Tom had used for his didactic: it had been telegraphed from The Eagle to Central City's news desk; from there, the wire services picked it up and broadcast it along their distribution lines; finally it wound up in the paper his uncle bought.

A few days after Gerald received the clipping, news broke that an airplane was lost in the Alps. Gerald researched the origins and pathways of the daily accounts of the hunt through treacherous, snowy terrain. Reports wired from Switzerland to the New York bureaus then reached the feeder service for <u>The Eagle</u>. Tom included this riveting, harrowing story on the front page of the paper. Gerald interviewed his fellow townsmen about the effect of the tragedy on their thoughts and moods and found that each person he encountered during his meanderings through town was eagerly tracking the rescue efforts. That meant they were avid readers of Tom's newly added two-page daily sheet.

Responses varied significantly. Ben Jacobs, the local baker, told him, "Whoever's crazy enough to ride in one of those newfangled flying machines is suicidal at heart." Dan Evans, recently returned from the Great War, chatted enthusiastically about watching the aeroplanes overhead and dreaming of their future possibilities. The veteran hoped to learn to fly so he could join one of the traveling groups that performed stunts for audiences and sold rides. Dave White, the postmaster, predicted that the whole country would send letters by air; but his sister-in-law, Mildred White, who overheard the discussion as she waited to mail a box to her brother in Kansas, interrupted to insist she'd never trust her packages to leave the safety of the ground. Gerald wove the quotes from his hometown community into a feature that numerous publications copied — again with his byline.

Locating the downed plane and the three survivors became the lone topic of conversation at the breakfast tables when the wire service information appeared in the morning <u>The Eagle</u>. Gerald was proud to be part of the fraternity responsible for the flow of news around the nation and globe. An inner drive surged through him and energized the development of the feature series Tom had assigned. His comprehension of his singular contribution in human interdependence proved a profound enlightener; perhaps he could extend his sense of participation in the universal scheme to his fellow townsmen when he traced their interconnections across the nation and maybe world. Jodi and he discussed all the inferences and Tom's early lesson with all those circles and dots on the map really sunk in.

Ted meanwhile passed his summer in the fields with his father. Side-by-side they planted, tended, harvested, and talked. At summer's end Ted intended to matriculate at the state university: the first step on his quest. Ryan tried to persuade his son, subtly and, not-so-subtly, to relinquish his plans to pursue religious studies. The man had spent all his days on the farm, taught the trade to his four sons, and believed nothing beneficial could come out of formal education. High school was "more learning than he'd got" and should be "good 'nuff" for his boys. Honest enterprise mattered and came from using one's hands plus one's wits to figure out the mechanics of equipment. Ted's older brothers were happily married, already producing grandchildren, and tending farms of their own.

However, Ryan recognized Ted's talents in construction and would have been elated if his son entered the building industry. Since middle school days, he'd involved Ted in projects ranging from assembling cupboards to raising the new barn. He had the boy draw up the designs for such enterprises: the productions proved praiseworthy and the results made his father proud.

Ryan, though taciturn, mustered whatever words he could find to argue his willful boy out of his intention to pursue such strange goals. "Luke Barlow, you know, he built the Jason home; he's advertising for an apprentice. You'd do good with him," Ryan suggested one day as he and Ted devoured sandwiches and tea, sitting in the shade of a willow while resting from their labors in the fields. "You got the talent boy. Look how good you plotted that new barn. Besides building it sturdy, you kept the cost down. And that was without an apprenticeship. Gotta think about it: think hard, son."

"Dad, I could build and Luke would teach me well. But that's not how I'm driven to use my life." Ted's voice resounded low, measured, and confident.

Frustrated, his father threatened to disown Ted if he shamed his mother — to no avail. By the end of the summer, thoroughly exasperated, he desisted and simply shook his head. His boy had always had such a stubborn streak. With grim foreboding, he obsessed over where he'd gone wrong with his recalcitrant son. Ted behaved respectfully but remained obstinate.

The final day before Ted's departure – an early September Saturday — the four up-till-then inseparable friends gathered for one last confab. As they sat around their bonfire, crickets chirped and crows cawed. The aroma of burning embers mingled with the fragrances of the newly mown hay. The sky darkened as late afternoon edged into evening; stars twinkled into view offering the new moon companionship on that clear night. An owl hooted. Hot dogs were eaten; marshmallows roasted. A pack of distant wolves howled across the fields while hunting.

The light cast by the flames flickered on the figures of the four young adults: hard not to believe in the supernatural on such a still night! Ted's expectant visage displayed a little trepidation as well as much determination; Gerald's remained fixed and hardened as he anticipated the grayness of his milieu without Ted. By throwing himself into his series, he had forestalled thinking about the imminent departure. The time had come when he could no longer avoid the inevitable.

Gerald acknowledged two personal problems with Ted's quest: the loss of his lifelong pal and the acceptance of his own decision. By all rights, he, the journalist, should be participating in this adventure that Ted undertook. He hadn't the foggiest notion why he'd elected to stay behind. It wasn't like him. Yet he could not convince himself to join his buddy.

No one spoke. Repeatedly over the past years the group of four, together and individually, had discussed Ted's theories and his decision to acquire a ministerial degree as his first action in his exploration of the unseen and unknown on the planet.

"Hey, I demand the first news scoops on your findings." No longer able to mull over his gloomy thoughts, Gerald sprang to his feet and leapt toward the heavens. At the apex of his jump, he produced a make-believe pencil from behind his ear and, when his feet touched ground, he dramatized scribbling into a pretend notebook while glancing at Ted, the interviewee.

"Of course. You're the only person who'd publish my crazy ideas," laughed Ted who rose to his feet and performed a stately bow during which he mimed sweeping off an imaginary top hat.

Robin, who had loved Ted from that initial day in first grade, dreaded her impending loneliness. She had known deep inside, since Ronnie's death, that her sweetheart didn't aim to settle down, marry, and pursue the career toward which his talents directed him. How she'd hoped and prayed he'd change his mind. Her contagious laughter concealed the dreaded hollowness she anticipated occurring the minute his absence from her daily affairs became real.

That night they could no longer postpone the unwelcome farewell. After extinguishing the bonfire, Cindy and Gerald strolled away to allow Robin and Ted a private good-bye. As the two walked hand-in-hand toward Robin's house, she promised, "Ted, I'll...I'll... wait ... for you."

"No, Robin. You mustn't. I envision myself wandering the planet, scrutinizing different theories and beliefs. I'll never earn enough to support a family nor will I remain in one spot for long." He spoke tenderly and turned to gaze into her eyes. The moon looked down from above and the stars winked in and out. The scent of chrysanthemums filled the air. A tomcat on the prowl hissed as it happened upon his next door rival and the howls of their fight shattered the silence of the night air. An owl hooted as if reproving the felines for contaminating the otherwise peaceful ambience. And Ted swallowed hard, "I love you, Robin. It's not you. It's this compulsion inside. I must undertake this endeavor; I must hunt answers for humanity's miseries."

"Maybe what you seek exists in our town. Maybe your truths involve the growth and development of each citizen of Earth, including citizens of our community here." Robin's irritation at the futility of her attempts to reason with him increased with each try.

"Likely they do and probably I'm foolish." Ted shrugged. "But there's more than we humans and our Newtonian physics….You know that I believe there are universal laws that scientists can't even imagine yet." He stopped and again made eye contact. "Robin, please forgive me. In many ways, I wish I could stay and marry you. But I am driven to try to uncover what I can." He lay a hand on her shoulder; she looked at him through tear-filled eyes. "Maybe, if I'm lucky, I'll happen onto one or two cures – and perhaps those will help people someday. I beg of you to understand, please. It's a quest some are obliged to undertake. And, I sense that I am one of the seekers."

He mentally willed her to respond positively, to encourage him. He so much hated to hurt her. His tone pleaded. He'd spent years in contemplation, did his senior research paper on the broad area of metaphysics, was counseled by their pastor, exhausted the resources of their region's libraries. This passion consumed him. "Others have pursued these truths and many more will. But I need to contribute my efforts."

"You will…will write, to me, us, won't you? Let us keep up with what you discover?" Robin's voice caught; tears spilled forth. She squeezed his hand with her entire strength. She, at that moment, couldn't even begin to imagine how she could function apart from him.

"Definitely and write me even after you're married and surrounded by children. We will be old buddies; warm friends; sister and brother." He knew he'd also miss her intensely. But no one, especially he, could control this over-whelming need which was forcing him to abandon his beloved.

At the end of her lane, under the stars, the couple stood side by side and faced the hill toward the distant plains on the horizon. Ted took Robin in his arms, brushed away her tears with his kerchief, and placed a kiss on her lips – a kiss that translated as farewell. When the two arrived at her porch, her younger siblings threw open the door and lined up for hugs from their sister's boyfriend whom they so admired. Her parents, who likewise adored the seri-ous, conscientious, if stubborn Ted, said their goodbyes with the anguish typ-ical of adults predicting a looming youthful error.

"Still think you're taking the wrong road, son," Robin's father added one last time. It was tough enough to witness his daughter this desolate, the man was fond of Ted — plus, he could attest to the youth's architectural gifts ever since Ted designed and constructed the addition to their old barn. "Listen, I know this isn't the first time I've said it and Lord knows a lot of people agree with me, but America's mushrooming — incredible buildings are springing up all over, not only in the metropolises. Seems to a lot of people who know you that God put you on this planet to erect them."

"Yes sir, thank you sir. You compliment me, sir — but I'm drawn toward the university and away from the trades." Robin was gratified by her father's intervention but knew it would be of no avail. Ted's goal had not wavered since her little brother's death: a death that carried two losses into her life. Silent tears coursed down her cheeks. Her mother thrust a box toward Ted. "Some-thing for your journey. Now don't forget to eat on your quest," she admon-ished.

"Thanks, m-ma'am." He spoke through the frog in his throat. With one final wave to the family, Ted fled down the path. Robin stood at the threshold watching. Her mother came to her side and grabbed her hand, holding tight. When they could no longer distinguish him in the dim light, she pulled Robin to her and hugged her tight. "Thanks, Mom. I'll, I'll be okay. It'll just take a while." Then the young woman stumbled up the stairs. Once in the bedroom, she slumped into the rocker and let it gently move of its own accord. She no longer attempted to stifle the sobs. She felt as if her insides had been ripped out.

Cindy appeared in their room and stooped down to hug her fiercely. She'd left Gerald earlier than usual; her twin needed her. "Cindy, we're together — I've got you. He's totally alone." Robin, at that moment, committed herself. She gulped and clasped her sister tightly, "Cindy, I'm going to wait for Ted. He loves me – he said so – and I'm sure he'll let me join him as soon as there's a way."

The summer following the posse ride had been a quiet period for Jodi despite the emotional pain of anticipating and then experiencing Miguel's loss from her life. There had been no close calls. She'd been relaxing in the calm when, a few days after Ted's send-off, Gerald shattered her serenity. Bent over his desk, he had appeared to be industriously organizing material for his feature on their baker, Ben Jacobs. Ben's original recipe for apple-orange-raisin pie took first place in a national contest and was published in a major cookbook. Gerald planned that the lead paragraph of his article would acclaim Jacob's contribution to American cuisine. For several days Gerald had collected information concerning the baking industry. Mint he learned was grown locally while most cinnamon and more exotic spices came from the Orient. Salt was mined just north of them beneath the city of Detroit. He thought about traveling to see the salt mine but decided that detail wasn't necessary for this article. But, maybe, some day.

Even with all pieces gathered and only a final assembly needed, Gerald's mind wouldn't focus on baking. Instead he announced, "Jodi, I'm marrying Cindy."

"That's news?"

"Just wondering what you think about it. In the past you and I confronted life's challenges. In the future Cindy and I'll do that. It's an enormous – and, uh, really confusing change, right?" Gerald, jumped to his feet, flung his pencil on the desk, strode to the window, and opened the shutters. "Will you feel left out? I mean, uh, it's been you and I since I turned four. What'll you do? And what about Cindy's angel? How do guardians work together when a couple marries? I mean, uh, you're not going to watch over us every night, are you?"

"Yes, I'm a slight bit nervous – but we guardians have guarded through all sorts of situations, most especially marriage."

Gerald paced, then flopped back at his desk, and spun his pencil on the surface. This habitual game required his stacking various papers to make room. He'd note whether the pencil, on hitting various piles, stopped dead or rotated in another direction. Even in deepest thought, he couldn't keep from fidgeting.

"You're supposed to marry Cindy – my role is to guard you," she interjected into his restless activity. Jodi imaged herself perched on his desk's edge; she drew up her legs and rested her chin on her knees. Perhaps if she showed herself in a relaxed pose, his agitation would abate.

"Aw, c'mon, Jodi! There's plenty more to our liaison than guarding and being guarded." Snatching the pencil, he doodled couples — human, angelic, and angel-human combinations. The lines quivered as he scrambled to put into clear words a multitude of emotions about his omni-present companion, mentor and dearest friend.

"Yes. I am a little nervous." She portrayed herself leaning closer to him. "It's true that you won't be as available for me – but, Gerald, you've known Cindy since you were six and our partnership hasn't interfered with your and Cindy's friendship and love. So, how will our relationship change?"

"Guess it won't. But – but, what will I tell Cindy about you?" Gerald finally got out the question that had ignited his emotional dilemma.

"Why tell her?" Jodi creased her forehead with worry lines and felt inwardly apprehensive. Would this be yet another complication caused by her unconventional approach to guardianship. The upheaval created by her introduction to Ted left her chastened for years: that meeting had altered the course of his destiny. Jeff's fury and the session before the Angelic Council had instilled caution!

"I can't keep secrets from my wife, and, if I could, I wouldn't." Gerald stretched toward her, spread out his hands, and pleaded. "You're such a huge part of my life. We must divulge your existence." He gripped his pencil; his eyes didn't blink, "Uh, you will, uh, let her meet you? Er, like you did for Ted?"

"I don't think so, Ger." Jodi's psychic patterns, which after years of constant communication allowed him to sense the angel's emotional state, carried the confusion the angel felt.

"Why not?" Gerald crumpled a piece of paper and threw his pencil down. "Ted and I grew closer and understood and loved each other much more completely than we ever would have if I had kept you secret." Gerald's knack for persuasion had matured. Jodi acknowledged that his rapport with Ted was probably deeper and more honest as a result of the boys sharing their angelic companionship with each other.

Although Jodi was well aware that of the prerequisites for intimacy, truth formed the foundation and must be the a component of Gerald's marriage bond, she persisted in following the angelic rules and concepts imprinted indelibly in her energy patterns over years of Jeff's supervisory sessions. "For one, Cindy's a grown woman while Ted was a little boy when he met Miguel; she isn't accustomed to conversing with angels. I doubt she could envision me."

"Mother did." Gerald's confidence that Cindy would accept Jodi was based on his mother's story about her initial dream that Jodi implanted. His guardian's doubts seemed foolish.

"Your mother was open to receive my prompts; she welcomed anything that could assist her in managing you." Jodi grinned as she reflected on the early days of the mother's and angel's joint battle to keep the reckless boy among the living. Her hand rose to conceal the twitch of a smile. Gerald, seeing her amusement, emitted a half- chuckle.

"I was a real hellion, huh?" A mischievous mood overpowered him as he replayed particular adventures – the time he dared to scamper up to the tippytop limb of the maple in their backyard; he would have been around four. He recalled his fear and that his father had to retrieve him with a ladder because he couldn't figure out how to clamber back down.

"Was a hellion?" Jodi's right shoulder lifted in a teasing shrug.

Nevertheless Gerald refused to be distracted for long and doggedly resumed, "What if you introduce yourself in Cindy's dreams?" The young man had pondered this quandary for hours and intended to gain Jodi's cooperation.

Pointing toward his image of her, he employed the debating techniques he'd absorbed while on the high school team.

"I can't, Gerald. No way can I break the rules again." Face puckered and fingers alternately yanking at her hair strand or twisting her skirt seams, she pleaded for his understanding, "Please, Ger, we all must obey our superiors, even angels."

Gerald trembled as he felt something ominous, even threatening, envelop him. "What rules?" The two words were staccato: anger seeped in around their edges.

"You, know, the laws on how to guard humans." Jodi reached toward him, "C'mon Ger – remember! We've often talked about the negative effects that resulted from you encountering me, not to mention Ted encountering Miguel and me." When Gerald refused to turn toward her, she sprang into the air, flitted to the window and peered out into the night sky for several minutes. Gerald, stationary, gripped his pencil so tightly it snapped in two. Eventually, the angel rotated back toward her human. "My supervisor repeatedly – for decades now — reminds me of how I should never have l-let you…." Gerald had been oblivious to the many nights during which Jeff hammered regulations into her; her supervisor toiled tirelessly to prevent his impulsive guardian angel-in-training from instigating further catastrophes.

"But this is completely different! Passion imbued Gerald's voice. My wife needs to be intimately involved with you. It won't work any other way!" Gerald had carefully planned how Jodi would fit into his marriage; angelic rules should have nothing to do with their marriage.

"No, Gerald, I can't." Jodi's rigid posture expressed her adamancy.

Gerald stewed. What a bind! No way would he establish anything but one-hundred percent honesty with Cindy, the woman with whom he'd share his soul; he would not conceal a thing. If his bride had no inkling about his angel, he'd feel disloyal. He shoved back his chair with a screech, got up from the desk, and slammed down the remnants of his pencil; he stomped to the door and yanked it with such ferocity that it struck the wall with a loud bang and the knob dented the wall. Outside he plodded down the road, kicked stones, grabbed twigs from trees and bushes and snapped them off. A few travelers on the dusty road stared.

In the nearby woods, Gerald seized a rock and hurled it down the trail, followed by a second, then a third; he began to trot. "Leave me, Jodi! If you're not gonna reveal yourself to Cindy, I've gotta banish you from my life. I'm not gonna keep secrets from Cindy. You're the one who insists you messed up by introducing yourself to Ted and me. So you win: you messed up. Guess I'll be learning to get along without you, Guardian Angel."

For several days, Gerald refused to communicate with Jodi. He completed his newsroom duties mechanically, sulking and angry. He avoided Cindy, too. At first she was baffled, then worried about what she might have done, but after reviewing recent events she reasoned that Ted's departure had elicited inexpressible pain. Although Gerald appreciated his sweetheart's attempts to discuss his feelings, he ignored her overtures.

Sue was the first victim of his moodiness to reach the limits of her tolerance. "Ger, what is it?" his mother demanded.

Gerald, who had been sulking at his desk with his head propped in his palms, rose and paced when he heard his mother's question. He pounded his right fist repeatedly into his left palm, nonverbally phrasing an answer. Eventually, explanations burst out. "Jodi refuses to let Cindy know her! And if I marry Cindy, I can't keep secrets — especially one as enormous as Jodi; I don't want to give up Jodi but haven't the foggiest notion what to do!" At the last word, he struck the bookcase.

"What does Jodi say?" his mother's imperturbable demeanor interrupted the tirade.

"'Don't tell her.' He mocked Jodi's cheery, feminine voice. "But, I can't. I can't, Mom. You wouldn't keep a secret that huge from Dad, would you?"

"It's impossible, Ger, to force Jodi to act in ways she doesn't believe she can or should." Sue studied her fingers in thoughtful contemplation, "But you can recount Jodi anecdotes for Cindy, can't you?"

"What? I don't understand, Mom?"

"Just because Jodi won't talk to Cindy doesn't mean you can't tell your sweetheart about her, right?" His mother's measured words contrasted with her worried expression. Sue was tacitly agreeing that the marriage might be shallow if Cindy were left in the dark about Jodi. And, no, she couldn't fathom keeping such a secret from Dan. She thought back to her reluctant decision to share with him that first adventure with Jodi — the afternoon Gerald toddled into the woods. Her husband, initially incredulous, promptly forgot the exchange until he spent his unforgettable day with three-year-old Gerald.

"Mom, I love you! Of course! You're the greatest. Thanks." His spontaneous hug lifted her off her feet; he twirled her, causing her dress to fly out from her ankles.

Gerald's euphoria held steady … for a few minutes. Then an aspect he hadn't considered deflated it. He and Cindy had been chums forever. She'd revealed her innermost thoughts and trusted him, while he had been hiding a sizable portion of his everyday reality from her. He felt like he'd lied to her for years. During the many discussions of possible unseen phenomena — the occult, guardian angels, and the like — the boys had never hinted at their partnerships with the omnipresent Jodi and Miguel.

In fact, although Cindy loved Ted as a dear childhood buddy, he didn't compare favorably to Gerald in her opinion — and, frequently, she shared that feeling with Gerald. Her conservative self could not justify his planned meandering course. She was scheming to find a decent suitor for Robin and couldn't forgive Ted's abandoning her.

Sue returned to her chores downstairs, unaware of Gerald's renewed agitations, *Cindy'll never give credence to my Jodi stories or, if she does, she'll be hurt I didn't disclose them before.* A peculiar timidity swept over him; in the days to come, beleaguered with imagined consequences of ambiguity – or past deceptions – on his engagement, he avoided his fiancée. *Will she ever trust me again if she believes me? If she thinks I'm crazy, what'll happen then?*

Jodi felt miserably to blame. After all, if she hadn't introduced herself to Gerald and if she hadn't assisted Sue and if she hadn't petitioned to transfer to the Guardian Division in the first place.... *But, why shouldn't humans personally communicate with their guardians?* The old questions tumbled through her brain anew.

Jodi and Gerald enjoyed a deeply fulfilling friendship. True, during his childhood, she functioned more as nanny. But as he matured the connection resembled one between equals: an achievement possible precisely because of their intimacy.

Restlessly she zoomed about the office as she examined her options. What would be the consequences of Cindy's entering the angelic-human partnership while simultaneously oblivious to its existence? *Gerald and I will be like the "kitchen cabinet" we studied in his American History course. But will that harm the marriage?*

The more Jodi pondered, the more she respected Gerald's point of view. *Shouldn't I introduce myself to Cindy? But, if I do, after years of Gerald's apparent forthrightness, how can Cindy not feel betrayed?*

And fear agitated her considerations: *If I do that, Jeff will be as furious with me as Gerald currently is. I'll forever lose the chance for Guardian Angel Licensure. They'll never trust me with another human.* She glanced at Gerald's cluttered desktop. *But, that's selfish. The priority must be Gerald's and Cindy's marriage.*

Jodi's enthusiasm bubbled with a momentous inspiration and she leapt into the air. *I'll request a replacement Guardian for Gerald. He won't be intimate with his new angel; no secrets will derail the marriage.* As she examined this scheme, Jodi ascertained it the best one for everyone — except her. She would miss him. Gloom descended. Gloom she'd feel again some sixty years later. But she resolved to delve heavily into Special Forces' assignments for a while. *Boy will I be lonely! After this wonderful experience, can I ever be happy in Special Force? But I have to be. It's the only answer.* Psychic tears washed out her original jubilation at conceiving a plan; desolation again pervaded her being.

When Gerald fell asleep, Jodi sent a telepathic flash to Jeff who arrived shortly. There in the young man's bedroom, Jodi hesitantly elaborated her dilemma and the solution she believed necessary. Jeff's pride in his trainee shone sincere and his empathy with her felt genuine. He agreed that she'd reached the correct decision; he promised to locate another angel to assume her duties. "I'll need a few days to sort through the profiles of available guardians. When a suitable choice appears, I'm obliged to obtain a release from the overseer, then ascertain if the angel is willing to guard a human of Gerald's age and unique angelic awareness."

Angelic bureaucracy was as convoluted as those that contemporary humanity invented. Jeff was one of a plethora of supervisors. In the tier above supervisors were the regional directors; eventually the pyramid narrowed to the Overseer of Guardian Affairs, the ultimate authority over all jurisdictions of Earth for the Guardian Division. The multi-layer structure allowed for an orderly process in angelic governance; however, orderly processes take a few days. And free will and choice were prerequisites: an assignment must be accepted by the recommended angel.

During the delay Jodi shared her strategy with Gerald. At first, the notion of a foolproof solution relieved him. "Jodi, I'll miss you – but, you're right. This is the best way." His tension abated somewhat. A little bit at least. He returned to his work on the bakery article. Yet he wasn't ready to dance a jig: something, somewhere inside him felt pretty dead.

As he tossed and turned that night, his conscious mind began to recognize what his unconscious had already perceived: the utter barrenness of life without Jodi. Her subtle encouragement – naturally, Cindy would be able to provide that, but often a married couple is separated by physical space. Jodi remained ever present, that second pair of eyes and ears in the tight situations or dangers in which he plummeted perhaps more frequently than most people. His heart was shattered. Torn between the two females, he reconsidered: he would keep Jodi, relinquish Cindy.

Satisfied in his resolution, he spoke again to Jodi, "I love Cindy — but I can't function without you. I've chosen you."

Jodi wouldn't hear of it. His choice was unacceptable to her. "Ger, I'm honored. I mean it." *S*he imaged herself robed in blue satin with angelic wings inset with stars; a golden halo and wand visually emphasized the distinction between herself and Cindy, a human mate. However, that still didn't prevent Jodi from hugging Gerald and kissing his cheek. She murmured, "You and Cindy will marry. That's your destiny."

"Jodi, you've reiterated, as has Miguel, that Ted deviated from his fated way of life. So, why do I hafta pursue mine? And, I've got free will. Right! So I hereby choose to retain my affiliation with you." His intention had not been diverted by her visual attempt to distance herself into the angelic realm.

From their countless discussions about free will, Gerald apprehended that Jodi possessed the right to exercise hers, too, but he depended on her love for him to persuade her to stay. Nevertheless, he understood that she, too, could exercise her will over her destiny: she must be permitted to remove herself if that should prove her choice.

"But what about Cindy, Ger? You'd profoundly affect her destiny. Can you do that to her?" Jodi designed her question to initiate a dialectic. With her eighteen years of mentoring him, Jodi could produce the arguments that would influence him to deliberate all facets of an issue. As she spoke, she depicted herself lightly squeezing his shoulder as she habitually did during difficult moments to portray that she cared.

Gerald was stumped. He realized the correctness of Jodi's argument. What an imbroglio! Would all adult decisions end up being this complex?

"Oh, for a confab, Jodi — Ted and Miguel are gone. But there must be a better idea. Some answer that I'm – I mean, we're – not seeing."

"Jeff offered no other options." Jodi dejectedly slumped to the bed as she continued, "I don't want to leave. This is hard for me, too." Her outfit shifted to a basic brownish calico as she resumed peer status, no longer acting the mature authority figure.

Gerald stepped over to the bed, plopped beside his vision of where she sat, and laid his hands on his knees. Long ago he'd learned the futility of putting his arms around his perception of her shoulders. Nothing tangible occupied the space, merely empty air. "Jeff is a bureaucrat. He obeys each rule. C'mon, Jodi. Innovative inspiration is needed." Gerald felt irritated — and scared — and depressed — and worried and – and he couldn't fathom existence without Jodi.

"Soooo — what do you recommend?" Jodi's dejected tone told him that she was drained of proposals.

"Let's ask God. In His infinite Wisdom perhaps He'll devise a creative solution." It had come full circle! Gerald was six when Jodi taught him the variety of assistance Jesus could bestow during those frustrating first days of school. This time Gerald initiated the action grateful again for Jodi who had taught him so well. Together they prayed for guidance.

Afterward, Gerald reasoned, "Jodi, maybe Mom and Dad could advise us. We should request a confab with them."

With that plan settling his mind, Gerald nodded off to be abruptly awakened by Sally teasing him for lazily lying in bed.

"Darn!" He'd overslept and missed the opportunity to request a confab; by then his father would be out in the fields and his mother shopping. Frustrated, he hopped on his bike and raced to the newsroom, trying to trust that the situation would resolve: that God could and would provide an answer.

Focusing on the town council meeting that afternoon proved impossible for him. The reporter saw the logic of both sides. Many citizens dreamed of installing lampposts with the new electric bulbs that lined streets in bigger cities. The cost triggered significant debate. Several people spoke on either side of the issue. Gerald's quotes necessitated accuracy; but his incessant fretting derailed his finished product, which he dashed off sloppily.

"Gerald, this is not your best piece," criticized Tom.

"Yessir, I couldn't keep my attention on task. Sorry, Sir." He watched as the editor transposed quotes to their correct sources and modified several sentences. Although grateful that Tom had attended the council meeting and thus could fix his commentary, he berated himself for his loss of concentration.

"Next time better take even more notes," snarled The Eagle publisher who had been careful, unknown to Gerald, to document the proceedings. *When will these young lovers resolve their current spiff so the paper can function normally again?* Tom growled under his breath.

"Yessir," Gerald, vowed to himself that he would never again be distracted. That chronic weakness, inattention, sure kept trying to defeat him. And it worsened when he was under stress.

As he left the news office that night, he spotted Cindy rushing in his direction. "Ger, you'll never guess what I found at the bookstore! See, a book on angels! I bought it for Ted, but scanned it first, and – Hon, each of us has a Guardian Angel. I'm going to pray that mine will communicate with me. You should try, too, Ger, but you already know her don't you." Enthusiasm overflowed from his usually unflappable and circumspect Cindy. She thrust a book at him.

Gerald scanned the title incredulously. "Sweetheart, how d-did you find this? This is incredible!"

"You'll think I'm crazy, Ger," Cindy giggled nervously. "I had this dream last night. And," her voice exuded defiance, "after what happened in the bookstore, I believe it's real." She glanced sheepishly at her fiancé, then squared her shoulders, "I was at a picnic in the dream. Don't laugh, Hon, please. Jesus came up to me with a man in tow, 'Cindy,' her voice gentled into the soft refrains memorized from her celestial encounter, 'meet your Guardian Angel, Sam.'"

"Sam and I strolled out into the woods; he dressed so ordinarily, Ger, no halo or wand or robes. He looked like any other young man. He said that you – you, Ger! — have an angel named Jodi. And, he told me you know Jodi!" Gerald studied her wrinkled brow and perplexed frown; he fleetingly wondered if she were telepathic.

"Do you?" But, without pausing for his reply, her words raced on, "Sam promised me a sign to prove himself trustworthy. He advised me to search in a particular stack in the back of Ott's Bookshop for a book with this title that would explain himself to me."

As the miraculous phrases penetrated, Gerald's affect brightened. His whole body felt lighter. He grabbed her and hugged her regardless of the public display, smack in the middle of Main Street. People turned to stare and several grinned no doubt with wistful notions about young love. His kid brother, Johnny, biking home from a game of basketball with his buddies, smirked to his pal, Paul, who rode beside him, "Wait till I tell Jimmy and Janie."

Gerald's heart pounded; his love radiated. "Oh, Sweetheart! I'm so glad I could dance right here in the middle of the square."

With Cindy's dream story told, he started in on a detailed account of his own; he narrated multiple tales of Jodi, including Miguel and Ted anecdotes. While he talked, the couple strolled into the soda shop. After they ordered sandwiches, he continued to recount adventures. He concluded by divulging Jodi's horrible decision to leave and his fear he couldn't have both his wife and his angel.

The young lovers, adored by many in town, had caused great distress by the apparent tension between them. No special edition newspaper needed to proclaim that Cindy and Gerald had reunited that evening. The grapevine carried the message to the farthest reaches of the county before the couple, arms around waists, exited the soda shop and strolled toward her doorstep. They parted with a long goodnight kiss late that evening.

That night's outcome: their formal engagement. The wedding, unbeknownst to most guests, would include an angelic component.

Chapter 3

Cindy paced the bedroom. Pangs of jealousy gnawed at her. At the mirror, she fussed with her new bobbed hairstyle and her tension eased briefly. But her next thoughts stiffened her: *I'm his sweetheart and yet Jodi has been intimate with him for almost his whole life. I'll never be that close to him — even after we're married.* With her silver hairbrush, Cindy attacked her scalp with brutal strokes, then threw down the brush so harshly it bounced. She stomped to her bed where she yanked sheets and blankets here and there. *After all, Jodi's an angel.* Cindy folded the upper edge of the sheet over the blanket and smoothed out wrinkles. *Their relationship is different. But she seems human, like a sister, or ....* She jerked the quilt with a quick tug that disarrayed her tidying. *Are her feelings for Gerald the same as mine?* Memories of sibling rivalry flooded her consciousness

Twisting from the bed, she glimpsed the flash of a safety pin against the dullness of the braided throw rug and bent to retrieve it. *Never noticed before; it's like a symbol of being in love.* She opened and closed the clasp. *Two pieces that connect together. Two coming together and locked together. So where does an angel fit in?* She detoured to the dresser and placed the pin carefully with the other safety and straight pins in the third drawer down on the left; she strode to the window.

Although she stared toward the branching oak, Cindy didn't notice the baby wrens who vied for their mother's attention. Instead her mind recalled a period of strife with Robin during childhood. *We wanted to wear identical dresses but couldn't agree on the color. As I remember, Robin insisted on hues of pink while I demanded canary yellow with forest green.* Her lips twitched as she relived their long-ago contentious quarrel. Eventually their mother intervened and ordered, as a lesson, colors neither twin liked: chartreuse with a bright orange floral design. Cindy blushed at the revived waves of shame; she recalled her dread of the mocking she anticipated from peers teasing about such awful costumes.

She walked to the desk, settled into the straight-backed chair, reached for her sketchpad and outlined two identical dresses. *Jodi and I are in the same type of argument over wedding colors. It's crazy.* With the yellow crayon, she filled in one sketch; then, as carefully, shaded the other with the blue pastel that Jodi preferred. *Why am I acting like this? I like the blue. I'm being despicably perverse, but why? What's wrong with me?*

Deliberately she added a background for the dresses. *I adore this combination. Why not use both? But, if I submit, does this mean I will forever be forced to compromise with … her?* She picked up the black crayon and formed dark clouds. *It's my wedding. Not Jodi's.* She jagged a lightning bolt between the two figures.

Snatching a second sheet of paper, she began a list, titled, "How did this battle begin?" She scribbled: "1. I desired to include Jodi so I asked her opinion about the wedding colors I chose." Staring at the words in front of her, with the red crayon, she circled each 'I'. A candid young woman, Cindy admitted she'd provoked the controversy. Still entranced by the presence of Guardian Angels, she hadn't foreseen the inevitability of competitive feelings.

But she's partly to blame. Insisting on her way ever since I asked her opinion — well, it's true, she's only promoting her preference – but at every single chance! Cindy fussed with her pencil lead before doodling two figures in different poses. At first, awed by the heavenly being, she'd been inclined to obediently agree. She added motion squiggles between the figures hinting at the current separation from their initial proximity.

This is my wedding! Cindy's jaw clenched as the adrenalin of anger surged through her system. *I'm going to choose my own wedding colors! Jodi's his angel but I'll be his wife.* She scratched out a few marks of her cartoon; as a result, the dark haired woman stood tall and no longer appeared to edge backward. A coldness toward Jodi permeated Cindy. Her caricatures turned their backs on one another.

I'm putting up barriers to keep Jodi out, the bride-to-be mused. *Nevertheless if I shut her out of my life, she's still always with Ger; she can invade his thoughts whenever she chooses.* "Darn him!" That never-before-spoken phrase exploded into the room. *He's the one who permitted Jodi this extra closeness: he let her run rampant through his everyday affairs.* She stabbed at the paper; the pencil lead snapped. "Nuts!" Cindy searched for the little knife the girls reserved for sharpening pencils. *Ah. Here it is.* The irritated slices she shaved off the offending wood, which surrounded and shielded the interior lead, dissipated her edginess although she nearly cut her finger.

Cindy had been employed at Bernard's Ladies Ready-To-Wear since her high school graduation. The newspaper office stood kitty-corner from Bernard's, so Gerald and she routinely stole a few minutes together during their lunch hours. One noon they were discussing their evening's activity: he suggested the current movie at the cinema; she preferred a stroll alongside the river. "So, why not ask Jodi to make the decision for us," burst from her lips; the vehemence of her retort shocked her and her hand sprang to her mouth.

Gerald, baffled, interjected, "What…?"

"Well, you consult Jodi about everything, don't you? She has a special spot inside you. And, she knows exactly what you'd most like. And …." Cindy burst into tears and fled down the street.

Gerald gawked after her. "Women!" He shook his head and sought answers from his angel. *What's wrong with her?* But Jodi, equally puzzled, had no clues.

Along the path of the town square, among the fragrant aromas of innumerable flowers and accompanied by the chirpings from chickadees and wild canaries, Cindy stalked oblivious to the peaceful surroundings. Fury at her fiancé's dragging a long-term intimate liaison into their marriage reigned supreme and rage roiled internally. *I will not be a member of a harem!* She groped into her pocketbook for a hankie. *But, if I am marrying into one, I will be first wife. This is crazy. Jodi isn't even tangible.*

That Sunday's sermon focused on forgiving "seventy times seven:" the words seemed directed personally at Cindy. As she eagerly absorbed each point, she analyzed the recent few weeks of negative obsessions. *Why don't I plunge in with a frontal attack? But how should I broach this — through Gerald or Jodi?* As the sermon ended, she rose with the congregation to sing one of her favorite hymns, "Take my life and let it be, consecrated Lord to thee…" During the chorus, inspiration struck, *A confab, tonight, that's the answer. Phooey on the cinema!* Cindy's spirits lifted once she had a plan. *I bet Jodi's been secretly involved in previous confabs — now, I'll insist she participate openly.*

She adjusted her bonnet then turned to Gerald who sat in the pew next to her, "Gerald, Jodi, I'm calling a confab. Tonight. At my house. Seven o'clock. Mom and Dad'll be at the Johnson's with the younger children and Robin's babysitting at the Kitredge's. Be there."

That afternoon Cindy, feeling uncharacteristically manipulative, baked Gerald's favorite cinnamon teacakes coated with vanilla frosting. With an intention to look romantically alluring that evening, she pulled one outfit then another out of the wardrobe and held it up to her as she gazed in the mirror. Finally she selected her scarlet sundress with embroidered roses outlining the bodice: sleeveless, it showed off her trim arms.

When Gerald arrived, Cindy coquettishly swirled her skirts as she led him into the sitting room. Gerald followed without hesitation, nonplussed by this novel aspect of his conservative fiancée. Obediently, he slumped onto the sofa; she'd set the teacakes on the table and the enticing cinnamon aroma wafted into his nostrils. Cindy settled into her mother's rocker opposite him; she carefully arranged her skirts and crossed her ankles in imitation of the actresses in the student plays when they attempted to create a seductive image.

Blinking her lashes and folding her hands, she perceived she'd attracted Gerald as she intended. *I retained something out of the hours of theatrical coaching I witnessed,* was her tacit commentary on her own behavior as she audibly continued, "Jodi, join us: this confab's about you and me. We're going to reach a reconciliation once and for all. Have a teacake, Gerald."

Although Cindy languidly gestured toward the tray, her chilling implication made Gerald lose what appetite he had. His muscles tensed; all he could think to do was pray. He heard the words, "Jodi, I'm unreasonable but I can't stop myself. I'm terribly jealous. Your rapport with Gerald is such as I can never have. I come in second place. I'm feeling left out. Why should he marry me since he already has you."

The very problem he'd hoped to avoid by introducing them had occurred. What had been his mistake? His sweetheart drew a shaky breath then leaned toward him. He realized she had been acting a role and observed with relief her abandonment of the obviously rehearsed performance. Still her next words hit him hard, "Either, we figure this out or call off the wedding."

Jodi was stunned. Why had she not intuited Cindy's inner turmoil? Jodi sifted through recent interactions and realized that Cindy had unobtrusively distanced herself. Exhilarated by the new experiences of human interaction, Gerald's angel had been oblivious to the widening void. How could she have been so obtuse? Why did she neglect to empathize with Cindy.

"Oh, Cindy," the telepathic response resounded contritely through the young woman's mind. "I didn't dream you'd suffer this way. You probably believe that Gerald and my bonding is more intimate than yours can ever be. But, would you believe? I envy the connection you'll achieve — a physical closeness. Gerald will be your husband."

Jodi imaged herself attired in a plain smock with her blond hair tied in a ponytail. She ensured she sat on a separate chair, not beside Gerald. "Cindy, I'm sorry. I see that I've insinuated myself into the wedding arrangements. This is your wedding. I imagined it to be mine, too, because I can never have one of my own." She smiled at Cindy. "You're right! We have to seek out ways to coordinate. I love you. And I want you to love me."

Gerald felt hopelessly confused. He loved both. He conceptualized the dichotomy easily: Jodi occupied the role of angel and Cindy, fiancée. That the two females would compete seemed unfathomable. Both were essential to his happiness and should relish each other's company. The conflict Cindy described was alien to him.

Gerald had no idea how to proceed with this confab; stunned he slouched and fiddled with his ever-present pencil stub. He discovered he'd unconsciously scrolled question marks on his notepad. What did those "?????" mean? "Cindy, I didn't guess a problem existed. Remember, I figured it'd be necessary to abandon one of you if Jodi and you couldn't become acquainted. It never dawned on me that you wouldn't be friends. You're both so special to me." With that, he wanted to mutter an inaudible, "women!"

Gerald's remarks exacerbated Cindy's confusion. She sprang to her feet and paced; her hem swished against the furniture; the wide skirt swirled with each pivot to the opposite direction. She felt guilty. What caused her negativity toward Jodi? Didn't Jodi or Gerald detect that she couldn't tame these fierce emotions?

Although Gerald envisioned her and Jodi in separate roles in the marriage, Cindy couldn't discern many ways in which her part would differ from the angel's? To be serene, she needed clearly defined responsibilities; Jodi's function must be clear; and an outline of how the inevitable intertwining would occur was essential. Gerald couldn't delineate their individual tasks – that was up to them!

Facing the spot where Jodi pictured herself as sitting, Cindy pleaded, "Don't you recognize the problem, Jodi? After all, both of us are presuming to participate in this union. What will you do and what about me?"

Sam, in his several thousand years of guarding humans had never previously witnessed a situation like Jodi's with Gerald. Dumbfounded by their naturalness with each other, he had closely watched their communications. Gerald would pose a question and listen for Jodi's answer. Over the eons Sam had relied on flashing intuitive messages or attracting rescuers or, in the case of a few ancient mystics, interjecting insights into dreams. Jodi's concrete involvement in Gerald's daily routines to Sam seemed nothing short of astounding.

For some years, he had studied the relationship between Cindy and Gerald as well as that of Jodi and Gerald. Significant differences distinguished the partnerships. Although he felt awkward at phrasing his insights, he conquered his qualms and dove into the fray. "Gerald, how do you interact with Jodi?"

Gerald frowned as he considered the question. "Uh, let's see, I depend on her for warnings." He stared at his pencil, "Er, let's see, uh, she provides new ideas when I don't have a hint." Scratching his chin, "Well, she's a companion when I'm lonely." He chuckled, "and sure is an honest critic of my schemes – uh, I mean, she forces me to reality test, and…, you might say, she keeps me in check."

"And how do you interact with Cindy?" Sam next asked, surprised that talking wasn't so hard.

"Why, Cindy's my fiancée. She's going to be my wife. She'll build a home with me and we'll raise children together. She'll give me proposals for my articles and I'll encourage her endeavors. We'll be a team facing the world together."

"What are the differences between Cindy and Jodi for you?"

"I see it!" Jodi exclaimed. "I make the everyday safer for Gerald. He provides me with a service I can give him but doesn't share my angelic realm." She jumped up and flitted around the room as her words rushed on, "Cindy and Gerald share each other's lives in material activities. They'll build a concrete home and family together."

Cindy twirled her wide chiffon sash and, studying it rather than her surroundings, traced its embroidered roses with her forefinger. Eventually she reacted, "I don't understand. What do you mean?"

"You'll build a home together. I'm limited to the mind; I don't participate in physical reality. Cindy, you share both. You'll bear children together. Raise them together. I offer suggestions that you accept or reject. For example, I won't participate in day-to-day parenting. I can't cuddle the babies, feed them, change their diapers. I actually have no say or control. I'm like an adviser who helps you achieve your goals through insights and ideas but is compelled to accept your free will decisions."

Cindy's stress abated and the excitement that ensued almost over-whelmed the staid, practical bride-to-be. Words tumbled out, faster and faster, as she spoke through what she was assimilating.

"I see what you're saying; I'll be Gerald's physical partner." She resumed her pacing albeit less with anxiety than enthusiasm. Her gestures contributed to her delivery as she took a step closer to Jodi who'd perched beside the fire-place. "You serve as a guide but," she nodded to Gerald and touched her chest, "we finalize the projects." Her hands spread out expansively. "You can guide both of us as a unit as opposed to Gerald alone. You and Sam can act as guardians for us as a pair instead of individually."

Sam experienced a unique joy as he recognized the power inherent in an angelic-human problem-solving session. And he'd played an integral part in what Jodi called a "confab".

From that point on, Cindy included Sam in the manner she'd witnessed Gerald employ the resourceful Jodi. One day while trying to decide the dinner menu she implored his advice; her mother, although genuinely busy, figured her soon-to-be-married daughter should design and prepare an entire meal. Normally Cindy, with her twin, assisted their mother or cooked what she had requested. Today Bertha Eldrick accompanied Grandma Smythe to her doc-tor's appointment — no human remained at home. The usually competent Cindy experienced a profound sense of inadequacy.

She slipped the apron off the pantry hook, fastened it, and flipped through menus in the cookbook. *What to select? Hey, I'm not alone, Sam can assist me! Gerald trusts Jodi; I'll try with Sam.*

"Sam," she spoke aloud "would ham and sweet potatoes, beans and car-rots for vegetables, and apple pie for dessert be acceptable?"

Sam, never much intrigued by human diets, much less food combinations, felt out of his element. Menus varied to a significant extent from culture to culture and age to age. A neutral response — *Sounds fine to me* – didn't ap-pease Cindy.

"Or should I cook Swiss steak and mashed potatoes since we ate sweet potatoes a couple days ago?" Cindy, faced with multiple reasonable choices, was filled with ambivalence.

That should be okay, too.

"Do you think Dad would appreciate biscuits with his potatoes? I could bake biscuits to cover with the gravy."

Sam wanted out. Instead he remarked, *You're obsessing,* and continued in a firm but empathetic tone. *I bet they'll enjoy whatever you cook. Why not pre-pare what sounds good to you?*

That advice proved correct and inspired her trust in his wisdom: they developed a comfortable camaraderie with Sam providing insights. He pre-ferred to speak into her thoughts rather than adopt Jodi's self-imaging method. Jodi had first portrayed herself to Gerald the child. Visual images fostered a sense of reality in the little boy. Later she and Miguel, who operated as a team, perfected conversing with each other's charge visually as well as audibly. Sam would need to practice the skills that had evolved for Jodi and Miguel over the years. In the meantime he cautiously involved himself in daily affairs with slight nudges from Cindy. Over the years she and Sam would chuckle at the amazing truths hidden in such mundane humdrum as dinner menus.

Sam's new status produced many disquieting moments, such as occasions he must trust Jodi to guard both Cindy and Gerald while he sought a human rescuer: a collaboration to which Miguel and Jodi often resorted during childhood crises. Jodi related an example to Sam one evening while Cindy and Gerald discussed their future home. As she remembered, the boyhood chums would have been eight. They were playing sheriff and robber in the old field behind the abandoned Bartlett farm; Gerald, the robber, snuck from bush to hedge, until he stepped on and fell through the rotten well cover. Down he shot, more than ten feet before he hit water. Jodi shouted into his fear, *Tread, Ger, c'mon, start treading.* Hearing her words, he peddled his feet thus bringing his mouth above surface. Since the near-drowning at age six, Dan had drilled his children to gasp for air as they submerged, then not to breathe until they bobbed up; thus Gerald had pulled no water into his lungs.

How long could the boy tread water before exhaustion settled in? And, Teddy couldn't run the couple of miles to reach the closest farm — Gerald wouldn't be able to float that long. Jodi and Miguel, having as much fun as their charges, had let them venture quite a way from nearby farmsteads. On that occasion she and Miguel received supervisory reprimands; the first dressing-down he'd experienced in several centuries. Participation with Jodi included some consequences.

Miguel had to fetch rescuers since Jodi needed to remain to support Gerald emotionally. Miguel instructed Teddy, "Stay at the edge of the well. You can help Jodi. Gerald might stop listening to her. You, Teddy, keep yelling at him to tread water." With such an important assignment, the eight year old stood where ordered so Jodi could guard him too.

Miguel spied Sheriff Jenkins out for a ride with his hounds about two miles away and influenced a family of rabbits to run through the tall grass near the hounds; that action incited the dogs to dash across the fields; the sheriff followed in close pursuit of his recalcitrant terriers. Later the lawman repeatedly reflected on the unusual set of circumstances that led him to a child leaning over a well while sobbing for his buddy to keep treading.

Sam, on the other hand, had never before lost sight of a human charge. Although Jodi told him how she had convinced Miguel of the wisdom of combined efforts during that long-ago cave adventure, Sam wasn't sure he could ever do the same.

One spring afternoon, however, the wisest solution was to split duties. The newly engaged couple were hiking through the hills along the river's course; they merrily plucked bouquets of daisies as well as rummaged for and snacked on wild strawberries. "Hey, Ger, over here!" And, as he glanced in Cindy's direction, she tossed him a ball of blue moss.

Caught by surprise, Gerald reached for the fluffy object. As it hit his hands, he stumbled backwards, "Wha—at!" Never the athlete, in fact a little uncoordinated, the weight of what he presumed moss made him lose his balance. On the gravelly path his boots couldn't dig into a solid footing; he slipped over the edge of a rock and twisted his ankle. Excruciating pain pervaded his consciousness.

Moaning, he dropped the moss-covered stone; he heard a shattering crack; more stabs of hot pain radiated from his big toe; *was that toe fractured?* He collapsed to the ground and clutched his injured foot with both hands: the application of pressure relieved a smidgen of the agony.

Cindy's voice resonated vaguely, far away, as the wilderness grayed around him and throbbing followed those initial stabs. His ankle and toe stuck out at odd angles. Beads of sweat poured off his forehead and nose. Hot tears swam in his vision. Cindy's fingers forced him to loosen his grip on the ankle. Her fingertips gingerly inched along until they pressed the fracture; his body shuddered; he vomited and lost consciousness.

"Ger! Ger, answer me!" Cindy's urgent tones were dim – ringing from a great distance – similar to how Teddy's resounded above that well. The sharp pebbles under his buttocks and shoulders dug into his flesh: he wasn't lying on his soft bed. As he reoriented himself, he recalled climbing rocky paths with his fiancée. Why was she calling his name and shaking his shoulder. He couldn't see her. A few seconds passed before it occurred to him that his lids were closed. Forcing them apart caused blue sky, trees, sun – Cindy — to swim into his sight. How strange! He felt as if he were returning from a long voyage.

The fiery stabs shooting up his leg quickly evaporated that mental fogginess. "My ankle, how bad?" His dry throat produced hoarse rasps.

"It's broken," Cindy's response penetrated.

"Oh no!" Anxiety overwhelmed him. He tried to lift onto his elbows but Cindy gently pushed him down. She'd created a pillow from the dry leaves and pine needles and blanketed him with the picnic cloth. "How long was I out?"

"Just a few moments. Oh Hon. Gosh, I'm sorry. I thought it such an unusual formation with the moss encasing that rock. And I never considered its weight when I threw it. I meant it as a fun tease. Forgive me, Ger. Please, please forgive me."

Gerald empathized with the remorse his conscientious fiancée poured out and weakly reassured her, "Sweetheart…an honest mistake. You'd not have tossed it if you thought I'd fall. Besides, I'm clumsy. Don't worry. I forgive you. I love you."

"I've got to go for help. Water's right here. Are you warm enough?" Cindy's voice quivered.

Jodi interrupted, "Wait, Cindy. One of us can travel a lot faster while you care for Gerald."

The stunned Sam perceived that Jodi's 'us' meant one of the two angels at the scene. What could she be up to? In similar situations over the centuries he shadowed his human who sought help; he'd prodded his charge to leave clues to retrace later. He'd flashed intuitions of correct branches and re-minders to spot landmarks at forks.

But, Jodi, if we handle this your way, the humans will never learn to survive without angelic assistance.

And why should they? We'll always be with these two. So why not cooperate as partners?

Sam, reeling from the novelty of his new reality, couldn't refute Jodi's logic. But the law — Guardian Angels remain with their humans under any condi-tions until death – was engrained so indelibly into his psyche that panic rose at the thought of abandoning Cindy. So Jodi flew off to seek rescuers while Sam guarded. In Jodi's absence, Sam contemplated the situation. What a dif-ferent method for dealing with humans! Trusting another angel to protect Cindy was perhaps the most difficult method he'd need to integrate into his guardian armamentarium.

In about half an hour the thud of hikers' boots alerted them to approach-ing rescue. Jodi explained to Sam that she located the party a few trails away. "After all," she said, with a nonchalant wave, "if one flies high to better scan the area, it's easy to detect the best source of assistance." She explained to Sam that she attracted the group's attention to yellow pansies by the wayside at one fork and the lilacs farther along the trail appeared of a deeper hue when she energized a white cloud to dim the sun's rays. Sam was uncertain of his opinion.

The next day, while the soon-to-be-newlyweds rested in the sun to permit its warmth to penetrate Gerald's casted ankle, Jodi and Sam floated close by. Sam shared his confusion with his colleague, "It's strange: this partnership. We guardians seldom are acquainted with the angels assigned to our charge's mate or siblings, parents or children. The supervisors teach that socializing among each other distracts from our duty." He paused, took a deep breath, and ap-peared a tad shy. "I kind of enjoy chatting with you but … oh, it feels uncom-fortable. Jodi, are you aware – do other guardians collaborate in this way?"

"I don't know," Jodi shrugged, "But, since it works, what's the harm?"

Sam hesitated before deepening the discussion, "It negates the human re-quirement for innovative survival skills. And, and, I, uh, worry my acquain-tance with you will cause me to be careless in tending Cindy." While Sam betrayed his private concerns, he experimented with projecting his image as a youth, roughly their humans' age, clad in denim overalls and a flannel shirt similar to Gerald's. This, his first attempt at appearing in garments of the cur-rent fashion as opposed to the traditional silvery guardian robes, was fun. The straps extending up and over his shoulders from the top of his bib enticed him; his fingers repeatedly slid their length.

"Sam, perhaps they are acquiring a different set of abilities – such as skills at calming worries in order to listen to our voices? Maybe the potential for survival augments when angels and humans cooperate? Seems to me we're teaching interspecies collaboration and, at least in the case of us angels, intraspecies." Jodi exuded confidence, expounding on her favorite topic – intimate interaction between humans and their angels.

Lost in thought, Sam mused over her ideas. Far too complicated a topic for facile answers.

Chapter 4

What a novelty! Progress had invaded their rural community: first the electric streetlamps and then Bernard's Ladies Ready-To-Wear opened. The concept of a finished dress waiting to be carried home sparked conversations in sewing circles and the grocery shop. Several liked the convenience while others bemoaned the lack of individuality in mass-produced garments. Cindy found a job assisting the town women who valued her practical insights into color combinations and becoming styles: skills she had acquired during her days designing costumes for high-school dramas. And she loved helping each find exactly the right frock.

Jeannette Smith wandered through the new shop fingering the various garments: she scrutinized seams and visualized each item in her wardrobe. Clothing of different colors and sizes hung on racks. Against the back wall were arranged a discreet display of petticoats in the current styles. The lush blue-green carpet into which Jeannette's feet sank and the soft moss colored wallpaper enhanced the rich and serene atmosphere.

Since the guests at her daughter's wedding shower would include a number of Jeannette's own peers, along with the younger generation, she had decided to splurge on an impressive store-bought dress instead of making a fresh one or letting out an older frock. Besides, creating the wedding gown consumed her sewing time. Although this thirty-eight year old matron had grown a little plump after five children, she regarded herself as young and attractive: her hair, with no gray streaks, was fashionably bobbed - in contrast to the braided buns traditional for women of her age.

As Mrs. Smith browsed, Cindy empathized with her evident fantasy of owning this red dress versus that golden one. Hadn't she shared that feeling when she wandered the aisles during periods when no customers were present? The young salesclerk watched Mrs. Smith pull the embroidered blue dress from the rack, position it in front of her and gaze in the mirror. The woman was, it appeared, enraptured.

Cindy knew that her customer, like most women in town, was accustomed to purchasing fabric, then designing an outfit suitable both for the material and her figure; thus, with these ready-made garments, she was attracted to the material and ignored the cut. And that blue sheath didn't suit her matronly pear shape. Cindy suggested how lovely she would look in the pink linen intended for the more mature woman. Jeanette agreed, but nevertheless was enticed by the embroidery on the blue one.

Annoyance edged aside Cindy's innate diplomacy — *It won't make that much difference whichever she chooses. How ridiculous for such concerns over a mere garment!* Bursting forth, with no tact, the horrified Cindy heard herself exclaim, "Oh, Mrs. Smith, it's your daughter's shower. Either dress is fine. It doesn't matter."

Jeannette flushed, "You're right. Of course, you're right. I suppose you think I am a foolish school girl." She stormed out of Bernard's Ladies Ready-to-Wear, climbed into her buggy, and, with an agitated tug on the reins, forced her chestnut into a trot.

The following day Mabel Clark came in to look for something appropriate for the banquet at her husband's upcoming convention. "This is Timmy Smith," she introduced the five year old alongside her. "Timmy, say, 'Hello,' to Miss Eldrick." The child interrupted the yoyo tricks he was practicing long enough to mumble a bashful, "Hello," to Cindy. "Timmy's mother caught the city train this morning to hunt for an outfit for Mary's shower." Mabel ruffled the boy's shaggy locks, "He's my godson. Spending the day with me and as soon as we finish here we're going to get sodas. Right, Timmy?"

Cindy's neck grew hot and her heart pounded. She castigated herself for the previous day's rudeness. As the young woman obsessed on the reasons for her despicable salesmanship, she perceived an uneasiness that had intensified over the last several weeks from a single bubble somewhere in the pit of her stomach to an all pervasive irritability. She couldn't seem to control her tongue.

Her inability to ascertain a reason for her disquietude was only worsening it. Nothing was blatantly wrong. Why was she being like this? She hadn't a single clue. And her sleep was restless. Dreadful dreams concerning Robin plagued her nights and drained her energy. In one, her twin filled her steamer trunk; Cindy foresaw she'd never see her again. Cindy urgently desired to accompany Robin; but, for a reason she couldn't recall when she woke, she was compelled to stay behind. In other dreams Robin became lost; and though Cindy searched and searched, she didn't locate her sister. In some snippets she waved goodbye to her.

After one particularly agonizing night, Cindy brushed her hair so vigorously her head stung. Since a recent article in the woman's journal recommended a hundred strokes a day to stimulate her scalp and promote a healthy shine, Cindy had dutifully incorporated that advice into her morning ritual. "I bet I'm trying to brush away the bad dreams," slipped out after an especially rough stroke.

Robin pivoted from the mirror at which she had been applying her powder. "What dreams?"

As she steadily, but less harshly, continued to brush, Cindy described the most recent terror; one in which Robin departed on a schooner. But the vessel, drawn by dark horses, rose out of the water into the sky. A skull crowned the body of the captain-turned coachman. As she recounted the details, she glanced at the mirror and saw Robin's reflection sitting rigidly on the stool seemingly hypnotized by Cindy's recitation; a few tears rolled down her cheeks.

"Robin, what's wrong? It was my nightmare, not yours."

"Nothing, got powder in my eye."

"You're lying." Laying her brush on the dresser with a click, Cindy abruptly swiveled toward Robin.

Sobs that Robin had suppressed for a month engulfed her as she shuffled to her bed and flopped onto its rumpled sheets. She crossed her legs, elbows on knees, and propped up her head in her hands. Her words slurred together in a long sigh. "I'm so alone. All our days, every single minute of them, even before we were born, we've had each other. And, now, you're gone, or...I mean...you will be gone. And you should be, it's right. And Ted's gone," she gulped. "And...I'm s-so alone."

Cindy's haunted mood and the angular lines of her body softened as she reflected on the truth her twin expressed: Robin was alone. Cindy discerned a simultaneous loneliness weighing heavily in her own heart. In spite of Gerald, Jodi and Sam, an enlarging void existed within her as her twin, an integral part of her lifelong identity, withdrew from her. Cindy, caught up with her job and engagement, hadn't been conscious of her sister's absence.

But, in a quick shift of mood, she refused to accept the blame for the estrangement, "Robin, you're drawing away from me. It's not actually my fault." Indignation flooded her at the notion her bout of irritability was the product of Robin's steady distancing from her.

Robin seemed to shrivel further into herself. "On purpose, Cindy. You're engaged. I've gotta extricate myself from your everyday affairs or, at the least, remove myself from the intimacy we've shared."

"Oh no you don't – you can't!" Cindy's tone was strident. "Robin, you're wrong! Definitely wrong! Just because I'm marrying Ger's no reason for you to stop being my twin. We've been together forever." The necessity that Robin accept her error in logic triggered an urge for motion; Cindy jumped to her feet and marched along the curve of their oval rag rug. "C'mon, Robin. Stop this absurd talk."

"It's impossible. It's all impossible don't you see?" Robin's despondency clashed with her twin's aggression. No longer sobbing, she simply wept. "Ger's gonna — and should — usurp our closeness. That's right – I mean that's proper. My intrusion might mess up everything for you – I have to get out of the way."

But Cindy refused to slide into the trap of choosing between Robin and Ger. This dilemma was reminiscent of Gerald's when he believed he needed to choose between marriage and Jodi. That unraveled marvelously: true reciprocal partnerships had begun to evolve. She'd achieve the same with Robin — expand their universe — not shrink it.

Draped in her navy blue robe, Cindy looked dramatic framed by the yellow curtains. On their wide window seat, Snow Kitten, the cat, nestled between two teddy bears nervously twitched his tail. The three supplied Cindy's audience; Robin hadn't lifted her eyes.

Cindy's scolding posture relaxed, her hands fell to her side. She drew a deep breath and continued in a gentler tone: "Robin, listen. You're wrong. You've been a part of Gerald and my relationship since we were six." Cindy's absolute certainty lent power to her words.

"But there was T-Ted, too. I didn't in-intrude on you and Ger because I had, well, Ted and I had each other." Robin curled up into herself; her arms encircled her knees; her hands cemented together.

"Robin, if you say 'intrude' once more—I... I... I'll throw this bear at you!" Cindy punctuated her real threat by grabbing one of the soft toys and raising it overhead in an about-to-throw gesture. She meant to win this argument no matter what – but Robin remained in her dejected pose and didn't even notice. Cindy started to feel silly holding the bear.

"I can't be part of a husband's and wife's bonding? Oh, Cindy!" Her tears flowed anew. Cindy rushed over, squatted beside her sister, pulled her lifelong confidante into an embrace, and mentally debated what to say. Ultimately she decided on honesty and plunged right into her recent experiences.

"Honey, sweetie. I'm sorry. Please listen now. I have such an incredible story. And, please, you can't interrupt. You might think I'm crazy. At first, that is." She paused and peered into Robin's eyes, "The relationship isn't only Gerald and me. There's Jodi and Sam too." Without hesitating for Robin to react, Cindy recounted in detail her meeting Jodi and Sam, how Gerald had communicated with Jodi most of his life, Gerald's refusal to keep his angel secret from her, her own jealousy. She shared how Jodi invented the human-angel partnership and its conflict with angelic law, and the dream in which Jesus introduced Sam to her. "If there's room for two angels in our marriage, there's plenty for you — my twin and Gerald's childhood playmate."

As Cindy's statements tumbled out, Robin's tears dried up and an eerie peace permeated her body and dispelled her anguish. Cindy needn't have worried: Robin expressed no doubts about the miraculous events her twin related. "Cindy, will my angel talk with me? Can my angel and I join the four of you? That way I'd have someone; maybe not someone I can see or touch but I won't be the odd loner."

"Honestly, I have no idea." Cindy's face creased, "The angelic hierarchy forbids guardians to reveal themselves to their humans. A lot of this is brand new to me, too. But Jodi first broke that law; then Miguel introduced himself to Ted and Sam to me." She stared at her hands folded over Robin's. "Jodi told me that God intervened for Ted and me; I mean, He apparently instructed Miguel and Sam to reveal themselves."

"We must ask Him to permit my angel and me to become acquainted." Robin sat tall; she grasped Cindy's shoulders; her eyes pleaded. And so the twins knelt, earnestly prayed, then hugged once more.

"It'll work out – it has to – you'll see." Cindy's optimistic tone concealed her apprehension. Lacking knowledge of how such requests are decided, those prickly feelings of anxiety returned as she waited. Cindy craved the ability to control events of her life and sensed her uneasiness at relinquishing control to other beings – in this case to God Himself.

But, in His omniscient compassion, God instructed yet another angel to break universal law and befriend her human. Robin's exclusion wasn't part of His program as He tinkered with the workings of the universe.

Because during sleep a human's consciousness quiets itself and the unconscious has access to the foreground, the sleeping mind usually perceives intuitive whispers first. Therefore, Chelsea, Robin's angel, initially spoke into her dreams. However, it took a couple of nights before the young woman heard: her fear that God would deny her prayer interfered with Chelsea's messages. The Guardian Angel struggled to pierce the insidious anxiety that clouded Robin's mind and thought for the thousandth time how much more aware humans would be if they rid themselves of that tyranny!

And soon a group of six were celebrating together – but their total was eight, with Ted and Miguel merely absent physically. While they composed a joint letter to inform Ted of the new membership, each tacitly wished he would forgo his spiritual pursuits and come home.

Robin's spontaneity reemerged as she no longer felt the outsider. She and Chelsea spent innumerable hours chuckling over past mishaps during which the angel lent discreet aid. Before long, angel and human were fast friends as they sorted through mutual likes and dislikes.

Chelsea's insights into culinary possibilities fascinated Robin. Her angel suggested peculiar combinations such as adding a bit of cinnamon or red pepper to form the most unusual taste sensations. Recipes they devised were alien to Midwestern cuisine and her family served as less than enthusiastic guinea pigs. After all, Dad liked his meat and potatoes plain, but how could he gripe with his daughter's reacquired cheerfulness? "If only her joy of living would manifest on something other than my supper," he muttered to his wife as he ate something Robin called moussaka which she explained originated halfway around the world in Greece.

Jodi relished Chelsea's companionship: the male angels just didn't relate to some of her interests. Robin's Guardian, at first timid around the very social Jodi, relaxed into a comfortable friendliness, though no Guardian Angel could match Jodi's gregariousness. Chelsea, awed by her counterpart's innate social skills, deliberated one night while her charge slept whether the former Special Force's Angel could ever be a typical introspective guardian? *Such a role doesn't seem possible, given her personality. But she's managed this long. God must have reflected on Jodi's nature when He assigned her to Gerald? Maybe He planned to spice things up a bit?*

Everything seemed perfect for the sextet, except that they missed Ted and Miguel.

A few months later, clouds of dust swirled behind Gerald as he biked vigorously down the road; he veered left then right dodging boulders along the route. His movements resembled a well-rehearsed dance as he sped down the familiar country lane. When he reached the twins' property, he swerved to avoid the pine which marked the corner and raced along the curving drive shaded by tall oak and hemlock. After a hundred yards he sighted the whitewashed, two-story house, with its large front porch and the broad swing where he and Cindy delighted in private chats, hugs and stolen kisses. He rode toward the kitchen entrance, threw down his bike, and leapt the half dozen wooden steps.

The peaceful house filled with the rich aroma of pot roast was jarred awake with his shout, "Cindy! Robin! You won't believe…" Every human and canine resident rushed to the commotion. Felines fled to their hidden recesses for clandestine observation.

Mrs. Eldrick pivoted from the stove where she was thickening gravy; the liquid dribbled from her stirring spoon and stained her red-and-white checked apron then hit the floor. The twin's mother responded immediately to crises and forgot such niceties as replacing a spoon on its saucer. "Gerald, what's wrong?"

He startled the woman by sweeping her in a huge hug and spinning her around. "Nothing! Nothing's wrong. Everything's right! I've received incredible news – it's marvelous! Ted will be at our wedding. He'll be my best man."

"Oh, Ger — how wonderful!" Cindy, breathless from her race to the kitchen, embraced him. Robin beamed: Ted, best man and she, maid-of-honor. She no longer worried about feeling awkward at the festivities.

"His response arrived in today's mail. He'll be finished with school and return home in plenty of time."

During that evening's confab of six, Gerald read aloud the letter.

> Dear Ger,
>
> Of course, I'll be your best man. Would never forgive you if you didn't ask. Exams end in late May; I'll certainly be free for your June date.
>
> Can't wait to share. Somehow it doesn't seem right here at college. We know God is in charge and miraculous and all that. But the marvels of His munificence that we eight share aren't included in the lecture courses or the books. We are absorbing the Latin and Greek origins of the words, the ins and outs of the doctrines, the whys and whatnots of the dogma — but, there's an infinite amount that's never discussed.
>
> Is this what all new students feel? It probably takes a while to sort it out. I've made some associates among my fel-

low classmates. We study together and go out for hamburgers and sodas on Saturday nights – but it's not the same camaraderie as with you. No girl matches Robin, that's certain.

How exciting your news! And I envy you the togetherness. Say 'Hello' to Jodi. Can't wait to meet Sam and Chelsea. It's awful lonely here away from you all. I'm terribly homesick. I think of you as the sextet but wish it could be an octet with Miguel and me a part too. Keep wondering if it's worth it to pursue my quest. In many ways it feels as if your group has what I'm hunting for.

Sorry. A little melancholy in my aloneness but that will vanish as I anticipate your wedding and seeing you soon. Greet everyone for me.

Love, Ted

P.S.: Miguel reports that he's lonely too; he misses you and can't wait to meet you, Sam and Chelsea.

The three humans and three angels who encircled the picnic table listened intently. A melancholy fell over the group when the words ended. Ted's letter had intensified his geographic distance. Each was lost in his or her own musings. Gerald stared at the paper which had brought Ted into their midst for a brief few moments. Robin noted how morose the missive sounded and sympathized with how profoundly he missed his oldest and dearest pal. She wondered if Gerald, too, felt similarly alone without Ted's presence. *Of course, he has Cindy;* her gaze rotated to her sister who nibbled a hangnail and bit her lips, cues Robin recognized: *Cindy misses Ted, too.*

Her desperate loneliness, usually rigidly suppressed, pushed its way into her awareness. *I bet no one has the aching in their throat and chest like me. I'm glad they don't. But it's hard....*

In that misery Robin sank deeply into herself; she barely heard her sister suggest, "Let's formalize our group and include Ted and Miguel as absentee members." Cindy paused before asking, "What shall we call ourselves?" Robin's twin obviously intended to organize things then and there.

"How about 'Crazy Eights'?" Robin heard Gerald contribute. "After all, anyone who tried to figure out the composition of the club would deem us crazy. And our problem-solving methods are pretty weird by any mundane standards."

"But how would we explain 'eight' to a curious outsider?" The ever-practical Cindy triggered a fleeting annoyance in Robin: *She always needs to think of every possible objection.*

Then a sudden inspiration lifted Robin out of her depression; with a chuckle she quipped, "Oh that's easy. Remember how Mom used to say taking care of twins is like having quadruplets? How putting two together doubles the trouble? So if anyone asks about the club, we'll say that when you put us four together, you double everything."

"Love it," Cindy and Ger blurted out in unison, startled at each other, then burst into peals of laughter. Robin and three angels added to the happy chorus.

Ted and Miguel chuckled together when they received the charter drawn up by their friends:

> Now Hear This:
> On this First Day of May (in other locales celebrated as May Day) of the Year 1920 is hereby formed a group that shall forever after be named "The Crazy Eights".
>
> The membership of the Crazy Eights shall exclusively consist of pairs of human-angel partners.
>
> Bylaws yet to be determined. The principal regulation requires rules be highly flexible in order to accommodate unusual circumstances.
>
> Final authority rests with God. An attempt will be made to obey such lower celestial and human authorities as seems reasonable and possible.
>
> The Charter membership pairs, listed in the order of conscious pairing, are as follows:
>
> > Gerald and Jodi
> > Ted and Miguel
> > Cindy and Sam
> > Robin and Chelsea
>
> (In other words, there is no hierarchy to this membership — and women are equal to men in this here club.)

Chapter 5

Frustrated and discouraged Cindy had no doubt that she merited the award: World's Lousiest Mother. Her beloved Nancy clenched her tiny body into a ball and wailed. Both grandmothers provided assistance, as did her various aunts. Even fifteen-year-old Aunt Janie and her best friend occasionally stopped by to try to distract the poor infant. Uncles Jim and Johnny visited, grinned when the baby smiled and bubbled, then skedaddled, when the shrieks began.

The family's efforts allowed Cindy essential sleep — but the over-whelmed, conscientious mother suffered along with her daughter through every colic- driven scream. Cindy's and Gerald's mothers failed to persuade Cindy to stop berating herself for her inability to sooth her baby.

Another afternoon and again and again she circled the sitting room; she cuddled the disconsolate child against her breast, she raised the rigid bundle over her shoulder and patted the tiny back; she cradled her in her forearms and swung her back and forth. Finally, she sank into the padded seat of her wooden rocker which was painted in blue; yellow daisies climbed up the back and twined along the arms. She reminisced on the peacefulness before Nancy's birth when she sat by the fire in the evenings stitching needlepoint cushions to match the daisies that decorated her chair.

Slowly Cindy rocked, softly singing a tune her mother had used to calm her.

> Gently, gently my little girl,
> overhead the clouds do whirl,
> underneath the grassy plain
> with daisies playing in the grain.

You and I are safe indeed
for God succors our ev'ry need.
Let's rock and pray and go to bed,
Shhh, listen now to Jesus tred.

Wonder of wonders, the infant's taut form relaxed, she looked in her mother's eyes and smiled, then she nodded off against her mother's shoulder. For a few minutes, Mamma-Cindy experienced the joy of comforting her precious child. An hour later Gerald opened the door onto this tableau: his two most cherished humans, both sound asleep. He draped an afghan over the pair. What a priceless gift to witness them peaceful and, for a change, the little one free from pain.

He tiptoed across the room, gingerly unlatched the screen, and stepped outside. Strolling through the garden, he marveled at the miracle of their little darling and prayed yet again that God would furnish a remedy for her pain. He had already exhausted the newspaper files and the town library. After an interview in Columbus to gather background for an article on ham radios, he researched the university library. Every piece of advice he dug out, they tried. Ted popped into his mind and Gerald decided to dash off a letter. *Maybe he'll know an answer.*

Another day, as Cindy paced with the sobbing Nancy, she recalled her prenatal grand design to establish a perfect environment. When she and Gerald discussed their home, children were figured into the blueprints. During those first months of marriage and pregnancy her efforts as a homemaker created a comfortable, attractive home for her husband and its future little residents. They chose a rather large house on the edge of town with five bedrooms: one to serve as the nursery and, within not too many years, one bedroom would fill up with boys another with their girls. The fourth would perhaps provide a study for Gerald. Maybe one room too many, but the house was ideal in every other respect; she refused to fret about the extravagance of extra space since their budget could accommodate the mortgage payments.

Electric lights on the ceiling illuminated each room. At the outset, Gerald's thrifty wife meant to utilize wedding gifts and family donations to set up housekeeping. As they saved sufficient money, all sorts of convenient electrical inventions like vacuum cleaners could be purchased.

Soon after the wedding, she commenced crocheting and knitting layette items; before her pregnancy was established, she painted the nursery. Months in advance of the birth, Cindy methodically arranged the cradle, dresser, bottles, buckets, and a neatly ironed pile of diapers — ready for their child's arrival. She composed list after list and crossed out each accomplished task. If only organizational skills could vanquish colic.

On yet another tedious morning, with Nancy on the cusp of sleep, Cindy inched to her rocker by the window. Her vision drank in the pansies emerging from seeds she'd scattered in her last week of pregnancy. Soon her little girl would share her delight in colorful flowers. As she rocked monotonously, she studied the living room with the pale ochre walls and hardwood floors which she kept polished to a deep sheen; her eyes lingered on the midnight blue throw rugs she had hooked while she and Gerald enjoyed their radio's evening programs.

With a fretful infant often her sole companion, Cindy's anguish and fatigue left her mind prone to fuzzy reminiscences. Once, amid pacing, patting, nursing, she thought of her final day at Bernard's. Mr. Bernard, himself, valued her keen sense of customers' preferences and tried to convince her to continue at least part-time employment. But she planned to devote full-time energy to the roles of wife, homemaker and future mother and, although flattered, politely declined his offer.

Maybe I made a mistake, she added a new worry to her collection as she twisted to find a more comfortable position. She couldn't permit her physical or emotional distress to seep out: the hand that rubbed Nancy's back must stay calm. But the thoughts would not go away. *Maybe I should have pursued a career in sales or in fashion – forgotten about children. It certainly isn't fair that Nancy has to suffer as the result of an inadequate mother. Everyone I know, all my former classmates, can soothe their babies. Pshaw! so what that Mother says I was exactly like Nancy!*

Cindy grimaced. Trying to quiet a colicky twin while she cared for the other — how on Earth did her mother juggle her tasks! *She's an excellent mother and yet she had me. Could it be that this isn't my fault.* But that moment of clarity soon muddled as the long days and nights wore on.

One particular afternoon, after Cindy had repeated her unsuccessful routines, prayed for her daughter's relief and contemplated her own inadequacies, she began weeping. "Oh how I wish you could communicate with me," she mumbled to Nancy as she shifted her from lap to shoulder. "Maybe we could cure this together...." She giggled through her tears, "Wouldn't it be funny if you could tell me how to help? Maybe you'd say, 'I want pink instead of yellow swaddling. Yellow hurts my tummy. Pink is warm and jolly.' And I'd reply, 'But what if you'd been a boy? We couldn't use pink in the nursery.'"

Cindy's thoughts rambled in odd directions. She drifted back a year to when she and Gerald developed the skill of compromise. Give-and-take proved a necessity from the beginning of their marriage. He craved a red living room — a conservative burgundy, but still a shade of his favorite color. It would, he thought, be elegant to entertain in such an ambience. Cindy preferred a serene effect: a room decorated in hues that evoked peace. In her opinion, red stimulated, agitated, increased adrenaline.

"But Cindy, that surge of energy in our home would connect us with our modern age! Our own hub that links to contemporary centers– honey it would make our home a point in the communication network." His elaboration confronted her reluctance. She loved her man-of-the-world and urgently wished to please him. Yet she couldn't acquiesce to such a room — especially not the living room. She was hooking a rug for their bedroom during the argument. Deep blue yarn framed blossoms, including poppies and tulips, as she attempted to fathom a red room. And what would their friends think? "How ridiculous!" The women would whisper at teas when she stepped into the kitchen.

An inspiration floated at the edge of her awareness – after a few moments of calm breathing she retrieved it. "What about adding shades of red in every room to sort of energize the environment with a dash of stimulation? Rather than concentrate it in a single room, the motif could weave throughout the house." She pressed on more enthusiastically, "Like hang the two cardinal plates on the wall or design slipcovers from material with roses in the print."

Gerald refused to be mollified. His wife knew this craving was from childhood: he'd shared with her how his mother squelched his every plea for a red bedroom. Since he was the homeowner, he would have his room. The couple waited in stony silence, each entrenched in an opposite point of view. How to compromise? Cindy stewed. *This room should be quiet and serene in order to engender peacefulness in our children. Red would kindle squabbles. We'd be arguing worse than this. If we're irritable in this room, think how we'd battle surrounded by maroon walls, crimson drapes and cherry rugs and slipcovers. All the ladies' magazines advise use of reds to stimulate romance, not to elicit calm.*"

Cindy looked toward the nearby tabletop where Jodi projected her image, "Jodi, what's your opinion?"

"I'm not butting in this time. Home décor is no more an angelic function than the selection of wedding colors." The angel's tones were final.

"Don't wiggle out of this. You and Sam will spend many hours in this space. Let's be a team."

"Just one minute," a baritone interjected. "I'm not involved in this, Cindy. I won't be cornered into an argument about interior decorating. I will be content in any setting and have inhabited more than I can count."

"Sam, you ever dwell in a red house?" Gerald's tone revealed genuine curiosity.

"Certainly." Sam replied. "During what your western historians call the Renaissance, wealthy Europeans adorned their public rooms with red paint and accents."

"See. That's my point!" He seemed barely able to suppress his glee. "That was the epoch of mankind's greatest intellectual achievements and artistic advances."

Cindy bit her tongue. She stood and walked to the opposite wall to adjust a crooked picture. The profession of her husband necessitated his existing at the vanguard of information so anything that stimulated lively interchanges would be beneficial. But a red living room? He was serious. How could they resolve this conflict?

Robin coincidentally arrived as the two sulkily stared at anything but each other. After Cindy summarized the conflict, Robin, without hesitation, flippantly suggested, "Why not use all-red for Gerald's new office. He can be stimulated and motivated, and — when he's tired of the arousal — he can join you in your peaceful living area."

Humans and angels gaped at Robin. Why had none of them had that inspiration? Together the newlyweds had been setting up the extra bedroom for an at-home office: they'd hauled over Gerald's boyhood desk and added a comfortable lamp and chair. An old bookcase stored in his family's attic was cleaned up and already contained a dictionary and a dozen other books. In fact, Cindy had used crimson everywhere possible in the pictures, pillows and rugs she moved into his writing room.

Gerald had gained quite a reputation as a credible journalist. Several of his feature articles about how small-town tradesmen meshed with the nation had been carried by the wire services to newspapers, large and small, across the United States. Tom Walthers received word that Gerald's pieces had appeared in London and Paris, the latter in translation. As a result of his phenomenal rise in readership, newspaper publishers, impressed by Tom Walther's protégés, sent letters and dispatched representative to meet Gerald. But he did not intend to forsake The Eagle as had previous apprentices Tom had trained.

In exasperation, one of the most prestigious publishers declared, "If he won't come to us, we'll go to him. He's too good for us to get only the occasional reprint." And, with that thought, he personally made the trip to visit Gerald and negotiate a syndication contract. Tom advised Gerald on the terms and then brainstormed many titles with Gerald who, about two weeks later submitted, "What America Is Thinking." After running a few months, his were often the first words read at American breakfast tables, surpassing front page, sports and comics in popularity.

Gerald composed most of these pieces in his home office since at The Eagle's headquarters the bustling activity of the weekly-turned-daily with its added employees and new apprentice distracted him. Gerald's morning routine began at The Eagle where he took notes on pertinent information from the overnight wire releases. Then he chatted with and interviewed folks in town, chasing potential leads. He reached home for a leisurely lunch with his wife then disappeared upstairs into his private study to assemble stories from the material he'd gathered.

The unique quality of his column was his insightful depictions of the wisdom of the common person. In one article he invited the townspeople to opine about telephone usage. Farmer Jack extolled the convenience of telephoning his order to the local feed store for delivery, but bemoaned his decreased socialization "with real people" since he'd installed the machine. He reminisced about the old days when he dropped by the feed shop not only for supplies but to discuss weather, crops, children, life in general with his fellow farmers.

Grandma Maple relished her daily "chatterings with Grandma Jones." She remembered her own mother's isolation from her peers. She was surrounded by children and grandchildren but still felt lonely. But old Mrs. Perkins scolded that the invention was "the work of the devil" and criticized Bonnie for rushing to answer its ring. "You're under the control of that dang thing, Bonnie. Man should not be subservient to machines."

So on it went with one person's impressions jotted into his utilitarian notebook then another's. By week's end a simple question developed into a detailed commentary on one of the country's modern contrivances, both pro and con. Although the views Gerald presented derived from a single small town, they resonated nationwide with rich and poor, young and old, educated and unschooled.

As a result of the confab on the color red, Cindy ordered maroon paint and lovingly painted the walls and ceiling. A cherry slipcover protected the easy chair and the braided throw rug was from the same material. Cerise drapes could be tied back to let in sunlight. In all but the winter months, fragrant scents perfumed the air from the tulips or roses or whatever red bloom Cindy could pluck from the garden or discover in the fields.

Gerald reveled in his room. His desk was perennially strewn with piles and piles of paper. Open books or newspapers or journals inevitably settled beneath, on top, or beside each teetering pile. His student desk was soon replaced by one that took up a fourth of the room. Cindy never straightened his mess. If no one disturbed the heap, the writer could locate any item either by himself or with Jodi indicating the whereabouts of a necessary, but concealed, fragment.

Cindy's pleasant memories of the "red confab" faded when Nancy emitted plaintive sounds. Sighing, once again on maternal alert, the young mother responded to her baby. The scheduled feeding time was near enough; she put her infant to breast, relaxed, and enjoyed the nursing child. Nancy giggled and peered into her mother's eyes as she took a break from her busy suckling. Smiling at her child and sniffing the sweet downy head, Cindy prayed this colic would dissolve as did the color scheme problem. After ten minutes that hope shattered: Nancy rejected the nipple; her screams permeated her mother's psyche. Tormented, Cindy resumed the ritual of pacing round and round the house as she derisively reviewed her attempts to design an ambience designed to produce a contented child.

After her pregnancy was certain, in her favorite woman's journal, she read a recommendation to think pleasant thoughts and view happy scenes. Never a person to go halfway, she collected peaceful verses, inspirational poems and Bible passages for memorization which she affixed to the refrigerator, cupboards, mirrors and wherever her gaze might land. Each morning over tea she leafed through the photographs of forests, mountains, rivers and oceans she had put into a scrapbook. Images of cherubic babies were scattered through its pages.

Although she conscientiously maintained her regimen including eating the diet suggested for pregnant women, Cindy couldn't quell her fears. *Would she be a nurturing mother? Would the baby survive?*

Listening to the same shrieks over and over, Cindy concluded that all her prenatal worries must have caused Nancy's inconsolability. Finally, she couldn't suppress her dismay that she alone was responsible for Nancy's agony and sobbed, mingling her tears with those of her baby. Bertha Eldrick, walking in on the sad scene, gathered the two into a hug.

"Mom, I caused this, didn't I? I tried so very hard not to worry, but I worried so much when I was pregnant and I constantly worry and now look what I've done."

"Oh, you silly thing!" The grandmother's tender voice, overflowing with love, penetrated the screams. "Of course not. A lot of babies suffer from colic. Some worse than others. No one knows why." She nudged her daughter back slightly so she could peer into her eyes. "There's never been an answer. And it happens no matter what a mother's disposition: calm and placid, yelling and angry, or fretful and blue. Now you scoot; it's the day your group is quilting at church. My turn with my grandbaby."

Cindy obeyed her mother and escaped to an afternoon of quilting. But she felt herself a deserter. Although her peers tried to distract her from her obsessions about her inadequacy with her cranky baby, she collapsed into sobs and spilled forth her self-recriminations. The women launched into their own tales of frustrations with young children. By the end of the afternoon, Cindy's mood had brightened and she almost laughed at her attempts to assume the blame.

Still it proved difficult to avoid vilifying herself as the weeks stretched on and the colic didn't abate. Cindy stared out toward her vegetable garden in the early morning light; she reveled at the sight of the healthy plants that had grown from the seeds she planted in late April before Nancy's birth. As she labored in the thick loam, she enjoyed digging her fingers into the soil, extracting weeds, watering: in the garden she could be successful.

Soon the cucumbers, which already contributed to salads, would be ready for pickling. Beans and peas had been canned and the ripening tomatoes looked close to stewing quality. In her opinion a responsible wife preserved the family's food – certainly did not rely on store-bought produce for the winter. With modern devices invented faster than anyone could keep track, her mother gently teased and asked if Cindy intended to craft her own soap and candles.

She delighted in her kitchen set-up with its new gas stove, double sink, and ample storage. The cheery room, with yellow walls and countertops, contained the requisite splashes of red via rose motifs crocheted into potholders and towels that coordinated with the vivid throw rug.

In her reverie of pickles and canning, the early morning slipped by and her husband entered before she had taken the eggs from the icebox. He gave her a kiss. "Hey, what's for breakfast, Sweetheart? I've an appointment with Tom at 8:30 on the Bascom case. Have to get perking."

Shirking her duties, dreaming away the dawn, and breakfast not ready. Cindy flushed from the inferred criticism: the anger at herself projected onto Gerald. "Why did you schedule an 8:30 AM conference! I've been up two - no three - times during the night. I'm exhausted. You could be more considerate and set your meeting for later. What with Nancy not sleeping. It's not fair. Everyone thinks I can do everything!"

Gerald, incredulous at the outburst from his tranquil, overly competent wife, embraced her and whispered, "Honey, breakfast's hardly that important.

It's rough with Baby so fretful. I'll grab a cinnamon bun at the bakery. See you later." And he fled only to worry about Cindy throughout the day.

Guilt consumed Cindy: *I'm not only a lousy mother, I'm a lousy wife. A good wife sends her husband off, fed and relaxed to important business.* At dinner the evening before, Gerald had shared his concerns regarding the controversial article he needed to write about additional funding for the community poor-house. Paul Jones stated that the coffers would contain plenty of money even if the budget were trimmed. Eleanor Nichols and Mildred Cantor disagreed. On the annual inspection tour a day earlier, they had pointed out the chipped and peeling paint in the halls and most rooms; in addition, the stove, which Jake Curry declared beyond repair, sent smoke spewing through the building.

The teakettle whistled; Cindy jumped; her irritation increased another notch. *It will surely wake Nancy. I can't bare her screams just this minute.* The distraught mother swiveled to turn off the gas and stumbled over Rover stretched in the middle of the kitchen floor on the throw rug — his usual place. Her foot landed on his paw. He yelped. Nancy woke abruptly and shrieked. Cindy plopped in the middle of the floor and sobbed.

Sam advocated, "Take Nancy to your mother's; you and Robin picnic. You need to get away."

"But I'm behind on chores." Cindy whined. "The lack of meal planning and this dusty house and — I can't keep up." Rover licked her, but she shoved her faithful companion away. His head lay on the floor as his big sorrowful eyes regarded his beloved mistress. Her concentration rested on the golden re-triever who idolized her and whom she loved almost as much as Ger and Nancy. "I'm sorry, Rover. I'm lousy to you, too, aren't I?"

And she mercilessly hammered herself. "I'm probably increasing Nancy's colic by being so frazzled." She addressed her angel, "Is that the way with other mothers? What can I do?"

Sam repeated his advice, "Go for a picnic with Robin. You'll regain equi-librium and energy if you get away for a while."

Suddenly the side door slammed and Cindy recognized her twin's step. That inexplicable twin telepathy: Cindy realized that Robin had sensed her distress. "What's wrong?" Robin took in her sister's posture and urged, "C'mon, Cindy, what is it?"

Everything' s wrong. I can't do anything right. I'm frustrated. Tired. Anx-ious. It's impossible to be anything but a rotten wife and mother with a colicky baby. At least, impossible for me. Nancy cries and cries. I neglected Gerald's breakfast and snapped at him and he has an important meeting with Tom. I stepped on Rover. I'm failing as a wife, a mother, a dog-owner."

"Seems to me you're overwhelmed. Let's drop off Nancy at Mom's and pick blueberries and have lunch in the meadow. The berries are out in force I hear. C'mon, I'll get Nancy ready. You dress. We'll make sandwiches at Mom's."

Cindy, normally the twin who took charge, had no strength to argue; she tolerated her sister's ministrations. Up on the hill, under the sun, the pair ate sandwiches from meatloaf left over from the Eldrick dinner table. Blueberries, the perfect dessert, completed their meal. Laughter about the trials and tribulations of motherhood and homemaking gradually relaxed Cindy. Robin could empathize since she herself experienced little success during her attempts to soothe her small niece. Yet she cherished the times Nancy, free from colic, cooed and responded to her voice and touches.

As they enjoyed the fresh air and chained daisies into hairpieces, Robin manipulated the conversation's topic to Cindy's self-castigations. "You're feeling low about your inability to cure Nancy's colic. But, Mom says she couldn't cure yours and we both consider her a terrific mother. And she'd already three before us; she had plenty of experience."

Despite the logic, Cindy would not be easily mollified. "Come on, Robin, our classmates are capable mothers. Consider Jane — how well she handles three!"

"Ever seen her ironing? Or run your thumb over her tables? She definitely lets nonessential tasks slide," Robin threw out rapid-fire facts to counter Cindy's example.

"So, what about JoAnne? She's taking care of her grandmother after the apoplexy, keeps a clean house, and her four children are under seven. Jimmy isn't old enough to help."

"C'mon, Cindy, you're leaving out half the facts." Robin checked the length of the daisy chain she was making and reached for some more flowers. "You know as well as I that her sister and Doug's not only baby-sit but help tidy and cook. Really, there are three adults taking care of that house. A huge problem is your refusal to seek our help with other tasks besides tending to Nancy." The length of her chain apparently satisfactory, Robin tied it into a circle and threw it over her head. "JoAnne's not afraid to delegate. That's why it might look like she achieves more. Come off it, Cindy. If you're insisting on being so durn independent, you can't compare yourself to housewives with extra assistance." Her sister's arguments had merit, Cindy admitted.

Robin grabbed a stick and flung it across the meadow for Rover to fetch. "I think...," she took the stick from Rover and tossed it again in the opposite direction. "I think you're actually choosing to feel a failure; I think you're creating reasons with which to beat yourself up."

A hush fell over both; the sun had passed its zenith and the women organized their picnic items and resumed berrying. *Robin's right. My attitude must change if I'm to be happy. I can't be successful with Nancy if I'm fretful myself.* While they filled their baskets and hiked the path to the bottom of the hill, Cindy formulated a brief list of resolutions. *I must include things in my day I enjoy. I have to get away from those shrieks of pain sometimes. Robin and I are going to can and bake all these basketfuls of blueberries. We'll send Nancy to her grandmothers' houses.*

That afternoon's picnic provided Cindy more than a new proposal for action: she was much more relaxed and would consequently be able to better pacify Nancy. The sewing circle at church should prove an excellent distraction. She'd not attended since the birth assuming she couldn't neglect her unconsolable baby for self-centered fun. One of the grandmothers could care for Nancy since the older age group met on a different afternoon. She'd attend every one of those meetings.

One fall evening, Cindy, who was crocheting hot pads for the pre-Christmas church bazaar, blurted out, "Gerald, what are your recent findings regarding colic?" His wife appeared pale, tired, defeated. She hadn't sought his expertise for the last two days and couldn't restrain herself although she knew that, if he'd discovered something, he'd have started a trial immediately.

It had been five months – five interminable months with a suffering child. Nancy's father between other tasks, managed to interview physicians, priests, pastors and writers, peruse files and expand his initial investigation to topics only remotely connected to discontented babies. Since the grandmothers were stumped and since his darling Nancy felt no relief when with them when wracked with pain, he realized the problem was not the quality of parenting. Still Gerald wondered if he might be committing a sin for which God was punishing them. He frequently reflected on his various foibles and speculated on what he could fix to cure Nancy. He too felt inadequate. Although his job was to uncover information, he was a miserable failure for his own daughter.

Long ago they consulted Sam and Jodi. "I'm sure that you angels must have proposals for us to try," Cindy snapped at 3:00 one morning. Nancy had fallen asleep about midnight, cooing contentedly, waving tiny hands at her adoring parents. Then she awoke with piercing wails two-and-a-half hours later. Gerald offered, "Get some rest. Let me walk her, hon. I can go in late tomorrow." But after half an hour she arose to assist him: the tormented cries prevented her resting. A tiny little corner of her was kind of glad. Her feeling of incompetence would have multiplied if Gerald quieted their baby easily.

Cindy's mouth spread in another wide yawn as she berated Sam for not being forthcoming. Her guardian angel had experience with countless children; he must have known tonics. "You've been around for centuries; besides, I suspect you can work miracles. With your resources, you should be able to cure my sweetie's agony."

Sam, who had indeed witnessed dozens of similar situations, figured it to be a natural phenomenon of the universe. "Cindy, I know no answer. If I did, I would have divulged it to stop her crying for my own peace. But colic, so far, remains unconquerable."

She faced Gerald to confront Jodi. "I can't imagine that in Special Forces you didn't rescue sobbing babies from distraught mothers." She wrung her hands and rubbed her neck, "I get so frustrated, I want to...." Gerald shifted their daughter to one arm and stepped over to hug Cindy.

"Me too. And, my research shows inconsolable children exhaust the resources of their parents – even leads to infanticide. Join the normal human population, darling. The feeling is universal. It's tough, Cindy, really tough, really tough. All of us are ready to give up at times. Remember the responses we received to my articles on colic." While the adults discussed the situation's effects on parents, Nancy quieted, cooed contentedly, beamed at her mother and dozed off in her father's arms; and the family slept well into daylight.

A few days later, in Nancy's nursery which Cindy had decorated with merry pastels of cherubs cavorting with tots, Cindy reached under the basin and pulled out a soft rag towel. Caressing and tickling her little girl, Cindy tried to encourage that anxious little mouth to smile. And her little girl responded, with a chuckle, as she grabbed for the colorful rag. Even Sam was captivated by the little cherub and wished he'd accumulated more wisdom about human children.

Gerald, too, questioned if their angelic partners withheld information. "Jodi, there must exist a secret tonic. Can't you go investigate in that angelic library of yours? Are you holding back because some angelic law requires that we suffer through this?"

"That's not fair, Ger. I don't operate that way. I would reveal any remedy I simply hoped might prove worthwhile." Jodi conveyed her emotions through a picture of hurt expression, hair disheveled a bit and drab cocoa frock. "It's this type of enigma that sent Ted on his quest. Maybe some day he'll find solutions." Her eyes searched his for reassurance that he recognized her sincerity. He returned a cold, stony glare. Immersed in his belief that his angel might be dissembling, he clenched his fists and stomped out the door.

Jodi, likewise convinced of a solution, deduced that the worst barrier to its discovery must be the universal acceptance that this suffering would eventually resolve. In his heart Gerald acknowledged her honesty; but, as a first-time father, he refused to be appeased – a speck of him wondered if she'd search harder if he remained disapproving. He went into his study, slumped at his desk and surveyed the street outside his window. He studied the street lamps — one shone immediately opposite their property. The large globe lighted the area; its glow seemed to symbolize the knowledge that should guide him.

Reaching into his roll-top desk, he pulled out the letter Ted had sent and reread his advice — perhaps the hundredth perusal....

Dear Ger,

Boy, it must be tough! Miguel says colic is one of "those" things humans endure. Better answers must exist for these common dilemmas!

In a number of the Christian denominations, the elders pray and lay hands on a person who is sick. Sort of like Jesus instructed his disciples to do in the book of Mark. Other denominations teach that this manner of healing occurred during the first century for the purpose of founding the churches and the ability hasn't persisted into our modern era. Religions throughout the world seem to agree that prayer is an effective remedy for many health problems. But you're using that method, as are Miguel and I.

Still, old pal, can't figure out why God doesn't answer our prayers for a dear baby's relief from pain. If He did, would it make it too easy to believe in Him? I'm only half-facetious. Maybe it's supposed to be difficult to believe and answers to each prayer would make it too easy to accept that God is.

Certainly can't find any church leader who is supposed to have solved that problem.

I bet the right occult method could resolve these mysteries. The church leaders would be furious if they heard me say that but I am extremely interested in people who claim they can lay hands on those who are ill and achieve a healing.

I've been to a few of the revival meetings with people who appear to have truly been healed. There may be something to what they're claiming. One old gentleman invited me to his home when I was in Kentucky last month. Had quite a decent meal with him and his wife – chicken and biscuits with corn on the cob. What a treat — home cooking — eaten around a kitchen table instead of in the boarding house!

They told me about their congregation praying for their youngest child who couldn't walk and the child then did. I saw her, ten now, lively and laughing. She and her brothers let me join a game of softball. She not only walked, she ran and batted a home run! They told me other stories of their congregation. Were their tales of the miraculous or...?

I may end up deviating from the theology route and pursue philosophy and metaphysics to discover answers. Ger and Cindy, at this point all Miguel and I can do is add our prayers to yours, and we're petitioning up a storm.

By the way, stopped by the farmer's market in Moline yesterday while doing some evangelism – a practicum for my course. Met a marvelous, grandmotherly-type, woman. She talked about a healing of her arthritis. She also said she was acquainted with you; seems you were introduced in Chicago at some convention. She writes columns for the local press on different remedies. No, she didn't know a solution for colic; just said some maladies we have to muddle through.

I do miss you and Robin. Although – between us men — I wish she wouldn't wait for me. I am compelled to continue this quest. She is too wonderful a woman to be without a husband and children. Do urge her to give up on this unworthy itinerant.

Love, Ted and Miguel

Chapter 6

"I'd adore having a baby like you," Robin murmured in lullaby tones to the drowsy Nancy she tenderly cradled against her chest as she meandered through the rooms. "But my love seems reserved for your Uncle Ted; the suitors your mamma and papa force me to meet…oh, they don't make my heart leap in the way he does." She paused to gaze out the large front window. "A family isn't likely for me. Uncle Ted has set many goals and fatherhood isn't included."

Robin studied the oak tree that shaded the walkway of bark chips neatly placed by Gerald and trimmed with Cindy's myriads of colorful petunias, moss roses and a smattering of daisies. Her eyes dropped to Rover, who, parked in the center of a throw rug, was thumping his long tail against the floor; she insisted as if to her four-legged audience, "Really he can't. One can't be both an indigent spiritual researcher and responsible father." Rover yawned.

As she strolled around the room, Robin studied the child she cuddled. On that late July day she had taken charge of her three month old niece so that Cindy could luxuriate in shopping alone. "Nance, your suffering teaches lessons to all of us. Your mamma is learning she must relax and stop judging herself so harshly. Your papa is discovering that the mass media doesn't have every answer."

"And…" Robin poked Nancy's dimpled chin with her finger while she balanced the baby on her forearm, "I'm realizing more and more that I need little folk in my life. Ted won't give me children, but I've been considering: I'll be a teacher — hey, maybe you'll be in my class." Nancy cooed at her aunt. Robin giggled. "Think of that. You can regale your classmates with tales of your Aunt Robin minding you while your mamma was out.'"

Nancy's alert blue eyes examined each feature of her aunt's face. Usually Robin experienced no better luck with Nancy's colic than anyone else, but that Thursday afternoon, her niece seemed peaceful. "But what about you? What are you learning?" Robin lifted Nancy up to better scrutinize the baby's countenance for responses. The infant stared back — apparently fascinated by the depth of her aunt's gaze.

The firm, rapid tread of Cindy's approach interrupted Robin's monumental insight. "What are you two up to?" Cindy stooped and nuzzled Nancy's cheek, grinned at her cherub's welcoming smile, then walked over to the table and dropped her wrapped packages of flour and sugar. She went to the pantry for a gingham apron. "Staying for dinner, aren't you?" She didn't wait for a reply but searched in the cupboard for a pan, chose three large potatoes from the bin and started peeling. Apprehension seeped into her awareness; clutching her potato and peeler, she pivoted from the sink, "What's happening?" Robin's smiling lips greeted Cindy's query.

"Well, I, we've decided, Nancy and I that is — we decided that I should become a teacher. The university has a Teacher's College and, if I enroll this fall, I could maybe teach Nancy. Remember back when Miss James, our high school French teacher, mentioned her boarding house with the landlady furnishing meals and sort of watching out for her – and the friends she made? And, and, I would have real purpose in life and be surrounded by so many children. Even if none is mine personally...."

Cindy's expression had changed to horror. The woman cuddling her daughter looked sheepish, yet determined. "Robin, you can't!" Cindy's fled upstairs. Nancy peered after her mother's fleeting back, scrunched her face, and shrieked.

As her psychically synchronized twin, Robin read into Cindy's response the host of emotions it contained. Cindy took her presence for granted: her twin presumed she'd always be there for her; and Robin understood that the support was reciprocal. Cindy's not-so-secret goal — securing Robin a husband — had caused her to scheme, to enlist Gerald's assistance, and to try to talk Robin out of her fantasies of Ted's return. After futile attempts, Cindy opted to involve her sister as an active participant in her own family in lieu of the one Robin might never have.

If she attended college, it would be the first separation for the twins by more than a few miles. They had shared the same bedroom until Cindy's marriage. During Nancy's months of colic, Robin set up a cot in the nursery where she spent frequent nights to grant Cindy a full night's sleep. Her surprise decision would bring her personal fulfillment and happiness but at the same time require her to live hours away.

The morning after Robin told Cindy she walked into the kitchen where her mother was rolling out dough for berry pies: the church bazaar on Saturday included a baked goods booth. "Mom, what would you think if I attended the university this fall – if I studied for a teaching certificate?" The older woman pivoted abruptly, mouth moving wordlessly. That certainly hadn't been Bertha Eldrick's desire for her daughter — alone in a faraway city, no family nearby. Although stunned by the announcement, the twin's mother recognized that it might well be the answer to her prayers.

Resolutely she smothered her fears for her daughter being so far from home and hugged her child who'd grown into a young woman. The hug left white-powder prints on Robin's dark green bodice. "Darling," Bertha's voice filled with sincere encouragement, "That's a marvelous plan. You should select an occupation that's right for you. To be happy you'll need a place just for yourself."

Bertha, like Cindy, had married Paul, her childhood sweetheart, right after high school; her life revolved around raising children and managing their home. She'd experienced the joys of her children's accomplishments and the bountiful crop years, as well as, the sadnesses of Ronnie's death and a stillbirth. Her quiet life was the type she imagined for her daughters. For a daughter of hers to be denied marriage to her first love seemed incomprehensible. She prayed for Robin daily and tried hard to put the situation into God's hands. But still, the role of mother of grown children who must pursue their own way could prove worrisome. Tears glistening, she turned away to roll the dough into circular shapes.

She'd promoted Cindy's hunt for boyfriends and couldn't suppress her annoyance with some of Robin's polite rejections. Bertha was disgusted and so informed her recalcitrant daughter when Robin displayed no interest in Tom Hanes from Masonville. A handsome young man, he'd played high school football like Ted; a couple of years older, he'd completed a business degree and was employed in his family's store. He'd shared with Robin his dream of expanding it into a nationwide hardware franchise and next year, with his father, would initiate a second store in another town. He seemed an excellent match.

Losing Robin to the university was not on Bertha's agenda for the young woman; nevertheless she grasped it was a wise alternative. And, perhaps she would meet a suitable husband at school. And, in the meantime, a teaching certificate would provide her with worthwhile activity and an enjoyable profession. Rapidly sorting through the advantages and disadvantages, Mrs. Eldrick's pros outweighed the cons and her mind started listing Robin's wardrobe, noting what garments would require replacement as she completed baking pies.

Not that these optimistic plans eliminated maternal worries. Was Robin mature enough to leave home? What of the knowledge and wisdom to which her sheltered daughter was oblivious? How incredibly difficult to agree to her child's venturing into an enormous and occasionally unfriendly world! Bertha preferred her daughter remain under her wing in their hometown.

Despite her worries, she smiled at Robin who was carrying the pies to the oven and remarked, "We need to schedule a mother-daughter shopping expedition to supplement your wardrobe." Robin mumbled her gratitude — and sent a brief thank you to God for such a mother. They hugged and laughed at their flour covered selves.

Together they informed her father at the supper table; he applauded the decision. "Now see here. Don't think I like the notion of my daughter being so far from home. But I want you happy. And, if you're waiting on Ted, you have to find a meaning for yourself."

Robin began preparations to move to the state university. Throughout August, Cindy, aware her attempts were selfish, tried to dissuade her sister. But Robin felt compelled and remained committed to her plan.

The distance, although not exceedingly far, would separate her from her family. It was hard to leave Cindy especially with Nancy still fretful. Robin anguished at night: her love for her twin, for Nancy, her parents, all weighed against her decision. One restless evening she tiptoed out to the garden, trimmed roses and deadheaded the cosmos. She sought Chelsea's opinion as she snapped a dried flower from the bush by the porch, "Am I being selfish?"

"How can a human not be?" Chelsea replied. "You need to think of yourself too. You can only be useful to others if you do."

Robin shifted to a patch of weeds sprouting among the lettuce. She stooped and, with her fingers close to the ground to avoid breaking the stems, one by one, extirpated each, shook off the loose dirt and tossed it onto a pile she'd later carry to the compost heap. "Maybe I should wait until the colic subsides. But, if I do, I can't enroll for another year. " Robin's thoughts swam with doubt as she was carefully clearing the patch. What would be best for her little niece?

"Nancy has a mother, two grandmothers and a large assortment of eager aunts," Chelsea's logic rang true. Robin knew how much Gerald's sisters, Sally and Janie, loved their niece as did her younger sister, Pris. But qualms lingered. This had to be the most difficult decision Robin had ever confronted; she was nervous — but Chelsea would always accompany her.

The day before enrollment, Cindy and Gerald drove Robin to college in Gerald's new model T of which he was mighty proud; Nancy remained with her grandmothers who assured Cindy they were capable of adequately tending her.

Among other arrangements over the past month, Robin had located a suitable boarding house. A former teacher recommended the place and wrote a letter of reference for Robin to submit with her request for room and board. Mrs. Brown, the landlady, responded by return mail and accepted Robin as a tenant. She enclosed a brief summary describing the other women who would reside there during the upcoming school year.

Gerald parked. The boarding home, freshly painted, with ruffled curtains and a flower pot on each sill, seemed perfect for Robin. Marjorie Brown, a graying woman in her early fifties, greeted them at the front door with a welcoming smile and showed them to Robin's room. After they helped lug her trunks and paraphernalia upstairs, Cindy and Gerald each hugged her goodbye, Cindy tearfully. Then, the young parents abandoned Robin to her new life and retreated homeward before night darkened the roads.

Upstairs, alone, Robin viewed her room; it was decorated in her favorite combination of pink and white: *perhaps a sign I've selected the right course,* she mused. She pulled out her pillow, covered in pink satin with white lace ruffles – *perfect for this room;* she felt comforted having used it since she and Cindy redecorated their room as a prelude to their adolescence. Just a year ago she had sewn a new cover so the pillow was fresh enough to bring to college but old enough to represent home in her boarding house bedroom.

She hugged the feather-filled symbol of security before positioning it, propped against the wall, in the center of her bed. Her second priority – her photographs of her parents, her sisters, Ted, Gerald, and of course, Nancy – each neatly framed and ready for hanging – made her eyes well up. Through her homesickness, she perceived a sharp rap and gingerly stepped around boxes to her door; a plump, cherubic-faced girl about her age greeted her.

"Hello! I'm Marilyn. Welcome. I'm your neighbor – from just across the hall." The words trailed behind as the young woman burst into Robin's room. One glimpse of Robin's damp cheeks aroused Marilyn's maternal instincts. Her sentences gushed forth, "It's my second year. Where're you from? I'm from Akron." She glanced over at the stacked boxes and trunks, "How about I take out clothes and you put them in the wardrobe and drawers?"

"Oh, yes. That would be nice," Robin gratefully murmured.

Marilyn's efficient aid and incessant chatter left no room for sorrow. Robin had the impression that Marilyn babbled more than any person she'd ever met. Eventually the verbosity might grow tiresome, but at that moment the fast-flowing phrases distracted her from succumbing to homesickness. Marilyn plucked out items and handed them to Robin who located a proper spot for each; she filled the empty drawers with hankies, panties, stockings, corsets but saved the top one for her few pins and bracelets. Combs, lipsticks, powders and hairpins wound up there also.

"There's not much space." Marilyn hardly came up for air, "Better keep the towels and washcloths on the shelf in your wardrobe. And, here, this set can remain in your basin; thataway it'll be handy." Marilyn handed her the blue ones Robin's mother found among the family seconds stored for just such a day as a daughter setting up housekeeping.

Robin hung her dresses as her housemate's commentary continued, "Hey, this is sure a super shirtwaist!" Marilyn admired the pink dress with coral buttons and braid which Robin herself had trimmed. "Wear that tomorrow. You're pretty in it, I bet." Out came extra pairs of shoes from another box, "And these go on the floor. Thataway they won't waste your shelf space." When Marilyn pulled out the bed linens, the two made the narrow cot with the sheets embroidered with pink roses and laid the set with daffodils on the shelf.

Working together, Robin's possessions found homes quite quickly. Her new friend fastened each case or trunk when emptied and stacked them in the corner. With all unpacked, she balanced two cases on one arm, "The luggage is stored in the attic. Here, I'll take these; you grab as many as you can carry. We'll find a space for your stuff and then fetch the trunks on another trip."

Marilyn and Robin required three trips to stow so many containers in the attic. "Just in time," panted Marilyn, "Dinner's in fifteen minutes. Mrs. Brown serves at six sharp — have to wash up. Be back in ten."

And with that, Marilyn disappeared across the hall. Robin filled her basin with water from the hall bathroom's faucet and washed her face before brushing her hair and powdering. Gazing into the vanity's mirror she thought, "How distant my own dressing table!" Tears threatened to resume but she blinked hard to force them into submission. She slipped into her favorite rosy frock with its lacy accents and placed the matching bow in her hair.

During dinner, she found herself at a large round table in the dining area with seven other girls, plus their landlady. Mrs. Brown had a plump face, brown hair speckled with gray, and an apron embroidered with daisies girding her ample waist.

"Well now. We have four new girls this term. Shall we introduce ourselves? Let's go around the table and tell a bit about who we are."

"Oh! Pardon me." First we should say grace so we can eat while we talk. How about you, Marilyn, since you're an old hand in our dining room?"

"Thanks God for all these blessings. Help us this coming semester do our best. And thank you for our four new sisters. For Jesus' Sake and in His name. Amen." Okay, let's dig in girls," Marilyn wasn't one to linger in meditation at the end of a prayer.

After they'd eaten and cleared the dishes, Robin's vivacious housemate suggested the entire group tour the campus so the first-year students could locate the different buildings and not feel lost. Later, as they strolled toward their residence, they stopped at the coffee house bulging with reuniting students. Old comrades gave hugs, shoulder thumps or hand shakes. Clusters formed to share summer adventures. Marilyn joined several of her buddies from the previous year and introduced her first-year housemates. With everyone bubbly and congenial, Robin felt welcomed.

Curfew at Mrs. Brown's house was ten; by that hour, Robin, overwhelmed with a variety of novel scenes and strange people, craved the solitude of her room. She bid Marilyn good-night as the amiable chatterbox appended, "Breakfast's at seven. See you there. We'll proceed to registration right afterwards."

Shutting herself behind her bedroom door, Robin plopped on her bed to sort through the events of the momentous, lengthy day with Chelsea. "What did you think of Marilyn?"

"She'll be able to supply information we'll need for solving university related dilemmas. She's a fund of practical details." Chelsea portrayed herself sitting with crossed legs opposite Robin. "If I'd attempted to ferret out those pieces of information, it would have taken quite a while. She's already been a great help."

"But, she's so talkative – I can't think clearly with her prattle." Robin crossed her legs, picked up her big pillow and hugged it. "It's true. Her ramblings did keep me distracted from feeling so far away from home. But her verbal onslaught might be too much to handle in the future."

"Let's not predict difficulties before they occur," Chelsea warned.

"You're right. I must be careful not to avoid her without a reason. Even though she seems too intrusive, I may feel otherwise after I'm used to her."

Robin ran her finger over the pillow's scratchy tatting and recalled the hours spent choosing the remnants to fit exactly. As she studied the contours, she once again thanked God for allowing her to know Chelsea. *Could I survive this separation from Cindy without my ever present angel?*

Thinking of her twin produced fresh trickles; she brushed them away with her sleeve. "What did you think of Janie-Mae?" asked Robin. Heavy-set Janie-Mae, a second year student like Marilyn, barely spoke. "Do you think she's shy or that she doesn't like us?"

"Why are you asking*?"* The question apparently caught Chelsea by surprise – her response was uncharacteristically sharp.

"Well, uh, sometimes people shun others out of fear, hmm, other times from boredom, occasionally, I suppose, they take a disliking ..." and with that Robin spread her hands in a gesture connoting, "You understand, don't you?" With her thoughts being so muddled, Robin sought to clarify her feelings. "She acted pleasant enough; she told us her family lives in Mason, Georgia, and she aspires to a teaching career. She just seemed...uh, aloof."

"Janie-Mae didn't feel well; her head ached."

Robin had learned during her two years with Chelsea that an angel perceives much that humans can't; still she was flabbergasted. She stood and tiptoed to the closet to avoid making any noise that might disturb sleeping housemates. Her cheeks flushed; her hands trembled as she listened to Chelsea. Her prejudice shamed her.

Chelsea continued, "I wondered about her behavior so I checked for clues in her energy levels. I sensed the hint of pain. Then I observed her twist her neck and rub it as if to relax her muscles."

Robin never ceased to marvel at angelic awareness. When they first met, Chelsea, although unaccustomed to fluent communication with humans, strove to untangle her assessments in order to better explain her analyses. And, as a result, Robin's ability to decipher people had improved. Nevertheless she totally misread Janie-Mae. Maybe that reflected her own angst over leaving home.

Chelsea sympathized with her charge's discomfiture, "This milieu is utterly strange to you. You had to match unfamiliar names with faces and determine how to communicate with each individual. You couldn't be expected to figure out Janie-Mae's circumstances tonight. No human, without a long term acquaintance, would have." Chelsea broadcast an image of herself with her long brown tresses pulled back with a hair band that coordinated with her yellow dressing gown. She'd adopted Jodi's practice of inventing fashionable images and outfits for herself and delighted in assuming new appearances.

"Janie-Mae hid her discomfort well, apparently didn't want to bother anyone." The angel paused and pictured herself rubbing her nose. "She didn't realize how she would be perceived by not being open about her pain." Chelsea gazed into Robin's eyes, "I've always been amazed by how humans' attempts to keep their problems to themselves often lead to misunderstandings."

Chelsea grinned at Robin, "In a few days Janie-Mae might say 'Golly did I have a wicked headache after that day-long journey. I wonder if it came from that cloud of coal smoke the locomotive spewed into our car.'"

Chelsea was right; Robin, on the verge of chastising herself roundly for such insensitivity, backed off. "I am hard on myself, aren't I?" she tacitly mused as she picked a nightgown and robe off the hangers.

While Robin stepped out of her dress, Chelsea brought her out of her self-recrimination by switching the subject. "What did you think about Ginger?"

"Is she the returnee from last year with straight hair and large glasses?" Robin turned to where Chelsea projected herself and looked into her angel's green eyes for validation that they referred to the same girl. Robin removed her petticoat and pantaloons while Chelsea confirmed the housemate's identity.

"Her dress appeared so...uh..."

"Prim?" Chelsea completed Robin's thought with a grin.

"I guess that's what I'd call it. She seemed odder than anyone I've known." As Robin pondered, she extended her arms into her nightgown. Statue-still, she envisioned Ginger once again. "I couldn't decide if those sharp, angular features create her, uh, critical appearance?" Robin toyed for the appropriate way to express her disquietude. *There is something unusual about her – but what?* "At first when she said her field was home economics, I heard her say economics. That meshed with my impression of her. But, home economics? Somehow that doesn't jibe." Robin automatically examined herself in the full-length mirror. She couldn't quash her curiosity about whether or not Ginger ever looked as feminine as she herself did at this moment — decked out in her beribboned nightgown.

"She's the kind of person it's tough not to form a snap judgment about — and a negative one at that," Chelsea offered with a self-deprecatory smirk. "I sure have often enough, and frequently in error."

"Yes, I bet she's another we should wait a few days before categorizing."

Robin picked up her hairbrush and continued sorting the mental list of her new peers. "I did like Annie but she sure acts homesick." She saw the girl trembled at times. "She doesn't look old enough to be out of high school. She claimed she's dreamed of being a teacher since her earliest childhood, but with such timidity and loneliness...."

"We'll reach out to her." The angel's reaction would have differed radically a year or two earlier. This entire concept of observing and assisting humans other than the one assigned was weird. She could appreciate Jodi's questions about the universal regulations that she'd obeyed for centuries. By following them, she had maintained a high level of alertness and an intense focused awareness of her exclusive charge — but dropping the exclusivity to help other humans might be a better way.

Robin used slow long strokes with her brush penetrating into her scalp; the method Cindy taught her. "Chelsea, if I succor Annie, I'll probably assuage my own sadness."

"And Melanie, too, will need a friend," responded her angel.

The shy Melanie was another who barely spoke. Robin's heart went out to her. Her few soft remarks proved hard to hear. She confessed to Robin she hoped to be a poet. Her father insisted she matriculate; his daughters would be as educated as his sons. Melanie, the youngest, grew up quite sheltered. "Yes, and Melanie," Robin agreed.

"Boy, I envy Linda. She has it easy." Robin compared the exuberant, laughing woman who displayed no trace of homesickness. Robin had learned that Linda was long accustomed to boarding schools and being away from home. Her parents situated their home deep in the woods with no school nearby. A rather famous author, her father lived the life of a recluse. Linda's parents educated their children at home through eighth grade and thereafter boarded them out in the nearest city – some fifty miles away.

"Will I ever be as comfortable away from home as she is?" Robin mused. She laid her brush on the vanity shelf, climbed under her bed covers and blew out the lamp. But her mind refused to quiet. She clutched her pillow close to her face and wept into it. Despite Chelsea's comforting presence, loneliness overcame her. She reviewed the previous two years: her discovery of Chelsea, the beautiful wedding, fun confabs with the Crazy Eights, Cindy's pregnancy and then lovely, dear Nancy. "What a full life I've experienced regardless of the separation from Ted! Why do I feel such abandonment?"

Dreams that night ferried Robin to an ethereal world. She entered a celestial palace and, from there, a room like a library full of tomes. An angel with shimmering wings was stationed behind a mahogany desk. Robin approached her and requested her records. The angel presented her with a thick leather-bound volume and, as Robin leafed through it, her future unfolded. She would be a beloved teacher and would write children's books. Photographs depicted an older Robin surrounded by a multitude of unfamiliar gleeful children.

In the dream, a door opened and in floated another angel who glided toward her, saying, "Robin, you can realize fulfillment and contentment. You would serve others and grow yourself in knowledge and wisdom. Or you can opt for sorrow and weep for what you lack. Or you can have children of your own, a supportive husband, and a home. But if you choose the path of mother, your mate cannot be Ted. The choice is yours. Make it wisely." And the setting faded with the voice.

Robin discussed the dream with Chelsea in the early morning and her guardian angel advised her to write it out but not try to fully fathom its meaning. And that Robin did.

Then, she wrote a letter to her parents with a sequel to her twin detailing that first day away from home. She included the dream in Cindy's note where a splotch from a tear smeared the ink.

Chapter 7

"I'll miss you when you return to school next week. All these quiet evenings, relaxing together, are so far beyond mere sisterly chats. There's something, uh, some kind of feeling between us...." Cindy poked at her crochet, her brow creased in lines of confusion.

"Yes, it's like there's something intangible, uh, tangible...some kind of special tie?" Robin dropped the bonnet she was knitting for her newborn nephew's excursions into autumn winds; she looked out into the night sky.

The twins were swinging on the porch, relishing a few quiet moments together. The air was saturated with late summer fragrances of asters and zinnias. Nancy and her baby brother Ronny, named after his uncle who died so young, slept soundly in their bedrooms just overhead. Since the women would hear any whimper, they could relax without apprehension. Gerald was on the road that evening, seeking opinions of various men and women in neighboring communities for a series regarding the effects of Prohibition: the country was three years into its experiment with legislating morality.

"And it's different from the feeling between me and the children." Cindy jabbed her hook into the next row of the afghan. "The sense of a tie between me and Ronny is somewhat different from that I feel with Nancy but they're more similar to each other than the uh, knot?... bond? ...the two of us have. "

"It is a bond, isn't it? And when we're separated it's like ...uh, like," Robin studied a pair of eagles soaring together in the distance, "I'm sort of floating, not tied to the ground...."

"Or," Cindy held out the afghan inspecting the last few inches for any inadvertent holes, "like a hole in the crochet, an emptiness."

"Yes, a void that no amount of diversion can fill." Robin shuddered as she gulped in a deep breath. "Cindy, I'm rather relieved that Ted didn't think marriage possible with all his traveling. I'm not certain if I could've stayed happy, always on the road, away from you, even if with him."

Cindy reached over and laid a hand on her twin's wrist. "Gerald and I have a tangible link between us, but it's not like yours and mine. A husband can't fill the empty space created when you're away."

Robin grasped her sister's hand, "We've been together since conception; he only turned up at age six, much shorter togetherness," and both doubled over in suppressed chuckles to avoid waking the children.

The twins' conversation triggered Chelsea and Sam to telepathically exchange anecdotes. Chelsea described Robin's struggle being away from home and family even after her first-night's dream and decision to refuse to complain. Sam reminded Chelsea of her charge's sanguine personality which was rarely cowered into gloominess for long.

Sam tendered his conviction that their distance proved equally, if not more, distressful for Cindy who was entrenched in the commonplace, not distracted by a novel environment, new faces and an array of activities. He argued that the collegiate experience supplied a plethora of diversions to alleviate homesickness: the establishment of friendships with peers from diverse backgrounds and the acquisition of knowledge and skills.

Chelsea conceded that Robin's acquaintances supplied companionship, Mrs. Brown nurtured and listened as would her mother, and her homesick and timid housemates, Annie and Melanie, allowed her an opportunity to succor others. "But," Chelsea reminded Sam, "Cindy is surrounded by individuals providing the same services for her."

Neither Guardian won the debate that one charge had an easier separation than the other and the angels concluded that both twins suffered equally. As a result of the discussion, Chelsea made what was for her an uncharacteristic journey. One night after Robin fell asleep, she flew off to the Angelic Library, materialized on the landing of the floor containing references to human bondings and found the section on twins – she did keep a close psychic ear attuned to her sleeping charge.

The separation of twins was described in one book as a perennially delicate matter. Due to the intimate entwining from the moment of conception — even in fraternal twins like Cindy and Robin their psyches often became enmeshed. Speculation abounded about positive effects early separations might engender. For example, school populations that educate their children might increase in number to the point where twins could be in separate classrooms. Would that perhaps smooth their eventual partings?

During her research, Chelsea pondered her own bonding with various charges over the eons. The tie felt tangible even when she lacked a frank rapport with her human as she did with Robin. And, when her charge died, the void inside herself was never totally filled by the next neonate assigned to her. *Yes, there's a bonding between Guardian Angels and humans*, she mused, as she flew back to Robin's pillow and cherished the relief that permeated her, once again settled in close proximity with her human. *I felt like I stretched the link precariously thin while in the library. Is that how the twins feel when apart?*

When Robin graduated, summa cum laude, she returned home to meet another set of twins, Jill and Bobby. Cindy greeted the college graduate with an embrace and the half-joking whisper, "Thank You Father. Now I can stop bearing babies in an attempt to replace my absent twin."

Robin had decided to settle once again in her hometown: she'd had enough aloneness for a lifetime. The principal and school board members rejoiced on receiving her application for the third grade opening in the newly consolidated county school which would have a classroom for each grade. Many of the staff were acquainted with Robin and avidly promoted her merits to those who weren't. All who knew Robin loved her. And she earnestly desired to inspire a love of learning in each individual child who entered her room.

On a stroll with her mother during Easter vacation of her senior year, Robin elaborated on her goals for her students, her home, her life. Pointing out a "For Sale" sign, Bertha suggested they wander the premises since they had no particular destination. "What a perfect home," exclaimed Robin. "Look at this kitchen, Mom, see how the sun dances in those windows. "

"Isn't this a cozy sitting room?" remarked Bertha. "There's even a mantel over the fireplace. And what a nice study this second bedroom would make."

"Some day, Mom, I hope to have a home like this one. When the job begins, I plan to budget a down payment." But Robin didn't wait a few years. Her mother's choice of routes had been intentional; their daughter's delight in the charming dwelling convinced her parents of the appropriateness of the down payment as a graduation gift. Robin's congratulatory card from her parents contained the house keys.

Chelsea and Sam agreed that the separation had forced the individuation of their charges and each proudly bragged of their human's ability to locate the silver lining in seemingly negative experiences. During a confab following the graduation, Chelsea and Sam shared Chelsea's research into twin bonding. The twins discussed their own attempts to compare the gamut of human bondings. Chelsea spoke of her realizations regarding the tangible nature of angel-human liaisons.

Jodi mulled over this new mystery that Chelsea and Sam inadvertently contributed to the Crazy Eights' increasing awareness of Divine Mysteries. She questioned, "I wonder if a bond is involved with miraculous cures? Do you think a person can form a temporary bond for the purpose of healing?"

Meanwhile Gerald thought about Ted's comments on healing ministries, "Do you think the one who heals and who is healed need to be believers?"

Robin questioned, "Is there a special attachment between teacher and pupil that allows extraordinary achievement to occur?"

Gerald's speedy mind whirled around these questions and he started a series on human bondings including parent-child, siblings, twins and private bondings with God. He formulated a question to permit serious, but hypothetical, speculation on what it might be like to experience a conscious bond with one's guardian angel: If you and your guardian angel were good friends, what do you suppose your friendship would be like?

Mary Jane Caruso, the librarian, grinned and said, "Well, we'd discuss literature throughout the ages."

Johnny Jellico, the athletic coach, mused, "Guess I'd expect her to calm me down when I've the compulsion to punch an umpire." No response suggested an ability to envision long-term personal relationships involving every aspect of their day-to-day routines. Gerald suspected the concept was too foreign for those who didn't participate in conscious communication with such a celestial companion.

Cindy contrasted her bonding with Sam, with each of her individual children, with Robin and of course, with Gerald. Robin pondered her bond with each of her students. As a result of the general discussion, the group wrote to Ted who'd become a preacher on the evangelism circuit.

> Dear Crazy Eights,
>
> The situation is unfathomable. Here we have a bountiful and generous God Whom we preach to the nations. And yet there is sadness, loss, separation, isolation and death for His people as well as the heathen.
>
> I'm convinced He created the bond that exists in different human relationships. There has to be some type of energy involved that is most palpable when the two are in close proximity but exists even at distances. I've discovered I can feel each of you — even this distant from you. And there's a difference depending on which of you I'm sensing.
>
> Does bonding exist to promote socialization? Or is individuation to be encouraged? But yet, think about it: why then should a twin link exist if individuation of each person is the divine plan? What does the twin bond offer when so much pain is involved in the breaking? Why not simply have sibling ties?
>
> By the way, speaking of siblings, Jed and his family came to my revival in Tennessee last month. Can you visualize the foothills of the Smokies with the dogwood blossoms sprinkling white among the pines that cover the rising landscape — and in that paradise a Biblical revival with the music echoing off the hills? Even the birds sang with us I do believe. It was one of the most glorious events — so full of mysteries and miracles.
>
> Jed seemed impressed by the spirit of the group, more than a little different from our staid Methodist assemblies. I think the eloquence? — bravado? — of his kid brother also stunned him. He probably remembers digging us out of the cave.
>
> My six nieces and nephews got into the laughing and singing and had jolly good fun when everyone jumped up,

raised their arms and praised God. It's not possible that my oldest nephew, Ryan, is ten. The years certainly speed along. The children were privileged to discern God in a different light during the service. More like the kindly, but powerful, Father our angels taught us to revere.

We truly don't possess all the answers. I understand a variety of sects of extremely religious people dwell in the Orient. Some of them worship Buddha. I may journey to the East to seek answers. And in Egypt there supposedly exist many secrets for alleviating human misery. But, I doubt the bonding questions are resolved in that country either.

I'm constantly hearing about universal laws. For example, Christian tithing is based on a law of abundance, "That which you give, you receive." I'm learning that most religions teach a similar tenet. Could the Law of Abundance govern as completely as does the Law of Gravity.

Are twins some type of universal law? Is their bond to instruct others that such an intimate tie is reality? Or are they simply learning to individuate and teaching citizens around them about the process of being a unique individual with free will?

Seems too deep for me some days so I shelve the books and wander through the streets of whatever town I'm visiting. I observe the children to discover if there are differences in their treatment of each other between towns, the wives to determine if they function differently as they conduct their household chores and the beggars – but I perceive little difference in the basics — at least here in America. On the east coast, the west coast, and in the Midwest, people pretty much follow similar patterns of daily life with the major variances occurring between different levels of society.

I'll be in the area on the 17th. Will stop over to chat with whomever is around. Do hope we can schedule a Confab of the Crazy Eights while I'm in town.

Love, Ted and Miguel

No one would miss a Crazy Eight confab with its eight charter members together. One of the grandmothers was enlisted well in advance to watch the children so that the group could use Cindy's and Gerald's home. Late into the night they caught up on each others' activities, examined current concerns, and fantasized distant futures.

Instead of pulling apart because of their differing paths, the chums grew closer. The confabs, held at least quarterly, allowed the participants to broaden by partaking in the others' circumstances.

Cindy permitted each to vicariously enjoy motherhood. Robin brought in the path of a young educated woman with a career. Gerald escorted the group through a stable, traditional career and Ted – well, Ted offered them the world far beyond the reaches of their community. But the local residents in his or her individual way contributed an equally large adventure to share with their wanderer – and each empathized with and respected the others' trials and tribulations as well as joys and expectations.

And Jodi, Miguel, Chelsea and Sam diversified their understandings of their roles by sharing adventures. The angelic contingent was acquiring new insights into human-angel collaboration. The scope of their definitions of Guardian Angel had widened. None would be able to participate in future guardianships in the former rigid traditional way: a fact which caused general consternation for them. What would they do at the end of their current guardianship?

No human is ever the same after a set of experiences – if only subtly, individuals modify their paths a bit following fresh challenges. And so it seems, also, with angels.

PART III

Chapter 1

Jodi reviewed her work: the dark years were next to outline. *I can't do it in the library. I must have space.* The ancient remnants of human accomplishments drew her to Athens: wonders produced by men without intimate familiarity with their angels.

Jodi meandered the streets. She yearned for a brief respite from writing and watched a shaggy dog chase a squirrel, a mother amble to a market, children empty from a schoolhouse. She wandered with sunglass-wearing tourists from all over the globe through the Parthenon and wondered, *Ancient Athenians suffered through years of blackness, loneliness, bleakness, are such times an essential part of a human's experience on earth?*

She recalled the treatise, <u>Dark Night of the Soul</u>, in which St. John of the Cross had so eloquently recounted human despair. *Will angels be obliged to experience such negative phases if the human-angel bonding is reciprocal? Well, I sure did after all with Gerald.* Jodi took out her notebook and pencil from the bag slung over her shoulder, and, basking in the sun on a tourist bench, began to jot down notes.

Her mind reeled back to that day some fifty years ago when the first incident of the chain reaction occurred. A wisp of thought suggested the initiation of that cycle really could be traced to when she introduced herself to the four-year-old boy. How to vividly and concisely portray the whole series of events?

The particular day she must focus on occurred in late August. That warm morning with the sun shining brightly and the birds singing merrily, she lounged on a freshly-mown rise in the field. Endless rows of hay as yet unmown gently swayed in the breeze: the fragrance still lingered in her memory. The cacophonous roar of the tractor rose and fell as Gerald cut straight swaths through the field. In his wake were strewn hay stalks that, after drying in the sun, would be baled by other volunteers.

Gerald had offered to cut the hay after his next-door neighbor, Ralph, fractured his leg. When Ralph protested, not wanting to burden his journalist-friend, Gerald insisted. Typical of a farming community, men pitched in for the harvest: each did a share. Although Gerald loved the outdoors, his writing afforded few opportunities to devote an entire day close to nature. The hay had ripened; the weather was dry; this would be the weekend. Jodi couldn't tell whether the antsy Gerald could wait until Saturday so keen his desire to relive his boyhood farming adventures.

Finally the eagerly awaited morning dawned. Gerald had retrieved the community tractor the evening before from George Kenning and parked it in the driveway, behind his Model A coach purchased the previous summer. The vehicle had front and back seats so the entire family could travel together.

Right after dawn Gerald pulled on the faded blue coveralls that he'd bought a few years earlier when Don Gallagher was suffering from pleurisy. Since then they had been worn whenever he helped various neighbors or fished with his children or pals. A straw hat protected him from the fierce sun; he grinned as he reflected on his childhood tantrums to avoid such a similarly itchy hat.

The farmer-for-a-day dashed through the kitchen to grab a couple cinnamon rolls and a bottle of milk. "Want some bacon and eggs?" Cindy offered.

"No, honey, not today. Want to get started." Cindy smiled fondly. She'd predicted that he wouldn't want to waste the beauty of that glorious summer morning dawdling over breakfast. Still tall and wiry, he sported no middle-aged paunch and was as speedy and restless as she remembered him back in high school. She watched him jog outside and through the window saw him hop on the farm machine and poof, in a cloud of smoke, rev the motor. She chuckled as he began mowing the instant he'd crossed their grassy lawn and entered the hayfield; she resumed her baking. She'd make bread first, the pies for the next day's church social and last the cookies.

The tractor, recently purchased by farmers who pooled their money, had a power take-out. Gerald had written an article about the device that powers mechanical equipment such as the sharp blades of the mower that the tractor towed. He'd described how the device worked and warned of the serious injuries that had resulted when unwary farmers neglected to turn off the motor prior to working at the rear of the tractor.

Jodi checked on her charge. *Gerald's labored two or three hours*, she calculated, *cut about half the field – he'll stop for lunch any minute now*. Dust streaked his forehead from pushing strands of hair back underneath that hat. His unruly hair never did stay in place.

While Gerald, the proud master of the modern machine, dreamed of days gone by riding behind Blackie and Butterball, Jodi manipulated the fleecy clouds in and out of recognizable shapes. With the energy of her psyche, she deftly nudged a little here and tugged a bit there. The composition-in-progress depicted her favorite theme: human-angel relationships. A mixture of figures, some with wings, surrounded what could be perceived as a bonfire composed of a base of a dense formation with stick-like strips jutting out at odd angles; puffs of cloudy flames scrolled upward in the scene she created. *Maybe if I add more waves in the lake — will balance the distant hills on that far shore*, she mused.

A scream pierced the air and shattered the peace. Startled, Jodi whirled from her celestial canvas to witness the machine shredding Gerald's hand. Without first switching off the motor, he'd attempted to dislodge a stone at the rear of the tractor and his arm was caught. His paucity of familiarity with the newfangled equipment and his lack of circumspection had contributed to disaster.

Blood spurted: Gerald's face paled to a chalky white. The hay, the ground and the emerald green machine glistened with streaks and splashes of bright red from the crimson rain.

"Stop! Don't faint! Gerald!" Jodi attempted to bombard him into awareness with psychic stimuli. Deep in shock, he neither heard nor responded.

The angel endeavored to solidify herself to shut the thing off. But materialization was impossible. "It's my fault. I was absorbed in cloud sculpture. I neglected to remind him. He's not accustomed to such machinery. Oh, God, dear God, help! Please help!"

Johann from Special Forces interrupted her prayer by shutting off the power switch. "Jodi!" he scolded. "Not again! Can't you keep better track of him? You're responsible for preventing these accidents. You're in real trouble, Jodi."

Jodi ignored the acrimonious criticism; Gerald was her top priority. Her actions became those of a top-rate Special Forces angel. She ordered, in a no nonsense, take-charge fashion, "Press his artery; he's losing too much blood!" She sent a psychic message to fetch Cindy into the consciousness of Sport, the family collie. The dog dashed off toward the house, howling and barking. Cindy came running.

As she approached her husband, she spotted the tall stranger with his fingers clamped on Gerald's upper arm effectively staunching the jet of blood that struggled to burst from the severed artery below the elbow; she ripped off her apron. During her frantic dash across the fields, she tore off a tie. "Thank you," Cindy panted between gasps as she struggled to control her breathing. Looping the apron string around Gerald's arm, she tightened it to occlude the artery.

Johann released his grip; no blood squirted out. "You're in my prayers, Cindy."

The words of the Special Forces Angel reverberated through her soul as she murmured, "Thank you, thank you." Johann stepped back, observed her mood and behavior a moment; apparently assured she could assume Gerald's caretaking without Special Forces' assistance, he dematerialized.

Cindy busied herself stabilizing her unconscious husband. Sport's wild barking attracted their oldest two, Nancy and Ron. "Go get the wagon," she yelled as they sprinted toward their parents. Gerald had commenced mowing as he entered the acreage, so a clear path extended straight to their own neat lawn.

Ron, by then thirteen years, abruptly pivoted; his mother must plan to haul his father to the house with the brown wagon in the shed. But, spying their automobile, the boy detoured toward it instead. He drove back roads with his father beside him and was confident that he could steer over the hay-strewn field. As usual, the key was in the ignition.

Nancy continued on toward the scene; the horror of the situation sank in as she drew close – her father on the ground; her mother bending over him; blood spattered everywhere. For a second, *Is he dead?* flashed through her mind; she fiercely suppressed the terror. She refused to panic. *The twins – they mustn't see this* crossed her awareness; she turned and spotted them bolt from the door and rush toward the site, "Bobby, Jill, grab your bikes. Go find Doc. Tell him to come quickly." Nancy fully possessed her mother's common sense.

The scene was the substance for nightmares: her father ashen, albeit breathing weakly; his arm wrapped in her mother's blood-soaked apron. He'd lost a lot of blood. A spluttering sound behind them signaled the arrival of the Model A; with her mother Nancy straightened her father's crumpled form. Ron skidded the vehicle to a halt, jumped out, and pulled the front seat forward to access the back. Absolute horror mixed with a genuine pride for his speedy contribution.

Cindy positioned herself at the center of Gerald's body, "Nancy, support his legs; Ron, his head. When I count to three, we'll lift him. One. Two. Three." Ever the efficient mother, she organized the children's exertions effortlessly. "Now, Ron, climb into the car and scoot along on your knees. Yes, that's it." And so, the family transferred Gerald into the vehicle. "Nancy, sit next to Dad and keep his arm on his chest; he mustn't roll off the seat." Cindy barely paused for a breath; "Ron, you run ahead and look for big rocks, I'll drive back."

"Mom, the field's fine!" Ron broke off his fleeting protest when his mother shot him a glare that compelled instant obedience, and, sure enough, he spied a dangerous stone almost immediately. *How'd she predict it'd be there. I just missed it.* Chastened, he scouted vigilantly while the others rode behind.

Doc MacNamara's car spun into their yard pursued by a cloud of dust. The country doctor burst out the door, snatched his medical bag, and hurried as fast as his arthritic legs permitted. Nancy edged aside to give him access to her unconscious father. The doctor checked his pulse and the tourniquet.

Deeming the artery clamped adequately, he hunched back out of the car. "Okay, to extract him." Doc's elderly body no longer possessed sufficient strength. Cindy grasped her husband around the middle as Nancy supported his head and Ron his legs. "Move him toward Ron. Now, Ron, back up and you, Nancy, ease through the car. Don't let go! Not too fast there. Careful of the arm."

Beads of sweat glistened on her brow as she issued orders while creeping along the floor of the car on her knees. Ron understood why she'd requested the cart – lifting his father in and out of that would have been a cinch. His cheeks reddened as his pride vanished; the automobile hadn't been the wisest choice.

Mick Johnson and Darrell Morris had dashed for the Daniels' place when they heard Doc's car backfire. Mick lifted Gerald by the shoulders and cradled the unconscious man's head in the crook of his arm; Darrell grabbed the hips and upper legs. With Ron supporting his father's feet, they maneuvered the unconscious man into the kitchen and positioned him on the table which Nancy and Cindy had rushed ahead to clear and cover with a sheet.

There Doc cleaned and dressed the stump of Gerald's left arm severed just below the elbow. Pastor Drake, notified by parishioners who had witnessed the sobbing twins biking home, arrived in the kitchen and prayed silently.

When her younger children flung themselves through the doorway, their mother cornered them. "Jill, Bobby, come, we'll fix the bed." Cindy bustled them through the kitchen quickly which permitted only the briefest glimpse of Doc stitching Gerald's arm. That activity cheered them: at least their father was alive. In the bedroom, their mother kept the pair busy smoothing out a rubber sheet against the mattress and adding sheets and blankets.

Their two neighbors slid the center leaf from the dining room table beneath Gerald's body to form a stretcher and carried him upstairs into the bedroom which soon smelled of the familiar and somehow comforting medicinal odors that always accompanied Doc's visits. The curtains were drawn together; the room was dim and quiet. Cindy sat beside the bed on a straight-backed wicker chair, gripped Gerald's wrist and prayed softly.

Jodi, perched on the foot of the bed, marveled at Cindy's tranquility and once more appreciated her charge's spouse. Jodi knew that Gerald's wife, who normally curbed anxiety with relentless practical tasks, was forcing herself to maintain a calm vigil. The angel realized that Cindy hoped her serenity would help her husband, somehow, as his body struggled to overcome the shock and compensate for the blood loss. Jodi, who prayed with Cindy, tried to slake her own nerves as completely as the human seemed capable of doing.

Meanwhile in the kitchen, Ron, humbled by his earlier miscalculations and weighted down with apprehension about his father, slouched against the counter; his hands thrust deep in his pockets. The strong, typically self-confident, teenage star of the sandlot softball team, wore no shirt or shoes in that day's summer heat. Although he had his mother's dark brown hair, it curled like his father's and sported an identical lock that incessantly slipped awry.

Before operating, Ron had keenly observed Doc roll up his starched shirt sleeves to above the elbows and vigorously scrub his hands and forearms at the kitchen sink. The green elastic suspenders, revealed when the elderly man removed his coat, was an anomaly that fascinated the lad. Doctor MacNamara, in the tradition of his profession, was typically clad in a black hat and coat, with a stethoscope dangling from the pocket: "my uniform" as Doc called his outfit.

When he completed the suturing, the physician returned to the sink to meticulously cleanse his instruments with the wire brush he drew from his bag. Spellbound by their doctor's thoroughness, Ron examined the man's reddened hands vigorously brushing and re-brushing.

Although a former athlete, everything about Doc grew comfortably round as he aged—worn trousers covered his ample belly. The doctor's eyes most attracted Ron's attention: depending on the occasion, they twinkled with joy, radiated genial empathy, or teared with sympathy. Ron thought that one day he might be a doctor like Doc MacNamara.

At the opposite end of the kitchen, Nancy brewed tea for Doc and Pastor. *Why is she setting out a plate of peanut butter cookies?* Ron frowned, bewildered by his older sister. *How can anyone be hungry? Dad could be dying.*

During the surgery, while Ron watched their doctor clean and suture the wound, Nancy baked the dough their mother had been mixing when Scout barked. A strong healthy girl, sturdily built, she often helped in the kitchen or around the house. Even under the stress, she'd remembered to pull on an apron and secure her bob with a band which permitted no stray hairs an escape. Always clean and careful, practical in her dress and movements – she mirrored her mother. Ron couldn't fathom how Nancy serenely cleaned up the kitchen and prepared tea and cookies with milk for the youngsters. He was oblivious to how ordinary tasks aided his mother and his sister to cope with fear.

Another incomprehensible achievement to Ron was his sister's management of their siblings; she so easily kept them busy and out of trouble. Jill, in her cotton playsuit, was plopped on the porch swing shelling peas for supper, and Bobby, with his brown curls falling across his forehead, shucked corn. Whenever Ron tried to keep the twins settled and out of the way, they refused to cooperate. Ron admired Nancy's ability, and envied her, too.

A bubble of anxiety rose in his throat; he pushed away from the counter. "Doc? Will he be okay?" His voice broke the somber stillness of the room. His siblings, alert for any nuances, intently studied their physician's demeanor.

"I believe so, Ron, if an infection doesn't set in. He didn't lose too much blood." Doc's words sounded firm and knowing.

Through the tedious afternoon his father's blood pressure hovered low—in the 80's — according to the bedside log that Ron continually consulted. The journal contained notations of the doses of morphine Doc administered, as well as the temperature readings; the pulse rate hovered near 110 because of the blood loss the genial old man explained. Ron glanced at their doctor questioningly when asked to fetch some boards from the shed and push them under the foot of the bed while the adults lifted the bed. Their medic described how gravity would facilitate blood flow to his father's brain. The physician frequently examined his patient and administered shots of morphine when his father moaned and became restless. Doc told the family he had to be careful not to sedate Gerald too much what with the blood loss and lowered blood pressure. Ron nodded with an anxious frown and partially understood.

The red and gold quilt his mother finished before Nancy's birth fourteen years ago covered his father. The blanket didn't seem that old; whatever mom sewed lasted. Her words, "If you intend to spend valuable hours on a project, don't employ slipshod techniques," were indelibly written into his brain. The four poster bed on which dad lay once belonged to Ron's great-grandparents. Mother said it exemplified the endurance of careful craftsmanship. The curtains with their crimson sashes matched the bedspread. But his pale father contrasted starkly against the red. Ron tensed from the fear generated in him each time he looked at the pallor of his beloved father as he slept under narcotic tranquility.

Grandma Sue and Grandpa Dan appeared shortly after the surgery having heard the news broadcast through town. Unobtrusively his grandmother and aunts assisted nursing his father, preparing supper and monitoring the twins. His grandfather retrieved the tractor, cleaned the equipment and finished the haying.

Ron, impressed by how the adults continued routine activities and took the episode in stride, couldn't pull himself away from his father's bedside. Nor could he convince himself to assist his grandfather. He felt compelled to stay nearby as if his presence might somehow facilitate his father's survival. By nightfall, Gerald rallied; Doc deemed him safely past the crisis. In the evening, the invalid sipped soup from the spoon Ron's grandmother Sue held.

Their physician declared he could leave, but promised to return in the morning. Aunt Robin collected the twins and an overnight bag. Gerald's parents slept that night in the former nursery long since converted into a guest room. Ron snatched a pillow and blanket and curled in the corner, his recuperating father within sight. The adults sensed his need and none questioned it.

Fifty years after the accident, Jodi paced around the Parthenon, her cheeks fiery with shame. The ancient structures could not distract her as her memory replayed the supervisory reprimand that followed that horrific day. Jeff had issued the anticipated summons as soon as Gerald was stabilized and sleeping soundly. Together, supervisor and trainee, flew into the woods behind the house. The second floor window with its curtains pulled back to admit the fresh night air was in view. A single light glowed from beside the bed where Cindy held vigil.

Hours earlier Jodi had switched from her day-in-the-sun outfit to somber woolens; a bronze cross encircled her neck. Fifty years later Jodi realized that, at the time, unconsciously she'd been doing penance through clothing selection to rid herself of some of her guilt. The more seasoned angel came close to a laugh as she acquired insight into that suppressed motivation, but shivered as her supervisor's words resonated in her head again.

"Jodi," Jeff rebuked. "He's impulsive; constant monitoring is vital. You must never allow your focus to wander." Jeff, who had dressed in his tan supervisory robes resembled an eighteenth-century friar as he clasped the cross dangling from his neck.

Jodi ducked her head. *Why did her attention stray? What was wrong with her?* She clenched and released her fists, then clutched at her skirts.

"I've been thinking, what about a relief? You've been at this thirty-five years now. How about reentering Special Forces?" Jeff's abrupt, stern voice and his black eyes bore through her.

The trembling fingers of one hand leapt to her cross; her other reached out as she turned toward him and pleaded desperately, "Oh, no! Please not that! Surely that isn't the answer. You can't separate us. Please, please, Jeff." Her nails brushed his sleeve until she became aware of the impudence; she immediately thrust the offending hand into its pocket. Barely able to stand, Jodi implored, "Please let me continue!"

"How many times, Jodi? Different assignments utilize different talents. You're remarkably capable at solving crises of the type presented to the Special Forces Division, quick in and out emergencies, but this guardianship job mandates unrelenting alertness. Your mind tends to charge off in a hundred directions." His accusations resounded, kind but firm. What should be his course of action? If only she'd request a replacement! But, no, not his headstrong trainee; she would never apply for a change of assignment.

Although Jodi realized that her negligence warranted dismissal, she beseeched him, "Please don't banish me, Jeff." Again, unthinkingly, her impulse ridden fingers extended to grasp his sleeve but she yanked them back.

"Jodi, your vigilance is crucial. Gerald's human; he can die; he has destined tasks to accomplish." Jeff's words were seconded by the hoot of a nearby owl. "His children are to grow up with their dad alive. Gerald has much more to teach them. He listens to you, to God. He talks with God." Jeff's hand pushed back his hair and their eyes locked.

"Gerald must pass along his ability to communicate with God to his progeny." A pack of wolves howled in the distance; a nearby cat pounced on a mole; scents of the newly mown hay filled the air. Jodi drank in these normal sights, sounds and smells of her familiar environment that couldn't supplant her sense of shame.

"Ron should learn so that the daughter he will sire, Carol, will teach her daughter, Jean, who will be the mother of a saint." Jodi was distracted by the owl stalking a rodent then diving to ensnare it. "Saint Ron, named after his great-grandfather, Gerald's son, will heal many of a dread disease. If Gerald completes his fated lifespan, the process is simplified since he will participate in training his granddaughter and great-granddaughter to walk with God." Jeff turned aside and looked at an abandoned nest. "Don't you see Jodi? Of course, there are contingency plans but if your charge manages to survive the duration of his allotted years. Jodi? Sometimes... sometimes, Jodi, I've wondered if you possess the same attention deficit as Gerald does."

On and on Jeff lectured. Jodi started to think him a bit unfair. Didn't he appreciate how difficult it was and how hard she'd worked to keep Gerald alive? Suddenly Jodi noticed silence: Jeff's lecture had ended. She only caught his final question, "Do you understand, Jodi?" She nodded but, despite her promise to concentrate more, she'd missed much of what Jeff had said. Furious with herself she realized that she'd failed to keep herself focused — precisely what the lecture railed against.

That night, beside Gerald's bed, Jodi prayed with Cindy and Sam for his recovery. As he slumbered, Jodi noticed his lips and fingernails regain a faint degree of pinkness, an optimistic sign, yet it would require weeks for his normal color to return. Jodi each day vowed fervently to never again lose vigilance. While contemplating Jeff's admonishment, Jodi wondered if other trainees needed dressings down from their supervisors like she did from Jeff.

Chapter 2

Jodi doodled in the margin of her notes; relived guilt and inadequacy flooded her spirit. Up until the accident life had seemed complete: Gerald's career, his happy marriage, their children's development, the Crazy Eights, Ted's sporadic visits, and Robin's teaching and book-writing. But after the amputation Jodi's reality upended.

She remembered how Gerald, during his recuperation, slumped in the front porch swing and gazed into the woods and fields. His expressions varied from a pensive frown, to a scowl, or a fleeting wry grin, but mostly Jodi observed an increasingly hardened set to his jaw. His right hand rubbed stiff muscles in his neck; his left followed suit which meant a miniscule movement of the stump upwards. When he pulled out of his deep contemplation and recognized the disparity between thought and reality, he angrily shook his torso and dropped both shoulders. The convalescent shielded his inner quagmire against angelic penetration and seldom permitted Jodi telepathic entrance into his reveries.

But, one late September day, Gerald did open his thoughts to his Guardian Angel while he studied the birds which had flocked to the field of mown hay for their flight south. He sipped his tea as he listened to their calls and watched other avian formations already on the move from farther north that passed overhead.

He reached for a biscuit and nibbled a corner, "My days are charmed, like those birds. There's a seasonal, annual rhythm." He glanced at the cardinal pair who would stay behind, eating from the feeder; their summer's offspring had flown off. "I'm blessed with a marvelous wife and children who are healthy and maturing splendidly. I've a successful career; people like me and value my opinion. I doubt I could have achieved any of that without my angel's constant guidance." His thumb traced the rim of his teacup. "You've been a miracle."

He squeezed his cup with such force Jodi feared it might break. On the verge of crying out, she prudently subdued her impulse. In this mood, he'd never tolerate an extra reminder of his dependence on her.

"I'm of the opinion..." his eyes fixed on his fingers as they enclosed the cup; he paused. Jodi prayed he wouldn't again submerge into himself. She sat tensely quiet.

"I'm of the opinion," Gerald repeated, "that a man my age should guide himself – oh, with help from God, of course – but, oh — you know what I mean...."

"What do you mean?" Jodi interjected; she was surprised and dismayed. To her, Gerald functioned as one of the more competent of their acquaintances.

"I have assumed no personal responsibility – none." His harsh staccato tones pierced the scene. "I'm impulsive. I don't reason out solutions. I perennially rely on you. This time I lost my arm. What will happen next?" Abruptly he glared toward her image, "And, no more apologies for not paying attention! I'm thirty-three: that's not a child. I demand to be held accountable for this predicament."

He stood and strode across the porch leaning slightly to the right. "Time and again I'm distracted, but I rarely suffer consequences because of your interventions, Jodi. Other people develop checks and balances — not me. When I was a child, I blithely meandered into danger without a care in the world. Now, I still act like a careless and carefree child. My behavior is inexcusable."

As he soliloquized, his words were emphasized with animated gestures; those produced on the left caused his stump to jerk. Histrionically he traversed the porch, as if on stage. Anger surged. He thumped heavily down the porch stairs, stomped across the lawn and smashed his fist into the trunk of the old oak; he glowered at the reddened area. He examined his hand on one side and the opposing empty space. His unconscious urge to rub the bruise and relieve the sting didn't register. Instead, the hollow left sleeve refreshed the tumult of emotions – grief, rage, loss.

Jodi breathed slowly, deeply, to control her agitation; she could find no words to assuage him. For all her training by Jeff and in her pre-guardian class, no one prepared her for this. The car engine heralded Cindy's arrival home from the grocery; Jodi heard the woman carry packages in through the front door. *Maybe she can calm him.*

On hearing her husband's angry shouts, Cindy rushed out the screen door. It banged — a crime for which she often chided the children. "Honey, what's happening?" She interrupted his tirade by grasping his shoulder. Irritably he shrugged her off. A wave of distress washed over her; she clutched her skirt. Backing off a few steps, she pleaded, "Don't reject me, Ger, please!"

Cindy, unaccustomed to such disturbed behavior, bit her lip. Usually Gerald, the unperturbed husband and father, handled crises with competent ingenuity. She cast through possible explanations for his rant. *Is it the pressure of article deadlines while still recuperating? Has a late infection set in? Did I do something to upset him? Did one of the children?*

She glanced toward Jodi who portrayed herself on the picnic bench. The angel's face wrinkled in frustration and she shrugged. Cindy turned back to Gerald; her eyes penetrated into his, cutting through the glassy fury; his eyes immediately dropped, unable to meet hers. A rueful smile pulled at the corners of his lips. "Cindy, maybe I'm being dramatic but admit that I'm a failure. I've been thoroughly reviewing my inadequacy as your husband — can you visualize a more atrocious role model for your children?" Apparently he discerned the absurdity of the depth of his disparagement for he peeked toward her sheepishly. "Honey, seriously, I'm defective. I don't look before leaping. I'm continually protected. I'm only partially a responsible person!"

"What are you babbling about?" As Jodi had anticipated, Cindy refused to concur with his self-appraisal: Gerald was talented, respected, and loving. Jodi fervently hoped Cindy could assist him to own up to his silliness.

As Jodi listened, Gerald outlined his perceived failings. However, his wife repudiated the dialectic. "What's the harm in your dependence on Jodi? Your life is worthwhile; you contribute to your community. Tell me why it's wrong to count on your angel."

Cindy tromped over to the rose trellis and snapped off a dried flower from one of the vines. She wandered over to an errant weed adjacent to a daisy. Although she gently tugged, the stem snapped. She disgustedly flung it down into the grass.

"Sweetheart, it's my inner development that's stunted." Gerald approached her. Though not impervious to her need for release of her own nervous energy, he craved that eye contact he moments ago had shunned.

"Remember two years back when Ron and his buddies raced their bikes down the back lane. He didn't spot the rock, flipped off his bicycle, was thrown into the roadside thorn bushes. All scratched and bruised, he vowed to take more care in the future – and he did. He's had other potential catastrophes — like his neglect to trail blaze when spelunking with Tim last September. Since that episode he's acted more prudently. But me? After Ted and I were rescued from the cave, we didn't function more wisely. I knew that ever-present Jodi protected me. My thirteen-year-old son is more circumspect than his thirty-three year old father."

"But, Ger," Cindy managed to break into his monologue on her third try. "You're forgetting the two of you have different personalities. Ron's cautious like me. I doubt you'd be much different with or without Jodi. You're much more like Bobby. You and he would tie in an impulsivity contest. In fact, I often think we erred when we decided not to pray for him to know his angel. He deserves the same support as you've had." This time she caught his eyes to ensure he understood. She did wish she could persuade him to concede for Bobby's sake.

Gerald disagreed. He released her arm and marched to the rose arbor where he twined a recalcitrant vine into the lattice. "No, Cindy — it's different." His expression appealed for her to acquiesce. "It is. Bobby does pause before he leaps, at least a lot more than I did at his age. Probably more often than I do as an adult and he's only ten."

Abruptly he switched to the declaratory tone he used in public speeches to sway an audience to support his position. "You judge my assessment inaccurate. Tell me then, why did we elect not to teach our children about their angels? Why is it we did not petition for their angels to meet them? What are the reasons we didn't deem it wise to inform them?"

Cindy was baffled and stalled to mull over the queries by proposing, "Let me brew more tea." On her return, while she poured and added sugar, she burst out, "Oh, Honey! I've never been sure of our decision. I question it most strongly in Bobby's case – but, for all our children – their lives could be much richer." Without pause, she tacked on, "I want a cookie." And she popped back in the house.

Gerald, accustomed to his wife's method of backing off to cogitate, watched the screen door bang as she stamped into the house. He resumed pacing the lawn; his agitation steadily increased. "Maybe a stroll by the river," Jodi suggested. But he would accept none of her interference. "No! That's precisely what I don't need: your advising me on my activities. No, I'll mosey along to my study and fiddle with my current article — that's all I'm capable of on my own — writing to instruct genuinely responsible people how to become more competent. My efforts haven't contributed one iota to increasing my personal responsibility and I'm the supposed expert who feeds the public recommendations."

Jerking his chair to his desk, he lowered himself into it, positioned paper in front of him and grabbed one of the pencils from the bronze trophy which served as a container. Another tribute to his professional advancement, the inscription spelled out his name, followed by the title, Syndicated Columnist. His efforts to secure the paper with his stump caused him to lean at an awkward angle; a throb shot through the healing limb which aggravated him further. Scanning the room, he spied his thick dictionary and positioned it on the paper's edge. When he rested his stump on the book, he wound up with a suitable posture. It was tough for Jodi to refrain from pointing out that she had not recommended that solution to a real problem.

Rather than writing, however, Gerald continued to obsess on his weaknesses. *Jodi deserves the credit for my so-called success. I'm less than a man.* He slapped the surface of his desk and stabbed his pencil over and over into the page in front of him until it was riddled with blackish holes and the lead snapped. He couldn't write a dozen paragraphs about real people achieving their goals: *I don't even know how a real person functions.* He recognized the harsh exaggerations in his self-vilification, but he yearned to act less erratically.

Jodi felt frustrated. *Ger's partially correct, yet... What's so wrong with humans relying on their angels?* "Ger, please – reflect on the beneficial in our partnership," she implored. She transmitted a picture of herself seated in the chair opposite him: supplicant, not authority.

Gerald refused to acknowledge the words that could resume the debate. After all, this was his suffering. "How in the world can you predict who I'm meant to be? I'm the first human you've guarded!" He reread Ted's response to his request for advice.

Dear Ger,

Interesting questions you pose. Pondered that subject myself —then decided it ridiculous to speculate on life without Miguel. That's a life in which I didn't participate: I'm leading this one.

I've accepted my existence as it is and refuse to worry about what it's not. Strongly urge you do the same. Where's the benefit of asking, 'What if....'

I've been delving deeply into Eastern traditions. Guess I'm considered somewhat of an expert on the varieties of spiritual phenomena. Been lecturing at a few universities.

Honestly, Old Bud, I'm not competent enough to be considered an "authority." I've only studied their literature — what others witnessed. I chatted with one of the professors in whose class I presented my conclusions. Yes, my book expertise impressed him and he pressured me to accept his university's offer to teach in their Comparative Religion's department. In fact, I'm being solicited by several university recruiters.

But how can I consider myself qualified without personal experience. Sort of an armchair philosopher – not sure I fit that image. As we debated various theories, sitting in two oversized armchairs in his comfortable office, warmed by a pleasant fire, I recognized I must acquire firsthand knowledge before I can justify that type of lifestyle – the one of professor I mean.

So I've determined to travel through India during the next few years and endeavor to comprehend the yogis. I've read Merton's descriptions, as well as Brunton's, on Eastern concepts. I'll submit my findings for your analysis before publishing them. Then, when I'm back in the states, I'll accept one of the university appointments and humbly propose to my childhood sweetheart who's been waiting so patiently. Heh, heh. Can you envision me – settled in one locality, married. I intuit Cindy saying, "About time." Please don't share this with Robin. What if I don't return? Don't get her hopes up.

My advice old buddy: Stop fretting about who you'd be without Jodi and proceed with your life as it is.

Love, your oldest buddy, Ted
And your second longest, Miguel
(After all, Jodi's a girl!)

Ted's letter didn't sway Gerald: he'd never achieve that complacent acceptance. And, Ted's compulsion to personally verify his library research added ammunition to Gerald's formulating plan.

Finally one October night, as he lay awake, troubled by the phantom pain from his missing arm, Gerald reached a decision. He quietly climbed out of bed and tiptoed out of the room, then strode resolutely toward the front door. His pajama sleeve flapped in the breeze as he marched purposefully across the porch in his bare feet, down the steps and over to the giant oak. Once there he turned and unconsciously imitated the strength of the mighty tree in his stance: back straight, head erect, he stared out into the infinite night sky. "Jodi, I demand you leave me." His voice resounded firm, measured, insistent.

"W-what are you s-saying?" She portrayed herself running her fingers through her hair; her brow creased as she grappled with his order.

"1 demand my independence. I'm determined to play the role of real human for a change. You must abandon me; I *will* learn to function on my own." Apprehension permeated his resolve as evidenced by the beads of sweat that dripped off his forehead. Simultaneously he discerned within himself a sublime certainty regarding the wisdom of his judgment and an excitement stirred his emotions. What trials would the future bring for him to face alone?

"B-But, Ger. All humans are guarded by angels. Please don't force me to disappear." His ears deafened to her entreaties; he willed himself not to concede.

"Of necessity I'll be laboring to develop skills I've never required. But you have to be elsewhere if I'm to become proficient as an independent individual."

"Ger, I've been assigned to you – please, don't banish me." Her image sprang into his awareness as she thrust her whole self toward him. Her hands stretched out in pleading gesture; she wore her trainee shift to convey an ultimate humility.

Her persistence only enraged him, "Why can't you just go!" He stormed away from the tree toward the picnic table and plopped down on its bench. He scanned the edge of the woods, at a world of perpetual nighttime – the darkness into which he resolved to venture alone. "I need to become a complete man: able to handle emergencies, figure out crises, and maintain vigilance." He whirled around, muscles taunt, voice anguished.

"Can't you see, Jodi? It's imperative. I demand to talk with your supervisor." As his voice grew more decisive, the words were brusque.

"I'll consult him." And the dejected angel vanished.

Jodi's arrival startled Jeff. "Why are you here, Jodi," he barked. His critical tone shifted to gentle concern when he witnessed her drooped shoulders and forlorn face. "What is it, Jodi? What's wrong?"

"Please, Jeff. Convince Gerald that I should remain with him. He's of the opinion he's an incomplete human because of our partnership. Please speak with him — he asked for a meeting with my supervisor. He wants me t-to leave."

"Well, he has free will – humans do — and that includes the right to dismiss you if he chooses." Jeff's warning was mitigated with empathy for his trainee's desolation. "But, I'll debate his arguments with him."

A couple hours later, Gerald slipped into a fitful sleep, excited but yet fearful of his momentous decision. Jeff left his current project which involved both the supervision of guardians of homeless orphans in India and the gathering of statistics on the best methods of helping parentless children. The goal was to determine what approaches achieved the most enduring results in that forsaken population: Guardian researchers were eager for some actual numbers to process. Although absorbed by the implementation of current experiments, he responded to Jodi's request and flew to the opposite side of the globe. Entering Gerald's dream, he greeted, "Hello, Gerald, I'm Jeff, Jodi's supervisor. How can I be of service?"

"Give her a different assignment. Don't misunderstand. She's wonderful. I love her – she's a valued companion. But my independence from her is a requisite to my overcoming my deficits. I guess...uh, she's too resourceful – I, er, haven't developed survival skills with her superhuman assistance."

"Did you thoroughly consider the ramifications, Gerald? Are you confident this is what you desire?" But Jodi's supervisor, as he formed the question, recollected his prophesy from some three decades back. He realized the prediction was coming to completion and he could change little.

"Very definitely! How can I develop each part of me when my angel's continuously on the scene to save the day?"

"So how much harm is there in collaboration? Together you are assuredly accomplishing much: the audience for "What America Is Thinking" gains inspiration and empathy with each column. Your family thrives and your community adores you."

"I'm blessed: there's much for which to give thanks. But what am I deep down inside? Only a distractible child!"

"Gerald, as you are aware, you were born with deficits in your concentration that contribute to your impulsivity. Those difficulties are unrelated to Jodi."

"But because of her I'm not overcoming them. Reassign her, Jeff, and furthermore I demand there be no replacement." Gerald's tone left no room for compromise.

"As you request, Gerald, Jodi will be reassigned and no guardian will take her place. You possess a free will and a right to exercise it. But do you realize you will be the only person on the planet without a guardian?"

"Yes, a bit grandiose. But I must do this. I'm compelled."

Jeff had no other choice. The decades old prophesy had been fulfilled. Nevertheless, the supervisor was saddened: who enjoys being proven right in such disconcerting circumstances?

Jodi was dispatched to Special Forces. Gerald was left unguarded.

Chapter 3

Jodi wondered if any other humans in history had elected to proceed without the aid of a Guardian Angel. She expected that this potential consequence of reciprocal relationships would be a topic of intense debate during the Angelic Council. And she was slated to address the august body in only a few days. Leaving Athens, she rematerialized in the library research area and strode to the index files where she flipped through cards seeking any pertinent reference.

Umm, probably nothing in these volumes on How to Guard...would there be something in Guardian Socializations with other Angels...probably not ... yes, here...this section on Guardian and Human Pairings...here's a subsection on Human/Angel Relationships...subgrouping on mystics...oh...one on saints...here a section on ordinary people....not much in this section....hey, here's a reference... Life without angels.... Section VII...B...3...a. That's this floor but where...?

Jodi rotated to check the aisle markers and sighted the B's, then hunted out 3 and finally reached the row marked VIIB3a. She scanned titles that covered the millennia of human existence under the guardianship of angels. There — that one – she pulled off the shelf a thin volume which contained the musings of an angelic philosopher, Ima Misanthrope; she flicked through the pages until the following passage caught her attention:

> Humans are such an unaware, yet independent, species that to successfully guard the creatures would necessitate artificial habitats similar to the zoological parks in their cities. Their young especially, but also a sizable portion of the more physically mature, constantly plunge pell-mell into crises while pursuing their fancies. The assigned angel can't possibly provide true safety using simple psychic nudges — an impossible mission, my fellow guardians. Even the mystics who quiet their minds enough to hear — seldom listen.

Jodi chuckled, *Yes, know exactly what you mean, Ima.* How to crash through the distractions persisted as a challenge though Gerald knew her voice well. Anxiety, fear and simple refusal could prove impenetrable barricades to psychic hints. She randomly flipped to another page:

> What if angels abandon humans? Would it pose a problem – even make much of a difference with this recalcitrant mob? Oh, reader, don't tremble so – meditate on the implications of such an experiment. Of course, one problem would be my unemployment! Now how would I spend my years if not guarding those characters? Probably be obliged to write more rubbish like this.

Laughing quietly, Jodi remembered her despondency after Gerald rejected her. *We angels do require humans as much as humans require us. The charge gives a purpose, a sense of usefulness, even a joie de vivre.* Skimming Ima's pages as she strolled toward her cubby, she read,

> What effect would this have on the humans? Probably little... they tend to listen so poorly. Yes, perchance a few more lost souls ... not winding their way to our Lord. And, more accidents, perhaps, would lead to a few more premature deaths. But, seriously, wouldn't we, Guardians, minus our mission, feel more bereft than humans would without their angels? Ponder this, my reader, while I catch a forty-year snooze.

Jodi giggled as she imagined Miss Misanthrope settling in for a four decade nap while the realm of angels wrangled with these outrageous concepts. *Who did write this? Didn't dream many guardians had a sense of humor – maybe someone was frustrated with a particularly recalcitrant human. Or maybe a light-hearted angel was poking fun at our seriousness. But does her book have ideas for my presentation?*

After Jodi had analyzed the bleak period of separation thoroughly would she feel obliged to concur with her more tradition-bound peers? Their reservations about the potential negative implications of her unusual guardianship methods deserved consideration. Yet, just maybe, her novel techniques with Gerald supplemented the overall armamentarium available for angel-human encounters. Her own discoveries certainly overcame several of Ima Misanthrope's laments on the difficulties inherent in communication with humans.

Jodi hunkered down for serious recollecting and note-taking. She had to assemble Gerald's trials and accomplishments from second-hand reports. She'd be as accurate as she could and at least recalled vividly the stories she'd been told of his first few days.

The morning after Jodi's departure, Gerald awoke to an ineffable difference in the room; it took a moment to recognize the angel's absence. Every day since he was four, a cheery "Good morning, Ger," and a brief report on the rain, snow or sunshine greeted his opening eyes. The utter silence that morning provided a first clue of the void he'd created.

The dream — his decision – popped into his brain. Despite how necessary and appropriate the choice, he couldn't squash the lump in his throat and the nervousness that percolated inside. His heart raced; his stomach churned; his throat ached. Throwing off the quilt, he crawled out of bed and struggled to the window to take in the late October vista with its bright sky. The scents of coffee and freshly baked cinnamon buns wafted up from the kitchen.

He dressed quickly in sweat pants and shirt and sneaked out of the house without breakfast – not yet ready to defend his resolution to banish Jodi. And the indoors felt too depressing without the sanguine Jodi brightening the ambience. His steps took him in the direction of the riverbank: another first, a hike without Jodi. At the sight of two deer drinking at the water's edge, he whispered, "Hey look," before he recalled that no one with whom to share his observations accompanied him.

Gerald found himself swept into an abyss of loneliness: the depth of which he hadn't dreamed possible. He fought the urge to scream out a change of mind, only his willful wish to survive unassisted by a heavenly crutch prevented him.

For hours he stumbled along the wooded trails, physically unsteady from the loss of weight and the asymmetrical swing of his arm and emotionally off balance from a plethora of inner-turbulence. Motley mums appeared drab and colorless. Birds emitted husky rasps. Trees drooped. Every inch of his being craved a huge storm to act out his inner maelstrom.

Late afternoon grayed into evening as he roamed. Overpowered by frustration, Gerald began punching a tree which caused a nested squirrel to jump clear, chattering angrily. His fist emerged reddened from his battle with the trunk but some rage had dissipated. With the ounce of self-control that he had regained, he became conscious of the late hour and anticipated Cindy and the children fretting. He lengthened his stride but pitched to the left on an unstable rock and, unable to break his fall, hit the ground hard.

Intense pain coursed through his leg. He couldn't organize his brain — couldn't focus. He wavered on the edge of consciousness, probably faded in and out for some minutes before the fuzziness cleared and severe stabbing pierced his awareness; then came the throbbing. He contemplated the odd twist of his knee.

Several minutes passed before he fully appreciated the situation: without Jodi to alert Cindy, he would possibly be stuck in the woods overnight. *I didn't tell Cindy I intended to trek along the river. Never before needed to write messages. Jodi and Sam functioned as celestial messengers. Sure had it easy with their assistance,* he honestly summarized.

Being October, the evenings turned cool no matter the warmth of the daylight sun. Worries entangled themselves with the throbs: *how many hours or days before a hiker arrives? This path's used frequently. But It's late in the day and it's autumn. Probably no nocturnal hikers.*

He swallowed against the lump in his throat and sank into despair. *I've never been this terribly alone. Can I succeed without Jodi?* He shook himself and gritted his teeth against the spasm of pain. *Your misery almost feels good, Mr. Leg – your agony sure lessens this ache in my throat.* Gerald giggled at his whimsy– *Heck, watch out Robin, I'll soon be writing children's stories — competing with you.*

"Jodi, can you imagine me writing a story about limbs gossiping with each other?" No laugh met his query: again the reality of his dependence confronted him. Chatting with Jodi stabilized him when his feelings ran wild. Since that day he and Teddy became lost in the woods and ended up trapped in the cave, the sequence of events that preceded the late-hour fall, the rush home, and the fracture wouldn't have occurred. Jodi and he had spent hours developing skills of interaction to prevent such recurrence. Jodi would have intervened; he'd have listened; and his agitation would have abated hours earlier. He'd be home eating supper at that moment.

I've more to acquire than prudence, right God? Must figure out how to soothe these run-away emotions. Sure going to need Your help. Bet I'll be increasing my prayer-time. How do others survive without conscious communication with their angels? A self-disparaging grimace crossed his pain-creased face, *Guess I'm about to learn, huh?*

The evening chill permeated his body as he lay on the rocky ground. He shivered and licked his dry lips. His stomach growled: a wild apple tree had provided lunch, but hours ago. He surveyed his surroundings for a branch to splint his leg so he could hobble home and spied a suitable one sticking out between two trees just a few feet from him. But his attempt to pull his body toward it inflicted an explosion of stabs and throbs — his last conscious sensation.

Meanwhile, miles away, Cindy sent the children to their rooms for homework and finished the dinner dishes. Her stormy look hastened their retreat. Alone, she banged pots and pans together. Her vehemence frightened her children: after all their mother would yell at them if they dared be so noisy in the kitchen.

Of course, I feel badly about his arm. But his incessant reservations about Jodi – hints of asking her to leave – she's my own dear friend – she's more than his guardian. How dare he even consider banishing her. Her best platter hit the counter and cracked; she dissolved into tears. *He didn't even show up for his favorite pot roast and mashed potato dinner. And he left this morning without coming in for the cinnamon buns I baked especially for him. And he didn't show me the courtesy of sharing his plans for today.*

Nancy, unable to bear her mother's anguish sneaked into the kitchen. "Hey, Mom, Dad's probably out inspecting the river. His mood's been so gloomy since he's been cooped up with his arm. Bet he'll be in better spirits after he roams the woods."

Ron, who followed his sister, chimed in, "Yes, Mom. I'm sure that's where he is. How about me and Nancy following the bank of the river to locate him?" Her son's breaking voice and anxious expression belied his confident words. He'd scouted his father's every move since the amputation and unobtrusively tried to ward off obstacles. Unaware of Jodi's existence, he, Ron, was determined that his father convalesce with no complications. But he'd been at school that morning and couldn't nonchalantly appear at his father's side with the offer of an apple.

Cindy smiled appreciatively at her two young adolescents. "Your dad wouldn't appreciate us pestering him this evening. He's a lot on his mind. Trying to sort out a new series," she lied. *After all,* she justified herself, *if I'm truthful with them, I'll be unilaterally breaking our decision not to introduce them to angels. I will reopen that whole argument — but now's not the time what with Gerald enraged at his dependence on Jodi.*

She hugged her empathetic offspring, "That's thoughtful of you two. But he'll be fine." She reiterated, whether for herself or the children's sake she couldn't be certain, "Dad's fine; probably he's outlined most of his series and is so deep into his ideas he's forgotten the time. He'll arrive home when he finishes." Her explanation satisfied Gerald's children who often witnessed their father in reverie over a new concept. "How's the essay, Nance, and your math assignment, Ron? Either of you need help?"

Cindy, by restoring her household to its normal after dinner routine of homework, baths, and bed, regained some of her own inner serenity. However, she still hadn't heard from Jodi when the clock signaled bedtime. Putting aside her knitting, she restlessly paced the sitting room and chastised herself for declining Nancy and Ron's offer to track their father earlier in the evening. "Where are you, Gerald?...Jodi?" She broadcast her question into the empty night. "Sam, what should I do?"

"Pray and then try to sleep. He'll be fine and you'll not find him in the dark. If there were a serious problem, Jodi would have sought our assistance." Even though Sam reassured her, he too wondered at Jodi's lack of communication: the unprecedented lack of consideration was positively uncharacteristic of his comrade.

Where did she go last night after Gerald fell asleep? She usually informs me before she flies off to investigate a fact for him. Since Jodi did spend frequent nights in the angelic library researching history for Gerald, Sam had not been concerned at her absence – just a little hurt that she hadn't admitted him into her confidence.

Chapter 4

Jodi dabbed at her tears preventing them dripping onto Ima Misanthrope's ramblings regarding human-angel relationships.

> So my friends, imagine your consternation if you were prevented by an official decree from guarding your human. Perhaps, another divine experiment like the one God and Satan conducted with Job. How would you deal with your loss of meaning and purpose? Would you fret about the consequences for your human? Would you ask Special Forces to subsume you into their operations? Join the library staff? Apply for administrative positions? How would the first day, month, year progress?

"Tough, that's how," Jodi spoke aloud as if Ima had directed her ancient query directly toward Gerald's former guardian.

"Shhh...." the officious librarian glared and Jodi reddened.

With her back to the room's center to conceal her distress from other angels, she rested her forehead in her palms and wept silently. Then, with a shake of her body, she returned to outlining that first horrendous day of separation. At least she didn't have to search out an assignment as Ima wryly suggested might happen if all guardians abdicated simultaneously.

Reassigned to Special forces she was dispatched to one rescue after another and each required her total involvement. Most memorable were the four children stranded in the foothills of the Rockies when their parents' plane crashed. The thought of those lovely children brought a half-smile to Jodi's trembling lips....

Jake peered out the window. Trees mixed with bushes surrounded the perimeter of the grassy, daisy-speckled opening immediately outside. Shards of metal lay strewn in the field. Since the frightening plunge, he felt wobbly. One arm dangled funny and wouldn't cooperate. The throbbing tried to snag his attention but his fear refused it admittance. He reached across, slipped the catch and pushed out the pane. Bright red blood on his wrist attracted his attention; checking his arms, he spotted no cut, even on the arm that wouldn't move.

Robbie stirred. Jake recalled hugging the little imp when their father yelled to hold him tight. Blood trickled from a gash on Robbie's scalp. Jake unfastened the bandana around his neck and pushed it against the cut like he'd seen their mother do. His little brother shook his head. "Hold still, gotta stop this bleeding." Robbie looked at him and surprisingly obeyed.

"Janie, you okay?" Jake asked as he pressed the cloth firmly. Across the aisle both his sisters were motionless. Janie continued to clutch Katie, who sat between her sister's wide spread legs. Then Katie's body shifted and she stared at him. Finally, Janie's eyelids fluttered open; Jake breathed easier.

Robbie cried, "Mommy! Mommy!" and wiggled around in his seat to climb down. Jake reflexively grabbed the back of the toddler's shirt and held on, "No. Stay here. Mommy'll come soon."

Robbie snuggled against him. *What's gotten into him? He's never listened before. Why isn't he struggling more? Is he hurt worse than it looks?* Jake inspected his brother but he seemed okay even if uncharacteristically docile.

Anyway, where are Mommy and Daddy? When are they coming for us? His parents had been up front; Jake could distinguish the back of their chairs and a lot of twisted metal — a huge jumbled mess with sharp edges. *Are Mommy and Daddy under that?*

Their father had shouted, "Jake, Janie grab Robbie and Katie! Grab your armrests; hold on tight as you can!" Immediately Jake's tummy acted funny as the aircraft dropped fast. There was a loud noise. The jar of the bumpy halt bounced him and Robbie into the air even as he squeezed the armrests.

Then it was quiet. The chairs tilted at odd angles; the four children were up higher; the floor slanted toward that debris. "Robbie or Katie might slip off the seats, Janie. We can't let go of them." Jake pointed, "We can't climb down to Mommy and Daddy. There's too many sharp pieces." He pointed toward his window, "The wing's right outside. I could step onto it. Janie, we could lift Katie and Robbie out. I betcha Daddy is sure to say it's okay. It's not safe here with so many places for Robbie or Katie to get cut."

He scrutinized his twin; she just had to agree. "We'll find Mommy and Daddy better that way. They must be stuck underneath; otherwise they'd be here by now."

Janie studied the aluminum hazards and nodded. "Katie, crawl to the edge of the seat; hang onto the arm." Janie pulled herself after her sister, dragging her left leg and moaning. She held onto Katie stoically until Jake could grasp the little girl and steady her across the crazily sloped aisle. Once their sister was secure, Janie used the arm of her seat to hop toward Jake; spasms of pain almost knocked her to the floor. Jake reached for her; the two nearly toppled together until Jake wedged his shoe around the foot of the chair to steady them both.

Appraising his twin, Jake remarked, "Your leg doesn't move; it's like my arm. Hurts bad, too, doesn't it?" Shock had dazed Janie enough to produce an analgesia that allowed her to move; Jake's comments made her aware of her limb. She nodded stiffly.

"Can you take him?" Jake gestured at their younger brother. "If he breaks free, you can't catch him." Both older children knew the challenge of keeping track of their active and willful baby brother.

"I guess so. But, maybe...," and she looped her arm through the toddler's suspenders so the elastic stuck in the crook of her elbow. "There, I can ... do ... it now." The words came out through clenched teeth. Jake assumed his most authoritarian style, "Get between Janie and me, Katie. Now, don't budge an inch!" Jake climbed through the porthole to the wing. The feelings in his dangling arm disoriented him; his vision became blurry and gray as the stabbing was aggravated by the movement. Janie noticed his condition and stretched across Katie to give his shoulder a firm pinch. Color returned to his ashen face. His fingers wrapped around her wrist until the strange shakiness ended.

When he felt balanced, he told Katie to climb out. Janie boosted her up then Jake ordered, "Get your arms around my neck," as his good hand supported the younger girl's bottom. She passed from one twin to the other without mishap. "Katie, sit here," he plopped her at the joint between wing and fuselage. "If you move, you'll fall off." She could be trusted to mind. "Okay, now." Robbie would be an ordeal, what with his temperament and Jake's single arm.

With considerable effort and pain, Janie positioned her hands on the boy's hips and lifted him to the round window. "Robbie! Hug Jake!" she yelled. Familiar with that command from bedtime rituals and laughing play, Robbie automatically responded. Jake planted a knee against the fuselage and braced himself with a wide stance; then he put the child beside Katie. "Don't lose hold of him, Katie!" he ordered as he slipped Robbie's suspender over her head and shoulder and pulled her arm around his waist.

Jake then focused on his twin. Without use of her left leg, he'd have to drag her out. She scooted over. "Put your arms around my neck," he demanded. He tugged. Her right leg eased through, but her other foot caught against the frame. He figured that, if he stepped back, he might be able to pull it free. "Janie, I've gotta move back. Can't you lift your leg at all?"

She tried again but the pain made her dizzy for a moment. The situation was desperate; they recognized the dangers if Jake slipped. She whimpered and her forehead beaded with perspiration. How much longer before Robbie got antsy and fell off the wing? A sturdy boy, if he tumbled off his lithe sister could go with him.

Jake yanked hard, but Janie's foot remained stuck. The first wave of panic permeated his being. *What's taking Mommy and Daddy so long?* "Janie, kick it with your good foot; maybe you can free it." And she did. The twins simultaneously shrieked as hot stabs exploded into their consciousnesses when they toppled onto the wing's surface. Katie sobbed in terror on hearing her older, trusted siblings' screams. Robbie's countenance grew wary; he studied the others then howled.

Jake recovered first. Janie's eyes briefly glazed. But, in a few moments, she moaned, leaned away from Jake and vomited. Jake pulled her away from it and told Robbie and Katie, "We're okay. Now, gotta figure out how to get down." It seemed a huge distance even for a big five year old. How could he manage to get the little ones down? And, Janie, with one leg working? They couldn't just sit up there — Robbie would never stay still for long. Jake needed to solve the dilemma alone; Janie was too sick to help. But what he felt like doing was cry.

He bit his lip, "Janie, you better? Can you tend Robbie while I find us a way to climb down? Gritting her teeth and with Jake's assistance, she slid awkwardly to sit beside their two younger siblings.

"You did good, Katie. Now let me help you." And she slipped her arm through the useful suspenders of the little boy.

As Jake crawled toward the wing's edge to examine their height and locate a means to lower his siblings to the ground, a flicker of color caught his attention. A lovely lady was strolling into the clearing. He definitely wasn't acquainted with this person who wore a white gown decorated with blue-and-yellow flowers. She carried a large wicker picnic basket; her dark brown hair blew in the gentle breeze; she approached the wreckage.

"Hi, folks. You're a ways up there." Putting her basket on the grass, she stretched her arms to grasp the wing, gave a jump, and sprang up beside them. Mouths agape, the children then reflexively relaxed in the company of an adult. Even Jake, after scrutinizing her, trusted and let go of his fear. She could help them move off their precarious perch.

"I'm Jodi," she shook his small hand.

"I'm Jake. This is my twin, Janie, and that's Katie and Robbie. We were inside with Mommy and Daddy. They're down there and I have to get them but we couldn't do it from the inside. There's lots of sharp metal that Robbie or Katie could fall into. And, maybe now, if you help us down, I can get Mommy and Daddy out." His words rushed out to explain their predicament.

"Well, getting off this wing does seem like a wise first step," Jodi stooped down to his level. "Shall I jump you down first?" He breathed in relief that she asked his advice; he could assure himself his brother and sisters would be safe. His gaze met hers. "That way you can prevent the little ones from running off into the trees, can't you?"

"Yes, ma'am. Sounds good."

Jodi scooped him up, leapt to the ground, and set him in the weeds. When the woman cradled his fractured arm, the throbbing disappeared and the creases of pain scrunching his little brow vanished; but the worry frowns lingered. Pleased with her ministrations, Jodi smiled genially at the precocious child.

Jake eyed her every action as she bounded back on the wing to fetch Robbie. The instant Robbie landed on the grass, Jake hooked his healthy arm through the child's suspenders to prevent that perpetual-motion machine from dashing off to explore and get lost or hurt. Their mother had explained that, at his age, his brother's job was to explore his world. Jake wished the imp would take a break from that monumental task which, in Jake's opinion, the little boy performed too seriously. "Hold still," Jake irritably chided as the scalawag struggled to wriggle free.

Katie nervously stuck her thumb between her lips while the stranger transferred Jake and Robbie to the ground. She nestled deeper into Janie's protective embrace when Jodi approached.

"I won't hurt you, Katie." The love this beautiful woman radiated seeped into the girls. "Jake and Robbie are safely off the wing. We're so high up, please let me carry you."

"It's okay, Katie," urged her older sister, releasing her embrace. "Jodi's our friend. You saw her take Jake and Robbie, see, now they're safe on the ground."

Although Katie's rigid posture begged, "No," she slightly nodded her permission. Jodi cuddled the timid three year old especially close on the descent. Although soothed by the hug, Katie kept her thumb in her mouth as she snuggled against Jake.

Jodi next headed for Janie. No longer distracted by caretaking responsibilities, the elder sister had submerged into partial shock from the wrenching pain coupled with her apprehension about her parents. Jodi bent and caressed the thigh precisely on the spot where it tortured her. A soothing peace surged through the girl's body; the horrible discomfort disappeared; color flushed her cheeks. "Thank you," she murmured. This must be one of those angels from the storybooks her mother read to her. Jodi deduced that Janie recognized her and nodded her confirmation; the little girl brightened as she hugged the angel who, gently supporting the broken limb, brought her off the wing.

"How about we walk over to that knoll," Jodi pointed to a grassy mound that Nature had decorated with several varieties of daisies, white mixed in with gold and red.

"What about Mommy and Daddy?" Jake mumbled. He should obey this adult but he'd been studying the portion of the plane collapsed beneath the wings. The entire cockpit area appeared crushed flat; it was tough to figure out where his parents' seats were.

"I don't see any holes to peek into." Jodi crouched next to him and pretended to examine the crumpled surfaces intently. "We could investigate what's on the other side. Will you and Katie sit here a few minutes while the boys and I walk around it?" Jodi gazed into Janie's green-brown eyes and the girl nodded fervently; she realized she couldn't participate in the search with her leg not working.

Jodi held Robbie's hand and circled the destroyed craft with Jake. A barricade of jumbled metal extended the circumference with no breaches through which to peer. "We'll have to wait on the rescuers to free them," Jodi concluded.

Jake peered up at the wondrous stranger called Jodi who had materialized so unexpectedly. Her voice sounded soft, warm, and confident. He yearned to trust this adult. But he desperately needed to locate his parents buried under that mass. They were probably wounded – they couldn't escape or they would have assisted him with his sisters and Robbie.

All morning he'd been excited and hardly able to wait for the fun afternoon he was to spend with his best friend, Todd. The two boys would hunt for tadpoles at the pond on Todd's ranch. Their parents had arranged a late fall picnic – the last before the winter cold. His mother had prepared an abundance of food and everyone wore play clothes. He and Janie had helped their father load supplies and the family of six had taken their seats for the trip to the neighboring ranch.

But, instead of landing at the Jensen ranch, they'd crashed into the brush; Jake hadn't the foggiest notion where he was. Maybe Jodi could help. "Excuse me, where are we?" He spoke out in his clear voice. "Are we near the Jensen ranch? If we are, I can go fetch Todd's dad. He could get Mommy and Daddy out. The ranch has to be close by because we can fly there quickly and we were in the air a long time."

Jodi squatted, "Jake, some men are cutting in through the brush with a jeep and tools. A hatchet would be necessary to cut through these thorns and I have none. Come! I packed a picnic you can share with me."

Jake, enchanted by the woman's melodious tones, forgot his worries and followed with no further protests. Jodi carried Janie with Robbie and Katie each clutching a fold of her skirt. The Special Forces Angel organized the group in a circle, spread out a cloth, and laid out sandwiches and apples. After eating, she taught the children how to construct flower garlands while she regaled them with tales of elves who dwelt in a place she called Ireland. Robbie and Katie dozed off for afternoon naps with their heads on Jodi's lap. The distractions and her voice helped Robbie and Janie to forget that their parents lay pinned beneath the wreckage.

Jodi performed her afternoon's assignment with her typical dedication and aplomb. But, while supervising the flower braiding, her thoughts wandered to Gerald. *What compelled me to petition to be a Guardian anyway? Look how I botched it! Has anyone else in the history of mankind banished his Guardian?* Waves of mourning and shame washed over her, but the four children captivated her and unwittingly eased her dysphoria. She thanked her superiors who had compassionately dispatched her to such all-consuming initial assignments.

Hustling outside upon hearing the "Mayday," men had viewed the plummeting plane spiral to ground. Todd's father rapidly rounded up a rescue party with hatchets, scythes, and first aid supplies. The men chopped a swath through the thorny brush to the impact site. When her celestial senses picked up the snapping and slashing of the rescue team's tools, Jodi hummed a lullaby which put the twins into a deep slumber beside their younger siblings. The angel vanished with her picnic basket just as the men cut through into the natural clearing.

The ranchers fearfully approached the four small bodies sprawled on a rise somewhat distant from the wreckage and audibly exhaled a collective sigh upon ascertaining the children were simply sleeping. After splinting Janie's leg and Jake's arm, Todd's older two brothers hoisted the children on two of the pack mules and led them back to the ranch while the men tackled the wreckage. The youngsters were some distance from the knoll when the bloody corpses of their parents were extracted from the disaster site. There had been no suffering: death occurred on impact.

For years, Jake and Janie would relate stories about the special lady who picnicked with them. Their aunts and uncles were convinced the twins had hallucinations from the shock of the crash and their injuries. Nevertheless, they thanked God for taking care of them and providing them with such very pleasant memories — thus avoiding permanent emotional damage. But those intricate daisy garlands were a mystery.

Chapter 5

Cindy got a wink of sleep; it was fitful. She continuously expected Jodi. When the downstairs clock cuckooed 4:00, she knew that rest was an impossibility, dressed and headed for the kitchen. She caught herself selecting the green rick-racked apron and a wry grin spread across her face. *Am I trying to attract Ted? Is that why I grabbed the green one. His presence sure does calm Gerald. But our quixotic adventurer is away on some quest. Guess I'll make chocolate cake or maybe brownies or – no, I want to knead dough.* She pulled out her bread making bowls and utensils. As dawn broke, she was punching down the risen ball of dough.

She washed up again and then paced. Concerns and prayers somersaulted through her consciousness. *Where is Gerald?* She returned to the kitchen sink to rinse her hands. *And, where is Jodi? Oh God, please, where are they?* She stepped outside in the cool autumn air to wander the dying gardens and saw that the residual tomato and cucumber vines were ready for the compost heap and the four remaining pumpkins were ripe for the upcoming church potluck. *Why hasn't Jodi informed me he's fine?* Worries furiously surged; her vision blurred from frustrated tears so dense that she could hardly detect the dried flowers that she was snapping off and discarding.

Robin habitually rose early for a couple hours of writing before she dressed for her day. But on that morning she sensed her sister's anxiety. A foreboding prevented her settling at her desk. She hurried to dress, fed her cat and dog and hooked the leash on her golden retriever's collar. Miss Caroline pulled her down the path and onto the street. Spurred on by her mistress's urgent stride, Robin's dog trotted along the familiar route to the place where her own buddy, Scout, dwelt.

At the gate, the sensitive animal picked up the scent behind the house of the person they routinely visited. As soon as her mistress replaced the latch, she yanked Robin around the bushes that she'd learned to avoid after a thorny encounter when chasing a rabbit. She guided her human right to the other one whose smell she knew so well then whimpered for her owner to disconnect her leash. Once free, the dog, barking for Scout's attention, sprinted across the yard. Within a minute the two were merrily tussling over a newly fallen branch.

Robin focused on the woman who distractedly tugged at the dried flowers while agitatedly muttering. "What's the matter, Cindy? You look as if the world were about to end."

"He's probably okay..." Cindy gulped, then blurted out, "But why didn't Jodi fly back last night? Why? She's never left me clueless! Why?" Her frenzied hunt for dead plants to extract resumed. Abruptly she halted and stared out toward the woods as if her vision could penetrate through the trees.

"Hey! Hon, What *are* you talking about? Something's horribly wrong, isn't it? Cindy, what is it?" She was accustomed to her twin's anxiety, but this was abnormally intense. No matter how distressed, Cindy cogently enumerated her worries. This time phrases scattered hither and yon as if Robin would intuitively infer her full meaning.

Cindy paused, inhaled deeply, wiped her clammy palms on her apron and started over, "It's Gerald. He's probably okay, but didn't come home yesterday. He went for a walk along the river in the morning. No idea where he is. He's probably okay." Her fingers picked at dirt on the apron. "But Jodi didn't come tell me what's happening." Her haunted expression frightened Robin. "It's all wrong. What if he's dead? Is Jodi prohibited from visiting me before reassignment? He's probably okay."

Robin threw her arms around Cindy and hugged her to her chest. She could not imagine Gerald dead. Not with the resourceful Jodi around. "Of course, he's okay. But, it *is* odd that she didn't reassure you while he slept." She, too, glanced toward the woods. "How 'bout we take a sisterly stroll along the river bank paths since that's where he was heading? I doubt there's a serious problem, but — it has been a spell."

Robin's suggestion felt right. Cindy raced indoors, dashed upstairs, awoke Nancy, "Honeypie," she asked, "keep an eye on Jill and Bobby, will you, sweetheart: Aunt Robin and I, um, need to go out for a while." She kissed her firstborn on the forehead and joined Robin, Sam and Chelsea to locate their wayward friends. The minute the group stepped on the path to the river, the noise of a backfiring vehicle made them whirl around. It was Ted: he leapt from the green roadster that braked at the end of the drive.

"Hey, no fair picnicking without me!" he called. Disbelief, mixed with relief, flooded Cindy. Had he sensed her musing about him? Or had she foreseen his coming? Deep inside she submerged herself in the ever-present, yet suppressed, irritation which was bubbling up unchecked: *Why couldn't he have shown up sooner? He is consistently too late!*

Robin shouted "Ted", ran and flung her arms around his neck. *Plus, she's perennially waiting for his return. Why can't he appreciate how much she loves him and just settle down?* As Cindy angrily edged toward the couple after giving them space for their initial embrace, she experienced an infusion of gratitude on behalf of her twin that he did visit occasionally. *Still, I wish he came more often.* Cindy drew a deep breath and deliberately relaxed her shoulders.

As he aged, Ted's appearance had developed into that of a well-fed, sanguine, bespectacled, itinerant preacher. Cindy gave him a quick, obligatory hug which Ted recognized as less than enthusiastic. "Cindy, what's the matter? You're looking mighty upset." He massaged her shoulders gently. Scanning the area, he noted that Gerald was nowhere close. "So, how is the ol' boy? And, where is he? Still sleeping? The lazy loafer... Miguel and I resolved to cheer him up. Been driving all night and wanted to surprise him. What's with all his crazy ramblings about banishing Jodi? Is he losing his marbles? So, where, out back?"

Softening under Ted's kindly concern, Cindy's body went slack. "He's been missing since yesterday. I last saw him hike toward the river; he didn't tell me his plans. And, and, J-Jodi hasn't flown home to re-reassure me." She twisted the apron strings. Her desperate anxiety resembled the nerves of youth; nerves that had for the most part vanished as she matured into a confident matron, soothed and calmed by her angel while trusting her Lord's protection.

"We were about to search," Robin added.

Ted wrapped an arm around each sister's shoulders and hugged before he put into words their unspoken fear. "What if Ger's dismissed Jodi?"

Cindy shuddered. "He'd be in the woods alone. Now. We must hunt now."

Ted's voicing the unthinkable allowed Cindy to stop berating herself for behaving foolishly; she telephoned the sheriff to request an official search. The three humans and their angels fanned out to cover nearby paths.

While Cindy had been kneading her dough, Gerald awakened with the sunrise; shivers from the chill air aroused shooting pains that coursed through his body. He could not shift position by even an inch without aggravating the wrenching throbs. By moonlight, he'd examined the leg and discovered no broken skin. He hoped there'd be no infection.

The plan to splint his leg dissolved when the branch he reached for turned out to be so dry it snapped. No other suitable ones lay nearby. If he tied his fractured leg to the other, he'd have no use of the good leg to push him along the ground. During the evening hours he'd gradually dragged himself into a patch of leaves beneath a tree. Each effort was halted by harsh spasms which caused some brief lapses of consciousness; each time the throbs abated, he pulled himself a few inches farther. Finally, he reached the pile, which he tossed over his body for extra warmth; a survival skill Jodi taught as they wandered together through the hills and forests.

Throughout the long night each fitful doze was disturbed by stabs produced by chilled tremors. Every bone felt stiff; he was hungry and thirsty. How stupid he'd been! Every muscle in his body ached and the incessant pain was unmerciful. An owl kept him company overhead and Gerald listened to various creatures during their nocturnal roamings. The noises seemed magnified in his solitude. No large carnivores were indigenous to the area, yet his imagination swam with horrific "What-ifs?"

At the first glimmer of daylight, he faced a conflict: to wait for rescue or to attempt to crawl home. If no one came and he had no nourishment, would he possess the strength to try tomorrow? *Cindy's bound to search this morning.*

The sun rose; the songbirds sang; fluffy clouds smudged the azure sky. Gerald, embedded in the fragrance of autumn foliage and pine needles, should have enjoyed the promise a fresh day imparts. Instead, he lay despondent and suffering. Crawling was so physically intolerable that patient waiting proved his sole option.

Time crept at a snail's pace. His ability to think rationally faded. Drops of dew from nearby blades of grass quenched his thirst when he awoke but, by midmorning, the sun evaporated that wetness. Where could he find liquid?

In retrospect, Gerald would question why he hadn't shouted. Potential rescuers might have located him. *Why did I forget? I'm a bright person. I write articles on people who survive disastrous events.* But when had there been an occasion to cry out before? He concluded that the shock and pain muddled his reasoning and, thanks to Jodi, he lacked the reflexive survival skills. Thus Gerald justified his resolution to dismiss his angel and insist his children grow up with no awareness of their own guardian angels.

Nuts on the ground a few feet from him caught his eye. But, after he maneuvered toward them, he had to spit out the one rotten bite he sampled. If only a hiker would happen by! He spied wild raspberries out of easy reach. With a stick he hooked the delicate branches to bend them closer. The juicy berries provided moisture as well as nourishment.

But his body sensations overwhelmed him; he sank into a nap and dreamed of being alone – utterly alone at the bottom of a deep well. Teddy yelled from the rim far above urging him to hang on a little longer. Jodi related stories about wells that illustrated their functioning and benefits. Teddy called encouragements. Keep treading water and all would be fine. So, why did his pal keep calling his name? Surely he knew he was right there in the well. Why did his leg hurt?

"Ger! It's me, Ted. C'mon, Ger. Speak to me! You all right, buddy?"

Later that afternoon, lying with his casted leg elevated on pillows, Gerald, calmly and coherently defended his banishment of Jodi to Ted who sympathized with this exercise of free will yet thought it a big mistake. And Gerald's adamancy thwarted any hope of changing his mind through mere one-on-one debate.

A seven-member Crazy Eights' meeting was held that evening: each missed Jodi and wondered where in the world she was. It was impossible for the group to know that she was working in India at the scene of a train wreck. Residents of an orphanage were relocating by that train from one village to another. Four angels had been dispatched to comfort and protect the children while awaiting human rescue squads. The two chaperones could not prevent the little ones from wandering away. Because Special Forces Angels so frequently care for children at disaster sites, a majority of their educational seminars are devoted to that topic.

"First of all, I forbid any of you to let your angels help me," Gerald was resolute. "I must acquire normal survival skills. Robin and Cindy were adults before they had any knowledge of Guardians. Even you, Ted, lived two extra years without angelic awareness. You were six when you met Miguel. I was only four when Jodi introduced herself to me in that dream." He slid into a momentary despondency as he replayed that mental game of catch. He shook off the reverie and his expression transformed from wistfulness back to determination.

Cindy sat rigidly; none of the Crazy Eights displayed a hint of acquiescence. Gerald broke the stony silence and pleaded with them, lifting his neck from the makeshift bed to make eye contact with each. Cindy intentionally sat farthest from him in the semicircle of three humans and three Guardian Angels gathered around the overstuffed sofa. His study had been converted identically to when he convalesced following his amputation. The upstairs bedroom proved impractical with a leg injury, and anyway, this time, Cindy preferred the room to herself.

"You will not dictate what resources I employ as your wife," some of her suppressed fury leaked out. "If I need Sam, you pigheaded oaf, I'll use him. You can be as imbecilic as you wish, but I'm not forced to join in your stupidity!"

The entire afternoon she'd devoted to necessary pragmatic duties for his benefit without a single kindly gesture in his direction. He received no affectionate touch or light kiss. Instead she supervised the children who rearranged the home office, put the scattered books into the bookcase and fetched supplies. They brought in dining room chairs to enable their father to hold business meetings and to entertain visitors.

Ron had sat by his father for hours and ran for whatever was requested – another pillow, another beverage, his glasses. The boy had been there since Doc set the leg. He apologized as soon as Gerald regained consciousness from the anesthetic, "Dad, I'm sorry I didn't hunt for you after school yesterday."

"Ron, stop it. This is not your fault. I'm the fool who stayed out too late and then rushed home too fast. Never blame yourself for my stupidity." The paternal firmness relieved some guilt. Nevertheless, the lad felt miserable. Why hadn't he quietly slipped into the woods, located his father, and prevented the injury. That sense of responsibility, of missed opportunity, kept him in the downstairs study. He couldn't be enticed into playing even when his best friend biked over with his bat and softball.

To get some time alone for a private chat about Jodi, his Uncle Ted had sent him on an errand to the other side of town. At his house Ted had a box containing treasures for his godchildren. "Bring it here. Don't you peek inside," he admonished.

Cindy, relieved of contact by their son's vigil, kept her distance except when he reported his father's need for medication. Even as she administered his morphine, Gerald detected no compassion for his pain. Therefore the shock of her strong protestations during the confab was mitigated: Gerald acknowledged he must allow her and the others to function as they saw fit. "Okay.

You're right! I can't control your free wills. But, it is possible you – all of you — can respect my desires."

No one responded. Not one of the Crazy Eights agreed. Each deemed him wrong. "But," in a beseeching whine, "golly. Gee whiz, it's my life. I possess rights over my own self."

Gerald realized no one would concur and debate was useless. Drawing a deep breath, Gerald turned to his wandering friend and changed the subject, "Ted, what's this I read about you? Gee gosh, my childhood buddy, the keynote speaker at a fifteen-thousand-person rally? In Atlanta last week. That number accurate?"

Ted shrugged a bit self-consciously, "Well I guess I'm a pretty popular preacher on the evangelism circuit. Seem to have a knack for arousing the spiritual side of those who listen." He examined the backs of his wrists. "There's a power when Christians congregate in large numbers and unify in prayer; amazing healings can happen at such rallies.

"I relish the spirit of community I feel during the potlucks; the same sense occurs with the families that provide rooms for me. People regale me with extraordinary tales of God's interventions on their behalf. Stories I pass along to others." He paused and sipped his tea as he gathered his thoughts. "Last week I spent with a family in Ontario. The father had lost a leg in a logging accident; instead of wallowing in despair, the family praised God he had lived. Now the man plans to attend school and become a minister; he considers the loss of his leg a divine impetus specifically designed to push him to that transition."

"I'm confident one of the arcane laws of the universe involves the effects of group, as compared to individual, prayer: like we discovered in the high school cafeteria when we prayed for family and friends in the Great War. And, of course, the Bible states that Jesus was most successful when supported by the collective faith of those among whom He performed miracles." Bashfulness spread across his face, he lowered his chin as he added, "The book you looked over for me, Ger, on that subject is scheduled for publication in the spring."

He stood, went to the window, and stared toward the stars. "There's so much more out there to uncover. I've spent years holed up in stuffy libraries researching the occult wisdom of the Eastern mystics; it's essential I actually witness their outcomes. I'm headed for India in two weeks. This vacation is sort of an interlude to say good-bye to you and my folks before my departure. Probably be in the Orient a few y..."

"You infuriate me, Ted!" The unexpected outburst came from Robin, who rose from her chair and marched up to him. Her hands squeezed against her hips, her eyes fixed on his eyes, she enunciated each word mechanically, "Right here in this house are all your grand mysteries of the ages: Here, in the marriage of Cindy and Gerald, in careers we've chosen, the growth of your very own godchildren, and our homes where we dwell, and ... So, Ted, why? Why are you combing the world for answers when they're unfolding in your own backyard?"

Staggered by the tangible force of her words, he knew her logic was irrefutable. He looked wistfully at the woman he loved and who loved him. With his hands upward, he responded, "The answers here are real. They're real for here. But findings of other cultures, combined with ours, are apt to broaden our knowledge and add ever-more-meaningful bits to our ability to intervene and relieve suffering and despair."

"You and Gerald! You two are identical twins with different parents. Both of you are just as stubborn and unyielding, as absurd, and," on hearing herself, Robin ran out of the room; the bang of the door heralded her departure home. How she loved him! How lonely her existence so much of the time!

Ted's skin blanched. Why couldn't she empathize – he missed her, too. What compelled him to continue this quest? But he couldn't stop. It was a commitment. His body sagged as he said farewell to Gerald and stepped out in the night.

Time passed slowly. Gerald endured an additional eight weeks bedridden, followed by several on crutches. Eventually conquering self-pity, he gathered a pile of paper and blew dust off the typewriter. He resumed his efforts on features for <u>The Eagle</u> and his column, "What America Is Thinking;" once again themes flooded him. His popular column, a lucrative source of income for his family and his newspaper, became a restorative for his morale.

While recuperating, he cranked out pieces on mundane issues dealing with marriage, family, injuries, recoveries: the outgrowth of his and his visitors' reflections. But he eagerly anticipated plying his village circuit once more. Activity, he was certain, would lessen his loneliness – both Ted and Jodi gone within days of each other. How was Ted coping so far from home? But, at least he had Miguel.

Chapter 6

"Dad, can Larry and I borrow the Olds next Saturday? We want to go to the county fair." Nancy's question shattered Gerald's contented mood. One month earlier he'd resumed his active routine after almost a year as an invalid and could walk anywhere he chose: with barely a limp, without a cane. He relished his independence and simultaneously the household settled into a serene ambience. He was calmly reading the newspaper when Nancy's benign question jarred him.

Words weren't forthcoming. With fatherly fondness, Gerald appraised his pretty daughter who had developed into a conscientious adolescent. This young woman — his little girl — hoped to drive across the county with her boyfriend. Although he'd considered fudging the truth and running off to war at her ripe old age of fifteen, she remained a child to her father. After all, roads are bumpy; cars break down; tires blow. "What's wrong with his Model T?" fumed Gerald, oblivious to the source of his sudden petulance.

"He has a flat; he's no funds to purchase a new tire."

I guess I'd prefer them in my roadster: it is in better condition. Aloud he responded, "Okay, but you both better be careful."

"Thanks, Dad. You're the greatest!" And she dashed off to inform Larry.

Inwardly her father obsessed about the two of them driving those *25* miles. *What if a tire blows? Must be sure to check them. What if the brakes malfunction? It is fairly new....*

Cindy stepped in from the garden; the basket she clutched overflowed with flowers. One glance at her husband raised her concern, "Why the scowl, Hon?" As she passed the cupboard, she pulled out her crystal vase, a fifteenth anniversary gift from Gerald, and strolled to the sink.

Gerald put down his newspaper and picked up a pencil. On an empty page in his notebook, with sharp hard lines, he doodled a cartoon of a car by the side of the road — a figure lay under it and another paced nearby. "Nancy wants to borrow the roadster for her and Larry to drive to the county fair. Isn't she too young to be traveling that far with him? What if the radiator overheats?"

Cindy noted the tension in her husband's tones and rotated from the vase of flowers. "Come off it, Ger. What's wrong with you these days? You never used to obsess."

"What's wrong with you!" he retorted caustically. "Don't you care about the children, maybe a little?"

"Of course I do; much too much. But I discuss situations with Sam, uh, I mean when you're not home. He usually laughs at me for fretting or tosses out a suitable suggestion." She chuckled, rather sheepishly it seemed to Gerald, as she inserted three smaller yellow zinnias into the slot from which she had extracted a gigantic red aster which she then used as the center of the entire grouping. When the bouquet of late summer colors met her standards, she carried the product to the table, plopped down across from him and poured herself some tea.

"Forcing myself to describe my uneasiness shows me the irrationality of my excessive concern." She paused and studied his creased brow, "But you've never been the worrier. You seldom mention misgivings." She caught herself, "B-but don't misunderstand. I'm glad you're sharing with me." She reached across the oilcloth and laid a hand on his. "Still, why now? "

Gerald recognized the accuracy in her observations. "Why the jangled nerves? Any idea?" He averted his eyes. "I'm so easily overridden by doubts… about Nancy at school. Is she safe? How are her grades?" He gripped her wrist as he enumerated the persistent intruders. "Ron's safe — in eighth grade — not at the high school, but what about another war? I mean I'm really ridiculous in my worries! But there is Hitler." A deprecatory grin curved his lips. "Or, will he be injured during football practice – there was that wire service last year of the boy who died after the second — apparently minor — head injury. And Jill — will she remember her lunch box? Or Bobby, will he run in front of a car or horse? Or will I be able to keep us afloat through this economic bad spell?"

He swiveled in his chair and gazed out the window. "Did the accident stimulate this onslaught of fantasies? I sure did gain an appreciation of the vulnerability of the human frame." He chuckled at his irony. Squinting into the distance, he saw a hawk pursue a crow then snatch it with a diving attack. He focused on his cup once more and examined its depths intently as if seeking his answers in the tea. Glancing at Scout who dozed at his feet, then Miss Cutie who napped in the window seat, he murmured, "You two are really lucky – no worries in your noggins." But the pets couldn't distract him as he returned to ponder why at that stage so many preoccupations bombarded him. When the cuckoo clock blurted its one o'clock chirp, he flinched before chuckling, "Gosh, I'm nervous!"

Cindy's eyes scrutinized her husband, then her fingers holding her cup, and finally the surface of her own tea. She sipped. "I doubt it's the accident, honey. After all, we've confronted similar episodes with our active daredevils...Ronny's broken leg? Remember? Age seven? Jumped off that wall — pretending to be Tarzan — intended to catch the limb ten feet away...." She grimaced as she recounted the scene, thankful it was in the past.

Gerald nodded. "You're right. That did force us to reassess the wisdom of not introducing the children to their angels —- but we decided against that. We were skeptical — but not that much. We reasoned such injuries were inevitable ... and ...well... beneficial."

"Think about it: If I'd hinted at imitating Tarzan, Jodi would have intervened in some fashion. I can picture her scratching her chin and, in apparent sincerity, remarking, 'Ger, down by the river there's a tree with the perfect branch to jump from and the vine will swing out like Tarzan's.' And, of course, under the tree there'd be dense moss to cushion my fall." He laughed fondly. "In fact I envied him his opportunity to undergo childhood misfortunes and develop more prudence than I ever acquired."

"Maybe that's the solution – actively encourage our children in their adventures, treat the wounds that result, and praise God for their mishaps – certainly sounds better than immersion in this agonizing disquiet. But, you're right. Why I waited until the age of thirty-five to fret is a conundrum. And, no columns are getting written while I'm puzzling this out. Back later — and, Sweetheart, thank you."

She smiled up at him, gratified that he looked happier though she'd hardly said a word. Cindy lingered at the table, "Sam, it's the loss of Jodi, isn't it?"

"Yep" was the taciturn reply. Her angel imaged himself to her wearing the lumberjack costume he'd adopted since that fateful morning they'd searched the woods for Gerald. If he were human, Sam had no doubt that he'd select that occupation. The tramp through the woods had reawakened memories of another charge, Pete, in the 1840's. When he reminisced on that human, the one just prior to Cindy, he visualized the burly man, who had spent his days in the logging camps of Maryland. Pete was congenial and gregarious — a popular addition to any crew. He didn't stand around and cogitate like some other charges but jumped into the fracas and straightened it out whether it be a brawl between men on the crew, a log jam, or an ornery child. But he once suffered such an injury as Gerald's and lay in the woods two days before being rescued. Sam recollected that Pete had also lost consciousness when the pain became excruciating. Most of all, Sam admired Pete's refusal to sink into despondency during those quiet, pain-filled days as he rummaged for nearby berries, nuts and morning dew.

That night Gerald tossed restlessly. *Are our savings sufficient for the children to attend college? Will those dismal city soup lines, portrayed so graphically in the wire releases spread to us?* He sat up, plumped his pillow and lay back down. *No! We can feed the town in some other way. What about the newspaper bankruptcies – my third contract cancellation? When will the economy improve? Millions out of work... I have to lie still. I'll wake Cindy.*

Despite that loving consideration, he couldn't prevent himself from shifting again to his right side; his wife mumbled in her sleep. Cradling his head in the crook of his arm, he drifted to the rumblings from Germany – *Hitler is such a madman. His speeches expose the hate that consumes him.* Gerald's muscles clenched and his jerks moved him from his back to his left. But on that side no arm could cushion his head. *How can I get comfortable?*

His mind wandered to Jodi, *How is she? What's her assignment? Guarding another human? Maybe a child of two or three – as wild as me? Does she miss me? Probably not as much as I yearn for her. What's so wrong with having my angel by my side?* Frustrated his body gave a sharp twitch that jolted the mattress and caused Cindy to stir. Then he abruptly slammed shut the insidious portion of his brain from which that errant whim had escaped.

I can't stay in bed. Gerald tiptoed out of the room and slipped into the garden. *Am I this apprehensive because Jodi isn't around?* He meandered paths lit by the moon and stars. *Her optimism encouraged my optimism. If I found myself in a stew, I shared it with her.* He glimpsed an owl on a branch and watched as its head swiveled, searching for prey then flew off in a minute for more profitable perch. Determinedly Gerald resumed the musings that the predator had interrupted.

Jodi supplied a sounding board for me. Judging a situation through her eyes usually forced it to evaporate. He blushed as he recalled how silly most fears seemed when her insights were applied: like when he felt sure his mother shouldn't take the train to Detroit to assist his sister. Too wearisome a trip. Train might be in a wreck. Jodi advocated that his mature, but healthy mother, might be less likely to experience an untoward incident than would her impulsive son.

If dilemmas didn't resolve into the ridiculous, the sharing cleared his confusion and provided obvious avenues for investigation and resolution. He thought about his apprehension for Tom Walthers, his editor, who as he approached eighty tired too easily. Tom would admit to no decline but Gerald, from his vantage, dreaded that an illness might be the cause of the elderly gentleman's deterioration and frequent naps. Jodi helped him devise ways to convince Tom he should talk to his doctor.

Doc MacNamara diagnosed diabetes and prescribed the recently discovered insulin and a special diet. Tom did hate the food regimen. And Doc encouraged him to delegate some of his duties: find time for more relaxation and fun. At first the newspaperman fumed but later became entranced with activities he'd never indulged –picnics arranged surreptitiously by Cindy and the children, fishing trips with Gerald, walks in the woods. Tom would survive another five fulfilling years.

Gerald swallowed the lump that rose in his throat as he relived the grief over his late mentor and friend. He recalled the day on the banks of the river while fishing with the beloved old man. "Ger, I've been pondering my probable demise." Tom never minced words. "Cindy's my niece. I have no children. It would make sense to put you in charge of <u>The Eagle</u>. But I'm not convinced that's best for you. You're an author of the finest caliber. It's tedious to publish a daily newspaper: it would hinder your career. Whacha think?"

Gerald had been considering his answer if the question were ever raised. "Tom, I agree with you. And also I don't possess the organizational skills for publishing. Though I'd hate <u>The Eagle</u> to dissolve and would take it over to prevent its loss."

"Appreciate that, Son, but here's an idea. A former student of mine is on the Tribune. In his forties. He's the night manager– responsible for the bulldog edition. But he's very unhappy in the city. Wrote last week asking if I'd a lead on a small town paper up for sale. He'd bring experience, enthusiasm, big city contacts ... the contacts probably aren't essential what with yours....but, whacha think? I wouldn't recommend this if I didn't expect you'd like each other."

"Have I met him? From around here?"

"Nope, he heard of me while working on his high school paper and requested an apprenticeship. Has always said it was the happiest he's ever been. But went on to the Tribune before you started. About ten years older than you." Following that conversation, George Guntler journeyed to town. If nothing came of the meeting, he reckoned the opportunity to meet Gerald Daniels would make his trip worthwhile. The two men took a liking and Janet Gunther and Cindy enjoyed comparing their hobbies and children. George and Gerald complemented each other and Tom confidently retired for another year before he succumbed to pneumonia in their guestroom despite the vigilant nursing of Cindy, Robin and Nancy.

Gerald, pausing in his stroll, swallowed back tears engendered by the memories of the man who proved so momentous in his life. He gazed at the gently flowing river, *How I wish I could flow through the days as you do.* But then he visualized the tumultuous waters at flood stages like the time he nearly drowned and swallowed.

If I share more with Cindy, will that help? Jodi's suggestions cleared the unease. Could Cindy's? He shook himself, tugged at his night shirt with his fingers. *Is this how people without reciprocal relationships with their angels subsist each day; full of constant discomfort? If I'm to write for that audience, I must acquire similar experiences.* And, squaring his shoulders, he trudged on in military posture: a soldier heading off to an invisible battle.

Although dawn eventually ended his night, the rays of rising sun could not pierce the thick cloud of doom. Shuffling into town with his mind bereft of ideas, he figured he might as well ask Jed, their town barber, to trim his scraggly hair. Cindy's hints had been intensifying. Jed surveyed the lines on his customer's face, "What's with you? Why so glum?"

"I'm trapped under an avalanche of cares," Gerald confessed. "What do you do, Jed, with yours? You know – your worries. How do you get rid of them?"

Jed assumed Gerald was gathering material for an article so he took a moment to mull over his response as he snipped unruly curls. "Guess I tell myself I can't do nothing about it no ways; might as well let things be." He stropped his razor before shaving the back of Gerald's neck. Jed knew that his customer, who frequently forgot to comb, preferred his hair trimmed short.

Gerald wasn't convinced that Jed's approach would help. He'd tried to argue the forebodings into submission without success. *But, maybe, if I increase my efforts*....He flipped to his anxiety about Nancy and Larry and the trip. *If the tire picks up a nail, the boy can fix it — after all, he does own a car. But he's only sixteen, lacks maturity. And that Olds frequently creaks and groans. I'm familiar with it; it can't cause me real trouble, but... Uh—— oh! Should I have them take the Buick Roadmaster. Why does that trip haunt me? I'm hopeless.*

That afternoon, Gerald slouched at his typewriter staring bleary-eyed at the blank sheet of paper. What should he select for the week's column? He'd dealt with moments when inspiration ran dry. A chat with ever-present Jodi used to spawn a topic to research. But he was on his own. How did writers without camaraderie with their angels cope with this mental block? *Maybe it's time to test out whether Cindy can substitute for Jodi.*

Scooting back his chair with a screech, he moseyed into the kitchen and perched on the stool by the counter. "How's the article coming?" Cindy turned toward him; her hands grasped the ends of the rolling pin with which she had been stretching out the pie dough. A few flakes of flour floated to the floor.

"Can't conjure up a storyline, not a single word," he moaned. "Worry about accidents, the Depression, Hitler, the children, automobile tires — you name it and it's bouncing around in my brain. No clear thinking can penetrate the tumult."

"How about taking one of those themes and expanding it?"

"My worries are mundane and common; they've been analyzed ad infinitum."

"What about a piece on how to enjoy summer events during a Depression or the effects of the Depression on small towns – all I've read is about urban problems."

Gerald's whine interrupted, "Cindy! Oh, you don't understand!" He stomped out the back door. The difference between his wife and his former guardian became apparent: Cindy, a pragmatic thinker, couldn't attain the creativity of Jodi's spontaneity. *Cindy's contributions are banal. She's so... human.* He stomped down the trail to the river and glowered at two rabbits that dared peek at him. His fury radiated at every creature on Earth, including —perhaps especially — himself.

He realized how unfairly he'd treated his wife; his cheeks flushed. *My real problem may be that I miss Jodi;* he stumbled, catching himself by grabbing a branch. *And with her gone I'm irritable; my reasoning's off kilter.* Suddenly he halted; he stood tall and beamed. *I'll write about how people manage their worries. Jed gave me my first entry, and ...and the article might end up benefiting me, too.*

Thrilled by the inspiration, he raced indoors; Cindy still stood in the kitchen baking pies. The therapeutic activity of the extra pounding and pulling had reduced some of the sting of his rejection so she wasn't half as cross as he expected and, he ruefully admitted, deserved. But she still felt annoyed and scowled when she heard his step, "So, you've returned?" And mimicking his tone, she quipped, "Oh, I don't understand!"

"I'm sorry, honey. I shouldn't subject you to my ill humor. Forgive me, and, please, could you supply input for my article on how to stop worrying."

"And how can I help with that topic?" Her usual common sense replaced her annoyance.

"I plan to research techniques that the town's folk employ to keep from bogging down in quagmires like mine. The feature can describe methods I learn." He grabbed a pencil and snatched a notepad from his back pocket, "So how do you do it?" His entire demeanor radiated enthusiasm for the first time in a year. The energy that punctuated his words seemed miraculous to Cindy.

"Yes, I like your idea. And," with a mischievous twist to her lips, "you'll jot down our techniques, then try some yourself." To see him approximating the Gerald she'd been missing felt glorious. Her floured hand made its way to that incessantly fondled strand of hair; she gave a tug and streaked it white before breaking into a giggle. "Well, hmmm, when I'm upset I enlist my Guardian Angel, Sam, for his assistance, uh, suggestions. Discussion unravels the problem. Perhaps because I have to clarify it for him, I do so for myself." Dramatically covering her smirk and with her eyes glittering with alacrity, she curtsied.

"Aw c'mon, Cindy. What about before you met Sam?" Gerald greeted his wife's stab at humor with a poker face.

She recognized that she'd struck a raw nerve and quickly grew serious. "We've been together over a decade and a half; hard to recollect the before.... Uh, I guess I shared in our confabs."

"So hashing out problems in a group would be one successful method?"

"Did it for uh, me," she agreed. "I became less apprehensive than my peers, except for Robin. She utilized the confabs, too. And Chelsea gets an earful even nowadays!"

After scribbling down, "Guardian Angels" and "group discussions", Gerald strode off for town. He entered the general store where Charlie tended the butcher counter and, without a preliminary greeting, questioned, "Hey, Charlie, how do you deal with your misgivings?"

The man's brow furrowed, "huh?"

"I'm researching ways we all handle worrying."

Without a second's hesitation, Charlie replied, "I sing." He pulled off a piece of brown paper with which he packaged some ground beef for John Garner's big order. John routinely dropped off the meat order while he made the rounds of the other stores. His wife, with ten youngsters and always, it seemed, another on the way, seldom accompanied him: she provided a weekly list when he trucked in their farm's produce.

"Sing?" That sounded a bit crazy to Gerald as he dutifully scribbled: "Charlie – sings."

"Yup. You know how Torn, Joe, Jed and I perform in the barbershop quartet? Rehearsing together relieves tension, although sometimes a few butterflies flutter at performances." On the slip of paper, he crossed off pot roast, then hunted for pork chops in his cold storage. "I also hum and sing while dressing, walking to the shop or working in the back room. Nobody can fret and sing at the same time ... er...at least I can't."

"Thanks, Charlie, I'll definitely write up your technique." And off Gerald trotted. The locals were accustomed to their famed columnist-reporter who, when onto a new story lead, might approach any resident. The first few he caught offered spontaneous reactions. Typical of a small town, word of the week's topic rapidly spread and responses grew less candid as the day progressed. At the noon meal debates over various possibilities for each query regularly occurred. Afternoons he received cogent reflections, often assimilations of others' ideas. Gerald figured he obtained unpolluted comments from perhaps twenty percent of the town if he raced from person to person at the inception of a fresh project. Thus his brisk pace signaled his fellow citizens that the next column was in the research phase and fascinating speculations ensued.

Jim, the baker, said he went fishing. The anticipation of how big a catch and the poundage of the largest "takes all my brain space: none is left for such upsets."

Grandma DeVito described how she fed the birds; she threw out a handful of corn on observing the arrival of two mourning doves. "How can you be unset while watching them?" Mrs. Smith, with whom she chatted, advised crocheting. Greg McBeth at the pharmacy said a Cuban cigar did the trick; while Tom Sonders, who was purchasing some tobacco, totally disagreed, and argued that a pipe was the way to go. By the time he filled and tamped and lit the bowl, his disquietude went up in smoke.

Bill Kramer at the feed store remarked that a beer hit the spot. Ruth Kramer advocated a good, long walk. Doc recommended a bicycle ride and Pastor Thompson advised prayer.

The completed article included quotes from numerous individuals. His favorite recommendation became "Get in a broil with your wife." Frank Knight, the miller, offered that suggestion with complete seriousness. Several folks mentioned substituting a positive thought for the worrisome one. And the most popular wisdom was to determine the worst possible outcome. "Once you do that," Joan Adams said, "you can stop obsessing since you've confronted the worst already." Gerald decided he'd best not include Cindy's thoughts regarding guardian angels but did say his wife shared problems with friends. She grinned while reading the article as she realized she had really helped him.

For his own anxieties, Gerald tried prayer first. Yet no matter how often he prayed that the pesky intruders would vanish, they still plagued him. So he opted for prayer followed by a positive thought replacing the negative. For practice, he prayed about the roadster and pictured Nancy and Larry merrily en route to the fair and, upon arrival, laughing and joking among the booths.

Nevertheless, during Nancy's trip, he fretted and paced with no ability to calm himself. He barely ate supper; he snarled at Bobby when the impulsive boy knocked over his milk while leaping for the rolls; finally Gerald escaped for a hike along the river. He returned to greet the young couple who appeared at nine, the agreed-upon curfew, jolly, safe, full of fun stories. And Nancy's father exchanged his fretting about the trip to self-castigation for his surliness and lack of trust.

And Cindy and Sam debated when Gerald would give up on his foolish, willful walk without angels.

Chapter 7

"Dad, do you honestly believe in God? I mean deeply, personally, uh, in the way you've taught us to." Ron and Gerald were fishing on the riverbank under the canopy of a large willow. Above birds chirped and flitted through the sapphire sky sprinkled with puffs of fleecy clouds. Dainty wildflowers — violas and columbines – wafted their spring fragrances on the gentle breeze. The two eyed their bobbers which danced merrily on the water's surface. Thus far they had caught two brook trout, one apiece, and thrown back a half dozen non-keepers.

"Whacha mean, son?" Gerald stalled, wary of his maturing son's intention, as he reeled in his line.

"Uh, I mean ...." Ron's rehearsed confidence sagged and he fiddled with his rod, "I mean, Do you, er, trust in God as much as you say you do or is that something good parents are supposed to tell children to do?"

"I truly believe and trust in God, Son. Honestly. No doubts." He'd noticed Ron's deepening insights so wasn't surprised by his question. The boy's recent contributions to dinner-table conversations pleased and fascinated Gerald. A week earlier the family had discussed Ted's letter describing Hindu marriage rites. The families of the bride and groom consult astrologers to determine the most auspicious date for the wedding according to Ted's account.

"Why would an ancient culture continue that custom; uh, you know – it's all hogwash," Nancy had commented. "Certainly the Hindu wise men have figured out that astrologers are just tricksters."

Ron's unexpectedly thoughtful, mature response floored their parents. "But are those astrologers frauds?" He slit open another roll and buttered it, then continued, "You're right that the Bible forbids reading the stars and consulting those who predict the future; but the Bible never states that the astrological predictions are inaccurate. In fact, if all those kinds of forecasts proved wrong, God wouldn't have been obliged to proscribe paying attention to them.

I mean why would He bother." During the animated and frequently heated words that followed, Ron persisted with his argument and the family reluctantly acknowledged that his observations had merit and no easy refutation was possible.

Such thoughts lingered in the boy's mind as he continued his questions. "But, why, Dad? How can you be positive that He's real? Can you, uh, prove it?" Ron persisted.

"That's a tough one, son." Gerald secured his rod between his knees, then with his finger brushed the new grass and examined the green shoots emerging from the ground. He plucked a blade to chew and played out his fishing line while he pondered what to say: how could he avoid patronizing his adolescent son or dismissing such wonderful inquisitiveness. "I guess I know God exists because of my first-hand experiences with Him."

"But, how? I don't understand how those happen." Gerald knew his son; the compulsion for answers was sincere. The boy's forehead furrowed as he regarded his father intently. "Dad, I want – no, I need — to know."

"Guess you and He have to figure that out together, Son. The process seems unique for each of us. Knew a fellow once who claimed the Almighty's voice traveled straight into his ear. For me, I prayed and examined the results that unfolded. After enough such occurrences no other answer satisfied me." Gerald's words were sincere. But a subtle wistfulness swept over him. Jodi deserved a large portion of the credit for the certainty of his faith — much of which derived from intimate interaction with the divine.

"What about examples Dad? Could you give me some?" Ron was posed in rigid concentration; he intently monitored his line, ready to react to the slightest jerk. But the physical tension betrayed a different anxiety. He'd planned this discussion for months, nervous to broach the subject, yet desperately longing to hear his respected father elaborate on his belief in God.

Gerald threw away his grass fiber and scrutinized the choices around him for another while he reflected on which anecdote would be the most convincing. He recalled his second, or perhaps third, day of school– when he was convinced he was a first-grade failure. The results of that evening's prayers proved incredible; he'd accepted God's presence and trusted Him to respond ever since. But, how to verbalize that series of events for his son – especially because he had to delete references to Jodi's major role!

He sighed at the end of a silent request for guidance in this most important conversation. Plunging into his tale, he described that day when school seemed impossible for a six year old who couldn't simultaneously sit still and pay attention. Ron paid rapt attention to his father's story, fussed with his line and reel, but ultimately objected, "Dad, sounds to me like Grandma and Grandpa persuaded your teacher that you'd tried as hard as you could."

"If it were that simple, why did Miss Smith dream the remedy before she chatted with them?" He emphasized his point with an abrupt jerk of his pole and, with a powerful side-arm fling, cast the baited hook on a wide arc. Ron's reservation deserved respect: how often through the years he'd analyzed each part of that miraculous series of coincidences! No wonder Ron expressed doubts. If he hadn't actually lived the events, would he believe they took place!

Gerald pursed his lips, scratched his ear and tugged the lobe. Shoving memories of Jodi away, he scanned episodes that did not include her, "One proof for me occurred at a time when Mom and you were recovering from influenza. Jill and Bobby were toddlers and Nancy too young to assume responsibility. I wanted desperately to hear the keynote speech of the '24 political convention; you'd both passed the febrile crisis so I knew you'd recover. Grandma Sue had traveled to Detroit to assist Aunt Sally with Jerry's birth. Grandma Bertha was recovering from the illness. Aunt Robin had a speech to present in New York at a conference for children's book authors. All I could do was ask God for help: ran out of ideas myself even though I'd pondered possibilities the entire day."

"So..." But Ron's line twitched. Had he hooked a fish on the end of the line or simply snagged a branch?

Ron manipulated the reel, observed the tip duck underneath the surface and, sensing the powerful tug of a probable keeper, jerked to secure the hook. As father and son gazed out over the water, a hefty trout flipped into the air. Gerald positioned their basket as Ron wound in the line.

"Steady now," Gerald cautioned but his son reeled in then let up in perfect rhythm. As soon as he spoke the words, he berated himself — the warning had been unnecessary; he'd trained his boy properly. Ron, almost an adult, could land his catch. As it neared the bank, the fish made a lunge back toward its beloved watery home; but the sharp metal embedded in the creature held. In one graceful movement, Ron flipped it onto the sandy bank.

While Ron strung his fish with the two already caught, Gerald continued. "Well, back to that convention, uh, where was I? Oh, yes, I prayed for a solution. Should leave on the 7:30 in the morning. Couldn't trust my sanity when your Aunt Jane pulled up in a taxi. She'd experienced an inexplicable homesickness at college and felt compelled to board the train to spend a couple days with us." Gerald remembered his astonishment when his sister arrived. He deemed that story clear proof of the existence of a compassionate God who responds to the entreaties of his children.

Ron remained unconvinced. At sixteen he was examining his childhood beliefs in preparation for stepping out into the world as an adult. "But, Dad, couldn't that be telepathy?' An embarrassed body twitch accompanied his reasonable demur. He did desire his father's respect and didn't want to be reckoned purposely difficult. Yet, those examples were insufficient. Part of him craved to believe as his father did; but he couldn't be certain about God. And he yearned for a life of honesty.

"How's that?" Gerald, unaccustomed to objections to his favorite illustration, felt a trifle annoyed.

"Well, uh, she read your mind. Then, uh, hopped on the train," Ron suggested. "Like Mom and Aunt Robin sense each other's emotions and so do Jill and Bobby — when they're not squabbling. I envy that kind of intimacy."

Ron's sincerity was apparent. If his parents had introduced the children to their angels, it would be easier. Heck, the conversation would never even occur. But, Gerald had decided it best they grow up without reciprocal spiritual relationships; *how do other parents field such questions*? "You want another example, I suppose."

Gerald fell pensive. The pole slipped as he delved into his recollections. Shifting his posture, he dug his heels into the sand and tucked his knees toward his chest which position created an effective vise for the pole. "Well, what about the fire at the Jacobs' place. You've heard the stories. Those flames were fierce. That house appeared sure to collapse any moment when Sammy's mother shouted that he wasn't in the yard and must be trapped indoors. The entire assembly of folks recited The Lord's Prayer."

"The crackling noises and unbearable heat distracted me from the prayer." Gerald's voice wavered as he relived the vivid terror. "I was just about to run in to hunt for Sammy when the crowd screamed. I followed the gestures to the boy in the second-floor window. Yelled for him to jump and we caught him. Rushed back as the building fell."

At the story's climax, Gerald grew more emphatic. "Sammy told us that he couldn't see a thing. He'd no notion which direction to go." Gerald glanced at Ron and, with a deprecating shrug, "The boy reported that a path opened through the smoke and an angel, that *was* his word, son, sheltered him from the flames."

Wish I could relate the rest, Gerald mused. Jodi had completed the details: God, on hearing the crowd's prayer, dispatched one of her Special Forces' friends, Sarah. The two angels acted in concert. Sarah materialized and led Sammy out while Jodi delayed Gerald the few seconds necessary until the child reached the window.

"Pretty wild," Ron agreed. "I've heard that story from neighbors and Sammy. I appreciate that almost every witness concluded a Divine Deliverer exists. Still, it's uh like hearsay; I'm having trouble with fact. And I know I wasn't there at the scene. But, you're basing your surety on a five-year-old's claim of an angel."

"Son. My encounters convinced me; my words don't carry the same assurance to you." He drew another breath, "I cannot insist you believe in God even though I do wish that faith for you." He pulled on the rod; the tip edged up and down a bit. "I can share my experiences, include Him in our lives together, and pray for you children to have similar personal opportunities. But, I guess, you'll need to discover God directly." You must find your own truth."

"How, Dad? How can I generate such experiences?" Ron persisted. He was eager to plunge into such an experiment.

"Why not pray for God to create ones designed to assure you?"

"I will, Dad."

Ron's questioning provided the inspiration for a series of columns whose concepts exploded across the nation. Shortly thereafter the favorite topic of conversation throughout America became, "How do you know there is a God?"

The journalist amassed countless tales of personal encounters with the Almighty.

As usual, he interviewed locals since he deemed his own Main Street a microcosm of America. Professionally – and personally – Gerald grew intrigued by the plethora of justifications cited as proof of individual beliefs. And the reasons matched the particular individual's personality.

Miss Melbourne, the second-grade teacher, explained that God guided her toward the most expeditious method to teach each child. Her principal, Mr. Arns, politely disagreed, "She has no idea how creative and intuitive she is."

The principal's conviction of God's existence rested on the fact that his three-pound baby daughter, Angie, survived with no abnormalities. He and his wife had yearned to become parents but three prior pregnancies terminated prematurely and a fourth was stillborn. The entire church prayed during the fifth: Arns claimed the congregation stormed the gates of Heaven on their behalf.

As Gerald collated his research, the most common persuasion was the accomplishment of a task the individual believed impossible without Divine assistance. However, to an outside observer outcomes seemed logical, coincidental or merely the supplicant's hard effort.

A whole category of interviewees insisted they sensed God's presence or heard His voice in a tangible way. And these people tended to be highly regarded in the community. For instance, Gerald approached Grandma Jennings, an unobtrusive woman, revered for acts of loving mercy; she replied, "Well, we discuss whatever is happening. He's real to me. As a little girl my mother taught me to be still and listen and, sure enough, I heard His Voice. Been talking together ever since." As she spoke, Grandma's fingers industriously knitted a blue piece – perhaps a man's pullover, the reporter guessed.

Did her communication with God differ from his past experiences with Jodi? "How can you be definite it wasn't, say, your Guardian Angel or your imagination, Grandma?"

"Oh! Well, my Guardian Angel speaks to me differently. See, I asked myself that same question. When I questioned Him, He clarified, 'No, I'm not your angel. Tillie's your angel. Want to meet her?' And I did. Tillie and I are like sisters; we gab a lot together." Gerald slouched motionless as a flood of desolation and abandonment smothered his ability to reason for a few seconds. This woman prattled on describing a relationship akin to his with Jodi. Her words barely penetrated the inner storm they generated. "But with God, well, — He's lots more serious."

With difficulty Gerald clamped down on his emotions and resumed his professional demeanor. Perhaps only someone with his background would receive Grandma Jennings' angel story uncritically, he thought. "Why don't you tell people about your personal contact with God, Grandma?"

"Now, son, can you honestly be suggesting that folks'd take me seriously? I'd be brushed off as a crazy old lady. No thank you. And anyway, each of us has to find God for himself."

"But you told me. Why?"

"He told me to," an impish grin flashed, "and you probably know why." Her green eyes twinkled.

"Have you mentioned this to others?"

"Occasionally. People He instructed me to tell. Ones who needed to hear or who would understand. Often enough that I realize I'm hardly unique." She peered up from her knitting with a quizzical smile, "In fact, because you're struck dumb, I reckon you know exactly what I mean."

Gerald blushed. "I suspect you're right," and he mumbled, "Thank you, Grandma, good day," as he rose from the bench and put his notebook in his pocket.

Gerald had written Ted about the plans for his series when he initiated his investigation. More than a month later, he received his oldest chum's missive:

Dear Ger,

Great to hear from you. Another interesting question you pose. Obviously you're not expecting me to describe how I know there is a God because you were with me eons ago in those woods when we were around six. I'll supply you with some of what I've uncovered.

Westerners usually rely on faith — Sort of "Well, I believe: always have; always will." The my-mother-and-father-did-and-so-do-I phenomenon. And, of course, many Westerners have special encounters with the Divine which help fortify their faith.

But I'm fascinated by the Eastern spirituality I'm learning about. Yes, there are plenty of charlatans who subsist on the pittance their circumscribed psychic skill earns. Yet what they achieve says a lot about the psychic abilities of the brain. Fascinating stuff.

Back to your letter regarding God and the relationship with or knowledge of or belief in Him. There are extremely spiritual people in the Orient who don't doubt that God exists. Although they deny our Judeo-Christian deity, they definitely worship a supreme being. They meditate rather than pray. Meditation for them is to let God flow into their mind in contrast to the way we actively talk with God in our prayers. The practitioner sits truly quietly and focuses the mind. They believe that if you totally stop thoughts, you can touch the divine. But to attain that ability can take years I'm told.

Ger, you ever try to completely still your thinking? I've dwelt in an ashram in the Himalayas the last few months. The guru who teaches here is regarded as one of the holiest.

Several times a day we sit on pillows in a large hall and endeavor to stop generating thoughts. Sometimes we assume unusual postures. Other segments of the day we serve the community. Many gurus and their followers raise the quality of life in the rural areas – really serve the people. But I had fancied participation in an ashram that teaches more of this inner control.

Can you imagine sitting for hours on a pillow, trying not to think? It's amazing how difficult this seemingly simple effort is. Thoughts are pesky varmints that persistently intrude. There are Yogi teachers who claim you can rise above your thoughts and survey them — witness them as they flow out as if coming off an assembly line in Detroit. We are definitely distinct from our thoughts — whatever it is that we are.

Miguel and I made a new acquaintance: Juanita, the guardian for Raul, one of my fellow students. Miguel met her the other day while we practiced emptying our minds. Juanita, a tad bored I bet, paid more attention to her surroundings than is typical for Guardians and noticed Miguel; they struck up a conversation. Since I'm a novice at this meditating bit, my concentration slipped away, and, I must admit, my patience. I started to chat with Miguel and he introduced me to her. Our reciprocal relationship fascinated her. After the meditation period, Raul and I discussed angels. Wonder where that will lead? Interesting universe, huh, old Buddy?

Heard from Jodi lately or don't you two contact each other nowadays?

Love, Ted and Miguel

Why did Ted's every letter mention Jodi? Ted never had agreed with his decision. *Obviously he continues to hold the opinion I should stop this walk without angels.* The void inside him insidiously nudged the edges of his awareness .... Gerald shook himself out of his gloomy reverie and reminded himself he chose this path through his free will; he believed he must exist without her constant attendance. It was the only way for him to comprehend the lives of others. That meditation Ted described might alleviate his unabated uneasiness. He'd try it. Maybe he'd write Ted for more instructions.

Interesting, though, how those people when they emptied their minds achieved contact with what they deemed a supreme being. *Obviously God is everywhere and in everything,* he mused as he stuck the letter into its cubby hole and drew out paper to organize this information into his series on encounters with God.

While Gerald was writing that existence of God series, Jodi was assigned to the homeless who sought refuge in Grand Central Terminal in New York

City. Smoke from train engines and travelers' cigars, as well as the stink of the unwashed, polluted the atmosphere. Some of those left penniless by the Depression escaped for brief periods to the warm terminal from the cold drizzle of their street homes above. Into the squalor of poverty the crystal chandeliers overhead cast an ethereal light on the pathetic crowd which rested on the rows of mahogany benches. The cacophony of children's squeals and whimpers, parental rebukes and commuters' chatter added to the atmosphere of confusion and unrest.

Jodi's instructions were to encourage the unfortunates to devise manageable plans to support themselves through those troubled years. Walking among the clutter of people and luggage, she spotted a thin young mother in a ragged coat with frayed cuffs and missing buttons. The girl clutched to her chest a dirty blue blanket wrapped around an infant; a cap made gray by embedded grime was on the baby's head. The child appeared gaunt; wide brown eyes stared from under a wrinkled forehead. There were no plump baby cheeks to shape a typical cherubic impression.

Jodi sauntered over, slid beside the mother, and greeted her. The tattered girl pulled out of her lethargy enough to say that her name was Cindy. Jodi blinked back tears as a flash of the Cindy she loved shot through her memories. She tucked away those thoughts and settled down to succor the mother and infant. Cindy put Billy to breast but she produced no milk. "I haven't eaten for a couple of days. Can't make milk for Billy. I guess I'm dried up." She told Jodi. "I'm afraid to go to the bread lines for fear they will take him away."

Jodi laid a comforting finger on Cindy's wrist and scanned the large hall where people dressed for journeying mixed among the shabbily clothed souls. The Special Force's Angel regarded a grandmotherly woman who sat next to them on the bench. The elderly matron, clad in a woolen travel suit, was harried by two little boys of maybe three and four, who chased each other around the bench. Her swollen eyes were reddened. Amid the coats and bags, Jodi saw that she was carrying more than enough sandwiches for one adult and two children: *she probably didn't dare risk scrounging for food on their trip,* the angel mused. *Those two feisty imps are wearing well made clothing with no patches.* Jodi looked from one woman to another: *Hmmm.*

Jodi engaged the active boys with a tale of pirates. Their grandmother, relieved of the necessary constant attention, randomly focused on Cindy. Though in these Depression years tragic circumstances were innumerable, she couldn't avoid noticing the starved girl trying to nourish her infant.

Groping into her visible supply of food, she extracted one of the sandwiches and an apple. Although the famished Cindy wanted to refuse, the corner of the bread entered her mouth without conscious volition and she gobbled the sandwich. "Thanks. Got tossed out of our apartment. Lost my job when I had Billy. Barely enough money before; could spare nothing for saving." Cindy bit into the apple. "Derek, my husband, went west to Illinois to find farm labor during spring planting. There's been no word all summer and now, me being without an address, he won't be able to find us. I don't know what to do."

"He went to Illinois, you say? That's a big place. Where in Illinois might he be, you think?" Grandma, concerned with the young woman's plight, leaned toward her.

"The last we corresponded he'd seen something in the paper about hiring farm hands in Moline."

"Amazing, that's where we're headed. You'll come with us." The response came with the firmness of a matriarch accustomed to giving orders and managing family affairs.

Billy whimpered; Cindy put him to breast and milk flowed into the starving infant. "I-I thought he'd starve. I, uh, didn't know milk could restart after it dried up." Her expression changed from despondency to wonder; she didn't realize she'd been touched on the wrist by an angel a few minutes previously.

"That is a might unusual," sighed Grandma in relief. "Was figuring what to do before we reach Moline where I do have a neighbor who's nursing."

"I don't have a ticket. There's no ...." The girl's desperation showed; her posture registered hopelessness. "I'm at the station because it's warm. I've no money for the fare."

"I must take these grandbabies to the farm." The older woman gestured in the direction of Jodi's entranced audience. By then five little scamps sat in a semicircle transported far away to days of yore on the high seas. "Their mother, uh, my daughter," the woman gulped and fresh tears trickled. "I mean, uh, passed away from consumption last Thursday. My son-in-law's in the Army."

An inhaled sob cracked her voice. "I could use extra help keeping track of them. After all, I'm a tad old to chase young'uns this size. Handling them on the farm will require an extra pair of hands. You'll travel with me and care for the boys. From home we can send out inquiries and find that husband of yours — if he's around."

Cindy, astonished at the offer — or rather the command — glowed. "Oh, th-thank you, Ma'am, thank you!" Her body quivered as she hugged Billy.

Jodi breathed a deep sigh. She'd only needed to spell the grandmother of her exhausting charges for ten minutes. Maternal instincts accomplished the rest. Jodi adored her assignment – one of the best ever.

The pirates captured, Jodi waved goodbye and moseyed through the vast building with its high ceilings and ornate carvings as she searched for another opportunity to serve. But, when she neared the wide ramp scrolling up toward street level, she overheard words that forced her to eavesdrop.

"Hey, you read Gerald's latest?" A middle-aged, stocky man, in a tweed overcoat skimmed the afternoon press. A brown leather bag lay on the floor at his feet. He spoke to the woman by his side whose brown hair was fastened by silver filigree clips. She tatted a strip of lace; her marquise diamond ring coruscated in the chandeliers' light as she flipped the shuttle back and forth.

"No, dear. I've only finished the society news," the woman held out the piece of lace and measured its length by encircling her wrist with it. She turned to her husband, "So, Dear, what is America thinking this week?"

"Fascinating what he comes up with." She nodded, interested. "He interviewed a lot of people about why they're sure there's a God. Listen to this one:

> My pal Jake, the town cobbler, replied, 'Well, it's like this. When the bank folded and my savings vanished, I felt desperate, scared. But a tiny voice inside said, "Open your Bible, Ecclesiastes 3." You know, the chapter on time and how there's a time for everything? I reckon this is a time to fret about money but later will come a time of plenty. And that's what history's been like. Everything has its season. With that reassurance, my fear let up. I figure only God knows the Bible well enough to tell me what chapter to read — out of the blue — just like that.

As Jodi heard Gerald's words, she realized God intended that she apply Ecclesiastes 3 to her current situation. This was her time for loneliness; Gerald's to walk without angels. Phases are finite. From that day on Jodi's heart lightened. Her current season had a purpose — and it would end.

Chapter 8

It was late, getting later. The afternoon sky hung heavy with dull condensation — not unlike the war clouds over Europe. Gerald pumped the accelerator yet again. "No gas. Might as well accept it," the middle-aged man with gray-tinged hair muttered to the universe in general.

Before his faithful Buick sputtered on the remaining drops of fuel, he had been immersed in the poetic landscape: scattered homes contrasted against the white snow; smoke rising from chimneys symbolized warmth to weary wanderers. Childhood nostalgia, before the ubiquitous automobile, meandered through his memory. *Our homes were separated somewhat like these. Though we did reside closer to town than any I'm seeing along this stretch; still we needed to be self-sufficient during winters.*

In the immediate aftermath of his car's demise, he clobbered the steering wheel — without effect – the starved engine couldn't be knocked back into service as occasionally could their erratic washing machine. He settled back and chuckled, *Now my car's become a stationary, isolated entity similar to those larger properties I passed. But, this modern era, although more hectic than my earlier years, does possess at least one advantage: I'll soon be rescued by a fellow motorist. Catch a ride to the next town... buy a jug of gasoline ... telephone Cindy of my delay.*

Outside of his warm refuge, he scanned the snow-crusted roadside and spotted a suitable branch in a windswept weedpatch. *That'll be a good pole and my red scarf will suffice to get attention. If I twist this corner into a knot, it will slip over the end. Now there should be wire in the toolbox. Yes. Here it is.* He fastened his makeshift flag to the driver's side window post. *Brrr. It's cold!* Shivering, he climbed back into his still toasty automobile to wait for a passing vehicle.

Over the next hour no cars came from either direction. Denser, darker clouds filled the sky; the landscape dimmed; trees faded from view. Winds rose in earnest. Snow fell. And an early spring blizzard struck in full force. Hardened by the frigid air, sleet and snow hammered the metal roof. The last farmhouse he remembered had been several miles back. Gerald realized he'd waited too long. It would be treacherous to venture out; probably lose his way in the wind-driven snow. Although extremely unusual weather for the region, it was happening. He'd have to wait out the storm's fury in the safety of his car. He pulled on the overcoat lying on the seat beside him and thrust his feet into his boots.

During those first hours, his irritation dissipated and his mind traveled back over time; the years had vanished rapidly. Nancy would be married in a few weeks. *Our colicky infant transformed into bride-to-be: one of the wonders of the universe. Cindy's right that everyday miracles surround us. So why can't Ted recognize it – doesn't have to traipse halfway round the world to find them.* Gerald shifted his position. *But, of course, he grasps that; he's just convinced there's even more. Already he's contributed a lot of information about vastly different cultures to Western knowledge. Every bookstore and library carries his books on Eastern customs and beliefs.* Gerald remembered with pride Ron's senior term paper. Writing on Hindu marriage ceremonies, his son researched astrological indicators and expounded on their reliability. The boy quoted his godfather extensively. The content of the school assignment raised eyebrows; yet its skillful construction merited no mark lower than an A.

Ted about to leave the Orient; how many years has it been? Eight, no nine, guess he's had enough. Can't wait to see the scoundrel. Should be here in time for the twins' graduation. A radiant smile spread across Gerald's face and his body slightly warmed as he contemplated the arrival of his itinerant friend. *Sure hope he selects one of the university offers in our region – like Columbus — though I guess Ann Arbor would be okay. Please, Ted, don't go to Harvard or Berkeley – I'm tired of your being so far away.*

He stirred uneasily as he pondered the bleakness since Ted left the States. *My best friend and my angel gone within days of each other. How desolate I felt – lying there with my fractured leg – Cindy solicitous but pretty unsympathetic.* He shook away the memories and forced himself back to Ted. *Will he choose a university's Philosophy or Comparative Religion department? Ryan bragged about that son of his the other day at the barbershop. Come quite a ways from threatening to disown the scalawag when he refused to enter the construction trades.*

Gerald hugged his arm around his chest, shivered and shuffled his feet. *Boy, I've missed him. Hope he'll finally settle down with Robin. That's what he's been hinting. She seems aware of some upcoming change. So secretive though. Afraid she'll be hurt I suspect.*

He fumbled with the coat's buttons and pounded his fist against his leg. *My little Nancy, a nurse, already employed for a year. And, marrying George.* Gerald was impressed by his daughter's fiance. The young doctor had come to their town to join Doctor MacNamara last year. Since Nancy was working in the clinic, she and George soon became acquainted. By Christmas they were sweethearts. Doc had learned he could trust the younger man's skill, compassion and conscientiousness and planned to begin his longed for retirement in the fall. *It will be nice to have them nearby. Cindy's going to adore being a grandma.*

Gerald pulled his rabbit fur collar more snuggly around his neck and buried his nose deeper into it. Mentally banging his forehead for his stupidity, he leaned over to the backseat and scrounged in his bag. *Yes,* he located the wool scarf that Cindy had packed in case he took a lakeside walk during the Chicago visit. Wrapping it around his face loosely would allow him to breathe warmer air as the temperature dropped. *Is it safe to turn on the engine for heat? Yikes I'm going senile! Can't turn on a darned thing!*

A terse, "Hi Dad and Mom, I'm fine," letter had arrived from Ron a few days ago. The young man had joined the Navy and was stationed in Hawaii — a gorgeous locale; he loved his role on board ship, docked at Pearl Harbor. But, from the news reports about the war in Europe, Gerald predicted America would soon be involved. *The world's a mess. Wonder if Ron's destroyer will be deployed in the Atlantic...*

He flexed his toes and fingers, then tightened and relaxed limb muscles. Ron and his namesake were so different: the sailor couldn't have been more physically fit; the other had been chronically ill. Yet little Ronnie utterly changed Gerald's and Ted's universe in eighth grade. *Will my Ron impact people as did his uncle?*

Gerald scooted his stiffening body in the hard seat as his mind wandered to the twins, *Jill and Bob. Graduating high school already. Just yesterday I changed their diapers. Now Jill hopes to follow Robin's footsteps; teach primary school and write; bet she'll do so admirably. Who will she choose for her husband? Doubt my little social butterfly will wait some twenty years.* Gerald smiled fondly: his youngest daughter idolized her Aunt Robin.

When the twins were almost a year, Bobby would crawl off to investigate his world — as would Jill — unless Robin was nearby. In that case, the baby girl invariably scooted over to her beloved aunt and tried to clamber up her skirt until Robin lifted her up. Cindy, exasperated one day, half-seriously suggested they share the twins; Robin could abscond with Bobby. Robin grinned at her sister mischievously, "That offer has little chance of working. Jill wouldn't let me reach the front door with only Bobby. You'll just have to give me both." Moments later, Gerald had walked in on the women doubled over with laughter. It was a pleasant memory: the children plopped on their round, diapered bottoms, thumbs in their mouths, curiously eyeing their caretakers.

Robin would have been such a nurturing mother; yet actually she's mothered hundreds easing them through third grade. She'd often talked of having seen a former pupil who stopped by her room to bring her an innermost secret — a new baby brother or the first crush or grandmother's death. Gerald curled his fingers into a ball inside his glove for greater warmth. And, what about the millions who've been nourished by the loveable characters in the books she painstakingly detailed for her avid, young readers? *If Jill is half as productive as her adored aunt, she'll be mighty successful.*

Gerald wiggled and pondered, *Should I climb out and walk?* A moment's thought and he acknowledged the foolishness. His worries roved to Bob. *That one's sure lots like me,* he said for the hundredth, maybe thousandth, time. *Except he's grown up without personal knowledge of an angel. Was that for the best?* Gerald had no answers, no clue. *A few years back – wow, no, almost two decades – I'd been adamant: no personal relationships with angels for my children. Was I right?*

Gerald had progressed through childhood in conscious contact with an angel. Memories of his experiences combined with Cindy's ingenious resourcefulness helped Bob. Their son behaved cautiously compared with his father. But did Bob know true happiness? He constantly restrained himself and suppressed every impulse. At the same age Gerald had acted more wildly because he trusted the safety net Jodi provided for sundry predicaments into which he rushed pell-mell.

Mother sure disparaged our reasons for not introducing the children to their angels, especially Bob. Gerald replayed Sue's long-ago apology for introducing him to Jodi. She'd flushed and clutched her skirts after he told her why he'd banished his angel. Gerald shuddered as he recollected the scene that occurred a week later. His mother stamped, truly rattled the floor boards, as she marched into his convalescent room. Fists on hips, the dignified matriarch of sixty-three, faced him as he lay with his casted leg elevated.

"Gerald, I've deliberated about Jodi. My judgment twenty-nine years ago has proven correct; I'm rescinding my apology of last week. You are successful, respected, responsible and...and you're ridiculous to consider yourself half a man!" Gerald grimaced as he pictured her expression while she delivered those words. With an abrupt pivot she left the room. A few seconds later the slam of the kitchen door echoed through the house. Tires screeched as she roared away. Driving like that she was furious.

What am I gaining from this self-imposed separation from Jodi? I've definitely learned how to worry! In fact I'm an expert fretter and wallowing in my fears has taught me to be more empathetic. He glanced at the storm through a peephole created on the window by the swirling wind which whimsically coated some areas as it avoided others. Those gusts, he surmised, probably shaped odd peaks and valleys outside.

Sure is cold; am I in danger of hypothermia? He bounced back to his enumeration of lessons without Jodi. *Am I more careful? Oh, shoot: look at me right this minute, stuck in a blizzard with a car that ran out of gas because I forgot to stop at a filling station. What will I have achieved by freezing to death in the middle of nowhere?"*

He jerked angrily. Recriminations were counterproductive. Maybe if he exercised his arm and legs more he could stir up his circulation and create heat. He kicked as much as the car confines allowed and socked the frigid air, picturing himself on a football field, punting and throwing. He grew a bit warmer and less nervous.

He'd cherished Jodi's companionship; there'd be no room for loneliness if she were here. She would engage him in a rigorous debate. Of course, he wouldn't be in this mess since his angel would have noticed the gauge and recommended he buy gas. Planet Earth — despite a loving wife, great children and congenial friends — could be profoundly lonely.

He thought of prisoners in solitary confinement. That was genuine isolation. *Not much different from in this car.*

Gerald attempted to clear his mind – to let himself float – a skill Ted had developed at the ashram. However, his consciousness kept straying. Ted described how yogis often focus on a candle flame or an object. Gerald elected to maintain an image of Jesus in his awareness. That picture soon faded supplanted by a shiver and another recrimination. Each time he realized he'd lost the image, he restored it until he slipped into a sound sleep.

He was spelunking. The cave's pitch-black interior resembled caverns he and his children explored along the river. He groped the walls of the low ceilinged tunnel. Light from his lantern was miniscule in the enveloping darkness. As he crept along, dread of the unknown permeated. Where would the passageway lead? What lay beyond the next bend? And why was he alone? A person should always explore strange caves with a buddy.

In a sudden flash his tunnel was a vast space. Ahead was a large party with numerous flickering lights; murmured comments reached his ears; fingers pointed at formations. He strolled forward. Who were the other spelunkers? As he closed the distance, he glimpsed Jodi among a host of angels. He paused, fascinated, and restrained himself from rushing to her side.

The enchanting beings, with golden wings and halos, were oblivious to his presence. The tips of their wands emitted balls of energy that lighted the geological features. One gestured toward the peculiar colorations in a striped rock outcropping; another exclaimed over a stalagmite that resembled an elephant's trunk then peered up into a corner where bats slept. The angels explored as a team while Gerald traveled solo; he envied the camaraderie, their freedom from loneliness. *How barren this human experience,* he observed, then with chagrin admitted, *I chose this austerity – this absence of omnipresent companionship.*

A drip landed on his nose; he gazed at a forest of crystalline stalactites and identified the source of the water directly overhead; he foretold that he would become one of the stalagmites that rose from that cavern floor. Terror insidiously permeated his mind as he realized he was destined to spend eternity in solitary repose, entombed in calcium.

He jolted awake as the nightmare merged into the horror of reality. It was pitch black in the car. No peep holes revealed swirling snow. Gerald presumed the blizzard continued: not one star shone through the windows. *Why am I warm and comfortable? Why can't I hear the raging winds?*

An urgency to relieve himself necessitated action. If he kept his hand on the car, he should be able to step outside. It would be awfully cold. He'd exit then reenter quickly. *Should scoot to the right. Can't imagine a moving vehicle in this storm. Still it would be insane to step into the path of an oncoming car.* Besides, modesty precluded his urinating smack dab in the middle of the road — regardless of the deserted area.

Gerald pushed; the door didn't budge. He pushed harder. *Stuck. Have to climb out the driver's side after all.* That too was stuck. *The edges probably iced over.* He cranked down the window. It moved easily — yet when he maneuvered to trace out the extent of the expected icing, his glove hit a soft wall; pressing against it, he made a space. "What the…!" his shout exploded into the silence. A cocoon of snow surrounded the vehicle.

He sat entombed — at least to the height of the car's roof. Sliding to the passenger window, he poked upward and determined that there were several inches of snow atop the car roof. No wonder it was cozy. The snow insulated him like an igloo. But a hole was necessary for fresh air.

My shovel – where? Crawling over the seat, he swept his fingers around the rear compartment until he touched the handle of the tool all prudent motorists carried in those climes. Once forward he pressed the flat of the small shovel through the window and pushed snow back to clear a space along the length of the door. After five minutes, he had packed sufficient snow to force the door. Each inch the door moved significantly enlarged the gap.

He poked upward; it was difficult to guide the handle perpendicular to the ground with one arm but it eventually broke through the surface. He twisted the pole and through the vertical shaft, he saw sparkling stars. The sight filled him with awe as well as reassurance. He gulped in mouthfuls of the fresh air; it tasted delicious.

Wisdom dictated he remain in his shelter until morning. The air and warmth would be sufficient; a handful of the white stuff served as beverage: *Guess this beats being stuck in a desert.* With that wry thought, he dosed off, more confident and comfortable. Come daybreak Gerald, with some effort, burrowed out and scanned the valley in which he found himself. An avalanche from the hill beside the road had buried his automobile. He retrieved the red-scarf flag and retied it onto the shovel positioned above the car to signal its location. *At least I remember lessons from my hikes with Ted's family: mark my trail.*

Gerald trudged to the top of the hill and saw a farmhouse about two miles in the direction he'd been traveling. He identified a first landmark: a trio of evergreens contrasted against the fields of white. Heading toward those tall trees would lead him in a straight line as he descended and his vantage point shifted.

After a half hour and a quarter mile of arduous going, he reached the three trees and paused until his breathing quieted. The extra woolen scarf wrapped around his forehead and the fleece-lined glove partially protected his vulnerable skin from the air unwarmed by the bright wintry sun. He hoped to prevent frostbite. He climbed another low hill to search out a next landmark: a fence post contrasted against the sky another quarter of a mile farther.

He estimated the snow rose four feet in places, with drifting and layering of the fresh fall on old stuff: those areas forced him to make wide detours.

Through it all he maintained focus on each landmark. Silvery ice decorated tree limbs. The silent ambience encouraged imaginings of an uninhabited alien planet. But after he passed several checkpoints, civilization emerged: he could distinguish chimney smoke from the old white farmhouse. Beyond stood a silo. The distant lowing of cows renewed his momentum; he pushed on.

It was well after lunchtime when Edna Smith spied the human figure that advanced across their property. She and her husband, John, had completed their routine winter chores early. Paths were shoveled first thing in order to feed the animals and check the chickens. During breakfast the Smiths listened to the radio newsman detail countless storm-related stories. Their favorite broadcaster couldn't make it to the station, so they listened to an inexperienced substitute emotionally report numerous missing people.

Amidst nose blowing and some muffled sobs, the young man announced, "Because of the frigid temperatures authorities have expressed concern that a number of those stranded could, uh, freeze before crews can reach them." With a swallow and a gulp, the voice valiantly stammered on, "Er, authorities assure that rescue efforts are in progress but they warn that the uh," he sniffled, "uh, survival of all the motorists stuck on the roadways is, uh, deemed unrealistic...."

Mrs. Smith spotted Gerald's imminent approach at the same moment as Buddy, their barnyard guard. The collie barked ferociously and prepared to race to the defense of home and family. Edna called him off. The well trained dog reluctantly, but obediently, retreated from his previous plan to scare Gerald away. Gerald reached the door just after Edna poured boiling water into the teapot. "Bet you're one of the blizzard's victims. Hear there's lotsa stuck vehicles along the highways."

Gerald faced a plump woman in her early sixties. Bundled in a woolen jumper with a tan sweater for extra warmth, her cheeks were rosy and her welcome genial. Her cheery kitchen was heated by a wood stove in the corner, and in its center stood a round table with a green-and-yellow checked oil cloth which matched the kitchen curtains. A teapot and three cups, along with a platter of cookies, aroused Gerald's hunger and thirst. "Come in; have some tea. You'll be half frozen. Give me your coat and gloves — glove. Here, sit in this chair next to the stove." She poured a cup of steaming liquid. "Here's the milk and sugar. Have a cookie."

"Anyone else with you?" Her husband entered from the barn, stamped snow off his feet and clapped his mittens together. He'd observed the last few yards of Gerald's trek and was ready, if necessary, to rush to the aid of others who might be behind. Also in his sixties, the man had ruddy cheeks and laughing green eyes. Although gray, Gerald suspected from his complexion that Mr. Smith once had red hair.

"Nope, I'm alone. Forgot to gas up and ran out; the blizzard hit while I waited. Now my car is buried under an avalanche." Gerald scowled into his teacup, "Don't think there's another automobile in the area. I scanned the horizon and saw your house but no evidence of any vehicles or hikers. Could be one buried under that snow along with mine. But I heard no sounds, so kind of doubt it." After he'd reviewed his visual memory of the landscape and assured himself he'd left no one behind, his brow relaxed but then tightened as he recollected Cindy, "How far to the nearest town — to a telephone? My wife will be worried."

"Canton, 20 miles thataway. No phones though. Lines down. According to the radio, the roads are impassable. Can't repair the lines. I submit, my new friend, we're stranded fur a day or so."

Oh no! In the past Jodi would relay a message to Cindy. That realization underscored how alone most humans truly are. And... how selfish he'd been to ask Jodi to go. How frantic Cindy would be!

Edna intuited that Gerald would be starved and busily assembled a lunch, "So, who might you be?"

"Oh, I'm sorry! I didn't even introduce myself. Fretting about my family. My name's Gerald, Gerald Daniels, from farther south, on the river."

"John Smith, this is my wife, Edna. Welcome to our homestead. So, what line of work you in?" John surveyed their guest's rumpled business suit. "Sales?"

"No, Journalism. I'm a reporter. Traveling home from a meeting in Chicago."

"Goodness, you're not the Gerald from, 'What America Is Thinking'?"

"Yes, ma'am, that's me. You read it?" Gerald's amiable tone encouraged honesty. Inevitably curious about his audience's reactions and candid critiques, in his opinion, trumped professional appraisals.

"Who doesn't read it?" Her voice rose; excited gestures emphasized her words. "John and I wouldn't miss it. Imagine, having you in our house! I'm embarrassed...a famous writer."

"Famous or not, I'm the dumb-dumb who didn't remember to stop for fuel," Gerald's expression relaxed his hosts who were flustered by the presence of a celebrity.

For three days he stayed on the farm and helped out wherever possible: he fed the cows and mucked out the barn. He carried logs to the fire and regretted his inability to chop wood one-handed. He felt at home with the Smiths and they relished his humor and tales. The sight of the snowplow brought a tinge of disappointment. Behind it drove Sheriff Green. "Morning. We located a car, buried a couple miles north, marked by a shovel. Seen anyone?"

"That's my automobile, sheriff. Gerald Daniels. Sure would love to send word to my family that I'm safe." He grinned sheepishly, "Ran out of gas before the blizzard hit."

"Lucky you stopped where you did, sir. Few miles on up the road the bridge collapsed. Drivers, blinded by the storm, plunged into the river. We lost several souls."

The journalist's mind took note: perhaps that coincidence could supplement his anthology: "Why I Know God Exists." Then instantly, horrified. What would I write about *the poor folks who died in the river?*

Those days that followed the ferocious blizzard had proved an inescapable nightmare for Cindy who snapped at everyone, including the twins when they tried to calm her. Even her four-year-old niece, Corrie, who came with Gerald's sister, Jane, to play dolls couldn't soothe Aunt Cindy. She believed that her husband's distractibility had resulted in his death; she was convinced of her forebodings when the sheriff's car parked in their drive, the deputy climbed out and walked toward their front door.

Her audible intake of breath showed the palpable relief that swept out her crazed fear when Deputy Perkins told her they'd received a dispatch from Sheriff Green not far from Canton: Gerald, although safe, couldn't yet reach a telephone. Two days later he phoned and reported that it took forever for the plows to dig out the road so he could hop a ride to make that call. He'd explained that he would be detained longer as his car must be extricated and he'd need to double-back and detour around the downed bridge.

Gratitude flooded Cindy temporarily when he described the bridge collapse. Still, if Jodi'd accompanied him, he would have been alerted to it; and he wouldn't have neglected the gas tank in the first place. And, Jodi would have alerted her of the situation.

Until that episode, Cindy had vacillated on their resolution not to tell the children about the angels, thinking Gerald correct — maybe his argument that a personal relationship with one's angel was inherently wrong should be honored. But she believed that he was wrong: their children deserved that marvelous privilege of a mutual relationship with their own angels. The circumstances surrounding his being stranded in the freak storm with no means of communication proved to her the last straw. The children should be informed.

Cindy sipped her coffee as she pondered her options. She restlessly rose and pulled out the bread-making equipment; if ever she felt herself driven to knead dough, it was then. As she worked the water into the flour, she weighed one idea against another. Should she tell the children before Gerald's return? Should she pounce on him the second he walked into the house?

Pounding the dough eased some tension, but she needed to concoct a scheme or she would never harness her fury with her husband's intransigence. Finally she picked up the telephone, "Robin, honey, we're going to convene our own private confab tonight." The command spilled out without an opening greeting. When her twins arrived home from school, Cindy readily agreed to a request to spend the evening working on a school project at Jordan's house.

The elder twins, satisfied after a quiet meal, lounged in armchairs by the fireplace and watched embers flare into brief flames. While munching oatmeal cookies made during the afternoon baking spree, Robin studied Cindy. Could the purpose of this confab be to decide how best to draw and quarter Gerald, or did her twin plan to learn hypnotism in order to persuade his unconscious to summon Jodi?

"Robin," Cindy, intense and rigid, leaned forward, "I've never fully agreed with the decision to conceal our angel comrades from the children. After all,

Sue introduced Jodi to Gerald. In my opinion our children's world is unnecessarily treacherous." She twisted her wedding ring so it caught the firelight. "Gerald's wrong in his analysis. This last disaster was totally unnecessary. He could've learned as much with Jodi at his side, plus been a lot safer. And, I sure would've lived through a much easier couple of days."

Jumping to her feet, she marched over to the bookcase, straightened a couple of books that appeared a bit crooked and realigned the picture of cardinals in the snow hanging on the adjacent wall. She whirled and spat out, "I've had it!"

Robin listened to the uncharacteristically fierce outburst with a mixture of thrill and concern. The exultation, *Finally*! rushed through her body. Robin carefully chose her words, "I've deemed you two mistaken ...." She approached her sister and placed a hand on Cindy's forearm. "I know the dressing downs Jodi got from her supervisor hit Gerald hard. And, he panicked because a huge consequence of their childhood companionships was Ted's taking a different route than God may've intended him to follow. But think about it: what's wrong with Ted's life? He's loving it and doing so much for the West's understanding of Eastern culture."

"It's not been fair to you." Robin was keenly aware of the concern Cindy held for her happiness and her sister's irritation toward Ted for sabotaging what she envisioned as an ideal marriage. Yet Robin felt differently: she accepted his quest. It had been charmed. His study of deep mysteries had benefited innumerable people and he exuded such an inner peace that she sensed it in his letters.

"C'mon. It's been my choice not to marry. There've been plenty of suitors." She grabbed her sister's arms and jostled her. "Do you comprehend? It's my choice. And you have to admit that I have a satisfying and productive role in society. Still Chelsea definitely helps complete my life." She released her grip and returned to her chair. "I would like my nieces and nephews to acquire the opportunity to walk with angels. A chance like I've had...," her voice trailed off as she again studied the embers.

Cindy stared. She'd had no hint how intensely her twin disagreed with her and Gerald. Robin had avoided entanglement in their parental decisions. She swallowed the hard lump in her throat, "Oh, sis, I wish you'd argued with me. But," she took a quick step forward, "I respect your lack of interference."

"Chelsea, Sam, what are your thoughts?" Cindy's imperious voice could not be ignored.

Sam spoke first, "Our camaraderie is markedly different from others I've experienced over the centuries. It was initially tense. But I've cherished the opportunity. Yet you and I entered this unique communication when you were grown, ready to marry. If your children had known their angels at a young age, they might not be as capable. Ted and Gerald had abnormal childhoods. Their familiarity with celestial beings disrupted their expected acquisition of skills and Ted's own life course. Your children are adults now: that argument is no longer relevant."

"And what was so wrong with their childhoods? It seemed ideal for them," Cindy reproached him.

Robin perceived that irritation and confessed to herself she'd often shared those opinions. Because she was curious about Chelsea's reaction, Robin faced the chair on which her angel lounged.

Chelsea's distinctive alto chimed in. Do you appreciate that we're living an experiment that could result in a major shift in the operation of the universe? Personally, I'm not sure how far this concept should be extended. The world functioned rather adequately for several thousand years without this sort of ... meddling."

Cindy sped up her pacing as she habitually did when in a debate. She went back to the shelves to adjust two more seemingly awry volumes. "Therefore," she leaned to straighten the picture of bluebirds on the branch of a maple, "if a better method pops up, we should ignore it because that's not the way it's been done in the past? What's wrong with progress and fresh ideas?" Robin, taken aback by Cindy's belligerence, gaped at her sister.

"You're posing questions that should be attended to at a far higher level. The four of us cannot – indeed, must not — resolve these issues. Your proposal effectively would double the number of humans who walk consciously with their guardians. Continue the multiplication and there's an exponential increase."

Chelsea's correct about potential numbers, Robin acknowledged as she sat with arms hugging knees. *It could become a very different world with more pairings.* After examining a piece of thread she'd plucked off the upholstery, she twisted it into random knots.

"So, what would be wrong if each person has a reciprocal relationship with his angel? Everyone over the entire planet?" Cindy's staccato comments shattered into Robin's mind like gun shots.

Sam hesitated then ventured, "I'm not certain. We should consult God. He must decide whether or not to increase the number of us. He actively involved Himself in each subsequent pairing after Jodi introduced herself to Gerald."

"All right," Cindy's agreement sounded reluctant.

But Robin hadn't the slightest intention of dropping the matter, "Let's ask Him – now!" And the emergency session of half the Crazy Eights adjourned after a prayer for guidance.

Chapter 9

Two days had passed since Robin's and Cindy's impromptu prayer session. Gerald telephoned at noon and promised to be home for dinner. Cindy had encouraged their twins to stick to their plans of attending the basketball game and an overnight with friends. She'd no desire to modulate the tone of that evening's reunion because of the presence of children.

But it was eight o'clock. Gerald had said he'd be home by four. Even if she allowed a couple extra hours for him to traverse the difficult roads, he should have arrived. She cringed at the thought: Would this prolonged nightmare end in his death on the still treacherous highways. Plows had created tall banks of snow at crossroads, obscuring visibility.

The twins' absence meant she had no distractions from the distressing wait. She'd opted to cook Swiss steak. Through the required pounding of the beef and the smashing of the potatoes, she could rid herself of some excess energy. However the meal was growing tough and cold. She tried to cross-stitch pillowcases, to crochet afghan squares, to leaf through magazines for new wardrobe ideas.

Finally, Cindy heard the car. She dutifully hugged Gerald when he bounded in the door grinning, eager for home and wife. Her body stiffened at his touch. Gerald trailed behind his wife as she returned to the kitchen to spoon the food into warming pans. "Took you long enough. You said you'd be here for dinner; it's eight: the entire meal has to be reheated. I prepared your special dinner – now it's ruined. I bet you feasted on better cooking at Edna Smith's." Pans banged against the stove. "Did you stop at every greasy spoon on the way for quotes regarding the effects of the blizzard for your next article?"

"Honey, the roads are blocked. And traffic is barely picking along. My estimate of the traveling time was way off – never imagined the conditions would be so adverse."

"Excuses, Ger, always excuses. Why didn't you telephone? You stopped for gas at least once."

Gerald replayed the afternoon drive: he'd figured that she'd recognize the impossibility of swift journeying after the havoc. Cars still buried by the blizzard limited stretches to a single lane. Accidents in which abandoned vehicles were not yet towed created barricades. Detours passed along unfamiliar back roads. Once he'd had to backtrack ten miles to reach an intersecting road. With slippery close calls, he hadn't considered his wife's isolation. "Sorry, hon. I thought you were aware of the traffic problems. Didn't realize...."

"That's the problem, isn't it? The basic one. You know I'm safe. Sam can tell you. How am I to intuit if you're alive or dead? Ooh, you're ... so self- centered, grandiose, impossible! I could scream...."

Gerald was confounded by her onslaught. *What's the matter with her? Does she believe I had fun on the farm — reliving my childhood — not thinking of the family? Doesn't she realize I couldn't contact her – not without Jodi. Uh-oh, this is about Jodi, I bet.* Even though he believed he understood her anger, Gerald thought it best to hear her feelings rather than spell out his deduction. "What is the matter, Sweetheart?"

"Why, nothing! Why do you ask?" Her words zinged. Her back remained toward him while she jabbed their supper onto dishes: the slam of the spoon against the edge of the metal pans clanged.

Gerald pressed, "You're either furious because I forgot to gas the car and subsequently was stranded by the blizzard or you're keeping some new problem from me on my first night home." He sat quietly, suppressing the urge to embrace her; he sensed she would not welcome any physical intrusion.

"Very well. For starters..." She faced him and with her left fingers and thumb dramatically pulled up her right pointer. Her eyes were as steely as he'd ever witnessed. "I've had it with you and your walk without Jodi. It's idiotic and dangerously deadly. Are you aware of your grandiosity? You say it's marvelous to, what do you call it, 'go it alone'. You're probably the only human being on the planet without an angel! Isn't there a flaw in your reasoning? A bit of arrogance?"

Gerald, although chastened, still believed it should be his choice. Why couldn't he choose his own life? He reddened and stiffened, but slumped with the next slam...

"And," she pulled up a second finger. "We had this fantastic camaraderie — we Crazy Eights. When you sent Jodi away, you banished her from *us*. Wasn't that a tad selfish?"

Oh...oh! She's right. I did banish her friend. And he hunched in his chair and nodded his comprehension.

"And third." As her ring finger rose, she stomped her foot for emphasis. "You and I are blessed by our walk with angels — and you won't give your children the same chance for partnership with celestial beings. They would learn much; yes, much more in conscious union with their angels than they can alone. Their own father has insisted on depriving them!"

At this denouncement, his jaw dropped; doubts festered; he couldn't form a response.

She positioned her hands on her hips and edged closer to deliver her summary whammy in a voice as hard as ice. "You're conceited, stuck up, rigid, inflexible ...and, I'm so mad at you, I could, could..." and Cindy rushed out of the kitchen; he heard her steps thud the stairs, the bedroom door slam.

Perplexed, he gazed at her departing back, shook his head as if the movement could clear the mental jangle, and pursued her to what – debate, apologize, acquiesce? But, when he turned their bedroom door's knob, he discovered himself locked out. He marched downstairs, through the living room and dining room into the library, where he fiddled with the books, sat at his desk, sifted through the recent mail — he couldn't read the first word. He went to the kitchen to refrigerate the uneaten food and wash the dirty dishes. Although he nibbled a piece of steak, the churning in his stomach made him nauseous.

His fury grew to match hers: how dare she treat him in such a fashion the evening he arrived home! But, during the kitchen chores his rage subsided and his mood slipped downward several notches.

He wandered into the living room and picked up one of the photographs on the grand piano. Taken during a Christmas pageant years ago, Bobby and Jill, about four, beamed in their angel costumes; Nancy and Ronnie portrayed shepherds. The staging suggested the twins were guarding the shepherds. He studied the children fondly and tiny doubts about his convictions regarding their angels pricked. Replacing the picture, he shuffled into the dining room and fingered the crystal sugar bowl and creamer: a gift from the other Crazy Eights to celebrate their, *was it tenth, wedding anniversary? Yes.* The ornate pattern reflected light in sparkling prisms. Robin and Ted explained that the selection symbolized the enrichment their angels added to life.

He stumbled back to his study and played with the smooth onyx globe Ted sent him from India. *Sort of symbolizes my reality for the past eight years – black, no sparkle — opposite of the crystalline years. Cindy's right.*

He plopped into his chair, rested his head in his palms and prayed. "God, I've been wrong. I apologize. I've never felt more sorry. I never should have sent Jodi away. Cindy didn't castigate me enough. My dear bride should add quite a few more pejoratives. Father, I am sorry for my sins and I pray that you, please, forgive me and, ...and, ...please, send Jodi back."

And, once again God kept His promise to forgive one of his children who sincerely regretted an errant decision and summoned Jodi. "Gerald requests your return; you are permitted to resume guarding him." Sitting at his desk, hands folded in front of Him on its gleaming surface, He reminisced to an era when He simply walked through a garden to talk with His children.

"Oh no. No, not right now!" Jodi's thoughts spun into turmoil. Although desperately longing to be with Gerald, her current assignment seemed vital. Her demeanor revealed her agitation. She wrung her hands as she stood before her God and Lord.

"What's wrong?" her Father asked in that melodious baritone; His compassion and love radiated such strong energy that she relaxed. God did not comment on her reluctance since he understood the conflict. But it would be best for her to verbalize her anguish.

"Lord, I can't leave Auswicz now. I'm safely in that bunker." Jodi was inundated with clashing emotions, ineffable joy at the promised reunion with Gerald and utter despair at the unspeakable horrors she would abandon and the helpless prisoners she'd desert. "The women depend on me. They're in dire straits." Jodi paced. Her thoughts leapt to images of the emaciated, lice-infested victims of a psychopathic dictator and his vile followers. She couldn't bear the pain of recollecting the unmentionable atrocities.

"Jodi, we'll dispatch a Special Force's replacement immediately. I'll perform a small miracle and none of the women will notice a change in angels. You are essential with Gerald." He spread out His palms as They have been reflected in paintings over human centuries. "Jodi, when you petitioned to serve as a Guardian, I warned that you could not participate in certain world events because of your duty to a single human. Each assignment is equally important."

"Thank you, Father. I know. I'm just caught up in the inhumanity." Jodi contritely considered the dilemma. She'd sworn loyalty to Gerald. But the imprisoned women were so wretched. Yet she knew the extent of assistance Gerald required.

"It hurts to abandon them." He beamed His kindly smile and Jodi realized he understood. "Janet will replace you. Detail for her what to expect and provide her with any helpful tips."

"Thank you, Father," she hugged Him and flew to the Briefing Hall on the Angelic Library's 85th floor, all the while replaying the emotionally numbing scenes she'd endured. She agonized over what to share with Janet and decided the stark truth best.

"It's awful there, Janet. You can't envision the horrors." She was breathless. The atrocities which flooded her mind impeded cogent presentation. "The prisoners are barely fed, but that, and the fleas and lice, are the least of their problems. The sexual horrors I can't describe – the mutilations, the nakedness – unbelievable — and the children – oh Janet — the children – gassed, killed alive. The guards are perverted animals. The barracks are filthy and the stench...." She restlessly strode back and forth in the immaculate, ornate conference room, one of hundreds, nestled in the vast building.

Jodi continued, "I've acted hopeful to boost their spirits and I've quietly sat beside those poor souls to listen and care. I've been striving for the maximum inner peace I can generate to quell their terror a bit. Anxiety is so contagious. A number of the women act like zombies, lifeless, wooden." She ran her hands through the dirty strands of hair which hung below her shoulders. "Janet, maybe I'm wrong, but I'm not trying to break through that defense. It's all they possess." Jodi's words begged; she needed Janet to fathom what she was trying to express and not condemn her intuitive approach. "It seems protective for them. The women seem, uh — maybe better off – their bodies are present but their spirits have vanished. Their behavior is mechanical."

Janet listened intently; her eyes reassured Jodi with their compassion. "I suspect I'll follow your lead, Jodi. It appears the most humane action."

"There's a girl named Gabrielle—16 years old! Her parents – her entire family – perished in one of the jam-packed cargo trains. I'm not sure how or why she survived. She's superb with the women. She sings to them and encourages them to join in. Another human with inner strength is Celeste. She worked with the French resistance. I try to shield those two from the guards to permit them more freedom of movement to aid their fellow inmates."

Jodi bent toward Janet; her replacement must thoroughly appreciate the situation. "One guard is Doris. She's atypical, not like the others, more compassionate. Often she can assist if she learns of a special problem. The authorities limit her but be grateful for any little bit."

Jodi jumped up and a shiver coursed through her energy fields. "Mabel, the supervisor is genuinely evil. It's crucial to prevent her from suspecting Doris. Though…" Jodi shot Janet a malicious smirk, which she covered with her fingers. "…it's possible to ward off Mabel by giving her a headache…." They couldn't suppress a nervous giggle. "She gets incapacitating migraines when the air is dense. That usually keeps her out of the barracks. I layer the air more densely around Mabel when she ventures in. She seldom lingers."

"And - oh, Janet! There's an elderly grandmotherly lady who hasn't succumbed to influenza or pneumonia yet. Usually women of her age rapidly sicken and die. She's fabulous with the younger ones. Try to sneak extra food to her — Grandma Schmidt. Last night, pneumonia set in— maybe she can survive. She's been a blessing for the others. She's sculpted from love."

Jodi gave Janet a warm hug intermingling her energy with Janet's. "I may be able to stop by when Gerald is asleep. Perhaps I can help even in guardian form."

"Thanks, Jodi, it sounds impossible but I'll attempt to replace you adequately." The Special Force's Angel gulped as she fervently embraced the Guardian. "I pray I can provide equal service."

Thus the two separated, each to her own assignment.

Jodi flew to the Daniels' home and sensed Gerald in his study. She looked down on the shaggy hair which had streaked with gray since she last saw him. Exhausted, he slept soundly, his head in the crook of his arm, his hand resting on his open Bible. *He hasn't undressed. Why isn't he in bed? How has he changed over the years?* She caught sight of citations and awards on the shelves and in the bookcase. *He's unquestionably successful. What about the children?* Again glancing around, she saw photographs of Ron and Nancy in uniform: Navy and nursing respectively. Next to that were the senior pictures of Jill and Bob. *But Cindy – where is she? Did she die? Is that why Gerald requested my return?* No, she sensed her agitated friend upstairs.

Gerald felt a presence, stirred and shook himself. Jodi sent him the image of the storybook angel with sandy hair clad in a white gown sprinkled with golden stars, complete with wings and halo, which she employed during her introduction to the four-year-old child, and she tossed the mature man a bright red ball. Gerald's eyes snapped wide open at the vision Jodi conjured. His light-initial chuckle developed into a hearty laugh, and, though aware it intangible, he grabbed the space in which he saw her and hugged and hugged and hugged. Tears ran down his cheeks.

"Oh, Jodi! How could I have been so foolish? And Jodi, from now on we will include the children in our confabs. All of them. Really. We humans need our angels."

Angelic tears trickled from the trainee's eyes: one shimmered and splashed onto Gerald's cheek, intermingling with his. Jodi was home.

~The End~